HUNTED

HUNTED

Emlyn Rees

corsair

Constable & Robinson Ltd
3 The Lanchesters
162 Fulham Palace Road
London W6 9ER
www.constablerobinson.com

First published in the UK by Corsair, an imprint of
Constable & Robinson, 2011

A copy of the British Library Cataloguing in Publication Data is available
from the British Library

ISBN 978-1-84901-882-1 (Hardback)
ISBN 978-1-78033-054-9 (Trade paperback)

Printed and bound in the EU

1 3 5 7 9 10 8 6 4 2

MIX
Paper from
responsible sources
FSC
www.fsc.org   FSC® C018072

To Jo – my partner in crime

THURSDAY

CHAPTER ONE

The willowy blonde sitting beside Colonel Zykov in the back of the black London cab was half his age, and twice as beautiful, he thought, as his wife had ever been. Stepping out into the warm June night, he held out his hand towards her.

'Such a gentleman,' she said, intertwining her black-gloved fingers with his.

Her name was Hazel. She was Scottish. A Glaswegian, she'd explained over cocktails in the fashionable bar they'd just left. Zykov had never visited the distant northern British city, but there was something about this girl's accent that reminded him of Eastern Europe and left him feeling quite at home.

He paid the cab driver, before steering Hazel towards his apartment building's well-lit entrance, on through its revolving glass door and across its polished marble hallway to the lift. He punched an access code into the security control panel. The lift's steel door slid smoothly open.

'Ladies first,' he said.

She didn't move. Instead she said, 'When we get upstairs, I'm going to do something very special for you. But first of all, I want you to do something for me . . .'

'What?'

'Call your office. Tell them you won't be going into work tomorrow. Tell them you're taking a day off.' She smiled.

'Why?'

'Because I'm not in the habit of one-night stands.' Her lips were now almost touching his; he could smell the champagne and kirsch on her breath. 'Which means tomorrow we're going to have a long lie-in. And then you're going to take me out for a very expensive lunch.'

At first he thought she was joking. But as the lift door began to close, she stayed exactly where she was.

He pressed the lift's hold button. He'd put too much effort into this conquest to risk losing her now. Taking out his phone, he made the call and left a message on his PA's voicemail.

As soon as he'd finished, she kissed him, briefly and gently, before stepping back and giggling drunkenly, clearly pleased at having got her own way.

It was a charming enough sound, he acknowledged, but not something he wanted to become a feature of their night. He hoped she'd not had too much to drink. The kind of sex he was antici-pating would be neither brief nor gentle. In fact, there was every chance this young Scottish woman would not enjoy it at all.

As they stepped into the lift, he pressed the button marked 'Penthouse', and was gratified to see a smile of arriviste triumph flicker across Hazel's lips.

It was a look he'd witnessed many times on many women over the years. Privilege and power, he'd long ago learned, were the greatest aphrodisiacs. Especially for the young.

The penthouse had, in fact, originally been earmarked for the use of the deputy ambassador, but the current incumbent was a married football fanatic who lived with his family in nearby Chelsea. Which meant Zykov had got lucky. As military attaché to the Russian embassy here in London, he'd been considered senior enough to move in here himself.

He caught his reflection in the lift's mirrored wall. The deep scar on his right cheek – a memento from a knife fight on a Moscow *elektrichka* as a boy – made him look quite the beast beside this young beauty.

He'd first met her three days ago in his preferred lunchtime café, around the corner from the embassy in Kensington Palace Gardens. The day had been warm. She'd been wearing a thin white blouse and no bra, he'd been delighted to observe, leaving her pert breasts enticingly defined through the near-translucent material. She'd caught Zykov staring. Frustrated, he'd had to look away.

And that would have been that, he supposed. Except for the thief. The bearded vagrant had been either drunk, or high on narcotics. He'd entered the café, staring wildly around, before lurching towards Hazel and snatching her purse from the table.

In truth, Zykov had done nothing. Even though he was a soldier, his position here in London was diplomatic. Which meant it wasn't his place to intervene in such domestic altercations. No matter how attractive the victim might be.

But the thief had stumbled sideways, catching his foot on the leg of Zykov's chair. He'd sent them both crashing to the floor.

Zykov had struggled – not to subdue the filthy degenerate, but to get away from him. The thief had scrambled to his feet and fled into the street. In his panic, he'd dropped Hazel's purse, which Zykov had then gallantly been able to return.

She'd been disproportionately grateful. So much so that it had completely slipped her mind that the colonel had been ogling her cleavage only moments before. She was a trainee accountant in a nearby office block, she'd explained. She'd insisted on taking him out for lunch the following day. To thank him. Of course, he'd agreed.

The lift slowed to a halt. Its door opened on to a black-and-white-tiled hallway. Without being asked, Hazel strode across it and on into the softly lit reception room.

The colonel flinched as he followed her, noticing that the heels of her stilettos were leaving deep crescent-moon indentations in the plush grey carpet. He considered instructing her to remove them at once, but instead decided to postpone the pleasure of punishing her until later.

He watched her gazing in silent awe at the sculptures and oil paintings that littered the dressers and walls. She'd clearly never encountered wealth like this up close before. He knew there was no way she would walk out on him now.

Proof of this came with the smile she flashed him next. She liked it here, she was telling him. Meaning, he also assumed, that she would do whatever it took to stay. She peered, one by one, through the doorways that led off into the bedrooms. He wondered how she'd look on her back.

'Why don't we start in here?' she said.

She'd chosen the master bedroom, he was pleased to see. The one with the biggest bed. He followed her through and switched on the lights, before turning the dimmer down low.

As she dropped her handbag on to the four-poster bed, he noticed her glancing up at the framed photograph of his daughter on the wall. Katarina was his only child. It occurred to him that she was probably the same age as this British girl he'd brought back here to screw. He felt a frisson of pleasure, reflecting that there was clearly life in the old dog yet.

Unable to contain himself any longer, he stepped up behind Hazel, snaked his arms round her slim waist and began clumsily unbuckling her coat. She gasped – in pleasure? in pain? He really didn't care which – as he roughly squeezed her breasts. Yanking her skirt up over her hips, he jerked her knickers down and groped between her thighs.

As she twisted round to face him, he reached up to grab her short-cropped hair, intending on forcing her to her knees. But the girl was wilful: she pulled free.

She said, 'Wait.'

The colonel quivered with frustration. Hazel kicked off her shoes. She shrugged herself free of her coat and slipped off her skirt, shirt and bra.

'So what is this special thing you wish to do for me?' he said, no longer addressing her face.

She stepped in close and began unfastening his black silk tie. 'I want to play a game.'

'What kind of game?'

Her brown eyes glinted darkly as she smiled. 'A tying-up kind of game.'

The colonel's pulse quickened. 'You like a man to be in charge, eh?'

'I was thinking more the other way around . . .'

His eyes widened. SHE wanted to tie *him* up?

'You cannot be serious,' he said.

'Deadly.'

The idea was absurd, of course. She clearly disagreed. Kneeling before him, she tugged his trousers and shorts round his ankles, before pushing him firmly back so he was sitting on the edge of the bed.

'Trust me,' she said. 'You're going to remember tonight for the rest of your life.'

He was tempted to strike her. To pin her to the floor and take her forcibly. To punish her impertinence.

But as her tongue began working steadily up the inside of his thigh, he decided that maybe there really would be no harm in indulging her suggestion. Reaching up, she gripped him in her fist. She was still wearing her leather gloves. He groaned with delight.

'Afterwards you can do anything you want to me,' she said. 'Anything at all.'

That clinched it; it must have shown in his eyes.

'Lie on your back,' she said.

He did as he was told, staring up at the gold-fringed, red velvet bed canopy, wondering if it might be possible to have a mirror fixed to it.

'But what will you tie me with?' he said.

He could have told her there were steel handcuffs and a restraining gag in the locked bottom drawer of his bedside table. Along with Viagra, Rohypnol, several wraps of pharmaceutical-grade cocaine and a loaded pistol. But she already seemed to know what she was doing; and he was intrigued to see where her imagination would lead her next.

Unclipping her handbag, she removed a crumpled pair of black nylon tights. She bit into them and snagged their soft material on her white teeth, tearing the garment in two.

Sitting astride his bare chest, she twisted one torn leg of her tights into a makeshift rope. She looped it round his right wrist and tied it to one of the bedposts. She used the second length of nylon to restrain his left hand. He noticed a small green rose tattooed on the inside of her right wrist.

He tried to pull himself free. He did it for show. To please her. He knew, from personal experience, that for any fantasy to work, it had to feel real.

At the same time, he felt the knots truly were secure.

He watched, fascinated now by the girl's concentration, efficiency and sheer speed, as she fetched his shoes and unthreaded their laces. She seemed utterly focused, no longer drunk at all, in fact.

She crawled on all fours to the end of the bed and got to work on his feet. Straining his neck to see over the swollen hump of his belly, he stared after her, keen to see how she looked from behind. Perfect, was the answer. *What is it the Americans say? Ah, yes . . . Just like a peach . . .*

But he couldn't help also noticing – and it struck him now as strange that he had not noticed it before – that her arms, legs and back were not merely slender, but muscular and toned.

No matter, he thought. It was good she was healthy. For what he had in mind for later on, she would need to be resilient and fit.

He cursed as a dart of pain shot through his right foot. 'Not so tight,' he said.

'Shut up.'

'What?' He tried to pull his foot free. He could not.

'I said shut up, you stupid old fool.'

What is this? he thought. *Part of the game?* It was not funny. She'd gone too far.

'Do not speak to me that way,' he said.

More pain. His left leg this time. She'd lashed that ankle to the end of the bed and was jerking the shoelace tight.

'Untie me,' he said. 'Now.'

He struggled to free his feet. They were pinioned as securely as his wrists. He watched helplessly as the girl clambered off the bed and bunched up his boxer shorts in her fist, before cramming them roughly into his mouth.

He tried to spit them out. She shoved them back in. She moved quickly then, clamping his mouth shut. She used his tie to gag him, wrapping it once, twice round his head before jerking and tying it tight.

His tongue was trapped, contorted. He tried yelling. All that came out was a groan.

Who the hell is she? How do I make her stop?

He bucked in an effort to free himself. His knee thudded into her ribs. In return, she struck him hard across the face.

He froze.

'Do that again,' she said, flashing a knife blade before him, pressing its tip into the soft flesh of his right nostril, 'and I'll cut your fucking nose off.'

His felt his genitals shrink as fear swelled inside him. It wasn't the razor-sharp blade that did it. Or even the threat.

It was the fact that she'd spoken in Russian.

CHAPTER TWO

As the black London cab's tail lights faded into the night, Danny Shanklin took Anna-Maria's hand and squeezed it tight, before setting off with her along the pathway into the park.

He'd not seen her in over a year. But he didn't reckon a day had passed without him wondering what she was doing, who she was with and whether she was thinking of him too.

It felt good having her this close, so close he could smell the perfume he'd sent her from Washington on her birthday, close enough to hear the soft rise and fall of her breath. But he wanted her closer still.

'Thanks for dinner,' she said.

'I'm just glad you could come.'

He'd only phoned her that morning. The first call he'd made after touching down at Heathrow. He'd hoped she'd be able and willing to cancel whatever other plans she'd made. He'd got lucky; she had.

But then that was how she always made him feel, he supposed. Lucky. Lucky to know her. Lucky that she still wanted to see him, even knowing everything about him that she did. Lucky to have someone as beautiful and bewitching as her in his otherwise most times brutal and complicated life.

'Will you be able to spend the night?' he said.

'Would you like me to?'

'What do you think?'

She didn't break stride. 'Thinking and knowing are two different things . . .'

'OK, then. Yes,' he said, 'I would.'

She smiled, leaning into him, slipping her arm round his waist. Whenever he was with her, he wondered how it was he ever went away. But he knew also that he would leave her again. And keep on doing it. Until one day he'd come back and she wouldn't be there.

'If you do stay, you won't regret it,' he said, stopping and pulling her in tight. 'I can promise you that.'

She softly moaned as he kissed her. He felt her body shiver up against his.

'Then I'll stay,' she whispered.

The noise of a car engine reached them. It slowed and idled nearby. Danny and Anna-Maria turned as one to stare back across the park in the direction from which they'd just come.

A lone gun-metal-grey Range Rover had drawn level with them on the dark road at the edge of the park. The bulky silhouette of a man could be seen hunched over its steering wheel, his face deep in shadow, making it impossible to tell if he was looking their way.

'Someone you know?' said Anna-Maria.

'No.' Danny was still staring.

'You don't sound so certain . . .'

He wasn't. Here in London, on a job, he never could be. The growl of the car picked up as it accelerated away. Danny memorized its number plate as it passed.

'I'm guessing you're not in town for a holiday,' said Anna-Maria.

'No.'

Danny knew she was teasing, of course, but he saw there was worry also in her eyes. She linked her arm through his as they set off walking again.

'Even more of a reason, then,' she said, 'for us to enjoy tonight as much as we can.'

He cast his mind back to when they'd met outside Covent

Garden tube station less than three hours before. How he'd thought that she never seemed to age. How each time they met after an absence, it was like he was seeing her again for the very first time. But how also always with the rush of desire came guilt, even though he no longer had a wife or steady girlfriend.

'Remember how we smoked our last cigarette there together,' she said, as they passed a wooden bench.

They'd turned into a series of ornate gardens, and were following a meandering gravel path between the flower beds. He nodded. It had been eighteen months ago. He felt better for quitting. No more waking up sweating in the night, trying to shake images of suppurating lungs from his mind. No more nightmares of him catching his daughter, Lexie, smoking, and her telling him she could because he did, because if her daddy did, then that meant it must be OK.

Yet still he pined for those selfish little moments, just him and a smoke, gazing out at some horizon, with the rest of his life put on hold.

'Do you miss it?' she said.

'No.'

He lied for her benefit. Quitting was something she'd instigated, something they'd done together, and which had survived the many months and miles they'd spent apart since. It was a part of him, he knew, that she felt still belonged to her.

They stopped at a heavy steel gate set into a razor-wired security fence. Tall pine trees reared up either side, blocking out the bright moonlight. No matter. Danny had returned here so many times after dark – either wired with insomnia, or trying to run off some bad dream – that manipulating the gate's heavy lock mechanism was now something he could manage by touch alone.

A row of barges waited on the other side of the gate, moored alongside the fat black stripe of Regent's Canal. Most of the vessels were permanent residences, festooned with bicycles, deckchairs and hanging baskets. Lights glowed behind their steamed-up portholes. Snatches of TV shows and muffled conversations drifted out as Danny and Anna-Maria walked past.

Danny's boat was the last in line. Its steel-plate hull was painted black and its name, *Pogonsi*, was stencilled in looping gilt letters on its stern. Even though it was officially registered to a Swiss holding company, the twenty-metre converted coal barge actually belonged to him.

It was one of his homes from home. He'd inherited it from Tony Strinatti, an old friend and comrade, now dead.

Danny stepped on to the small aft deck. He helped Anna-Maria aboard and unlocked the hatch. They climbed down the worn wooden steps into the main cabin. He'd put fresh linen on the bed and flowers in the tall cut-glass vase on the mahogany galley table. Not because he'd known she'd be coming back, not for sure. But because he'd seen enough bad things in his time to indulge himself whenever he could with life's little luxuries.

He took down a half-finished bottle of Jack Daniel's from on top of the fridge. Her favourite. He no longer drank. He'd had to stop. If he hadn't, he doubted he'd still be here now.

'You want one?' he said.

'I want you . . .'

He smiled, feeling the skin on his cheeks prickle, seeing her smiling too, no doubt enjoying this effect she had. Shaking his head, he turned to the fridge and took out a bottle of Coke.

He fixed her a JD, with Coke, lemon and ice, in a tall glass. Then he poured a straight Coke for himself, draining half of it in a single gulp. He was still jetlagged. Needed a pick-me-up. His journey to England had been the usual cramp-inducing, twenty-three-hour nightmare via JFK from his main home on the United States Virgin Island of Saint Croix.

As he drank, he watched Anna-Maria walk slowly round the room, trailing her fingers over the shelves that covered every inch of the boat's wall space. They were mostly crammed with old CDs and vinyls. Townes van Zandt and Dylan albums. Songs with stories to tell. The kind that took you out of yourself and into another man's life.

'It's good to be back,' she said, handing Danny a Shawn Mullins album, the same one he'd played her three years ago when he'd first brought her here.

He put the CD on the old stack system he'd never quite got round to replacing, lit an oil lamp and switched off the harsh electrics overhead. He noticed Anna-Maria studying him in the flickering golden light and wondered what was going on in her mind.

Sometimes he couldn't work it out at all, what an urban sophisticate like her could see in a guy like him. She normally looked like she'd just stepped out of a Chanel advert, him from a down-at-heel West Coast bar.

Back on Saint Croix, he normally wore faded T-shirts and ripped surf shorts, and kept his jaw fuzzy with a lazy half-beard, while his shaggy dark hair hung down past the nape of his neck.

But he'd got himself smartened up for the business meeting he was here in London to attend. Leaving him standing before Anna-Maria now in a jacket, black T-shirt and jeans, clean-shaven, with his hair cut short and neat.

She took his hands, and slowly looked over his tanned, weathered face before gazing deep into his dark brown eyes.

'God, I've missed you,' she said.

She said it in French, her native tongue, an occasional habit of hers when they were alone, and one that Danny encouraged. He was already fluent. A sliver of luck life had thrown his way was that languages had always come easy. But he knew too that there was always room for improvement. Fresh idioms and nuances to be mastered. Little things that might one day make a difference.

He gazed back into Anna-Maria's sharp green eyes. She was beautiful. Too interesting to be called just pretty. She combed her slim fingers back through her short, raven-black hair, and smiled as he pulled her towards him, drew her through the set of thin silk curtains and laid her down on his bed.

CHAPTER THREE

From where he was still trussed up on the bed, Colonel Zykov watched as the blonde girl pulled down her knickers and urinated into the toilet.

The bitch . . .

He wanted to kill her. He'd been set up. Marked. He could see that now. Right from the start. This woman – *this whore* – had tricked him, and now she had him trapped.

He could still taste the blood in his mouth. From when she'd struck him. His lungs were rattling with backed-up phlegm. and only years of training were stopping him from panicking. Training and fury and thirst for revenge.

Whoever she was. Whatever she wanted. God damn it, he would tear out her throat.

But what *did* she want? He still didn't know. For exactly fifteen minutes now – according to the antique French clock on the bedroom wall – she'd had him at her mercy. Yet she'd not even glanced at him.

He watched now as she stood and shamelessly wiped herself with a wad of tissue paper. She swigged from his mouthwash and spat in the sink. Only then, as she walked back into the bedroom and retrieved her handbag from the bed, did she look at him. She stared at him and slowly shook her head.

What is it? What do you want, you crazy bitch?

She took a phone from her handbag and made a call. She spoke a number out loud – in Russian – and the colonel's heart sank as he recognized it as the lift's access code, which she'd watched him type into the security panel downstairs.

So she is not working alone. Someone else was coming for him now. Another Russian-speaker. *Someone who knows where to find us.*

He cursed his own stupidity. No wonder her accent had reminded him of eastern Europe. That was exactly where she was from.

He thought of the tiny panic button embedded in the plaster rose on the wall beside his bed. He thought of the loaded pistol in his bedside drawer. He could reach neither.

He told himself he would survive. He had the might of his country behind him. He was a soldier. He would get through this, and then—

My God, he thought, remembering his phone call. The phone call to the embassy she'd insisted he make. No one was expecting him at work tomorrow. No one would miss him for thirty-six hours.

She stood and dressed. Taking his wallet from his jacket, she leafed through its contents. She took nothing. She tossed it aside.

So she is not here to steal from me, he concluded, although far from bringing him comfort, this only increased his dread.

Who's coming? What will they do to me when they arrive?

She began rummaging through his bedside drawers.

Is there something she thinks she will find?

He heard a drawer lock snap and then the drawer being opened.

'*Samozaryadnyj Pistolet Serdjukova,*' the girl said, weighing his gun in her hand before expertly checking its steel double-stack magazine. 'Twenty-one-millimetre armour piercing.'

Sitting on the edge of the bed, she jammed the pistol's cold barrel hard into the colonel's testicles, making him groan in pain.

'You know, if I fired this up your arsehole,' she said, 'it would blow off the top of your head.'

A wave of terror swept through the colonel's guts. Not because he thought she was about to pull the trigger. But because she knew so much about the weapon. There was no longer any doubt in his mind. She was a professional. Military or intelligence.

But who was she working for? That was the question upon which all other questions now rested, he knew. For Russia? Was that what this was all about? Was she here as the result of some counterintelligence operation? Was he suspected of somehow betraying his country?

Or was she a terrorist? Or in the employ of some foreign business multinational or intelligence agency? One of Russia's many enemies? Was she planning on somehow attacking or undermining Russia *through* him?

Noise.

Colonel Zykov's breath caught in his throat. From through the open bedroom doorway, he'd just heard the faint but familiar soft hum and click of the lift docking in the penthouse's entrance hall.

A clatter and rumble of boots.

'You'd better do what they say,' the girl said.

The bearded thief from the café – the one who'd sprawled into Colonel Zykov three days before – was the first through the doorway. Only now he was dressed in clean, neutral running gear and his black hair was combed straight back from his brow. He looked the colonel over dispassionately before unfurling a large plastic groundsheet across the bedroom floor.

Tears swelled in the colonel's eyes as he thought of the sheet and why it was there. To catch fluids. Urine, faeces, blood. To limit mess.

Two more men marched in. The first was mid forties, stocky and tall, with a shock of blond, almost white hair. He had tapered sideburns and was dressed like he'd just stepped out of an exclusive nightclub, in a smart dark suit with a heavy gold watch hanging at his left wrist.

His companion was older, perhaps sixty, balding, grey, unshaven, tall and extremely thin. He was wearing wire-framed spectacles and an oversized blue raincoat. He wordlessly set down a black attaché case on the bed and started to hum tunelessly, as if he were the only person in the room.

Colonel Zykov recognized neither man. Which wasn't true of the equipment the bespectacled man now took from his case's moulded-foam bed. Swabs. A loaded hypodermic. When he flicked the syringe with his forefinger, tiny bubbles spiralled to the top. A vein just above the man's left eye socket started to slowly pulse, like the throat of a lizard basking in the sun.

'Well?' the girl said in Russian. She was talking to the younger, blond man.

His hooked nose and gaunt face combined to give him a predatory, hawk-like look. He hadn't taken his ice-blue eyes off Zykov from the moment he'd entered the room. He hadn't so much as blinked.

'It's him all right,' he said, also in Russian. 'This is the one who fucked up my life.'

This man knows me? thought the colonel. He raked desperately through his memories, trying to work out where he might have seen him before.

He came up with nothing. The man must have made a mistake. Because those eyes . . . that face . . . there was something about it . . . a capacity for . . . *violence* . . . that . . . surely, the colonel thought, once encountered would be impossible to forget . . .

'Make the call,' the man said.

The blonde girl walked into the bathroom with her phone. The man with the glasses squirted a tiny jet of clear liquid from the syringe into the air. It pattered like raindrops across the plastic sheet.

'I've got a clear visual on the phone,' the girl said.

The hawk-faced man snapped his fingers first at the bearded thief. They lifted Colonel Zykov up and slid the crackling groundsheet beneath him. They pinioned him to the mattress, while the bespectacled man crouched beside him and gripped his wrist.

Zykov's breath hissed fast and shallow through his nostrils. Sweat prickled out across his skin. He writhed as the man injected him in the arm. *But with what?* screamed a voice inside the colonel's head.

He whimpered. He couldn't help himself. Up close he saw that the whites of the bespectacled man's watery brown eyes were yellowed and patterned with broken veins.

The colonel's stomach convulsed. Bile rose in his throat.

The hawk-faced man gripped him firmly by the jaw and twisted his head round so he could look him in the face.

'You've just been injected with an SP-17 hybrid,' he said. His tone was clear and measured. He looked like a snake about to strike. 'I'm sure you know what that means.'

Zykov nodded furiously, suddenly desperate to do anything to please. He knew all about SP-17, of course. It was a truth serum more powerful than regular Sodium Pentothal. It had been developed especially for the Russian Foreign Intelligence Service, the SVR.

But what did it mean? That this man was SVR? And the girl too? That the colonel was suspected of treachery? *Is that why they're here?*

'It's a notoriously reliable drug.' The man's pale, watchful eyes didn't blink. 'But you are an exceptional subject. You will have had occasion to deploy many truth serums in your career. It's possible your knowledge may reduce the effectiveness of this one . . . You may attempt to fight its influence . . . You may even succeed . . . So I have decided to introduce further incentives to ensure that you cooperate to the level of exactitude I require.'

The colonel's mind raced. When the drug kicked in, it would scramble his inhibitions and loosen his tongue. It would transport him into a nightmare state. A hell of paranoia and confusion and fear. He would start talking and he would not be able to stop. He did not believe he could fight it at all.

But what did that matter? Because if these people really were SVR – if that was how they had access to this drug – then he had nothing to fear. He was no traitor. He'd done nothing wrong.

Defiance flashed in his eyes. Let them ask what they wanted. Let them have their truth. Then they would have to set him free.

Then he would find out who had unleashed these animals. And make them pay.

The hawk-faced man clicked his fingers and the girl stepped forward and handed him the phone.

'Go ahead,' he said into the handset, before turning its screen round to face the colonel.

At first Zykov couldn't work out what he was seeing. The screen image was composed of grainy greys and greens. Night vision, he realized. A thickset man was staring back at him. Expressionless. Emotionless. Eyes the colour of computer screens with the power switched off. He was standing in the shadow of a grey-brick wall.

A hollowness grew in the pit of Zykov's stomach. There was something familiar about the brickwork. Something there filled him with dread. The man turned the camera away from his face to reveal the main entrance of the building.

Zykov twisted to break free.

His daughter. *How dare they?* Inside that building was Katarina's Moscow home. The colonel roared through his gag. Hot tears of rage rolled down his face.

SVR or not, he would make these bastards wish that they'd never been born.

CHAPTER FOUR

Danny and Anna-Maria took turns to shower. Then she sat on the arm of his worn leather chair, drying her hair with a towel, while he fixed her coffee, black and sweet, just the way she liked it.

Back on the bed, she rolled him on to his back and kissed her way down his body, the way she always did whenever she'd not seen him for a while. He sighed as her soft lips undertook their familiar, lingering journey along the pathway of his scars. Her touch was like a soothing balm.

The worst of his wounds – the missing tips of two of his fingers and the wide cicatricial scar on his right thigh – she steered clear of, knowing how he hated them being touched.

He'd told her he'd damaged his hand falling though a plate-glass doorway as a child. He'd lied about the injury to his thigh as well, claiming it was the result of a surfing accident, saying he'd snagged it on a reef off Saint Croix.

'I still don't understand why you won't get rid of it,' she said, gazing down at it now. 'Only last week, I met a Harley Street plastic surgeon who—'

'No.'

His answer came out harsher than he'd meant. But he'd heard it all before. From her and others too. He didn't care if the scar was ugly, or if it sometimes gave him pain.

Don't die, the man who'd given it to him seven years before had said. *Don't die. I need you.*

He'd needed Danny – *to watch*.

Danny felt the darkness rising up inside him. He turned his back on Anna-Maria. He didn't want to see her. He didn't want her to see him. He buried his face in the crumpled-up sheets. He breathed in her scent as hard as he could.

Be here, he told himself. *Just think of her, think of her, think of now. Just try to think of her and think of now.*

Anna-Maria said nothing. She waited for his breathing to slow. She weaved her fingers gently back and forth across his neck. Over and over. Before pressing deeper between the mass of knotted muscles leading down into his shoulders. Until finally he began to relax.

'So where is it you've been this time?' she said.

She was talking about how come he hadn't called her in so long, he realized. 'Africa,' he said.

The Democratic Republic of Congo, to be precise. He'd spent two months out of the last three as a consultant for a corporate security agency there.

She continued to work his shoulders. 'I wish I'd met her, you know,' she said.

Shifting on to his side, Danny looked up and saw she was staring at the photograph of Sally on the wall. Sally looking beautiful. Sally smiling in the sun. Sally who Danny had lied to Anna-Maria about, saying she'd died in a car crash. Sally who'd had the beginnings of a child growing inside her on the day this photo was taken. A son called Jonathan, who was now also dead.

Danny's wife Sally was the only woman he'd ever truly fallen in love with, the only woman he thought he ever *could* love too. Sometimes he felt that the year she and Jonathan had died was the last time he'd ever truly felt alive. Alive in the sense of wanting to move forwards, and not just keep dreaming back.

'Do you think you'll ever settle down with someone again?' Anna-Maria said.

It was a question she'd asked him soon after they'd first met. His answer remained the same.

'No, not with what I do.'

He'd told her some of how he made a living. Enough to sate her curiosity, without compromising either of them in any way. He'd told her that he used to work for the US government, but that he didn't any more. He'd told her that he worked for himself these days. That he helped people. That he got them out of bad situations. That he tried to stop them getting hurt.

'What about you?' he said. 'You're still with him, I suppose? You still haven't left?'

Her husband. He was talking about her husband of the last fourteen years.

'He still loves me,' she said. 'Not physically, I know. But with his heart. And in that way, I suppose I still care about him too.'

And yet here we both are, Danny thought. He felt a twinge of jealousy. No point in denying it. But no point in pretending either that he had any right.

They talked a while longer. About how they should meet up again some time soon. About how they should make a weekend of it. Go to the same quiet country hotel they'd visited the year before last. They'd made so many plans, so many times. But so few of them ever happened. Always, he knew, because of him.

Her words grew softer and the silences between her sentences longer. Until finally she slept.

He stared again then at the photograph of Sally. Again he felt it all – everything he'd ever loved – being torn and shredded and ripped away. He reached out for his jacket and slipped another photo from its inside breast pocket.

It showed a little girl riding high on a playground swing. She was laughing. Her long blonde hair was fanned out, fluttering in the breeze. In the corner of the photo you could just about make out Danny. He'd been pushing her higher and higher that day, but always he'd been ready to catch her if she fell.

Lexie. His daughter. Alexandra. His little princess. He still thought of her that way, even though he knew she now hated his guts. Lexie. His only living relative, his precious little girl who was nearly a woman now.

He put the photograph away. Anna-Maria knew nothing about his daughter. He had long ago decided that he'd never allow the complications of his own life to impact on Lexie's again.

He pulled back the curtain and gazed out through the wide oval porthole. A full moon shone in a clear starry sky, scattering diamonds of light across the glassy canal.

Next year would be the eighth anniversary of Sally and Jonathan's deaths. There'd been a time when all he'd wanted was to join them. A time of rage and confusion, before he'd found a reason to live again.

He tried to focus on Lexie and to think how one day things might be better between them. He'd never forgive himself for the way he'd let her down.

Images of how Sally and Jonathan had been at the end leapt into his mind. He fought the sense of panic rising in his chest. He tried not to think about what had happened. Or how much had been taken away.

But soon, he knew, the nightmare would come for him. The same nightmare he had every night. A nightmare that wasn't a nightmare at all. A nightmare that was a memory. One that began with a walk in the woods and ended with blood on the snow.

He stared into the night. Through dark, determined eyes. Old eyes in a young face. Watchful eyes that missed nothing.

The world was full of wolves, he knew. Good shepherds were few and far between.

CHAPTER FIVE

Colonel Zykov puked over the plastic sheet again. The girl wrenched his jaw open and cleared out his mouth with a sweep of her now plastic-gloved fingers. He tried to bite her and twist free. Someone punched him hard in the side of the head.

Thoughts chased through the colonel's mind. So fast, too fast to grip, spiralling like leaves tossed up by a storm. *What's going on? Why are they here? Who are these bastards? Why won't they let me go?*

He had lost all track of time. His spine and legs were locked with cramp. The ceiling and walls were shrinking and swelling and lurching left and right. Hot urine trickled down the inside of his thighs.

'Adrenalin,' a man's voice said, booming, reverberating, like he was yelling in a cave.

Someone seized Zykov's hair. A hard plastic gag was rammed into his mouth, pinning his tongue back to stop him from biting it off. Pain stabbed into his neck. A rush of clarity. Freezing water cascaded down on his face.

The man with the unblinking eyes and the hawk nose swung into focus. As he leant in close, Zykov again tried to tear himself free. The plastic beneath him crackled as his captors pressed down harder on him. A powerful fist seized hold of his throat.

Stop fighting it, a voice inside him screamed. *Remember: you have nothing to hide.*

'So now I'm going to try asking again,' the hawk-faced man said. 'But if you try lying again . . . if your answers become inconsistent in any way . . . your daughter will first be raped, then mutilated, then killed. You will watch . . . I will personally staple back your eyelids to ensure that you do.'

This psychopath bastard madman . . . he was telling the truth. Of this, the colonel had no doubt. *I'll give you anything you want.* He tried screaming the words, but all that made it past his blood-soaked gag was a gurgling sound.

'We originally only planned to kidnap you, Colonel,' the hawk-faced man said. 'What you knew was not important. Your rank and your position working here at the Russian embassy were sufficient for our needs.'

The man smiled, actually smiled. It was a smile of greed, of an appetite about to be indulged.

'But when I reviewed the dossier my people had gathered on you,' he continued, 'I saw your photograph and I saw this . . .' The colonel's whole body froze as, almost tenderly, the man traced the deep scar on his face with the tip of his forefinger. 'And that's when I realized I had met you before . . .'

Again, the colonel desperately tried to remember this man. Again, he failed. Other memories instead rose up inside his mind. The long-dead boy who'd given him this scar . . . his daughter in his arms, laughing giddily as a child . . . that man outside her apartment now, waiting for his orders to—

More freezing water sluiced down on his face. The hawk-faced man leered in.

'You will remember me,' he said. 'My colleague here will make certain of that.'

A tinkling of metal.

Zykov strained to look to his left. The bespectacled man was removing several stainless-steel surgical instruments from his medical bag. He laid them out neatly on the mattress beside the colonel's head.

The colonel fought again to break free, but the men holding him simply tightened their grip. The room's dimensions started shifting again. The bed canopy began melting like wax. A hissing of breath filled his ears.

The Adrenalin, he realized, it was wearing off. The SP hybrid was once more taking control. Zykov squeezed his eyes tight shut, as kaleidoscopic images burst like flak across his mind. He prayed that he'd black out.

He did not.

'I want you to think back to nineteen ninety . . .' The hawk-faced man's voice clawed deep into the colonel's skull. 'To the Biopreparat weapons facility you illegally raided with an anonymous armed group on the twenty-ninth of April . . .'

A bolt of clarity. The colonel's eyes flashed wide open in disbelief. What? *But how can this man know about—*

The hawk-faced man grinned down.

'You cost me my career that night,' he said. 'It's because of that humiliation that I'm here with you now. But more important is what you stole. That's what you're going to tell me about now, Colonel. What you stole. And where you took it next.'

No, thought the Colonel. *Not that . . .*

Because how could this be? What Zykov had gone to the Biopreparat for . . . what he had taken . . . its very existence had been classified . . . a state secret. Not even the SVR could have got access to *that*. And no one – *no one* apart from Zykov's six brother officers, whose loyalty was beyond reproach – knew that he had ever been involved in any kind of theft at all.

Suddenly Zykov knew in his gut: these people were not SVR. They had nothing to do with his government. They were not working for Russia at all. So who the hell were they? What were they planning to do?

He gasped. The drug had just dredged up another memory. From over twenty years ago. Of where he'd seen the hawk-faced man before.

The image of a zealous young officer rose up inside his mind with photograph-like clarity. A disarmed, humiliated young officer, kneeling on the cold wet concrete outside the Biopreparat facility, cuffed alongside the rest of the guards, turning and watching the colonel as he climbed back into his unmarked truck and . . . and pushed his balaclava up from his face to sneeze.

My God, he thought. *Can it be possible? Could this man truly have glimpsed my face? My scar? So very long ago?*

The colonel felt the hands holding him tighten, pinning him hard to the mattress. The man in the spectacles closed in and stared deep into his eyes. His pinched-up mouth left him looking hungry as a rat. A tooth of metal glinted in his hand.

When the colonel started to scream through his gag, it made a noise like rubber screeching on tarmac. It was the sound of death on the move.

FRIDAY

CHAPTER SIX

The VT Media van parked at the end of the small junction off Piccadilly had false plates that matched phantom records inserted into the two supposedly impregnable databases of the Driver and Vehicle Licensing Agency and VT Media Inc.

This was all thanks to 'the Kid', Danny Shanklin's regular tech support, who'd last night hacked both systems to ensure that his white Ford Transit appeared to be part of VT's engineering fleet, here on legitimate business. In case anyone cared to check.

Danny and the Kid were now sweating side by side in the windowless back of the van, wedged in a nest of comms kit and wires.

London was in the grip of a heatwave. According to the Kid's copy of the *Sun* newspaper, this was set to be the hottest day of the year.

But the van's air-con was broken. In spite of the fact that the same off-grid chop shop where the Kid had paid an extortionate sum to get its stencils sprayed and plates switched would most likely have fixed it for free.

The Kid's IQ was off the scale. But when it came to the mundane facets of day-to-day living, he had a tendency to let things slide. Meaning he'd not got the air-con fixed, because – quite simply – it

had just seemed like too much hassle at the time. Or to use his own
south London vernacular, because he 'couldn't be bloody arsed'.

Danny peeled the lid off the Starbucks cup the Kid had just
handed him and took a swig. Then winced. The coffee was
lukewarm, oversweet and stale. Something that clearly wasn't an
issue for the Kid, who now drained his own cup in one before
belching loudly. Twice.

The Kid was thirty-five years old, six two and sixteen stone, but
baby-faced with it, and pretty much wrinkle- and stubble-free.
Hence his nickname.

He was British army and GCHQ trained, and smart enough to
have lectured in encryption or coding at either MIT or Imperial
College, if he'd so desired. Lucky for Danny, he preferred being
out in the field, running his own show, for a few select, well-paying
contacts.

Right now he stank of smokes and last night's booze, and was
wearing a pair of blue VT Media engineering overalls with the
sleeves rolled up, revealing the legend *GOD IS A PROGRAMMER*
in fancy Gothic tattoo lettering across his ham-sized right forearm.

'You want one?' he said, offering Danny a brown paper bag
stuffed full of doughnuts.

'Thanks, Kid, but I already ate.'

Anna-Maria had fixed Danny an omelette up on deck before he'd
left the barge. Catching a trace of her perfume on his shirt collar
now, he felt a pang of regret, and wished himself still there.

But just as quickly, the feeling faded. Like a beautiful dream he'd
just woken from, which here in the daylight no longer made sense.

The Kid rummaged through his paper bag before selecting a
doughnut covered in chocolate icing and multicoloured sugar
flecks, from which he now took an enormous bite.

'You don't know what you're missing, mate,' he said, sugar snowing
down from his lips. 'This here's manna from junk-food heaven. I'd
have thought a Yank like you would have appreciated as much.'

This Kid's voice was gravelly, like he had a perpetual cold.
Danny had always joked that he could have been a late-night radio
DJ, if he hadn't been so busy going out and getting wrecked.

Danny had first met him in Basra five years ago, where they'd both been involved in training Executive Protection Units. Back then, the Kid had been able to run a mile in under five minutes and could bench-press twice his own weight – the same as Danny still could now.

But these last few years, working the private sector in Europe, mainly out of the back of surveillance vans like this, much of the Kid's muscle had turned to fat. It was a metamorphosis he embraced, rather than resented, though. His appearance didn't bother him one bit.

Most of the work I do could either get me killed or land me in prison, he'd once told Danny. *Which of course is part of the buzz, I admit. But meanwhile, right, I might as well just live life to the full. Eat, drink, gamble and screw myself senseless. Because none of us know when this ride's going to stop.*

'You know, nine times out of ten,' he told Danny now, 'I reckon I'd choose a good doughnut over a good woman.'

Danny couldn't help smiling. 'And that's a dilemma you find yourself faced with on a regular basis, I suppose?'

'Chance would be a fine thing, mate.' The Kid took another ruminative mouthful. 'But maybe that just means I'm hanging out at the wrong sort of clubs.'

'I can't even remember the last time I went to a nightclub,' Danny said.

It was true. Ever since he'd quit drinking, clubs had made less and less sense.

'Yeah, well, when this gig's over, maybe I should take you out for a proper session,' said the Kid. 'Show you the real London, eh?'

'Maybe.'

The Kid's offer was well meant, of course, but Danny doubted anything would come of it. He didn't even know where the Kid lived. The same as the Kid knew nothing about Danny's homes, or Anna-Maria, or even the fact that Danny had once been a married father. The work itself was to blame, Danny reckoned. The fact that it was messy. Most people he knew kept their private lives quarantined from it, uncontaminated, clean.

The Kid lowered his rectangular black reading glasses from where they'd been perched on top of his unruly mop of dreadlocked hair. His fingers absent-mindedly stroked the keyboard on his lap, like it was some kind of exotic pet, as his eyes flickered briefly across the row of monitors opposite.

'So who's the job?' he then said, killing the screens. He looked Danny dead in the eyes.

Who. Whoever it was Danny had travelled here to London to protect. Or get back. Because it was pretty much always one of the two.

'They haven't yet said.'

'Who's they?'

They. The client. The individual or organization who'd be paying for Danny's services, along with those of whatever team he saw fit to employ.

'I'm still waiting for confirmation on that too.'

The Kid grimaced, surprised. On account of the fact that he already knew that the client had first requested Danny's services five days ago. Because that was when Danny had contacted him here in London and put him on standby.

That the client still hadn't identified themselves, or briefed Danny any further as to the nature of the job, was unusual, to say the least. Danny would normally have been knee-deep in dossiers by now. Ensuring he could best engineer whatever outcome it was that the client required.

'What about Crane?' the Kid said.

Crane was Danny's ops provider. In the old days, he'd have been referred to as his handler, but the phrase had long since gone out of vogue. Crane was the guy who got Danny his assignments. And as per normal, the request for Danny's services on this particular job had come through him.

'All he knows is that the client's been forwarded to him from a US government source.'

The Kid openly sneered. Even before the Wikileaks fallout, he'd dipped into enough highly classified data files over the years to have developed a healthy cynicism towards governments of any sort.

'That's no guarantee of anything,' he said.

'Crane says it's someone he trusts.'

The Kid didn't answer, but it was clear from his expression that he didn't appreciate the lack of information any more than Danny did.

'I'm hooking up with him in a minute,' Danny said, checking his watch. 'To see if he's managed to dig up any more intel before I go in.'

In . . . into the meeting. The one Danny had asked the Kid to provide him with surveillance backup for. The one he was due to attend in just over thirty minutes. In Room 112 of the Ritz Hotel.

'I'm going for a smoke,' the Kid said, buttoning up his VT overalls to cover up the Aphex Twin T-shirt beneath.

Pushing himself off the bench, the big guy picked up a packet of Marlboro reds, and climbed out through the van's double back doors into the blazing sunshine, before slamming them shut.

Alone in the sweltering neon twilight, Danny checked his watch: 10.59 a.m. Better get a move on. He was due to rendezvous with Crane in Harry's Bar in less than sixty seconds' time.

CHAPTER SEVEN

Danny put his coffee down on the floor of the van, pulled out his phone and fitted his state-of-the-art Bluetooth to his right ear. He tapped the InWorld icon on his phone's screen, then waited a second or two until the website's home page popped up, before logging himself in.

InWorld was an open-world game accessible to anyone with an internet connection. Each day, more than 300,000 players were logged in globally at any one time. The game's vast environment included four virtual continents and twenty-eight virtual cities to explore, each of them containing thousands of individual locations.

It was a tough place to track someone electronically, in other words. Or eavesdrop on them. Making it the perfect place to host online meetings, if what you required was total anonymity and privacy. As Danny always did.

The virtual city he chose to beam into now was called Noirlight, and the precise urban location High Times Square.

Onscreen, a stylized realization of a crowded market square came into view. Ambient sounds – footsteps, street hawkers, distant car horns – synched through Danny's Bluetooth to fit the action onscreen.

InWorld allowed players to design the characters they controlled – their avatars – to look pretty much any way they wanted. Your avatar could resemble yourself, or a cartoon version of yourself, or look like someone else entirely. You could be tall or short, black or white. Or something more abstract, like an alien or a fish.

A system status message tickertaped across the bottom of Danny's phone screen, reading 'F8 IS NOW ENTERING HIGH TIMES SQUARE', informing the other nearby players that Danny's avatar was about to beam in.

Danny had chosen to call his avatar 'F8' for no reason other than that it had been the first key he'd looked at on his laptop when he'd originally been prompted to come up with a name. But he had to admit it had a nice phonetic ring to it, particularly considering the nature of business he was always here in InWorld to discuss.

A plain-looking cartoon avatar of a dark-haired man in jeans and a white T-shirt materialized onscreen next to the replica of the Trevi Fountain in the middle of the square.

Danny had designed his avatar to look as undistinguished as possible. He wasn't here to socialize with strangers. The less attention he garnered, the better.

'WELCOME BACK TO NOIRLIGHT, F8,' another system status message displayed.

Danny steered F8 quickly through the throng of other avatars milling around the square, before launching into 'Fly' mode, taking his avatar up into the permanently twilit sky.

Danny's 'Buddies' list at the bottom left of his screen showed the name 'CRANE' in green lettering, letting Danny know that his ops provider was already logged into the system and would no doubt already be waiting for him at Harry's.

If the real Crane was in North America – although Danny had no way of knowing where he might be at any given time – it would be early morning for him.

Danny tried to picture him sitting sleepily in an apartment somewhere, fixing himself a coffee, idly eyeing his computer screen, waiting for Danny to show. But when he tried to imagine Crane's face, all he saw was darkness, a mask.

Danny steered F8 over the skyscrapers and buildings of Noirlight before finally touching down in a heavily shadowed back alley, next to a dingy-looking doorway with the letters 'HA RY's B R' sparking and fizzing intermittently on a red neon sign.

The three-dimensional modelling tools available to InWorld players allowed them to construct virtual real estate – houses, restaurants and shops – and also to protect and control that real estate just like you would in the real world. Meaning you could decide who was allowed in and who wasn't.

Harry's Bar had been built and was owned by Crane. And as Danny steered F8 across to its rotting, uninviting front door, a virtual doorman with two virtual leashed Rottweilers stepped out from the shadows.

The doorman was a MOB, a non-player entity, part of the InWorld programme. Or more specifically, a security subroutine. He was visually impressive and intimidating. Perfect for steering unwanted players away.

Onscreen he towered over F8, all jaw and brawn, while the two Rottweilers boxed F8 in and began to growl.

What their programs were actually doing was data-sniffing, confirming that F8 was who he claimed to be and had a right to be here. Just as quickly as they'd appeared, the dogs now slunk back with their master into the shadows. The door to Harry's Bar swung open with a theatrical creak.

Danny steered F8 inside. The room was decked out like a speakeasy. There were no other avatars in sight. The only sign of life was another MOB, standing behind the polished bar. A grizzled old barman, straight out of Central Casting, with a waistcoat, a paunch and a greased-back slick of salt-and-pepper hair.

'Long time no see, pardner. What can I get you?' the barman said, his computer-generated voice emerging as a pleasing New Orleans drawl.

'Bloody Mary,' Danny said. 'Heavy on the spice.'

This was one of the access codes Crane had given him. The barman set about mixing F8 a virtual drink, while Danny waited, knowing that in reality his own voiceprint was now being checked, as a means of providing yet more proof that he was indeed who he said he was.

Finally the barman handed over F8's drink and told him, 'Good health.' Meaning Danny had been cleared to proceed.

A floor-to-ceiling bookcase on the wall to the right of the bar slid sideways, revealing a previously hidden doorway. Danny steered F8 through into Crane's private office, a windowless room with a wood fire crackling, blazing ruby red in a cast-iron hearth. Art deco ceiling lights bathed the exposed brick walls in a sapphire blue glow.

But Crane was nowhere to be seen. Looking round, Danny saw a virtual paper note left twinkling for him on the burnished mahogany desk.

He zoomed in on the message, until it filled his entire screen:

Have tried but failed to secure fresh intel on client. But have spoken to my govt contact and have been assured that all is fine. Sorry not to be here to tell you this face to face – or pixel to pixel, at least – but something unavoidable has come up. Yours, Crane

Both mildly surprised and irritated at having had his time wasted, Danny checked his 'Buddies' list, and sure enough the name 'CRANE' was flashing red, meaning that he had just logged out.

Danny had never met Crane in the flesh. Only online here in Noirlight. He'd been given details for how to contact him by a former colleague, who used to push work Danny's way from time to time after he'd first gone freelance.

Danny didn't even know if Crane was his ops provider's real name. What he did know was that he was reliable and had never let him down. He'd also never attempted to persuade Danny to take on jobs he didn't want. Meaning Danny trusted him and his judgement implicitly.

Danny would still go ahead with today's meeting at the Ritz, then. But even so, as he logged out of InWorld, he couldn't shake the sense of unease that had been dogging him all week.

He couldn't help wondering who this mystery client was. Or why they were insisting on meeting him blind. Or how the hell they'd managed to keep their identity secret from someone as connected as Crane.

He couldn't help feeling, in other words, that somehow something was wrong.

Which was why he'd brought the Kid in as backup. Because Danny knew better than to ever ignore his own intuition. He'd learned that long time ago. On a morning that had started with a walk in the woods, but had ended with blood on the snow.

CHAPTER EIGHT

'Do you like killing, Daddy?'

Like? It wasn't a question Danny Shanklin had ever been asked. Not one he'd thought about, either. Not once throughout his schooling or training. Never in all those hours he'd spent learning how to defend himself and his country, and how to attack.

Like had nothing to do with it, the way he saw it. Killing was about what was necessary. About what had to be done.

Icy wind stirred in the sycamore trees. Sunlight sparkled on the snow. In Danny's hand was a rabbit, dead not more than half an hour, its body still warm.

He glanced across at his daughter. Lexie was nine years old, swamped in a torn and battered camouflage jacket that had belonged to Danny himself when he'd been eight.

Her long blonde hair – fine, like her mother's – was matted from where she'd slept on it. Snow creaked beneath her waterproof climbing boots as she rocked back and forth on her heels.

A snowflake glistened on her button nose, beside the five freckles that never went away even in winter, and which Danny had gazed at more times than he could remember over the years, as she'd fallen asleep in his arms.

It was the fifth of January. Just gone eight a.m. Danny and Lexie were hunched down by the ancient hawthorn fence that partitioned the pastures in the snowy valley from the dark woods above. The air was heavy with the dank scent of pine.

Danny's father, the Old Man, had bought this rocky hilltop off a sheep farmer for next to nothing nearly forty years before, and had later built a log cabin on its summit the year Danny had been born. Danny had been coming here ever since, first with his parents, then his friends, and now with his own family too.

His wife Sally adored it. She thought giving the kids a taste of this simple life was an antidote for their New York city existence of boundaries, restrictions and TV shows.

'What I mean,' Lexie said, 'is we don't *have* to kill, do we?' Her voice was gentle but commanding, like her mother's. Danny could have listened to it all day. 'Because we're not poor like some people in the world are poor, are we, Daddy? And there were plenty of Wal-Marts where we could have stopped off and picked up meat on the way here.'

She was a preternaturally analytical child – something her school teachers had picked up on already, much to Danny's unspoken pride. And she was right about this, of course. Danny didn't need to hunt to eat. He was on a better-than-good government salary, and the home business Sally had set up – organic baby foods, frozen in sachets for busy working moms – had recently started turning a profit.

'It's not about rich or poor or going shopping,' Danny said. 'It's about doing something for ourselves. Without anybody else's help.'

It's about more than that too, he nearly said. *It's about who we are. About our place in the world. It's about learning to be hunters, not prey.*

'The way Grandad taught you.'

'That's right.'

Grandad. That was what Danny's kids called the Old Man. He'd been dead two years now, but Danny still sometimes felt that he was right here looking over his shoulder. He missed him like hell.

He loosened the noose of the wire snare from around the dead rabbit's neck. It had been a clean kill. The animal would have died quickly, garrotting itself as it struggled to break free. It flopped as

Danny lifted it up, like a glove puppet with the hand pulled out. Its dead black eyes glistened like olives. A cold breeze ruffled its fur.

'Killing it ourselves means we know where it's come from,' Danny said. 'Meaning we know it's not been fattened up with growth hormones. Filled up with crap,' he paraphrased, having listened to his daughter laughing along to enough *Simpsons* episodes to know better than to talk down to her now. 'Meaning we also know it's not spent its life in a cage either,' he said. 'And I don't know about you, Lexie, but I think it's going to taste a whole lot better for that.'

Lexie didn't reply. Danny didn't push her for an answer either. She had an independent mind and he respected that. She'd reach her own conclusions in time, he knew. And he hadn't brought her up here to mould her, just to hang out.

She walked ahead of him, casting a long, thin shadow before her, to where he'd set the last snare.

They'd walked the fence together with little Jonathan just before sundown the previous afternoon, with Danny pointing out the tell-tale tufts of fur snagged on the fence barbs and the smooth worn dirt of the rabbit runs beneath.

As he'd tied the snares, he'd explained to his kids how settlers and farmers had been hunting this way for hundreds of years, knowing how each dusk and dawn the rabbits would come creeping out of their warrens in the high woods to feed on the lush green grass below.

Danny had wondered when he'd woken today whether the snow might have deterred the rabbits from venturing out. Three inches had fallen overnight, and heavy flakes were drifting slowly down again now. But it seemed the snowfall had only made his snares that much harder for the rabbits to detect, because he already had two dead in the bag. And now a third. More than he'd hoped for. More than enough for the stew he'd cook and eat with Sally and the kids later on by the hearth.

It irked Sally, Danny bringing Lexie out like this on his morning rounds whenever they were up here at the cabin. But Danny had been even younger when the Old Man had done the same for him.

And Lexie wouldn't be left behind. She'd always been like a shadow to Danny. She wasn't afraid of anything that walked this earth. Not while she was by his side.

The Old Man had shown Danny more than the dead catch too. Danny had been taught how to skin the rabbits himself by the time he'd been seven.

No difference between this and peeling a banana, the Old Man had told him the first time he'd assigned him the responsibility of prepping and cooking supper on his own. *Take a hold of it by its hind legs. Lift it up. Slit it up the belly from top to bottom, then hook out the guts. See . . . that way they tumble down over the head and don't ruin the meat. Now snap back the head and see how smoothly the whole skin shucks off . . .*

The Old Man had been Chief Combatives Instructor at the United States Military Academy, where Danny's half-Russian, half-English mother had lectured in modern languages. Death had been in his blood, and he'd wanted his boy brought up the same.

But Danny was prepared to meet Sally halfway. He let Lexie come with him to collect the catch, but he always did the prepping alone, out back away from the cabin, only bringing the meat inside once it had been skinned and decapitated and washed of blood, so that it looked like it had just been bought from a store.

He dropped the dead rabbit into his drawstring canvas bag, unhooked his bowie knife from its scabbard on his belt, and cut the length of cotton holding the snare to the fence, his fingers already too numb from the cold to unfasten the knot.

He dropped the snare into his bag, on top of the other snares and the kill. No point in leaving traps out here when he was away. Not because they'd rust, which they wouldn't, but in case another animal got itself tangled in such a way that it wasn't killed outright and Danny wasn't here to deliver the *coup de grâce*. No point in causing anything any suffering, unless you had no choice.

A bird – a crow, he thought – launched itself up cawing into the sky over the trees near where the cabin was. Then another, a few metres to the left. Something must have startled them. Maybe snow falling off a branch, Danny thought.

And yet something didn't sit quite right as he watched the two birds flying off into the distance. Something he couldn't quite place. A tightening in his gut. An apprehension. He thought of Sally and Jonathan asleep back there in the cabin. He suddenly wanted to be by their side. To run there even.

You're just tired, he told himself. *Just tired and hungry.* But seeing his daughter shiver, he said, 'Come on, let's turn back.'

Lexie's pale skinny shins protruded like sharp white blades from her shiny black three-quarter-length leggings. This item of clothing had been all the rage at her school the last few months and had been her favourite Christmas present. She'd got them early, in time for a friend's birthday party, and had pretty much refused to take them off other than to be washed any time since.

'Do we have to?' she said. 'It's so beautiful out here.' She was staring out across the valley, past the winding black snake of the river, towards the distant Canadian border, with her eyes shining brightly, her cheeks rosy as apples and a trace of a smile playing on her bow-shaped lips, so clearly proclaiming to the world that she was glad to be alive.

She slipped her arm round Danny's waist and hugged him, making him realize how fast she was growing, and how one day she'd be standing here not with him, but with a man of her own, and how he wanted that happiness for her, the same happiness he had with Sally, but how at the same time the thought of her not being his little girl any more nearly broke his heart.

'I know, princess,' he said, thinking again of those crows, for some dumb reason not being able to stop himself now, 'but come on, let's go get that kettle on and fix your mother some coffee. Stoke up the fire a little too.'

Again Danny pictured Sally and Jonathan back there in the cabin. Jonathan had just turned five. He'd be curled up beneath the sheepskin cover on the pine bed the Old Man had built for Danny's mother so many years ago.

The snow began falling faster, big fat flakes drifting to the ground, as they set off tramping back into the woods.

The cabin – single-storey, asphalt roof, with wood smoke curling

up lazily from its solitary chimney stack – came into view through
the pine trees a few minutes later.

Seeing it there, safe and sound, he felt himself relax. He
remembered yesterday too, being out here with Sally and the kids.
How he'd promised her he'd start looking into changing his career.
Or at least she'd said he'd promised. What he'd actually said was
that he'd think about it. But in her books that was the same.

But what'll you do instead? That was what he asked himself now,
as he led Lexie past the old hawthorn clump and on towards the
cabin. He already knew he couldn't take a desk job, that he'd be
incapable of directing operations for any length of time without
wanting to get directly involved himself. *Meaning you'll have to
become a civilian.*

Only some people said you never quit the CIA. Not in your heart.
That it was a vocation, not a job. That the Company had chosen
you, not the other way round. And now that he worked for the
Company's Special Operations Group, specializing in the covert
collection of intelligence from hostile nations, he knew it would be
even tougher to walk away.

Danny stopped, brought up short.

He stood and stared.

The cabin was ten metres dead ahead. Cobwebs of
condensation – Danny's wife and child's breath – lay stippled on
the glass of the two windows either side of the door. The curtains
were drawn, red-and-white check, sewn by Danny's mother on
her old Singer machine. Icicles hung like the teeth of some
primeval creature from the eaves. Other than a collar of dark
wood around the smoking chimney's base, the slanted roof was
blanketed with snow.

But it was the snow on the ground that Danny's eyes locked on
now. The pattern of boot prints – right away Danny could see it
was wrong.

Two sets of prints – his and Lexie's, occasionally interlocking,
but mostly side by side – led away from the cabin door, showing
the route he and his daughter had taken that morning as they'd set
out to check the snares.

But now Danny could see a third set of prints – bigger than his own – leading in towards the cabin from the woods to the right.

He knew it for certain now. What his intuition had told him before. Whoever had walked this way, they'd scared those two crows into flight.

CHAPTER NINE

The foyer of the Ritz Hotel on Piccadilly smelt of designer perfume and fresh flowers. Danny walked past the liveried doorman without breaking his stride. He'd called in here early the previous evening to scope the place out, so he already knew where to go.

He walked straight past reception. None of the tourists or business people paid him any attention. This was something of an art with him, a point of pride. Whenever he was working, he liked to blend into the background, to become a distant figure in an Impressionist painting, just another blurred face in the crowd.

He'd picked out the suit he was wearing at Heathrow yesterday. Didn't even know its brand. It was grey, entirely unremarkable. A real IBM number. A garment he'd never have worn outside of work.

He'd chosen the black-banded straw trilby he'd seen on display in the airport store window because he'd known its brim would partially obscure his face. His Aviator shades served the same purpose. Meaning that none of the CCTV cameras he'd passed on the way here would have got even a half-decent shot of him.

If for whatever reason someone were to take a closer look at him now, they'd most likely mark him down as an accountant or a lawyer. But strictly middle management, nothing flash.

He pushed through the swing door of the men's wash room, slipping a standard size-four Phillips screwdriver from his suit jacket pocket as he did. When he reappeared less than two minutes later, it was without the small black Gor-Tex rucksack he'd walked in there with.

Room 112 was on the third floor. Danny took the stairs instead of the elevator, making note of the fire exits and other doorways leading off each landing.

'You still with me?' he said out loud as he reached the deserted third-floor landing.

'Every step.'

The Kid's voice had come through the Bluetooth audio bead Danny had slotted into his right ear. He was also wearing a transmitter sewn into his jacket lapel. He wanted this meeting recorded. The client's voice. Everything they discussed. All the information he'd been denied prior to the meet, he wanted to own by the time they were done.

'Happy eavesdropping,' he said.

He hooked out the ear bead and slipped it into his suit jacket pocket, knowing that as small as it was, anyone looking for it would soon be able to spot it. He checked his watch. Eleven twenty-nine. A minute early.

He stayed where he was. Staring up through a high window that looked out on to the bluest of London skies, he felt a stab of homesickness for Saint Croix, where the few neighbours he occasionally socialized with all thought he was a yacht broker with business interests in Miami and Saint-Tropez.

His mind wandered, remembering the warmth of the Caribbean sun on his skin and the crackle of twigs and dried leaves beneath his bare feet as he'd walked his four dogs two days before, down through the brushwood to the beach for their morning swim.

He hoped Candy Day was coping OK without him. His sixty-seven-year-old housekeeper had been working for him for four years, ever since he'd first begun restoring the dilapidated overseer's house on the old tobacco plantation out at Grassy Point. Even though Candy never complained, Danny worried that his dogs –

two Rhodesian Ridgebacks and two Dobermanns – ran her ragged whenever he was away.

He didn't yet know how long he'd have to be here, but he was already looking forward to getting back. He wanted to finish renovating the old tractor barn, where he hoped this summer Lexie would finally come to stay. She'd never been to Saint Croix, had never spent any of her vacations with Danny, not since she'd moved to England to live with her grandmother six years ago. He was planning on asking her at the end of her school term. He was hoping that having her own set of rooms out there might help to swing the decision his way.

He checked his watch again. Eleven thirty sharp. Time to roll. With any luck, the meeting wouldn't take too long. Lexie boarded at a school across town from here. In the sports day programme he'd been sent, he'd seen she was down for running the fifteen hundred metres later today. Even though he knew she wouldn't want to see him, he was still planning on watching her from the sidelines.

The residential corridor on the other side of the stairwell's reinforced glass fire door was empty, spotless and warm. Danny walked its length in silence. Outside Room 112, he took off his hat and put his shades into his jacket pocket. Then he knocked.

A woman with severe short blonde hair opened the door less than two seconds later. She was tall, athletic-looking. Pretty, but with bags beneath her eyes and grim, tight lines at the corners of her mouth. She was late twenties, Danny reckoned. Dressed in a neatly pressed fawn linen suit. No make-up. No nail polish either.

In Danny's line of work, usually the people he met this early on in assignments were lawyers, private detectives or the relatives of those who'd been kidnapped, threatened or worse.

But one look at this woman's face told him she was none of these. There was a coldness to her expression. An alertness, too, that made him think straight away that she was military. Or had been once.

'What do you want?' she said.

'Crane sent me.'

'And you are?'

'Sam Jones.'

As in Samuel Wilson Jones. Which was one of several fake IDs Danny used for work. Inside his jacket pocket were valid credit cards, a driving licence and the US passport he'd travelled to the UK under. All of which were in Jones's name. All capable of surviving any level of scrutiny. Danny never used his real name for work.

'Come in,' the woman said, watching him, stepping aside.

Danny walked past her into a small hallway. A neatly bearded man in his early thirties, with deep furrows in his cheeks and a long, narrow face, stepped out of a side door into Danny's path.

He was tall and sinewy, but strong-looking. Built like a basketball player, with crow-black hair combed straight back from his bony forehead. He was wearing a black suit, black shirt.

And if Danny staring right back at him bothered him in any way, it sure as hell didn't show.

At the end of the corridor, Danny glimpsed a well-furnished, brightly lit room. The severe-looking blonde woman closed the door behind him and then brushed past him and stood beside the bearded man.

'My apologies,' she said. 'And I'm sure you are not armed. But there are certain security protocols we must follow. So it will be necessary to search you now.'

A whole bunch of objections queued up on Danny's tongue, but he bit them down. He was here now. Was already committed. And besides, she was right. He wasn't carrying. He had nothing to hide.

He knew the drill. He faced the wall, spread his feet and flattened his palms against the silky embossed wallpaper.

The bearded man patted him down; found nothing.

Then Danny heard a beep. Then another.

He turned to see the woman gazing at him. In her left hand she held a palm-sized comms detector. As she reached out her empty right hand towards him, he observed that she had a tiny, intricate green rose tattooed on her wrist.

'We value our privacy too,' she said. 'So, please, I would like you to take off your jacket now until the meeting is over.'

The two beeps. The audio bead and the transmitter. She'd found them. She watched Danny patiently. Without emotion. Danny got the feeling she could have stared at him like that all day.

'Very thorough,' he said.

If the compliment pleased her, it didn't show. Danny handed over his jacket. She took his hat as well. He watched as she slid back a mirrored wardrobe door, revealing a large metal case on a waist-high shelf. She popped the case's lid and neatly folded Danny's jacket and placed it inside along with his hat.

The lining of the case consisted of a metallic mesh, Danny saw. Meaning, he guessed, that it was a Faraday cage, designed to block static electrical fields, including electromagnetic radiation such as radio signals.

In other words, all communication lines to the Kid had just been cut off. Leaving Danny now truly on his own.

The blonde woman snapped the case shut.

'This way, please,' she said.

He caught it then. The trace of an eastern European accent in her voice. Concealed. The way his own mother's voice had sometimes become at backyard Sunday barbecues with his father's military buddies.

Russian. If he'd had to hazard a guess right then, that was what Danny would have said.

And that feeling of unease that had been dogging him all week, it spiked sky high right about then.

CHAPTER TEN

The sitting room the blonde led Danny into was L-shaped, and much larger than he'd expected. Part of a suite. Antique furniture. Modern art. Ornate clocks. Two sets of wide French windows. Two balconies beyond.

Judging by how far away the buildings across the street appeared, Danny guessed this room had a view out over Piccadilly at the front of the hotel.

Two men were sitting side by side on the sofa. The first was early sixties, balding, with old-fashioned wire-framed glasses. He was dressed in a cheap dark suit that hung too loose across his wide bony shoulders.

Steam rose up from the black coffee he was pouring from a white china pot into one of several matching china cups arranged neatly on a glass table before him. He didn't look at Danny. He gave no indication that he even knew he was there.

It was the second man that Danny's attention locked on to. A hook-nosed blond guy in a red and white-striped tracksuit, with a gold chain glinting at his right cuff. Hunched forward with his elbows on his knees, he stared right back at Danny through hard, sharp ice-blue eyes. He looked like a boxer waiting to be weighed in for a fight.

Killer eyes. That was what Danny thought the second he saw him. This was no lawyer. No distraught relative or victim. Which meant that whatever the purpose of this meeting was, it sure as hell wasn't about getting anyone back.

Protection, then? It was possible. But Danny doubted it. Because who or what could a man like that need protecting from?

'I was told this meeting was going to be a one-on-one,' Danny said. No point talking to the woman or the bearded guy any more. The hawk-faced man was clearly bossing the show.

The man smiled, showing small, clean white teeth. He said, 'There's been a change of plan.' He was softly spoken, his accent Russian also, or perhaps Serbian, Danny guessed. 'Will you take a coffee?' he said.

'No.'

Wrong, Danny was thinking. Jesus, this all felt so wrong. Because why would a US government source be recommending a Russian or Serbian client to Crane?

'How about you just tell me why I'm here,' he said.

The man's blue eyes twinkled. 'You're not going to like it.'

'Try me.'

The balding man pushed his untouched coffee cup away. He picked up a black leather attaché case from the floor and placed it on the glass table. His hands were scrubbed clean, his fingernails filed. His thumbs rolled the case's dual combination locks. He kept the lid shut.

'You're here because of what you are,' said the hawk-faced man.

'What I *am?*' Danny didn't understand.

'A mercenary. A hired gun. A man with a reputation for dealing in violence for money.'

'I don't know who you've been talking to,' Danny said, anger mixing now with his nerves, 'but that's not what I—'

'You're here because it will be easy to hang the blame on you.'

'The *what?*'

'The blame. For what I'm about to do . . .'

Danny knew it then. He was in deep, deep shit.

The realization came too late.

A door clicked behind him. He turned to see a huge man in a black balaclava stepping out of an adjoining room. He was wearing an identical red and white-striped tracksuit to the hawk-faced man. A machine pistol was gripped in his hands.

No way Danny was going to get past him or overpower him. A weapon like that would kill him straight off. Would make enough noise to wake the dead, too.

Exit strategy. *Find a way out of here*, Danny thought. Now.

'You've got no sound suppressor,' he said. 'You pull that trigger and you're going to have every cop in London here in under five minutes.'

'Ah, but don't you see?' said the hawk-faced man. 'That's exactly what we want.'

Danny turned to see that the man was still on the sofa, but sitting back now, as relaxed as if he were watching a sequence from a favourite movie, where he already knew what was coming up next.

He gauged the distance to the door leading out of the suite. But the bearded guy with the slick-back who'd searched him was already standing there, pointing a Russian PSM pistol right back at Danny's chest.

He fought the panic rising inside him. This wasn't how it was meant to be. How could he have lost control like this? *What the hell do these people want?*

That was when he clocked that the balding, bespectacled man had disappeared from sight.

Danny heard him before he saw him.

A click.

His jaw locked so tight, he nearly bit his own teeth in two. Pain tore through him. Like he'd just been simultaneously torn in a hundred different directions.

His legs buckled.

As he fell, he glimpsed the bespectacled man, a Taser X3 stun-gun in his hand.

Danny tried to move. His muscles wouldn't work. He couldn't

call out. Shadows filled his peripheral vision. He felt something sharp slide slow and deep into his neck. Coolness spread through his veins. Darkness started to fall.

After that, he felt nothing. Danny Shanklin felt nothing at all.

CHAPTER ELEVEN

11.39, GREEN PARK, LONDON W1

Colonel Zykov was shaking uncontrollably. He'd heard raised voices and a thud through the wall.

He'd been gagged and tied to the radiator in the darkened hotel bedroom for over six hours. He'd had nothing to eat or drink. Dried blood caked his ribboned lips. His muscles felt like they'd been injected with lead.

Through his remaining good eye, he stared at the closed bedroom door, terrified of it opening again.

Across town in the colonel's penthouse last night, the bespectacled torturer had prised away Zykov's right cornea with a scalpel and rolled it slowly between his forefinger and thumb before crushing it flat.

Once the colonel had stopped screaming through his gag, the torturer had explained that he was looking forward to plucking the other eye clean out and examining its aqueous fluid – but that, tediously, he would have to wait until after the colonel had first watched his daughter being slowly raped and butchered.

The torturer had hummed softly to himself as he'd waited for the colonel's shock to dwindle and for the truth serum to intensify its grip once more.

He'd then asked Zykov for the location of what he had stolen from the Biopreparat weapons facility. Only then had he removed his gag.

The colonel's memories of what had happened next were a jumble. The SP-17 had claimed him again. It had felt like drowning. A struggle in dark, airless depths. Craving oxygen. Biting back vomit. Before hurtling back into the light. Hauled up like a fish. Babbling nonsense. Over and over. Then plunging into cold, howling currents again.

Zykov couldn't remember the exact moment he'd betrayed the oath he'd long ago made to his six brother officers. Bits of the truth had kept surfacing like storm flotsam spat out of a sinking ship. Until his torturer had at last put together the jigsaw of the colonel's secret past.

From snatches of conversation the colonel had overheard this morning, it was clear he'd eventually told these animals all they'd needed to know.

If there was a hell, he knew he would end up there now. If there was a God, then Zykov would be punished for the evil he'd potentially unleashed.

Again he tried wrenching himself free. It was no good. Some time during his torture, his wrists and ankles had been securely tied together with thick velvet ropes, so that now when he struggled, it didn't even hurt.

Dust motes danced in the sunlight filtering through the gaps in the closed curtains. The colonel glimpsed his gloomy reflection in the wardrobe mirror. He'd been dressed in his own clothes after they'd got what they wanted. His fountain pen – a gift from his wife – had somehow got broken in his pocket. He could feel its nib cutting into his chest. Black ink had blossomed across his shirt.

They'd moved him from the penthouse some time in the early hours. Prior to his transportation, he'd been injected with a different drug to the truth serum, one that had left him paralytic and tongue-tied.

They'd put a pair of dark glasses on him to hide the bloody mess of his eye. He'd then been escorted from their van and steered through the reception of whatever hotel this was.

When he'd tried calling out to the hotel's night porter for help, the hawk-faced man and the bearded thief had just laughed and told the porter that their slurring Russian friend had drunk too much vodka and needed his bed.

The bark and scrape of furniture being dragged came though the wall.

Again the colonel caught the medicinal tang of the healing balm the torturer had massaged into his ankles and wrists just after first light. As if the swellings there from when the blonde had first tied him up at the apartment had somehow been cause for concern.

He thought of his daughter. *Be safe, be safe, be safe . . .*

Muffled shouts.

Rapid footsteps.

The colonel's body tensed.

Please don't let them be coming for me . . .

The door burst open. Light poured in. A huge shaven-headed man in a red and white-striped tracksuit marched over to Zykov. He had a waxy, sick-looking complexion, and when he looked down at Zykov, he grinned.

He'd been wordlessly guarding the colonel all morning. Except for when the blonde and the hawk-faced man had come in here to mount each other like dogs in front of Zykov, and that *bitch* had used her knife to slash his lips until he'd fallen silent and still.

The skinhead now untied the colonel from the radiator, and hauled him by his bindings into the room next door.

'Be careful with him, idiot,' the blonde woman snapped in Russian. 'There must be no signs of torture or restraint.'

After what you've done to my eye? the colonel thought in disbelief. *After what you've done to my lips? Now you say no bruises? But why? In fact, why are you keeping me alive at all?*

It was this last unanswered question that confused him the most. Because surely these people couldn't be thinking of letting him go. Not after what he'd told them. Surely they must realize that – if released – he'd do everything in his power to prevent them from stealing back what he'd once stolen himself so many years ago.

The skinhead left him in a crumpled heap on the floor. Twisting his neck round, Colonel Zykov stared at the blonde woman.

The *bitch*. The *whore*.

She was crouched by a glass table, pulling on a pair of disposable plastic gloves. She took a surgical knife from a black holdall and held its blade up to the light.

Heavy footsteps pounded past. White trainers. Two people, Zykov counted. A blur of red and white-striped tracksuits. Black balaclavas. Black sunglasses. Assault rifles gripped in gloved hands.

More movement to his right.

A face from a nightmare. The torturer. Smiling down at the colonel now as he moved sideways towards him like a crab. Squatting beside him, he opened his case. He held a loaded hypodermic in his plastic-gloved hand.

No, the colonel tried screaming through his gag. *Please, I have already told you all that I know.*

Zykov felt no shame any more. He'd beg if he was given the chance. He'd do anything – *anything* at all that they said. He squirmed and tried to wriggle away. Fresh urine flooded out across his legs.

Then he froze. He'd just seen that another man was lying motionless on the floor with his back to him. Someone clearly either unconscious or dead. With two fingertips missing from his left hand.

The torturer kneeled. He locked one arm around the colonel's neck as he began the injection. He tightened his stranglehold when Zykov started to buck. As the paralytic agent took effect, the colonel's struggles weakened, then stopped.

The torturer rolled Colonel Zykov on to his back. He took out another loaded hypodermic and injected him again. This time in the wrist. The colonel didn't even flinch. The torturer shone a pen torch into his left eye.

Red flooded the colonel's vision. He tried and failed to blink it away. Then the torchlight receded and the blonde woman's face loomed into view.

'Is he dead yet?'

Am I dead? the colonel thought. *Is that really what she's asking? My God, has he killed me? Is that what he's just done?*

An urge to weep welled up inside Colonel Zykov. To shriek out in protest. But his tongue wouldn't move. He willed himself to break free from his bonds. To run across the room. To leap from the window. To fly.

The torturer shone the torch into the colonel's eye again.

I'm no longer breathing, the colonel realized. *Please . . . help me . . . please, someone . . . please . . .*

'A few more seconds,' the torturer said, removing the colonel's gag.

Pink spots danced across Zykov's vision.

A memory leapt inside him. From last night. Of the man who'd been stationed outside his daughter's Moscow apartment block. They'd shown the colonel another transmission of him later, during his torture. Only this time the dead-eyed man had been inside the building. In the darkness of the corridor outside Katarina's apartment door.

The pink spots before the colonel's eyes multiplied, expanded and swirled. Patterns as bright as butterfly wings began to emerge. His heartbeat suddenly accelerated. Cramp tore across his ribs.

In defiance of everything that was happening to him, a hope leapt inside him.

Please God, he prayed. *Please don't let that man have gone in to her. Please let what I told these people have spared my darling Katti from that . . .*

The torturer leant in and whispered in his ear, 'It took her over three hours to die. But you know what? From the look on her dirty little cock-sucking face, I truly think it was the best sex she ever had.'

The torturer pulled back and smiled. His lips pinched up like he was blowing a kiss.

Colonel Nikolai Zykov felt it then. Rage. A rush of blood. A fury.

A ballooning of his heart. A crippling pain. An agony that expanded inside him and would not stop.

My God, it's true, he thought. *This is it, I am going to—*

The pain vanished then, and Colonel Zykov felt his whole being shrivel up into a tiny black ball.

CHAPTER TWELVE

The bespectacled torturer watched the whole show. The light dying in the colonel's remaining eye. The tiny blood vessels rupturing there. If he had been here alone, he would most certainly have filmed the sequence. He thought he might even have clapped.

'He's gone,' he said.

'What was it you told him?' The blonde woman knelt down on the other side of the corpse. 'What was it you whispered in his ear?'

'That he didn't have to worry about his daughter any more. That she was perfectly safe and hadn't been harmed.'

'It's probably more comfort than he deserved.' The blonde woman unzipped a medical specimen bag. 'But I suppose, yes, he did spare her life, at least.' She glanced across at Danny Shanklin. 'Now deal with him.'

As the torturer left her, she opened a black holdall and took out two red and white-striped tracksuits. She threw one to the torturer and pulled the other over the colonel's suit, deliberately tearing his shirt and leaving both his suit jacket and the tracksuit jacket open to his waist. To make it look like someone had tried to help him after the onset of what would soon be diagnosed – thanks to the chemical cocktail the torturer had injected him with – as a fatal and entirely natural heart attack.

She swapped Zykov's polished black leather shoes for a pair of bright white Nike trainers. Using a set of bolt cutters, she lopped off each of the colonel's fingers, stuffing all but his right forefinger into the specimen bag. The forefinger she inserted carefully into a Petri dish of preservative jelly, which she then transferred into a dry-ice organ transplant container inside the holdall.

The blonde woman then set to work on Colonel Zykov's face.

She used a surgical knife to cut a deep diagonal line down from the right side of his hairline and clean through his nose cartilage. She repeated the same stroke from left to right. She slashed at his face randomly then, reducing it to a bundle of shredded red flesh and white protrusions of cartilage and bone.

Cocking her head, she studied her handiwork. It was messier than she'd imagined. But it had been just as adrenalizing as she'd hoped. In fact, she now felt almost high.

The main thing was, her man would be pleased. She'd done a good job. The former military attaché to the Russian embassy in London was now barely recognizable as human. His face looked like butcher's meat. ID-ing him would be impossible, until a DNA test had been performed and a corresponding database match secured.

All of which would buy the blonde woman and her friends more than enough time for what needed to be done.

She peeled off her bloodied gloves and dropped them into the specimen bag. Pulling its zip tight, she stuffed it into her holdall, along with the colonel's shoes. Then she pulled on a fresh pair of gloves.

Her heart jolted at the clatter of automatic gunfire. It came in short, controlled bursts. From out on the balcony. She wished she could be out there too. She wished she could feel that rush.

Forcing herself to focus on her own work, she put a black balaclava and a pair of black shades on the floor beside the colonel. She gripped his hair, raised his head and hung a 4GB data stick round his neck.

She made sure to leave it half visible there on his chest, so that only a fool could miss it.

Inside his suit jacket pocket, next to his monogrammed pen, she put an unmarked white security swipe card. In amongst all that spilt ink. Again where it would be easily found.

Silence. The shooting was over.

She realized she was sweating.

From outside on the street came a scream. Then another. It was the sound of people dying, crying out for help.

Another burst of gunfire from out on the hotel room balcony.

Then footsteps. Heavy breathing. A muscular man in a tracksuit and balaclava knelt beside her. *Her* man.

She adored his strong wrists, the robotic way their tendons flexed as he carefully positioned his rifle beside the colonel. He rubbed the dead man's palms between his own gloved hands.

She watched him, mesmerized, fleetingly remembering how they'd made love less than two hours ago. Through there in the bedroom, while the trussed-up colonel had twitched and whimpered on the floor until she'd taken measures to shut him up.

Being penetrated by this man was like being screwed by a machine, she always thought. Cold and ruthless and, *God*, yes, so pure. His touch made her feel elevated, like she was no longer human at all, but something much better instead.

As he kicked off his white Nike trainers and stripped off his tracksuit, she felt herself becoming so aroused that it was all she could do not to moan. He'd cut her off without regret, she knew, if it suited him. But surely the fact that he still tolerated her presence meant that he must still love her too? Oh yes, she'd do anything for this beautiful man. Anything to keep him hers.

Beneath his discarded clothes, he was wearing a well-tailored dark suit and white T-shirt. No logo. He accepted the polished English black brogues she gave him. Taking off his shades and balaclava, he stuffed them along with his tracksuit and trainers into her bag.

Only then did the hawk-faced man smile. She felt her heart swell with pride. So he'd done it. The shooting had been a success. She kissed him hard on the lips.

'Now move,' he said.

The balcony curtains had already been pulled shut. The torturer had Danny Shanklin's body prepared. Positioned on a chair facing the balcony. Slumped rather than seated. A black balaclava and shades covered the American's face. He'd been dressed in a red and white-striped tracksuit and bright white Nikes.

Shanklin's own clothes were in a pile on the floor. The blonde woman scooped them into her holdall. The giant skinhead tossed her his trainers, tracksuit and balaclava. He too had been wearing a dark business suit beneath.

He rubbed his gloved hands all over Danny Shanklin's, then carefully fitted his rifle into Shanklin's arms, propping the weapon's barrel up on the back of a chair that had been positioned in front of the American, so that he now appeared to be aiming its sight out through the window.

The skinhead joined the hawk-faced man and the bearded thief in the short corridor leading out of the suite. Only the blonde woman and the torturer now remained in the sitting room.

She stood to one side of the French windows before pulling their curtains open. A smell of burning drifted up from below. She wanted to look out and see for herself, but she resisted the temptation. She listened to the screaming instead. God, she felt so *wet*.

Crawling back across the room, so she couldn't be seen from the street, she joined the three suited men in the hotel suite's entrance corridor. They were now all wearing baseball caps and shades. The hawk-faced man led them out of the suite.

The blonde woman stayed. She took the Faraday case from the wardrobe.

'Now,' she told the torturer, who was crouched behind Shanklin.

The torturer sucked his lower lip in concentration. He shivered with pleasure, as he smoothly slid the needle of the syringe into Danny Shanklin's carotid artery.

The torturer had killed several Americans before. Most times for money. Twice purely for pleasure whilst on holiday in the Florida Keys.

It would be interesting to see how this one would die. Would he put up a fight? Would he scream? Would he beg? The torturer wished he could witness that now, and felt a temporarily crippling twinge of regret that he could not.

Then he pulled himself together, and pressed the syringe's plunger down hard.

CHAPTER THIRTEEN

Awake.

Danny Shanklin woke hyperventilating, his heart trying to punch through his ribs. Opening his eyes, he recoiled. Bright light. Burning red. He twisted.

Got to get away.

Pain.

His right forefinger. It was caught in something. Left hand too. He tried to see what. Saw more burning red. Forced himself to keep looking. The red fractured into a blizzard of pink dots. The pink dots faded into blue.

A rectangle of blue. Right there. Dead ahead.

'What the . . . ?' Danny's mouth was dry as ash.

He felt something solid behind his back. A chair? Was he sitting? His neck throbbed like he'd been stung. He couldn't slow his breathing. His heart kept hammering.

Where am I? What's going on?

A scream in the distance. Muffled shouts.

The blue was the sky, Danny realized. The rectangle was a set of open French doors leading out on to a balcony. The buildings across the street lurched into view. Rows of windows glinted in the sunlight. A hot breeze blew in his face.

Danny tried to stand. Faltered. Whatever his hands were caught up in slid sideways with a thud. He felt cold metal in his right hand. His left was entwined in what felt like a strap.

Even before he looked down and the object swung fully into focus, he'd already guessed what it was.

A rifle. Its barrel was now aimed down at the floor beside him. His right forefinger was wedged through the weapon's trigger guard. His left hand was bound up in its shoulder strap.

A Heckler & Koch G36 assault rifle.

But why am I holding it?

Heartbeat still racing. Muscles flexing. Buzzing now. Feeling crazed. Like he'd just been in a fight.

A voice inside him yelled, *Move.*

Tightening his grip on the rifle, Danny rose and spun. The short corridor behind him was empty. The door at the end was closed.

He kicked away the chair he'd been sitting on, then dropped to one knee and scanned the room. A glass table. A sofa. Expensive furniture all around. An open door led into what looked like a bedroom. No one in sight.

He glimpsed a flash of white on the ground. His own feet. He was wearing a pristine pair of Nikes he'd never seen before.

He couldn't remember anything. Was he hallucinating? Was that what this was? Some kind of a crazy dream?

The sounds of shouts and car horns drifted in on the breeze. A siren wailed. Another scream.

Danny's eyes locked on the sofa. Someone had been sitting there. He half glimpsed a memory. A mocking smile on a thickset, hook-nosed blond man's face.

Splinters of information pierced Danny's mind. This was the Ritz Hotel, he remembered. Room 112. Third floor.

But what am I doing here?

More screaming.

Outside.

Danny turned to face the balcony. He took a step forward. Another. Then froze.

A pair of white trainers was sticking out from behind a low

wooden table. Worn by a dead man, Danny saw, as he slowly circled round. The man's face had been slashed to shreds, his fingers cut off.

He was wearing a red and white-striped tracksuit. White Nikes. The same as Danny.

Another burst of memory. Of the blond man who'd been on the sofa. The one with *killer eyes* . . . Hadn't he been dressed the same too?

More shouts through the window. More screams. The siren was getting louder now.

A second rifle. Identical to the one Danny was holding. It lay there on the floor, just beyond the dead man's reach. Alongside it was a pair of black Ray-Ban Aviator shades.

Danny crouched down and checked the man's pulse. Nothing. The man's skin was warm. Not long dead.

Another scream.

Danny looked to the balcony. He didn't want to go out there. Didn't want to find out who it was who kept screaming. But he knew he had no choice. Out there was where the answers lay.

Keeping low, he edged through the open French windows and peered over the waist-high stone balustrade.

People were running wherever he looked. Away from the hotel. Into the street. Running awkwardly. As if they'd never done it before. Stumbling and tripping. In ones and twos. Hands above their heads. The further away they got from the hotel, the faster they ran. For cover. They were running for their lives.

Bodies were scattered across the tarmac. Broken and twisted. Twenty, Danny counted, at least. A scene from a war zone. Only these corpses were dressed in bright civilian clothes. And this was the centre of London. In the middle of a hot summer day.

Danny looked east and west along Piccadilly. The road was clear of vehicles for thirty metres either way. But then there was chaos.

Cars stood abandoned at crazy angles. Reversed and crashed. A red double-decker bus had slewed into a lamppost. A mangled motorcycle was half buried in a news stand that had mushroomed into flames. Further on, vehicles were still trying to slip free of the gridlock. Juddering like bumper cars at a fairground. Everywhere Danny looked, he could see people running, crawling, hiding.

More sirens in the distance. Car horns. A swarm of flickering blue lights was gathering in the east, nudging through the traffic, cracking through it like icebreakers on a frozen sea – police and ambulances, trying to get through.

A siren whooped much closer.

Danny edged forward and looked down three storeys below.

A black limousine was parked up tight against the kerb outside the hotel's main entrance. Its nearside tyres were ribboned, shot out. Black smoke billowed from its ravaged bonnet. Dozens of fist-sized holes had been punched through its roof. It looked like a tin can a kid had used for target practice with an airgun.

The driver's door was open. A man's body lay draped over it like a forgotten coat. A blood trail led away from the car's open street-side rear door to where a woman in a bright purple coat was crumpled in the middle of the street. Something was wrong with the shape of her body. Something was wrong with her legs.

The pattern of bodies . . . the black limousine was at its centre. Whoever had done this, the limousine had been their focal point. The limousine was what this was all about.

A police squad car had broken free of the gridlock. It was crawling along the pavement, hugging the nearside line of buildings to the east of the hotel. It angled into the kerb and stopped, blue light flashing.

The woman whose legs weren't right . . . she started moving then. Slowly, uselessly, flopping on the ground like a baby bird fallen from a nest, trying to work out how to fly.

She was the one who'd been screaming, Danny realized. She was the one who now couldn't stop.

The doors of the police car sprang open. Two uniformed police ran for her. They zigzagged, half-crouching. One of them lost his cap, but kept on going. He cradled his head in his hands like he'd just been slapped and was expecting the same again.

When they lifted the woman up, Danny saw that where her legs should have been there was only a bloody pulp. Her screaming grew louder as the police stumbled away from the Ritz, and bundled her through the glass doors of the building opposite. Out of sight.

More shouts. Directly below. Several women spilt out on to the street. In black and white. Waitresses or maids, Danny guessed. Hotel staff. They ran screaming with their hands in the air.

One group of people remained motionless in the chaos. Conspicuous because of it, Danny saw. There were three of them, crouched down low in a shop doorway opposite him. Glass glinted up at him. Something one of them was holding.

A TV camera, Danny realized. He was staring at a TV crew. And they were staring right back at him.

CHAPTER FOURTEEN

Danny backed inside and jerked the curtains shut.

He stared at the rifle in his hands. The one he'd just been holding out there in broad daylight. In full view of the world.

This was no dream. No hallucination.

So what the hell is going on? Why can't I remember why I'm here?

A flash of light. To the right. Another door. Ajar. Through it Danny glimpsed a sliver of brightly lit white-tiled wall. Another memory hit him. Someone had come out of there, someone who'd meant him harm.

Five soft strides across the deep cream carpet and Danny was there. He kicked the door hard, busted it open, his rifle already up.

A man in a black balaclava and Ray-Ban Aviator shades stared back at him.

Danny fired. A killing burst. The report was deafening. The man disintegrated into a hundred shards.

It's your own reflection . . .

Danny tore the balaclava from his head and stared at his face in the one jagged splinter of mirror left hanging on the wall. His eyes looked wired, insanely alert.

He was dressed in a red and white-striped tracksuit. The same as the corpse. He looked down at his feet. Nikes. Again the same. Box fresh.

He backed out of the bathroom. Checked the other rooms. A study. Untouched. A double bedroom with the bed still made. A dark stain on the carpet by the radiator. Looked like blood.

A diamond of sunlight sparked off the glass table as he went back into the sitting room. Coffee. Now he remembered. He'd watched it being poured. Another man's features flashed into his mind. Thinning hair. Wire glasses.

A Taser.

Shock and pain.

But then?

Lexie. The thought of his daughter swept through his mind like a flaming torch driving back the dark. A total dread that something so bad was happening to him that he might never see her again – it swept the last of his waking delirium from his mind.

Everything came back then. A deluge of memories that momentarily left him swamped.

Russians. They'd sounded like Russians. Or Serbians.

He remembered why he'd come here. For a meeting. One set up by Crane. He remembered the blonde woman at the door. The bearded man who'd searched him. The blonde woman had used a comms scanner. She'd taken his jacket. She'd taken his jacket to prevent the meeting being wired.

The Kid . . .

Danny ran to the entrance hallway and jerked the wardrobe open. The Faraday case was gone. Along with, he realized, his jacket, hat, credit cards, driving licence and passport.

He clamped his hand to the back of his neck, feeling the throbbing again. Another memory . . . he'd been injected with something. After the balding man had taken him down with the Taser, he'd used a hypodermic to knock him out.

Danny checked his watch. It was gone. He checked the clock on the wall. Eleven fifty. The blonde woman had opened the suite door at exactly eleven thirty. His conversation with the hawk-faced man had been violently interrupted just minutes after that. Which meant he couldn't have been unconscious for more than fifteen minutes.

During which time the limo had been ambushed, he'd been stripped and changed, and this rifle had been placed in his hands.

A rifle that had been used on the limo and those poor people, of that Danny had no doubt. Meaning that even prior to him shooting his own reflection, his hands would most likely already have been contaminated with gunshot residue. Something a counterterrorism trace-detection portal machine would sniff out no sweat, providing enough evidence to incarcerate Danny for life.

That's when Danny knew it for certain. What he'd already begun to suspect. Not only had he been set up, he'd been set up good.

And already he knew he would have to run.

But not yet, he told himself. *First take whatever you can from here that might help* . . .

He raced through the hotel suite rooms, jacket sleeves stretched over his fingertips, jerking open empty wardrobes and drawers, looking in bins and under chairs and beds.

But they'd left the place clean. Even the coffee pot and cups, which should have been here on the glass table, were now nowhere to be found. Because taking them would have been quicker and safer than wiping them free of prints.

All they'd left for the police to find were the rifles, the corpse, the carnage outside – and him.

Danny ran to the dead man. Wrong colour hair to have been the hawk-faced guy, or the man who'd searched him, or the one who'd taken him down with the Taser. Wrong build too for the man in the balaclava who'd come at him from the bathroom.

He quickly checked the corpse front and back for exit wounds. Nothing. No blood-spray patterns nearby either. Nothing to indicate he'd been shot.

So how the hell *had* he died?

The man's facial wounds hadn't killed him. That was for sure. The limited bleeding there and on the stumps of his fingers meant he'd already been dead by the time these mutilations had occurred.

Meaning he'd been disfigured to conceal his ID. Suggesting that maybe this was another member of the hawk-faced man's unit who Danny had never even seen. Implying that the others must have feared that they could be tracked down through him.

ID this guy and he might lead you to them . . .

Taking prints wasn't an option. Instead Danny hastily rummaged through the dead man's pockets. Chances were they'd already been emptied. But if the others had been forced into hurriedly mutilating him like this, it meant they'd been in a rush. And people in a rush made mistakes.

No wallet. Some loose change. All sterling. A broken gold pen, initialled 'NZ', sticky with black ink. Then something else in the man's jacket breast pocket. Something thin and rectangular. A credit card, he hoped at first. But what he found instead was an ink-drenched plastic swipe card.

He smeared the ink off. The card was white underneath. Unmarked. Could have been for anything. A gym or a launderette. But Danny hoped it might still have the dead man's name encoded in it.

He checked the man's wrists. No watch. Then something else caught his eye. Just there, where the bloodstained shirt had been torn open, in what Danny could only assume had been some attempt to revive him.

Danny jerked the shirt wider. A USB data stick hung from a cord around the dead man's neck.

Something for the Kid . . .

But even in the act of reaching out to grab it, Danny's fingers froze. First the swipe card and now this . . . Not one mistake, but two. Both items might have been left here deliberately for the police to find, he realized. To send them off on a false trail.

He took them anyway. What choice did he have? Any information was better than none. Yanking the stick free, he slipped it into his trouser pocket, along with the card, pen and cash.

He was up then. Running. Into the bathroom. Snatching up the balaclava and shades he'd been wearing. Rolling the balaclava up into a beanie hat on the top of his head. He put the shades on too. Turned up his collar. Hid as much of his face as he could.

He didn't know who might be waiting for him in the corridor outside the hotel suite. But he ditched the rifle anyway. Whoever had set him up must surely have fled by now. Because why bother going to the trouble of framing him at all, if they were planning on hanging around?

These were no martyrs, he was sure of it. This was no Mumbai. No hotel siege. This was an assassination. A hit. On whoever had been in that limo.

And this rifle they'd left him, it would only slow him down and further incriminate him. Or he'd be tempted to use it in self-defence against whatever British military or police got in his way. Which wouldn't end well for anyone.

He grabbed a shard of broken mirror from the bathroom floor, then used the alcohol-based boot-polish wipes from the room's welcome pack to clean his prints off the rifle and everything else he'd touched, including the dead man's wrist where he'd checked for a pulse.

It was the least he could do. But most likely not enough. If he'd contaminated the dead man's clothes with his DNA, then there was nothing he could do about it now. Plus for all he knew, the people who'd set him up could have put his prints and DNA – sweat, mucus, hair – in a whole bunch of other places. Leaving him circumstantially and forensically fucked if he got captured by the police, or tried turning himself in and claiming he'd been somewhere else in the hotel when the hit and the massacre had gone down.

He pushed down slowly on the suite's door handle with his elbow. Nudging the door ajar, he listened: heard nothing. He used the shard of broken mirror to peer outside. The corridor was clear.

Danny stepped out into it and started to run.

CHAPTER FIFTEEN

You're lucky you're not still back there slumped unconscious in that chair, Danny thought, already halfway along the corridor, not looking back.

That was just about the only comfort he had right now. He'd got out of that room where they'd left him to rot, before the police had showed up to collect.

Or – another sickening thought occurred to him – maybe they'd wanted him to wake as disoriented as he had. And stumble out on to that balcony with that gun. Or even try to fight his way out. So the police focused their attention right here on him, while the people who'd caused all that mayhem escaped.

Either way, they'd messed up on whatever drugs they'd knocked him out with. They'd not dosed him right. Because he was thinking clearly now. Clear enough to be getting away. Which meant they weren't as smart as they thought.

All of which gave him a chance. Because they wouldn't be expecting him to now come hunting for them.

Danny reckoned there was still a possibility of him slipping out of the hotel, before specialist police firearms and counterterrorism units arrived and zipped up the net for good.

The smiling hawk-faced man with the shock of blond hair . . . he was the one who was behind all this, of that Danny was convinced. He was the one Danny would find and make pay.

But the others . . . he'd find them too . . .

Glimpsing his blurred red and white-striped reflection in a wall mirror as he rushed by, Danny slowed and selected a door at random near the end of the corridor. He kicked it just below its handle as hard as he could.

He needed a change of clothes. That TV crew had got him good. He'd been lucky he'd still had the balaclava pulled down over his face and the shades on. But chances were this tracksuit would be plastered all over the networks in the next ten minutes. Meaning that dressed like this, he might as well have a target on his chest for armed cops to shoot at.

The door's lock shattered at the second kick. Danny burst inside. A single room, much smaller than the suite he'd left. A bed, desk and chair. The curtains were drawn shut. An open doorway led into a blacked-out en suite.

An unpacked suitcase stood open on the unruffled bed. Again covering his fingers with his tracksuit sleeves, Danny flipped through the case's contents. All useless. Female. Dresses, knickers, bras and heels. The only item that might have sufficed was a plain black shirt, but even that was way too small.

He saw her when he turned to go. Half hidden behind the chair. A woman in her late fifties. Curled up under a writing bureau. Wrapped in a white bath towel. Her make-up was smudged and her cheeks smeared with tears. She had ash-blonde hair, the same colour Danny's mother's had turned that last month in the hospital.

'Please . . .'

The woman stretched out her trembling right arm towards him, fingers splayed, like she was trying to block him from view. It was a gesture Danny had seen before. Dozens of times in dozens of countries. From old and young alike. She must have heard the gunfire. Or seen the devastation outside. She was trying to shield herself. She thought she was next.

Danny hated to see anyone cowering like that.

'It's OK, I'm not going to hurt you,' he said. He kept his accent neutral, clipped, as English as he could. Didn't want to mark himself out as an American, in case she told the police. 'And don't worry . . . the people who did that out there . . . I think they've already gone.'

'You . . . you're police?'

A flicker of hope in her eyes.

Dashed.

'No. But they'll be here soon. And until they get here, I want you to go into that bathroom and lock the door. You'll be safe there. Do you understand?'

Her mouth opened as if she were about to speak, but no words came out.

'You're going to be all right,' Danny said. 'I promise you. Everything's going to be fine.'

She nodded and started to rise.

Back out in the corridor, Danny felt his chest tightening. How could this have happened? How could he have ended up bushwhacked? *Crane* . . . Who the hell was his US government contact? Why had they led Danny into this?

No time left now to kick in any other hotel doors in search of clothes. Instead he ran to the end of the corridor and out in to the stairwell. He thought about busting out through the emergency exit onto whatever fire escape lay beyond, maybe trying to slip away down the back of the building. But just as quickly he dismissed the idea.

Before he made any decisions, what he needed was information. What he needed was the Kid.

He took the stairs two at a time. Round and down. Seemed like only minutes ago he'd been going the other way. He wished he'd listened harder to his instincts and the warning bells in the back of his mind that had told him not to come. He should have called the whole meeting off.

He remembered Anna-Maria last night. The peace and the warmth. She'd be opening up her husband's restaurant in Borough Market now. Less than two miles from here. Might as well be on another planet, though, Danny thought, for all their lives had diverged since they'd kissed each other goodbye.

Everything had changed in the blink of an eye. In the nothing time it had taken for the Taser's trigger to be pulled and its neuromuscular incapacitation pulse to slam into Danny's flesh.

He reached the ground floor in less than thirty seconds. He stared at the stairwell door. *What's on the other side?* A wall of police? Staff and guests cowering? Or a whole bunch of dead people? Frozen in horizontal cartwheels, blitzed by the same people who'd set Danny up as they made their way out?

Danny pressed the handle down with his sleeve and used the mirror shard to perform a quick visual sweep. No bodies. No police. Part of the hotel's main reception was visible at the end of the corridor to the left. Warm lighting. The only sign of a struggle was a single knocked-down chair.

Danny remembered the maids he'd seen running towards the waiting cop. Someone here must have done their job well. Got people out fast. After Mumbai, most of the big international hotels – particularly famous potential targets like this – had taken part in exercises arranged by security forums to brush up on their evacuation procedures.

Good for them. But bad for Danny. Because getting out was now going to be even tougher, if he was already one of the last people left.

He moved fast. Through the doorway. Away from the reception. Deeper into the hotel. His Nikes squeaked deafeningly with each step. He passed a doorway leading into the hotel kitchens. He caught a whiff of grilled bacon and freshly baked bread.

A short burst of radio chatter gave the cop's position away.

CHAPTER SIXTEEN

Danny wasn't looking for confrontation. He would have avoided the situation if he could. But it was too late. The cop – male, early twenties, square-faced, with a wide pockmarked brow – had already seen him.

He was staring out at Danny through the open doorway of a small windowless office, where he'd balled himself up into the corner beside a coat stand. The office ceiling strip light was out, but the screen of a personal radio unit glowed luminescent in the young cop's hand.

He was staring at Danny's tracksuit. He couldn't tear his eyes away.

Danny was no giant, but up close there was an undeniable sense of solidity about him, as if a whole building might collapse around him but he'd still somehow manage to walk away.

It was enough to give the cop cause for hesitation now.

Danny's eyes scanned the pouches on his black utility vest: CS spray, Taser. An extendable reinforced graphite baton, there at his hip.

Must have been passing by when the shooting had kicked off and had barrelled in here, unthinking, to try and help. A hero then. Bad news for Danny. Unpredictable. He needed to neutralize him fast.

Something in the cop's eyes told Danny he'd just come to the same conclusion himself. He scrambled to his feet as Danny stepped into the room. He was taller than Danny. Three or four inches at least. His eyes flickered up and down, looking to see if Danny was armed.

'You do not have to . . .' The cop's voice wavered and so he tried again. 'You do not have to say anything . . . but it may harm your defence if . . .'

Danny had watched enough UK TV shows over the years – and had also taken part in a carefully orchestrated takedown here in London four years back – to recognize the start of the verbal caution that British police were obliged to give citizens they were about to arrest.

He told the cop, 'Shut the fuck up and turn round.' He'd flattened his accent to English again.

The cop swallowed. His hands were trembling, but defiance now flashed in his eyes. He reached for the flap on his utility vest that was holding the baton in place.

'Don't,' Danny said.

But the cop did. Moved fast, too. Quicker than Danny had imagined he could.

But not quick enough. Before he had even got the baton free, Danny had stepped up close, grabbed his right lower sleeve and jerked it away from his body to prevent him deploying the baton.

The cop lost balance then. Danny spun him sideways. He slid his right arm inside the cop's right and wrenched his elbow up behind him. As the cop brought the baton up with his left, Danny shoved his knees into the back of the cop's.

The cop sagged, dropped two foot in height, allowing Danny's left arm to snake down over his left shoulder. Danny closed in behind him. He twisted the baton hard to the horizontal, bringing it up sharp beneath the cop's chin with a satisfying clunk. He jerked it tight against the cop's thorax. He didn't let go.

The cop struggled. Then weakened. A rattle of breath. A grunt. He tried rising, throwing Danny, but Danny just pulled back harder, redistributed his weight, then heaved some more.

The cop started shuddering then, fighting for breath. His arms flailed. He tried clawing back at Danny's face over his shoulders. He couldn't reach.

It would have been easy for Danny to finish him then, asphyxiate him enough to make him black out, or worse. But he wasn't planning on hurting him any more than he had to. He slackened off the pressure as the cop sank to his knees.

A voice burst out of the radio on the floor. Danny couldn't make out the words.

The cop gasped for air, tried turning. Danny flattened him face down. He jerked the cop's arms behind his back. Wrist-locked him with one hand and ripped the office phone off the desk with the other. He used the phone line to bind the cop's wrists. Then he stood.

'Please . . .' the cop wheezed. 'I've got children . . .'

Another cough of static burst from the radio. A man's voice hissed: 'Patrick? Are you still there?'

Danny snatched up the radio and muffled it against his chest.

'Tell him you're OK,' he said to the cop. 'Tell him your radio battery's nearly out of juice.'

He pressed the radio against the cop's face.

'I'm . . . I'm fine,' Patrick said. His lips were flecked with spittle. He was finding it difficult to speak. 'But my battery's out . . . it's out of—'

Danny switched the radio off.

'What's your emergency comms channel?'

Patrick stared at him in confusion, then seemed to remember. 'Four seven three,' he said.

Danny switched the radio back on, tuned it and listened in.

Straight away bursts of cop chatter started coming through. Different voices. Panicked, every one. Danny heard the hotel name mentioned twice. Piccadilly once. Green Park tube station too. The fact that it was being shut down.

Everything he heard only confirmed what he already knew: that the Metropolitan Police were zoning their resources in on this building.

Danny switched off the radio. No matter what useful information he might glean, keeping it on might end up giving him
away, the same as it had done this cop.

He quickly surveyed the room.

What else have I touched?

He cleaned the phone and its cord as best he could with the last
of the polish wipes he'd taken from the hotel bathroom. He slipped
the cop's radio into his trouser pocket, took the baton and hurried
out.

The men's rest room was at the end of the corridor. Danny
stepped inside and listened. A tap dripped. The air smelt strongly
of detergent and cologne. He checked all the stalls were empty, then
stood to the side of the wide frosted window.

Plenty of daylight shone through. Patches of pale green amongst
blocks of blue and grey. Meaning, he worked out, that this part of
the hotel offered a view south-west across Green Park. Outside he
thought he heard the sound of running footsteps. Then silence
descended again.

The Phillips screwdriver was where he'd wedged it down the
back of the radiator. He retrieved it and stood on top of the toilet in
the first stall. Unscrewing the ceiling panel directly above, letting
the screws rattle to the floor, he reached into the roof space and
hauled down his black Gor-Tex rucksack.

You drop your guard and sooner or later you'll end up getting hit.

One of the rules the Old Man had taught him. Danny had never
been more grateful for his advice than he was right now.

He took out his phone and Bluetooth earpiece from the rucksack,
cursing the fact that the blonde woman had taken his suit jacket,
along with its transmitter and audio bead.

Not only was the lost equipment's tech spec superior to what he
had now, but more importantly, if he'd got a recording of that
meeting, he'd be able to risk handing himself in to the police.
Alongside the recording, the Kid would then have been able to
provide testimony on Danny's behalf. But as it was, he had nothing.

He switched his phone on.

'The Kid,' he said.

The Bluetooth headset triggered the phone's voice recognition system, tripping its autodial function.

Less than two seconds later, the Kid's voice hissed through Danny's ear. 'Danny? Are you OK? What the fuck is going on?'

CHAPTER SEVENTEEN

'You've got to get me out of here. Past the cops. I've been set up,' Danny said.

'Jesus . . . You're still in the hotel . . .'

It was a statement, not a question. Danny's phone's GPS signature must have already flashed up as a map blip on one of the Kid's screens.

'I'm in the ground floor men's rest room.'

'I fucking knew this was going pear-shaped the second that woman found the bug,' said the Kid. 'It was them behind the shooting, right?'

'Right.'

'Well, listen. You can forget exiting out front. I'm piggybacking Westminster City Council's live CCTV feeds, as well as the Trafficmaster and Camerawatch systems. And the cops are kettling anyone they spot on foot into Berkeley Square. Quarantining them in a bunch of banks and car showrooms until they can work out who's who.'

No surprise that the Kid was already riding the data feeds. Post GCHQ, he'd spent four years working for the European Network and Information Security Agency. During which time – 'only out of sheer academic interest, right' – he'd illegally acquired copies of the master programming atlases and codes-and-procedure manuals for hundreds of police agencies, phone companies, government offices and banks.

Meaning that these days the Kid could break and enter into just about any system he pleased.

'I'm checking the back of the hotel now . . .' Danny could hear the Kid's fingers rattling across his keyboard. 'I've got squad cars showing on six of seven street corners to the east. Riot vans converging too. Busting up through Pall Mall and Marlborough Road. Uniforms on foot in the park, west and rear. Armed with MP5s, looks like. Fanning out and pegging down at three zero zero metres.'

Hardcore then, Danny thought. Most likely CO19 or SO15, the Metropolitan Police Authority's specialist firearms and counter-terrorism units.

The three hundred metres was standard. In case of IEDs. Which the police would be assuming that whoever had attacked that limo and strafed those civvies might also have rigged up to explode around the hotel.

'I'm telling you, mate,' said the Kid, 'it's getting hairier than a rat's arsehole out there. Looks like they're gearing up for a siege. Reckoning whoever did this is going to want to take a whole bunch more people out.'

'Yeah, well they're wrong,' Danny said. 'This was a hit. There's no more casualties here inside. The people who did this have gone.'

'OK, sit tight,' said the Kid. 'I'm trawling the council planning offices for the hotel floor plans.' There was the rapid scratch and hiss of a cigarette being lit. 'There's gotta be another way out.'

The Kid's voice had become garbled. Fractional delays had started punctuating his words.

'What's wrong with the line?' Danny said.

'I'm routeing us through an encryption filter. To make sure nobody's earwigging on what we've got to say. We're going to be jumping between networks from now on too. Just to keep us one step ahead.'

Danny was already moving. This rest room was a dead end. He switched the glass shard from his pocket for a telescopic mirror-on-a-stick from his rucksack. Convex-lensed. SWAT issue.

He guzzled from the tap. Didn't know when he'd get a chance again. Didn't bother washing his hands. It was going to take more than designer liquid soap to get that gunshot residue out of his pores.

He pulled a pair of neoprene SPECOPS gloves from his rucksack. As he held the rest room door ajar, the mirror gave him a fish-eye view of the corridor outside. Quiet as a church on Monday.

He slipped out through the doorway. Three metres to the right, he reached a crossroads. The corridors branching off it were deserted. He crouched down and watched and waited, as the Kid continued to type.

'So what the hell happened up there, Danny?' The Kid's voice crackled down the line.

Danny ordered the events in his mind.

'I got Tasered, then drugged. I woke up with a high-powered assault rifle strapped to my hands. Dressed in a red tracksuit, balaclava and Nikes. Next to a dead guy whose face and fingers had been hacked off. But it wasn't until I stepped out on to the hotel balcony and saw those massacred people out there that I realized how totally fucked I was.'

'Jesus, Danny. That was you out there? Gazing round like you'd just beamed down from Mars?'

'Sounds like I made quite an impression.'

'Too fucking right. And I only caught a glimpse. Had to get back to concentrating the hell on weaving my way out of that traffic, before it jammed up for good.'

'Where are you now?'

'An alleyway up the other side of Knightsbridge.'

Good news at last, Danny thought. Because if the Kid had already slipped the police net, he'd be able to work uninterrupted on Danny's behalf.

'Did you see the shooting?' Danny said.

'Couldn't exactly miss it, the way they went about it. Trust me, Danny. Covert is not their middle fucking name. There were two of them. Red tracksuits. Balaclavas. They rained down on that limo from the second it pulled up. Turned it into a sieve. Then started wasting the people on the pavements who were trying to get away. Just taking fucking potshots. Blowing them all to hell.'

Danny pictured the civilian bodies again. Their brightly coloured clothes. The sheer fucking *wrongness* of it all.

'And that's the last you saw of them? Out on the balcony?'

'Me and everyone else. I've been listening in on the police channels and they've not picked up anyone they think did it yet. Word is there's over twenty civilians who got killed, as well as whoever the fuck was in that limo.'

'The shooters were Russians,' Danny said. 'Or Russian-sounding, anyway.'

'What about your dead guy in the room? You got any idea about him?'

'I found a data stick and swipe card on him. But the card's pretty messed up. Covered in ink.'

'You let me worry about that.'

'It could have been left there on purpose. For the cops.'

'Or not,' said the Kid. 'Only way to find out is to let me have a look.'

The rattle of the Kid's keyboard stopped.

'OK, bingo,' he said. 'I got the hotel's schematics in front of me now.' A hiss of his cigarette. 'Roof to roof's a no-go. The building's a stand-alone. And you go trying any of those fire escapes and you'll get spotted for sure.'

Spotted or shot, the Kid meant. Police marksmen would already have had plenty of time to get in position. There'd soon be helicopters deployed too. With infrared detectors.

No point in trying to hide anywhere here in the hotel either, he'd already decided. The second the police had the building secure, they'd bring in portable heat-signature detectors and dog teams that between them would soon sniff out anything bigger than a rat.

Danny felt the walls closing in on him, as the prospect of prison swelled up in his mind. He thought about Lexie. About what something like that would do to her. Get caught and he knew she'd never speak to him again.

Again he cursed himself for not having listened to his doubts about the meeting. Again he cursed Crane for his shitty intel. Again he wondered who his US government contact had been.

'OK, Plan B,' said the Kid. 'If front, back and top are out, then maybe we should try down . . .'

'Down where?'

'Basement. I got some kind of delivery bay showing at the back of the building. Alongside the restaurant terrace. Steps leading up into Arlington Street. Might be a way to slip out there. Across into an office block. Even better, looks like there's a sewer maintenance point down there . . .'

Danny thought of darkness. Of cold and fear. Of a place beneath the ground he'd once been to long ago. He forced the thought away.

'How do you know it leads anywhere?' he asked.

'I don't. And I'm still looking for other options. But right now I reckon this is the best shot we've got.'

Danny weighed up the possibilities. The thought of trying to sneak out of some delivery bay and up into an adjoining street that was most likely already covered by snipers had to be a last resort. Even say he did then make it into some nearby building, if the police spotted him doing it, all he'd really have achieved was to swap one rat trap for another.

But the sewer . . . That might not yet have occurred to the police. Worth a try, then, even if the thought of it was like a punch to the gut.

Another of the Old Man's rules surfaced in his mind: *The longer you take to make a decision, the less time you have to act.*

Danny pictured his father's face the last time he'd heard him say it. The Old Man had been half eaten by cancer, about to board a round-the-world ship. As they'd hugged each other goodbye, they'd both known they'd not see each other again.

'OK, let's do it,' Danny said, rising, ready to move, knowing that even a sliver of a chance was better than none.

'Twenty-five feet to the right outside of the Gents, and there should be what's marked down here as a function room. Go straight through that and on into the stairwell at the end of the next corridor.'

Danny moved fast, stop-starting outside each of the open doorways he passed. He heard a radio playing through one. Jimmy Hendrix, a part of his brain recognized. 'All Along the Watchtower'. It was one of his favourite tunes, but it was nothing but background interference to him now.

The function room was right where the Kid had said it would be – which boded well for the accuracy of his schematics and the existence of the sewage maintenance point downstairs.

A dozen laptops and iPads glowed on a burnished mahogany boardroom table. A Regency couple stared out from a huge oil painting on the wall. A vast candelabra hung from an ornate ceiling, illuminating a meeting without people. Half-drunk glasses of water. Jackets on the backs of chairs. A coffee cup in pieces on the floor.

One of the room's three wide bay windows overlooking Piccadilly was open, indicating that whoever had been in here could well have bolted that way. Had maybe even bolted that way and then got shot.

Danny half crawled, using the table for cover, keeping well below the windows' line of sight. He pushed through the far door and hurried on down the corridor.

Just as he reached the stairwell, a deafening explosion ripped through the air.

CHAPTER EIGHTEEN

Danny hit the ground. He curled into a ball. Smoke billowed past a high barred window as he waited for the rumbling to pass.

What the fuck was that? he wondered.

A surge of doubt. The first since he'd left the suite upstairs. Eyes flickering, he checked his options. The stairwell led up and down. He could run either way, if that was what it took.

Maybe he'd been wrong, he was thinking. Maybe this was turning into a siege. Maybe the people he needed to find really were still here. They'd waited for the cops and ambulances to close in on the dead civilians outside and now they were letting rip with RPGs.

Or maybe the Brits had flipped and decided to storm this place early. FIDO – 'Fuck it and drive on'. That was the Paras' unofficial motto. 'Who Dares Wins' was the SAS's. It wasn't like the Brits exactly had a reputation for shyness when it came to hitting hard and fast.

But here in the centre of London? He guessed they'd be a whole lot more circumspect than that. More likely they'd be shutting this whole section of town down, hoping to snare whatever terrorist faction it was they thought had instigated this attack.

The rumbling dwindled to nothing.

No gunfire followed. No shouts or breaking glass.

'What the hell was that?' Danny grabbed his Bluetooth from where it had fallen to the floor.

'The limo out front,' the Kid's voice came back. 'Or what was left of it. Fuel tank went off. Flipped it on to its back.'

'I'm at the stairwell. Where next?'

'Head down to the first landing. Cut through the laundry. Then into the wine cellars and out the other side.'

Danny took the stairs three at a time.

'Good news,' said the Kid, as he reached the first landing.

The Kid's voice was cracking up again. Most likely the phone's reception dwindling as Danny moved deeper underground.

'I've cross-reffed the sewer maintenance point here on the building plans against the water board's records, and it's marked there too,' he went on.

'Yeah, well let's just hope it's not part of some Victorian system that got bricked up before we were even fucking born . . .'

The Kid didn't answer. Which Danny took as a fairly sure indication of his total ignorance on the matter.

Shit. Fucking great . . .

Danny reached the laundry. All bright ceiling lights and artificial floral scents. He looked round for clothes to change into, but all that caught his eye were wisps of black smoke rising in the corner.

A flat steam iron had been left switched on, pressed down on a bed sheet. Another few minutes and it was sure to catch fire. Danny ran across, raised the iron up from the scorched sheet and pulled its plug from the wall.

Then he was off again. No time to linger. He reached the wine cellar door. Tried it. Found it was locked. Saw it was reinforced too. No sense in trying to knock it down.

Opening his bag, he quickly took out and assembled the lockbuster. It didn't have a hipper name, on account of the fact that it wasn't on the market yet. It was a prototype, a thoughtful Christmas gift from an old Company friend now working for a Swiss weapons company that specialized in police, military and intelligence hardware.

Danny slipped the gizmo's barrel into the door lock and squeezed its trigger. It kicked like a mule, then buzzed. A high-pitched whine of spinning gears and blades was followed by a tortured metallic crack.

Then he was in.

Darkness. The hum of dehumidifiers. Danny took his torch from his bag and scanned the long, low room. An arched brickwork ceiling. Thousands of bottles of wine in deep alcoves. The torch's bright white beam flickered over their expensive labels as he hurried through.

Danny knew nothing about wine. Even when he'd been a drinker, it had mostly been spirits and beer. Anna-Maria, though, she knew everything there was to know about it.

And if I ever make it out of here in one piece, he thought, *I'm gonna bring her back here and buy her the best that they've got. In fact, fuck it, if I ever make it out of here alive, I might just drink myself into a goddamn stupor . . .*

The door at the far end of the cellars needed the attentions of the lockbuster too.

'OK, I'm in a service corridor,' he said, the second he got through.

The corridor branched left and right. More red brickwork. Crumbling mortar. He guessed he was right down amongst the building's foundations now. His headset only seemed to confirm this, hissing and scratching like a cat whose tail he'd just trodden on as its reception continued to fade.

'Fire exit should be just round the corner to the right,' the Kid's staccato voice came through.

Danny ran there, opened the door. Cold air and daylight flooded in. He used the convex mirror to sweep left, right and up. Apart from a scattering of cigarette butts across the ancient flagstones, there were no signs of life.

He stepped out into a stone trench. It was T-shaped, running ten feet east, west and south from where he stood. It was six feet wide and ten deep. To the east, a steep ramp ran up towards street level. To the west, a set of bowed stone steps ascended to the hotel garden.

Shafts of bright sunlight shone down through the slats of the interlocking cast-iron grilles above Danny's head. The hotel's rear wall stretched up into a burning blue sky.

A blitz of sirens all around. Danny's heart raced even faster, like any second it might burst.

He ran to a green-painted metal doorway set into a low brick arch. A fluorescent sticker was plastered across its centre. It showed a running water tap symbol, with the words 'Thames Water' printed underneath.

'I'm here,' Danny said.

'And is it?' The Kid's voice came down the line a little clearer now Danny was outside.

'Is it *what?*' Danny's fingers were already working feverishly.

'Bricked up?'

Danny smiled grimly. 'No, just locked,' he said, kicking it as hard as he could. 'But not any more.'

CHAPTER NINETEEN

Danny peered into the gloom. A maintenance room. Just like the Kid had said. Utilitarian. A wash basin, soap and paper towel dispenser stood in one corner. In the centre, two chairs and a table. A tabloid newspaper lay open at the sports pages. A rack of metal tools was screwed to the mildewed wall opposite Danny, alongside another locked door.

Danny stepped inside, torch in hand. He didn't bother switching on the bare ceiling light bulb. He shut the door behind him, snapped the thin curved wooden back of one of the chairs in half and then in half again, before sandwiching the broken pieces together and wedging them tight up under the base of the door leading back outside.

Stuffing his shades into his pocket, he checked the date on the newspaper. Only three weeks old. Meaning someone had been working down here recently. Which could only be good news as far as the possibility of this providing a way out was concerned.

Running the torch beam over the tool rack, Danny took one with a T-bar ending, and another shaped like a giant Allen key, assuming they must be for opening manholes and the like, and that he'd no doubt be needing them soon.

Right away, in fact, he now saw, as he examined the locked door set into the mildewed wall. The T-bar tool fitted its outsized keyhole. He twisted it once right round. Resistance gave way to a click.

He pulled the well-oiled door wide open and for a moment didn't move. He just stared into the cold dark mouth of the vertical shaft. The beam of his torch followed its metal ladder down for nine or ten feet before it faded into black.

There'd been a time when Danny had been terrified of places like this, a time when darkness had nearly swallowed him up for good. But it was a fear he'd learned to deal with. Not through bravery, but because he'd had no choice. He'd discovered words that had made him stronger. That had helped him block the terror from his mind.

I'll be there. Nothing can stop me.

'How's it looking?' the Kid asked, his voice half-crackle, half-hiss.

Danny was still staring, unblinking, into the gaping hole.

'Danny?' the Kid said.

'Wait . . .'

Move, Danny told himself. *Just damn well move.*

He did it. He took a deep breath and forced himself to climb down the ladder. Rung by rung. Into the dark.

He counted eighteen rungs before he reached the cold concrete floor below. The air was dank and cool. He shone the torch beam three-sixty and saw he'd now entered an eight-foot-high brickwork passage with a metal railing set into its right-hand wall.

He followed the railing for twenty paces until the passage opened out on to a raised brick walkway running the length of a much wider tunnel.

Danny shone his torch left and right. The main sewer tunnel was much bigger than anything he'd expected. Cylindrical. At least twenty foot in diameter. Plenty of room to stand. Big enough to drive a car through, in fact. It was built of Victorian brickwork, with plenty of patches of modern cement repairs in between, like stitch marks holding together an ancient and decrepit quilt.

The sewage channel itself was disused, Danny saw with relief, looking down. No rank, fast-running, icy black river, like he'd

imagined he might end up crawling through. A cold steady breeze
hinted at a much wider system of which this was only a tiny part.

More good news. Boot prints. Stamped right here in the dirt on
the walkway. Most of them led away from where Danny was
standing. Along the main tunnel. To the right. Meaning this
walkway had to lead somewhere, he decided, feeling a surge of hope.

Water dripped from the ceiling. Notes chimed everywhere, like
raindrops falling into bottles and pans.

'Kid? Can you hear me?' Danny said.

Nothing but a faint clicking.

He hurried back up into the maintenance room.

'Hey, Kid? You there?'

'I got you.'

'Looks like you might just have found me a way out . . .'

'Well thank Christ for that. But listen, there's no way your
phone's gonna work in there, Danny. So I'm patching you through
that water board plan I pulled up.'

An email pinged on to Danny's phone screen. An Acrobat file
began to download. Danny selected its icon the second it finished.
The sewer plans ballooned into view. Danny shrank them down
and then scrolled them across with his thumb.

'Christ, it's like a warren,' he said, suddenly daunted by the sheer
size of the plans. 'Which section am I in?'

'G three.'

Danny scrolled to the grid reference. There was only one dead
end in it. It had to be the same one he was standing in now. 'All
right, I got it,' he said. 'So which way next?'

'I'm looking at a street map I've superimposed on to the water
board's sewer map,' said the Kid. 'So I can kind of see where the
tunnels will lead you to above ground.'

'Only *kind of*?'

'The scales I'm working with don't match exactly. But close
enough, I hope.'

You're not the only one, Danny thought. Thought, but didn't say.
Because there was nothing to be gained from putting the Kid off
his stride.

The Kid said, 'Your phone's not got the grey cells to synchronize the two maps. So you're just gonna have to listen to the directions I give you and then make sure you stick to them once you're back inside.'

Danny traced his thumb across his phone, covering the route the Kid now read to him, memorizing it as he did. The exit point that the Kid suggested he use was nearly three-quarters of a mile away.

'Where will it bring me up?'

'A nice quiet spot round the back of a Royal Parks vehicle repairs outbuilding on the south side of Hyde Park, if my guesstimate's right.'

'Good. But one other thing . . .'

The smiling man in the hotel suite. Danny couldn't get him out of his mind.

'What?'

'The wasted limo. I need you to find out who was in it.' If he was going to discover who'd set him up, then working out who they'd come here to kill was probably a pretty good place to start.

'Already on it, Danny. I managed to scribble down a partial of the plate.'

There it was: the Kid walking one step ahead of Danny as usual. Yet another of the reasons why Danny thought he was the best.

'And?'

'I'm running the number through the DVLA's database now. We'll know who the car's registered to soon enough.'

Danny smiled, his nostrils flaring like he'd just picked up a scent. He felt fresh strength pump through him. So much better to be the hunter than the hunted. He looked back down the ladder. He could do this, he told himself. He *would*.

'Thanks, Adam,' he said.

'Oh Jesus, Danny, don't.'

'What?'

'Call me by my real name. You start doing that and I might start thinking that we really are in trouble after all.'

Danny smiled, in spite of it all. 'I'll see you on the other side,' he said.

'Good luck, bruv,' said the Kid.

Bruv. As in *brother.* As in *brother in arms.* Even though the Kid had said the word in a cod-American accent, Danny knew this was how he genuinely viewed him. As closer than a colleague. Closer than a friend. As *blood.* They'd been through too many tight situations together for it ever to be any other way.

And the feeling was mutual. The Kid was one of only three people left alive who Danny would trust with his life. There was no one else he'd rather have watching his back right now.

He cut the Kid off. Didn't want to wait any longer. He knew that if he did, he might not go in at all.

As he walked into the tunnel, he transferred the blank swipe card and data stick from his trouser pocket into his rucksack and zipped it tight.

In truth, he knew that these two small items and the Kid were the only real hopes he had left.

CHAPTER TWENTY

Danny set off south along the raised walkway of the main sewer tunnel. He shone the beam of his torch straight ahead and tried not to think of the darkness closing in behind him with every step he took.

He kept moving, following the boot prints. As if he were part of a bigger march. He tried comforting himself with the fact that plenty of ordinary civilians doing their jobs had walked this way before. But memories off the past kept strobing through his mind.

His Nikes crunched dirt and grit. He needed to go straight on for forty metres, the Kid had told him. Then the tunnel would divide into two. Danny should split right, then follow the gradual curve of the sewer through another four junctions, progressing south-west for nearly three-quarters of a mile.

What was going on outside? That was what he wanted to know. Was he even now walking beneath the boots of some watchful, waiting cop? And what if they too had someone who'd strategized smart like the Kid? What if they'd thought of the sewer as well? Not just as a potential route out of the hotel, but as a way in? What if, somewhere up ahead in this labyrinthine system, an infiltration unit was rushing towards Danny right now?

Just keep on, he told himself. *Don't give in to the fear.*

Time was still the most precious thing he had. He mustn't waste a second.

Somewhere below him, in the vast curved gutter where Victorian London's sewage had once flowed, he heard a tiny cascade of mortar dust and the squeaking of rats. The darkness was closing in. But he didn't break stride.

I'll be there. Nothing can stop me.

Again he remembered the words.

And this time he remembered, too, the circumstances in which he'd first used them. When the darkness had nearly swallowed him up for good. In North Carolina. In another cold hole in the ground. One from which Danny had thought he'd never escape.

After Danny had completed his masters degree in modern languages at NYC, majoring in Russian and Arabic, he joined the Army Rangers. Partly because he'd known it would have made the Old Man proud, because he'd served with them himself. But mainly so he could get away from his parents' empty New York house, which had long stopped being a home.

Three years on and Danny had been recruited by the CIA. Their Special Activities Division had claimed him soon after, training him up in everything from agent recruitment to defusing bombs. Until finally they'd sent him down the Hole.

It was meant to have been an exercise in endurance and bonding. For Danny and four other clandestine intelligence officers who'd shortly be working as a team operating out of Kuwait, gathering HUMINT as well as carrying out direct actions as and when required.

The Hole was local SAD parlance for the treacherous cave system located less than an hour's drive from the division's Harvey Point facility. Danny's team had been well trained and were equipped for any eventuality they might encounter down there.

But less than two hours after they'd entered the system – already a hundred feet below ground – a flash flood had struck, and Danny had got stranded the wrong side of a deep vertical chimney in a half-collapsed tunnel. He had no rope, no food, no map, and within forty-five minutes his torch flickered out.

He crawled blind. Any way up. Away from the rapidly rising water.

He tried mentally mapping his movements to begin with, counting junctions and inclines. He focused on his compass's fading luminous dial. He tried not to think of the cold rock against which he kept scraping his bleeding head. Or to listen to the asthmatic echo of his breath, or the rush, gurgle and spit of the water rising up below.

But soon his compass dial faded into the total blackness around him. And Danny found himself biting down on his tongue just to stop himself from screaming out.

He got stuck not long after. Jammed. Unable to go forward or back. Chest too tight even to scream. No way of knowing if the rest of his team had been killed. No way of telling how far into the system he'd now gone. Or when the water would reach him.

Hyperventilating, he was hit by the realization that he'd die down here. Entombed in rock. Drowned, suffocated, frozen or starved.

But he didn't quit. Something stopped him, penetrated his panic, gave him the strength to move first his fingers. Then his hand. Millimetre by millimetre. Rupturing his knuckles across that sharp knot of rock wedged into his side. Until he finally found himself able to ease off his knife belt and engineer the leeway to twist and turn and tear his body through.

Something kept him crawling. There in the depths of that darkness, inside his mind he found light.

A memory. Her. And a future. The same.

Something to live for, never to stop fighting for.

I'll be there. Nothing can stop me.

Down in that cave system, the words came to him as loud as if someone else were hissing them into his ear.

But in fact they were his own. The same words he'd called out six months earlier to a girl at the end of the first night he'd met her. And – as a kind of joke between them – every time they'd parted since.

Love at first sight. Back then Danny had thought it was a bunch of bullshit. Nothing but a myth. But the girl who'd sat down alongside him in the subway car late that Tuesday night, as he'd made his way home with several stops still to go, she'd caught his attention all right.

Short blonde hair. Deep blue eyes. Soft, fine features and a full-lipped mouth. Her smile kept breaking out like sunlight through a cloud-scudded sky, as she stared in rapt concentration at her newspaper crossword, and one by one filled in the clues.

Three stops later, and without thinking, Danny said, 'Diva,' out loud.

She looked at him confused, then back at her crossword. Her pen hovered mid air for a second. Then she turned to him and laughed. A mixture of outrage and amusement.

'Eleven across,' she said, staring back down at her paper and reading aloud the clue he'd just solved: *'Prima donna making an eager comeback* . . . You're quite right. Diva. Well done.' Her accent was English, the same as his mother's. London, he guessed.

She scribbled the four letters into the grid, then looked Danny over curiously, before offering up her paper and pen.

'You know what?' she said. 'I think I've already done as many as I can. So if you want to try finishing it off . . .'

Another smile, but this time with a challenge in it too, leaving Danny guessing from the fact that her pen looked expensive that she wasn't planning on walking away from him just yet.

He was right. Even though he only managed the one clue after that, the two of them started talking, and didn't stop.

He couldn't exactly tell her what he did for a living, but he told her a more honest version than he told most. Mainly, though, he just listened. And learned how she, like him, had dual citizenship, thanks to her English mother and recently deceased American father. She'd been living in the States now for just over a year, moving round. She'd studied history at college, but still had no real idea what she wanted to do. Currently she worked at a gift outlet at the Guggenheim museum, but she was toying with the idea of one day opening up a ceramics store in Greenwich. She'd moved here from her last place in California for the sole reason that *Breakfast at Tiffany's* was her favourite book.

It was only when the rest of the car finished emptying and the train stayed still that they realized they'd reached the end of the line.

On their way out through the darkening station, he said, 'So you live near here?'

She didn't answer. Instead she said, 'You?'

'I should have got off five stops back.'

She started to laugh. 'I was the one before that.'

Outside it was raining. Neither of them had an umbrella or raincoat. He stood out in the street and hailed her a taxi. He got the driver to pull right over on the pavement so she wouldn't get wet. He held open the door for her as she climbed in. Pulling it shut after her, she mouthed something at him and pressed the window button down.

But he never got to hear whatever it was she wanted to say. The taxi pulled away without warning, leaving him staring after her, watching her waving at him through its rear window as it faded with her into the rain-streaked night.

Only then did it occur to him that he hadn't even asked for her number.

He started to run. Kept on running. Slipping. Stumbling. Weaving high speed along the pavement, between people and bins, like some crazed NFL quarterback going for broke. Then out into the traffic. Forget jaywalking, he was jay-sprinting. He invented it right there and then.

Twice he nearly caught up with her. But twice the lights changed.

Third time he got lucky. At another set of lights, he collapsed panting at her taxi door. As his nails clawed at her window, she stared out at him with an expression of astonishment and delight.

The window buzzed down. Danny was too out of breath to speak.

'I finish work tomorrow at six,' she said.

He got to his feet just as the lights changed.

'I'll be there. Nothing can stop me,' he said.

Nothing had. He'd met her the next evening. The three evenings after that. That was how he'd started to get to know Sally Gillard, the woman who two years later had become his wife.

I'll be there. Nothing can stop me.

It was a mantra that had kept him going through that tunnel system in North Carolina. And three hours later it had brought him up gasping into the twilit air over a mile from where he'd gone into the ground.

Danny never did tell Sally how she'd once saved his life without even being near him. He'd often considered it, but a part of him had always made him hold back, thinking he'd just end up sounding dumb.

Then Sally had died, and the opportunity had passed. It was a secret that probably wouldn't mean a thing to anyone else any more.

I'll be there. Nothing can stop me.

As the words ran through Danny's mind now, down here in the London sewers, it was no longer Sally he was thinking of. He hoped there was a heaven, and that somewhere his wife and son went on. He hoped he'd see them both again one day. But he didn't know.

I'll be there. Nothing can stop me.

No, when those words ran through Danny's mind now, they weren't for Sally. Or Jonathan. They were for Lexie. Not because she needed his help now, or ever might again. But because if she ever did, then he would be there. For Lexie, he would always stay alive.

CHAPTER TWENTY-ONE

Danny shone his torch along the ladder leading up the dark concrete shaft. No boot marks on the rusty rungs. Didn't look like it had been used in a while. But according to his glowing phone screen, this dead end in the sewage network was exactly the exit point the Kid had described.

And sure enough, fifteen feet up at the top of the ladder there was a cast-iron manhole cover. Above which Danny hoped was fresh air.

Tempting as it was to stay put underground and try and ride out this storm, it was only a matter of time now before the police and military realized there was no one in that hotel and moved in and found the broken sewer maintenance point door.

He had no choice but to leave.

Zipping his phone and headset up in his rucksack, he gratefully started to climb. The stink down here had grown abhorrent. The kind of smell that no amount of exposure could acclimatize you to.

The spacious section of Victorian sewer he'd first entered by the Ritz had proved a false dawn. Not only in terms of air quality, but accessibility too.

After that first junction he'd gone through, all fears of being intercepted by the police had faded from his mind. Because only someone as desperate as himself would have considered such a means of escape.

Far from being able to drive a car through the rest of the route he'd taken, he'd have been lucky to squeeze a bike. The crumbling brick maintenance walkway had soon thinned out to such an extent that for several stretches Danny had been reduced to sidling sideways, and a couple of times he'd even had to crawl. In addition, he'd found himself negotiating ladders, stairs and an automated pump station, none of which had been marked on his map.

Modern sewer pipes had been fed through the old sewer gutters. Several had raw sewage bleeding from their joints. Danny had been forced to roll down his balaclava, as well as take off his tracksuit top and tie it in a makeshift filter round his face, just to stave off the risk of hydrogen sulphide poisoning.

As a result, his bare arms and back were now smeared with excrement and covered in cuts from where he'd scuffed his upper body on the pipes and tunnel walls.

At the top of the ladder, he stopped and listened. He heard nothing above. No traffic. Or sirens. Meaning that with any luck, the Kid had done his sums right and Danny was now beneath Hyde Park.

He hoped above all that this was the case.

Because it would mean he'd already circumvented the cops' main cordon. The one they'd be letting nothing and no one get by. And within which they'd soon be interviewing every person, and combing through every building, trash can and car.

Manage that and – so long as the police didn't find any finger-prints back in that hotel room to match up to his US State Department records – Danny might finally be in the clear.

It was the slimmest of hopes, he knew. But it was all he had.

Now get to the Kid's van. Then start looking for the scum who did this. Prove it was them and not you who killed all those people back there.

Holding on to the ladder with his left hand, Danny used his right to haul up the T-bar tool from where he'd secured it in his rucksack strap. He inserted it into the manhole cover. Turned the lock fully round. Then, leaving the tool hanging there, he gripped the manhole cover's handle and heaved it a half-turn anticlockwise. Until its open position arrows lined up.

Ignoring the of water rapidly dripping from its rim, he pushed up hard against the cover's cold metal surface with the flat of his hand.

Nothing. It wouldn't budge.

He tried again, his frustration turning to fear now, as it still wouldn't give. He couldn't believe it. He'd come this far and had got so close, only to now be denied. And by what? By rust? By some jerk parking their car on top of the manhole? By any one of a hundred other pieces of crap luck that Lady Fate have might just rolled his way.

Anger flared inside him. He ripped the T-bar tool free and threw it clattering down the shaft. Stepping up another two rungs, he wedged his right shoulder and the back of his neck up tight against the manhole cover. He brought his feet up another rung each, so his knees were up under his chin. He flexed his legs. Drove upwards with his shoulder, giving it everything he'd got.

A burst of surprise. The cover shifted, scraped, lurched to one side. A deafening rush of water crashed down. A flood that didn't stop. That battered him as if he'd just stepped under a waterfall and would any second get swept away.

Danny clung to the ladder for his life.

Only instinct saved him. Some primal part of him knowing what would happen if he let go. A fifteen-foot drop. Enough to fracture an ankle easy. More likely to snap his neck.

CHAPTER TWENTY-TWO

Blinded by sunlight, Danny clawed his way out of the manhole. He sprawled across slippery stone, coughing up water. Couldn't stop. Each heave of his chest tore at his ribs. He ripped his drenched tracksuit jacket from where he'd wrapped it round his face. Water poured from his nostrils. He vomited, gasping for air.

He tried to stand. He twisted his hip, skittered sideways on all fours, like a dog on ice. He steadied himself and finally rose. His legs were shaking. Arms too. It felt like every muscle in his body had just been stretched on a rack.

His vision swung in and out of focus. A million shimmering points of light. Then fixed.

Looking round, he saw he was standing in some kind of fountain. Some kind of *public* fountain, his brain filled in. People were staring. Ten or twenty of them. They were staring and starting to shout.

The balaclava. *Shit*. He'd rolled it down over his face to ward off the stench in the sewer. As if his rising up from the deep hadn't already been enough to freak these people out . . .

But there was no way he could risk taking it off. Any one of these tourists might film him on their phone and have his image Flickring out across the web at the touch of a button.

Danny tore off his rucksack. He jerked his tracksuit top back on. His scars and the tattoo on his right shoulder – of an Ouroboros, a dragon devouring its own tail – they were just as idiosyncratic as any fingerprint. They too might be snapped and get him ID'd.

The water in the fountain was already less than half a foot deep, and dropping all the time, rushing gurgling down that open manhole. Pulling his rucksack back on, Danny ploughed towards the fountain's edge.

The civilians started running then. Away from Danny as fast as they could. Who knew what had already leaked out to the public about the attack? They might have heard about the other massacred civilians. They might think that now he was coming for them. As they ran, they started shouting out.

But worse was what they were running towards.

Less than two hundred metres away, Danny saw police. Lots of them. Maybe more cops than he'd ever seen in one place in his life. That cordon he'd been hoping to slip by, he'd managed it all right.

But only just.

The police currently all had their backs to him. They were crouched down behind a stationary convoy of marked and unmarked vehicles, staring out across whatever road they were parked beside.

They must be facing Green Park, towards the Ritz, Danny thought. Due east. Which meant he had to run in the opposite direction. West into Knightsbridge.

And fast. Because the second those cops saw the civilians running at them, each and every one of those motionless black and white figures would flip like a line of dominoes and all end up facing Danny.

Hauling himself over the stone rim of the fountain, he hit solid ground and built up speed. He raced down a wood chip path.

To his left, through the trees, he caught glimpses of a wide empty road. Stretching between Knightsbridge and Hyde Park Corner, he guessed. The lack of traffic meant it must already have been cleared and blocked off either end. Meaning there'd be more roadblocks and police to the west.

To Danny's right and straight ahead, a vast expanse of rolling green grass dotted with sycamores and oaks stretched into the distance. Hyde Park. Meaning the Kid's directions hadn't been so far off after all. He'd got Danny into the park all right. He just hadn't brought him up anywhere safe.

The park was way too open for Danny to take cover in. Dressed like this. With those cops about to be on his tail any second.

Up ahead of him, there was no one else in sight. He rolled his balaclava up into a hat once more and pulled on his shades, so at least he didn't look like an actual terrorist any more. More like some jogger soaked through with sweat, about to have a cardiac arrest.

Panting, he reached sparse tree cover a hundred and fifty metres further on. Some kind of bower arrangement. Concrete pathways. Raised flower beds. Park benches.

There were people. Kids on rollerblades and skateboards weaving elegant lines between rows of plastic yellow cups, beat boxes pumping. None of them giving a damn about all the distant cop sirens.

Danny thought back to college. He imagined an asphalt track stretching ahead of him. He used to be able to do the hundred metres in thirteen seconds flat. Get anywhere near that now and he might still be in with a chance.

He stumbled after less than fifty. His rucksack felt like someone had packed it with bricks. But he picked himself up and kept on.

Ten seconds later and he was deep in trees and dappled shade. He notched down his pace to catch his breath as he rounded a curve in the path. Silvery water glinted through the trees to the right.

The Serpentine, Danny guessed. He'd once spent an afternoon on it with Anna-Maria, rowing up and down in a wooden skiff, smoking cigarettes and drinking cold Cokes in the sun.

Digging inside his rucksack, he pulled out his Bluetooth headset and phone. The Gor-Tex had spared both from the deluge of water.

He upped his pace again for a final burst. He focused ahead, forcing himself to run through a thick patch of bushes and shrubs, ripping his trouser leg on a rose bush, thorns tearing into his flesh.

This is what you train for, he told himself. *This is why you spend all those shitty hours in the gym.*

Gasping for oxygen, he finally slowed, his muscles crying out, laced with lactic acid. He saw the backs of tall buildings through the trees. Hotels and foreign embassies, if his memory served him right.

Another memory got dredged up right alongside. Of the SAS storming the Iranian embassy here in London in 1980. Operation Nimrod. The Old Man had talked Danny through it like he'd wished he'd been there himself.

Danny had worked with SAS guys since. Respected them. Enough to be afraid. Their regimental barracks was in Regent's Park. Only four miles from here.

'The Kid,' he said, picking up his pace again as he waited for his Bluetooth to patch him through.

'Danny?' the Kid hissed back at him five paces on. 'Why the fuck didn't you come up out of the exit I said?'

'I screwed up. I came out through a goddamn fountain.'

'A *what*?'

'Don't fucking ask.'

Dead ahead, through the bushes, Danny saw the stone pillars of an exit. 'I'm coming up to Edinburgh Gate,' he said, reading the pristine white sign set into the neatly mown grass.

'OK, I got your GPS sig back on my sat map,' said the Kid. 'I'm six hundred metres away. In Egerton Crescent. South-south-west from you. I'm patching you a route through now.'

'Better get the engine running,' Danny said. 'And Kid?'

'What?'

'Save me a doughnut, OK? I'm so hungry I'm about to chew through my own goddamn tongue.'

No answer from the Kid. Meaning no doughnuts left either, Danny guessed.

He pulled out his phone, saw the Acrobat file downloading. Slowing now, he opened up the map it contained and memorized the sequence of eleven turns he'd need to take to get to the Kid.

'Any word on the limo?' he said.

'Yeah, but it's not good news . . . Diplomatic plates for a start . . . I had to hack into the Foreign and Commonwealth Office just to pull them up.'

If there'd been anything solid nearby, Danny would have probably punched it. As it was, he settled for tearing a pathway through the undergrowth, down to the black park railings.

The plates being diplomatic meant the attack on the limo was almost certainly political, not just some criminal hit. Which in turn would explain how come that TV crew had already been camped out across the street from the Ritz. Not through chance. But because they'd been tipped off. By the same people who'd shot up the limo. To garner as much media coverage for the assassination as they could. It also explained why those civilians had been shot too. To guarantee blanket international media coverage of the kind generated by the suicide bomb attack on the international arrivals hall of Moscow's Domodedovo Airport in January 2011.

'You're not going to like which embassy the limo's registered to either,' said the Kid.

Danny tore through another row of shrubs. 'Try me.'

'Georgia.'

Danny slowed. 'I take it you're not referring to the Peach State bordering on Florida,' he said.

'More the former Soviet republic kind . . .'

Which even though Danny was covered with sewage, soaked through to the bone and being hunted by what looked like the entirety of the Metropolitan Police left him in even deeper shit than he'd previously thought.

The facts of the matter queued up in his brain. Georgia had gained its independence in 1991, as part of the so-called Rose Revolution. In 2008, however, Russian troops had occupied South Ossetia and Abkhazia, two buffer states that up until then Georgia had claimed as its own. The Russian and Russian-backed troops were still there. Georgia still wanted them out. And most of the rest of the UN agreed.

Leaving both Russia and Georgia looking for any excuse these days to put the other side down publicly.

But a hit like this could go further than that, depending of course on who had been in that car. A hit like this could mean war.

Which brought up the issue of who exactly it was who might have ordered the attack. No easy answer there. It could be anyone who'd benefit from an escalation of violence in the region. Arms dealers. Russian expansionists. South Ossetian separatists. Hell, even gas and oil companies. The hawk-faced man and his colleagues could be working for any one of these. Or he might even just be an individual with a grudge.

Once more Danny saw the man watching him from the sofa, so totally in control. No wonder. He'd been staring at the perfect fall guy, whom he'd clearly cherry-picked for the job.

An ex-CIA operative who now worked for money. Forget that Danny was choosy as hell who he worked for, the rest of the world would no doubt consider him a perfectly plausible assassin for whatever high-profile Georgian had been killed in that car. And for the mayhem that had come with it too.

You're here because it will be easy to hang the blame on you . . . For what I'm about to do . . .

'Yeah, asshole, well we'll soon see about that.'

'What?'

Danny hadn't even realized he'd spoken aloud.

'Nothing,' he said. 'You any idea yet who was in the limo?'

'No. But it could have been anyone with a link to the Georgian embassy. I've already checked the Ritz's records and there's no mention of any Georgians or Georgian diplomatic meetings being booked in.'

'What about the news feeds?

'Reports of the civilian massacre are leaking through now. On Reuters, BBC and CNN. And Twitter, of course. That's on fire. But no one's got any specifics on the limousine yet.'

'You let me know the second you find out what the fuck is going on.'

Danny reached flat ground and was grateful for it. A slick of sweat covered his skin, burning hot already in spite of his drenched clothes. He tried to ignore the aching in his thighs as he sprinted the last twenty feet to the gate.

He reached the gate, slowed, jogged through it. He saw a blonde woman getting out of a silver VW parked up alongside a grassy bank. A young couple walked by in the opposite direction with a spaniel puppy barking excitedly on a leash.

None of them gave him a second look.

Ten metres further on and he reached a junction between two service roads. He turned south, leaving only ten turns remaining before he'd get to the Kid.

That was when he heard the first siren approaching. Shrieking in from the east. The second he looked that way, he wished he hadn't. Because of the speed of the black car coming at him. It must have been doing ninety. Maybe more. It looked like a missile, like nothing could stop it. Two other squad cars fanned out in its wake.

CHAPTER TWENTY-THREE

Pulse racing, body temperature rocketing, Danny ran straight across South Carriage Drive. He didn't look back as he raced on into the city. From right up close behind him came a yelp of skidding tyres – those three cop cars kerb-mounting, handbrake-turning, almost on top of him now.

He jinked right, heart pounding, sliding between a row of parked cars. He used them as a shield, kept them between himself and the street.

The first cop car catapulted past him less than a second after. Unmarked. Black. It angled in hard right and slewed to a juddering stop halfway across the pavement. Five metres ahead.

Danny didn't slow. No point ducking into the chained courtyard of the building to his right. Too easy to get trapped. But he couldn't turn back either. Not with those other two cop cars no doubt already sealing off the road behind.

It was the driver's door of the black pursuit car in front of Danny that opened first. A man in his early forties with a hard, lined face and a short grey-black beard started to get out, pulling a pistol as he did.

Danny didn't mess about. While the plainclothes cop was still only halfway out of the vehicle, he dropped his right shoulder and hit the door as hard as he could.

The metal slammed against the cop's legs. The man cried out and crumpled to the ground as Danny let his momentum carry him onwards, spinning him across the car's front bumper, forcing him to throw his hands up just to stop himself from smashing his face against a blackened brick wall.

He turned, expecting the other cop riding shotgun to be coming for him. But all he saw was a blurred face staring out at him through the windscreen, alongside the manically strobing blue light on the dash.

Danny lurched panting away from there and out on to a wide gridlocked street, his right knee jarring with every step, the heel of his left hand bleeding from where he'd battered himself against the wall.

Fifty metres to his left, a crowd of people clung like a swarm of agitated bees to the outside of Knightsbridge tube station. Meaning, Danny reckoned, that the London Underground system must have already been shut down.

The secondary roadblock he'd predicted was there also, closing off the entire street. Traffic stretched back past him for as far as the eye could see.

And gridlock was good. For Danny, at least. Because no way could those police cars pursue him through this. Meaning the odds against him had temporarily been evened. If the police were going to catch him at all, they were now going to have to do it on foot.

He half ran, half stumbled diagonally across the street, away from the roadblock, heading west, zigzagging between jammed cars.

No one paid him any attention. They were all watching the police up at the roadblock. They'd realized something big was going down. Some kind of an attack. They'd probably heard details of the gunmen opening up on those other civilians on the radio by now. One guy was up on the bonnet of his truck, using his cell phone to film it all.

Danny kept his head dipped low beneath the line of vehicle roofs as he put more distance between himself and the police. He unrolled his balaclava another inch, so it was right down on his brow. Sweat trickled from it like a sponge. He reduced his speed to a steady jog. He tried to keep on visualizing himself as just another urban wannabe athlete out getting fit.

Something in his peripheral vision made him look right. Across the street were two armed soldiers. Household Cavalry, Danny saw from the uniforms. On sentry duty outside Hyde Park Barracks.

But they weren't interested in him either. The same as everyone else, they were wondering what the hell was happening to the east.

Danny glanced back over his shoulder. Didn't like what he saw. The police manning the roadblock were beginning to turn. Word of his arrival in this sector must have spread. In his direction.

Walk. Don't run, he reminded himself.

He spotted the junction with Trevor Street at last. Only then – when he had to, or else he'd pass it by – did he leave the cover of the stationary line of traffic and step up on to the pavement.

Don't look back.

It felt like crossing a spotlit stage. He remembered the last time he'd had to do that, in a nativity play when he'd been seven. His brow bled sweat. Each second stretched as his mind raced. He imagined the eyes of the police boring deep into his back. He waited for their shouts to start up, for the rumble of their boots to turn into a stampede. For the chase to be on again.

But he reached the entrance to Trevor Street hearing nothing more threatening than the frantic beat of his own drumming heart.

'OK, I've got a visual on you now,' the Kid's voice whispered in his ear.

Danny glanced up at a CCTV camera bolted to a set of traffic lights on a pedestrian crossing ten metres further up the road. A part of the Trafficmaster system the Kid was already jacked into, no doubt.

'I can't believe you've still got that tracksuit on, man . . .'

'Yeah, funny that, Kid,' Danny said. 'But there weren't exactly many clothes concessions down in that sewer of yours.'

As he turned into Trevor Street, the noise of the idling traffic behind him immediately dropped away. The small square was residential. Only parked cars. No cops.

'The only fashion I give a toss about right now,' said the Kid with a snort, 'is what's on your face. These images I'm getting of you now. The police can and will access these systems too. And once they start scanning back through the hard-drive records, tracking your movements street by street from where you came out of that fountain right up to here, any half-decent shots of your face they get, they're gonna set VIIDO on straight away . . .'

VIIDO. The catchy little acronym the British police had dreamt up for the Visual Images, Identifications and Detections Office at New Scotland Yard. Whose tech-heavy task it was to identify and help capture any suspects caught on CCTV.

'And the first thing they'll do is run that photo of you through all the major digital image databases they're linked up to, including those in the States . . .'

'Meaning sooner or later they'll match my face up to my name.' *And my address and my whole damned history.*

'Correct. So make sure you keep those shades and that hat on,' said the Kid.

Danny stepped up into a jog, having finally now got his breath fully back. He saw that nearly all of the Regency houses he was passing had CCTV cameras either high up on their façades or glaring out from their doorways. Bringing another UK tech stat rising up through his mind.

About how – in spite of recent pledges by the government to curb the epidemic – there were an estimated four point two million CCTV cameras in Britain. Half a million in London alone. Also meaning that your average Londoner, wandering around London on an average day, was likely to be filmed by more than three hundred and fifty cameras on thirty-five separate surveillance systems.

Leaving Danny's current chances of getting his portrait repeatedly snapped higher than anywhere else in the world.

CHAPTER TWENTY-FOUR

Danny cut through the deserted service alley linking Montpelier Mews to Montpelier Street.

He could hear a chopper hovering somewhere nearby. He stuck close to the residential buildings he passed, and used trees for cover where possible.

The noise of gridlocked traffic began building up again now. A tuneless chorus of blaring horns. The same as Knightsbridge, Brompton Road was jammed both ways.

The clatter of a road drill made him flinch as he stepped out on to the pavement. Sounded like small-arms fire. So much so that for a second he wondered if someone was shooting at him.

His stomach twisted with grim apprehension as he waited for a bullet to hit. Nothing came. He forced himself to stay calm and stay right where he was. He crouched down on the hot pavement and made a show of tying his trainers' laces, while really checking left and right.

Another roadblock to the east. Outside what looked like Harrods department store. More cops. Riot vans too. But no one was looking his way. They were all focused to the north, to where the pursuit cars had nearly run him down.

He turned south-west down Brompton Road instead and lengthened his stride, kicking off again into his jogging routine.

But the more designer clothes boutiques he lumbered past, the more frequently he caught sight of his ragged reflection in their gleaming windows, and the more he felt his confidence draining away.

No matter, he told himself. *You're going to make it. You're nearly there . . .*

Less than two hundred metres away was the turn for Egerton Terrace. Another fifty metres past that and Danny would have the Kid's Ford Transit clearly in his sights.

The thought of the cold water that would be waiting for him there left him light-headed for a second. He felt his legs nearly slip away.

Keep moving . . . Not long . . .

'We're going to lose contact for a second,' said the Kid.

'Why?'

'Cop chatter says they're about to jam the commercial phone networks. To isolate you fully, in case you're not operating alone. They reckon you and the others are being micromanaged remotely, the same as went down in Mumbai. I'm switching us to an emergency services network. But don't worry, I'll keep us encrypted. They won't even know that we're there.'

A crackle. A hiss. Four seconds later and the Kid came back.

'Word's also just out on who the target was,' he said.

'Shoot.'

'Nice choice of words . . .'

Danny was too busy focusing on not falling over from exhaustion to raise a smile.

'Madina Tskhovrebova,' said the Kid.

The name meant nothing to Danny.

'A Nobel Prize-winning journalist,' the Kid said. 'Due to ask the UN Security Council later today for their support in passing further resolutions demanding the withdrawal of Russian troops from her homeland of South Ossetia.'

Which of course was why she'd been in a Georgian diplomatic limousine, Danny realized. Because in truth she'd have been addressing the UN on their behalf. Because if Russian troops ever did pull out of South Ossetia, then Georgia would once more be able to claim the potentially lucrative territory as its own.

'And she's dead?' Danny said.

'Cops got her into the building opposite the Ritz. But she bled out once she was there.'

The woman who'd been screaming in the street. The only one of those prone civilians who'd been moving. The one whose legs had been blown away. So she'd been the target. And the shooters had let her live. The hawk-faced man had let her suffer a while longer, knowing she'd soon die anyway.

Something else for that TV camera crew to record. Something for news feeds across the globe to play over and over again. A world-famous pro-Georgian South Ossetian writer. An international martyr now.

'People are already starting to point the finger at the Russians,' the Kid said.

But to Danny, something about that didn't feel right.

He said, 'If they'd just wanted to shut this woman up, they could have done it a lot more covertly. Jesus, even another Litvinenko incident couldn't have brought them any worse publicity than this.'

Alexander Litvinenko was a former officer of the Russian Federal Security Service, who'd claimed political asylum in the UK to avoid prosecution in Russia, but who'd then been poisoned with polonium-210 and had died of acute radiation syndrome in London in 2006.

'Maybe,' said the Kid. 'But there's still plenty of hardcore factions in the Russian government who'd be more than happy if this led to a war.'

Danny could now clearly see the turning for Egerton Terrace up ahead. Fifty metres and closing.

A crashing sound on the other end of the line stopped him dead in his tracks.

'Jesus,' hissed the Kid.

'What?'

Some cop's just pulled up on a road bike at the end of the street I'm in . . . and . . .' – a note of panic rang out down the line – 'and, oh shit, Danny, he's walking my way . . .'

Scuffling. A muffled curse.

Silence.

Danny fought a sudden urge to spew. How the hell could a cop have got on to the Kid? And what would happen if the Kid was challenged? There was no way he'd just give himself up.

But then he heard the Kid sigh.

'It's OK. He's gone.' There was relief and surprise in his voice. 'Never even reached the van. Just turned and ran back to his bike. Set off faster than Steve fucking McQueen in *The Great Escape*. Like he really had somewhere to go.'

It didn't take Danny long to figure out where. Less than three seconds later, a cop bike burst out snarling on to Brompton Road, and reared up on to the pavement.

Its rider fixed his eyes dead on Danny, then sent the bike racing his way.

CHAPTER TWENTY-FIVE

Danny broke left. Across Brompton Road. Into Beauchamp Place. Every muscle in his body was burning, like he was about to burst into flames.

Pedestrians scattered in front of him like leaves before an oncoming storm. They weren't running from him. They were scared of what was chasing him down.

Sirens. Right behind.

Danny cut into the stationary traffic, using it again as a shield. Beauchamp Place terminated in a crossroads. He shot out on to Walton Street and lurched round to the right, gasping, clutching at his cramping chest.

Rounding a corner, he scrambled over a tall flint wall. Into a graveyard. A dark stone spire pointed like a witch's finger at the sky. Slipping on ivy and mulch, he staggered between graves and mausoleums to the opposite side of the church.

'How the hell did they pick up my trail?' he said, wheezing, chest rattling

'Someone must have seen you. That footage of you on the balcony . . . it's all over the news feeds now. For all I know the cops are already tracking you live on CCTV. I said it was just a matter of time.'

Meaning I'm screwed . . .

'They're reinforcing from the west,' the Kid continued. 'Establishing a line of roadblocks. They must think you're planning on heading that way.'

'In which case, I'll go east.'

Back into the fire . . . what they'll never expect . . .

'Good thinking. I'll guide you to Pavilion Road. Then take you south. Down past Sloane Street. Get yourself a change of clothes, and you might just drop off their radar for good.'

Danny threw himself over the wall. He landed hard on the pavement. It felt like someone had just struck his knee with a hammer. How much more could he take?

'Cross over into Hans Place,' said the Kid. 'It's diagonally opposite you now.'

Danny ran on into the leafy urban square. Tall, good-looking white houses. Bright floral window boxes.

A school playground up ahead to his right. The sound of kids playing, running. He remembered his own son's laughter. He pictured Jonathan's face. The gaps in his teeth. The way he'd sometimes giggle until he ended up gasping for air.

'There's an alleyway running down the back of a long square building to your right,' said the Kid, severing Danny's memory.

Danny heard the whoop of a siren behind him. He ignored what the Kid had just said. Instead he ran on.

'Forget it,' he said. 'It's a school.' He was thinking of the cops coming gunning for him. Who knew what weapons they were packing? Or how well or badly they'd been trained?

'Fucking turn back now, Danny, or you're going to get caught.'

A squeal of accelerating tyres. As Danny veered right at the end of the square, he glanced back and saw a riot van rushing up to his rear. Then – worse – a cop bike screeched up to block the road in front of him too.

He ran left. His only option now.

A cliff of ornate sandstone studded with windows reared up at the end of the street a hundred metres ahead. It had to be the back of Harrods, he figured, the taste of blood now rising in his mouth.

More gridlock. Engines revving. Horns blasting. Sirens wailing all around.

A thunder of rotors. Danny saw a helicopter directly above. An insignia was daubed across its fuselage. Sky News.

'I got a TV chopper locked on me,' he said, cutting right now into Basil Street, across the back of Harrods, past hotels and antiques shops.

A blur of motion in the window of a Sony store to his right. Twenty different images of himself stared back at him. All of him running. All filmed from up above.

'Kid,' he said. 'They're transmitting me *live*.'

Which meant half the country would be watching him now.

Manic bursts of sirens. Two, three – no, four, he counted – cop bikes slammed to a halt at the end of the street. Glancing back, Danny saw that another two had already circumvented the gridlocked traffic and performed the exact same manoeuvre behind him.

He ran for the entrance to Harrods – the biggest and most densely populated building nearby, and therefore his best chance of evasion.

'Oh, Jesus, Danny. You—'

Those were the last words Danny heard the Kid say.

Because right then he hit something. Hard. A man. The collision sent Danny spinning sideways, tumbling, sprawling.

His Bluetooth earpiece flew from him and smashed into pieces on the ground. He grabbed at them, stuffed them into his pocket. He couldn't leave them. They were covered with his prints and DNA.

Civilians were running from him like ripples from a rock that had just been hurled into a pool. He touched his face. Felt his shades were still in place. The same went for the rolled-up balaclava on his head, thank God.

They still haven't seen your face.

The thought gave him hope, sent him running again. Because there was no way the camera crew in that chopper would be able to get a decent shot of him from up there.

Just get under cover. Get off the street. Give these police the slip now and there's still a chance they might never track you down.

He staggered up on to the opposite pavement and careered through a bunch of empty metal bins.

Then *smack*. Another collision. This time with a young man in a blue pinstripe suit who'd been making a phone call. Danny kept his feet as the other man crumpled. But he still couldn't stop himself from crashing hard against the building wall.

As he tried running on, he felt himself jerked backwards. His rucksack gave an almighty rip. A drainpipe bracket had snagged it good. He twisted and spun out of its straps, plucking it from the air before it hit the ground.

But even as he turned back to run towards the entrance to Harrods, he saw something flutter free from the rip in the rucksack's side.

A faded square of card. It twisted over in the breeze as it tumbled to the ground.

It was the photograph of Lexie laughing on that playground swing. As he lunged for it, her eyes seemed to bore right into his, as if she were suddenly here by his side.

He would not quit or let her down.

His sunglasses had fallen. He snatched them up too with the photo and slotted them back on his face. Then he locked his eyes on the Harrods doors and ran.

CHAPTER TWENTY-SIX

Four minutes max. That was all the time he'd get, Danny was certain, before the police shut this whole store down.

He glanced at his left wrist, then remembered his watch had been stolen. By one of *them*. He'd get it back. It had been a present from Sally. Whoever had taken it would live to regret it. If he let them live at all.

He set an internal clock running instead. It wasn't something he needed to think about consciously. Just something he could do. Like he was operating on Windows, was simultaneously processing two sets of data. It was an old trick. A childhood trick.

The police baton slid easily from the rip in Danny's rucksack as he barrelled through the doorway into Harrods department store.

He'd straight away clocked from the look of the two liveried security guards blocking his path that they were both most likely ex-forces, the same as with so many of the security staff in London's bigger stores.

Certainly neither of them looked like they were about to let anyone with Danny's current personal standards of hygiene and attire get past them without a fight.

Three metres and closing. They'd still not seen him. A tall

brunette in a short black skirt and tight white top was hogging their attention, making them both laugh.

With two metres to go, as Danny accelerated across the polished floor round a chattering gaggle of foreign tourists, he brought the cop's baton swinging round and down in front of him in a wide arc, activating its extension mechanism as he did.

The first that the taller of the two security guards knew about it was when the full weight of the baton cracked down on to his collar bone, extremely hard and fast.

Danny knew that directly striking the man's neck, or indeed his skull or lower vertebrae, would have been a more efficient way of disabling him. But it would also probably have killed him. Or crippled him for life. And all Danny needed was to get past.

The blow he struck was more than sufficient for that. The guard sagged, his face scrunched up in pain.

His colleague – older, ruddy-faced, with a sinewy jaw – got a better look at Danny. At least long enough for his rheumy blue eyes to widen in alarm as Danny ripped his feet out from under him in a side-foot sweep, dropping him flat on his back beside his groaning friend.

Danny sidestepped the astonished woman and quickly built up speed. The store was busy. Plenty of human traffic. And over a million square feet of retail space to get lost in, if the stats Danny had once been told were true. All good news. But then the brunette started to scream and the customers up ahead of Danny shrank back.

These damn clothes. He had to get rid of them fast.

Air-con. Cool air. Danny sucked it up like a drink. But he also knew that if he didn't find water soon, he wouldn't need to wait for the police to take him down.

He ran straight past the staircases and escalators. His best chance of getting out of this building undetected, he'd already decided, was to stick to the ground floor. Get back out on to the street through another exit as quickly as he could. Hopefully blend into a crowd. Even better, a crowd starting to panic. Best of all, a terrified civilian stampede.

He just prayed that the cops hadn't yet got enough numbers here to seal the whole building off.

More noise behind him. Men's shouts this time. Or, more specifically, orders being shouted.

Danny jinked between a statue of Princess Diana and Dodi Fayed, and a waxwork of Mohamed Al Fayed, the ex-owner of the store.

The shouts were coming towards him. Meaning that whoever those guys were, they weren't just here to block his way back out. An operational decision had just been made to no longer simply try to contain him.

Danny weaved between pillars, desperately trying to conjure up cover behind his back. It was possible the police had already realized from his behaviour on the CCTV that he wasn't armed. Meaning it wouldn't be so hard to bring him in alive.

But there was also his rucksack – meaning they might now be thinking he was planning on blowing himself up, having cherry-picked an iconic and crowded department store as the perfect detonation point.

In which case they'd be looking to neutralize him as quickly as possible, in any way they could.

The shop floor widened out before Danny now. Ambient lighting. Mirrors. Rows of designer-label clothes fanned out left and right. Warm air. A tinkle of piano music. The scent of leather and floor polish and factory-fresh goods.

Shoppers stared up, startled, from the racks they'd been leafing through as Danny raced on by. Another liveried security guard – this one clutching a personal radio unit – spotted him coming at him like a bull, and hurled himself aside before he got mowed down.

Half running, half sliding past a display of ten faceless male mannequins sporting black jackets, Danny saw a frieze of dark silhouettes blocking the doorway on to the street which he'd been planning on exiting through.

Armed police, he realized a split second later. Not the mass of tourists he'd hoped to lose himself amongst.

One of the cops shouted, and Danny knew it without a doubt: he'd just been made.

He veered left, away from the doorway, deeper into the store. MP5 shots rang out. Blood burst across the shoulder of a woman rounding a corner up ahead of Danny. She slammed hard into a glass cabinet and slumped to the ground.

Danny ran on. A prefab wall, signalling the onset of a huge Ralph Lauren concession, cut him off from the cops' line of sight. But still more shots rattled out behind. People started screaming all around.

Over to the left, he saw a wide arched doorway. Up above was a brightly lit sign for the escalators. Stumbling, crashing through a cologne display, sending crystal bottles spinning, smashing to the floor, Danny rammed the baton back into his rucksack and then dug down deeper past it and pulled out his phone.

He burst through the arched doorway into what looked like a vast cosmetics emporium. Dozens of glistening counters. Hundreds of glinting mirrors. Shiny-faced girls with perfect make-up and hair. An almost overpowering collision of sweet and musky scents.

Anna-Maria flashed into his mind. Again Danny remembered saying goodbye, and the smell of her sweet perfume. But now with that memory came another. Of a date they'd once gone on. To a restaurant here in this store.

The bark of a megaphone brought him back. Everywhere he looked, customers were running, ducking, trying to hide. Danny tore a zigzagging channel through the stalls, past Dior and Karan and Ricci and Boss, their designer logos flashing subliminally before his eyes.

Another arched doorway up ahead. Beyond it, he saw escalators running up and down through the centre of the store, as sparkling and inviting as a waterfall.

'The Kid,' he said, panting, wedging his phone to his face.

A second later and: 'Danny? You're still there. Jesus, I thought you'd smashed your phone.'

'What?'

'On the TV footage,' the Kid said, 'taken by that damn helicopter. I saw it just now. You ran back for something outside the store. The same time we got cut off.'

'It was nothing. Just the Bluetooth.'

Danny didn't mention Lexie's photograph. The Kid didn't even know she existed.

'The building's totally surrounded,' the Kid said. 'It's worse than the Ritz. Jesus, Danny. Why didn't you go the way I fucking told you? You'd done that, by now I'd have got you in the clear.'

Danny vaulted over the handrail on to the escalator leading down. He took the sharp-toothed stairs as fast as he could, forcing his way past the protesting bulges of chattering civilians weighed down by shopping bags.

'Danny. I don't know what to do.' The Kid sounded panicked, completely freaked out. 'Jesus Christ, it's game over, mate. I really think it is.'

'No,' Danny said. 'Nothing's over. It's OK. I've got a plan.'

Anna-Maria . . . She'd told him how she'd worked here once. When she'd first come to England as a student. She'd worked here one Christmas vacation at the Oyster Bar, serving up champagne with a French accent and a winning smile to Britain's weary shopping elite.

And then, years later, she'd brought Danny here on that date. And after their lunch, they'd come down here to the lower ground floor, where she'd bought him a shirt and a scarf.

That was when she'd shown him something and told him a little-known fact she'd learned while working here. The same fact that Danny now hoped was about to save his ass.

'I'll call you back,' he said, noticing the low battery indicator on his phone beginning to flash.

'No, wait. You—'

But Danny was no longer listening. Cutting off his connection with the Kid, he switched the phone off and bagged it, then hit the bottom of the escalator running. Stretched out before him was a huge retail area studded with men's clothing concessions.

It was even busier down here than up on the ground floor, Danny saw, as he threaded his way into the loitering crowd. Anna-Maria had told him that the store was visited by more than thirty-five thousand customers a day. Leading to a possible thirty-five thousand cases of mistaken identity today for the police who were looking for him, Danny hoped.

On his way past a pay counter, he snatched a grey suit right out from under the nose of a stunned shop assistant who'd been folding it into a bag.

Danny rounded a corner. He slowed to a walk, counting the CCTV points he could see. Four in total.

A group of young American men stood laughing up ahead, trying on hats. Danny walked right up to them. He took a red baseball cap off the head of a mannequin, whilst simultaneously sneaking a plain black cap off a shelf below. He pulled the red baseball cap on in full view of the nearest CCTV camera.

Then he moved swiftly over behind a giant cardboard hoarding advertising Tommy Hilfiger jeans, which blocked him off from the CCTV.

He reckoned less than two minutes had gone by since he'd entered the store.

He crouched and took off the red baseball cap, along with the rolled-up balaclava, and shoved them into his rucksack. Face to the ground, he threaded his arms through the sleeves of the suit jacket he'd just snatched, then jerked the plain black cap down tight on his head. Pulling the stolen suit trousers on over his Nikes and soiled tracksuit trousers, he tore one of the legs, but there was no time to do anything about that now.

Then he was moving again, fastening up the buttons of the suit jacket to conceal the red tracksuit beneath as best as he could. His change of appearance, he knew, wouldn't fool anyone looking back through the CCTV hard-drive recordings. But with all the other confusion undoubtedly kicking off throughout the rest of the store right now, any misdirection might be enough to give him an edge. And he'd certainly stand a better chance of blending in out in the street dressed like this.

If he ever made it that far.

Again he fought the urge to run. *You're just some guy out shopping,* he told himself, forcing himself not to react to the first of the distant police shouts he now heard coming from back there near the escalators.

His eyes didn't stop searching, scanning everything he saw, as he cast deep into his mind, trying to hook any memories he could of that day Anna-Maria had brought him here.

Until finally he saw what he was looking for. There, dead ahead, was a small coffee shop. And yep – right there where he remembered Anna-Maria pointing it out was a double doorway.

The sign above it read 'STAFF ONLY'. There was a radio-frequency ID tag reader on the wall. Danny felt a swell of fear. He'd got no staff ID card to swipe. He'd have to try kicking his way through.

But then he got lucky. His first piece of luck that whole day. The door opened almost as he reached it and a stout middle-aged female exec in a three-piece charcoal-grey business suit looked Danny over curiously as she strode by. The redness of his face, the mess of his hair, something had snagged her attention all wrong.

Danny didn't hesitate. He didn't look back. He ducked on through the doorway before it swung shut.

CHAPTER TWENTY-SEVEN

Three minutes and counting since he'd first entered the store. Time was rapidly running out.

The little-known fact that Anna-Maria had told Danny when she'd brought him here on their date was this: Harrods owned a building across the street, to which the main store was linked via a short underground service tunnel.

The adjacent building had originally been used in the early twentieth century as a factory for goods sold in the main store, but was now mainly used for administration, coupled with six storeys of underground warehousing.

The good news for Danny was that the service tunnel between the two buildings was very much still in use. On account of the fact that most of the three thousand staff who worked in the main store exited the building this way once they'd finished their shifts.

The 'STAFF ONLY' doorway led through into a brightly lit, windowless corridor. An air-conditioner hummed.

Danny still stank of sewage. Even worse than before, he reckoned, down in this enclosed and sanitized environment.

He followed the corridor past a bunch of doorways and staircases leading off left and right. Hearing a muffled rumble of engines, he glanced up at the ceiling, and realized he must now be under the road.

Ten metres on and a security checkpoint loomed into view. Another RFID-controlled access point, he saw. And not just a wall pad either this time, but an electronic turnstile of the type used to gain entry to sports stadiums or underground train systems.

Just the other side of the turnstile, a tall, bearded uniformed guard stood stationed behind a wide table. A second guard – broad-shouldered and bald as Billy Zane – was sitting at a control desk, with a newspaper spread out in front of him, alongside a couple of lunchtime subs. A CCTV camera stared down from the ceiling.

A radio was switched on low, playing Sinatra. But the TV monitor on the desk beside the bald guard was tuned to what looked like internal CCTV of the underground warehouse system below. Not a news channel or any outside views of the building, thank God.

Past the guards Danny could see stairs leading up. To street level, he assumed.

A sign above the table read 'BAG CHECK'. Making this the kind of security inspection point run by lots of stores these days to keep track of their staff.

The trouble was, Danny's bag was way too bulky to hide. And once they looked inside . . . well, there was the cop's baton, to begin with . . . then the lockbuster . . . not to mention several other particular items that would inevitably stand out. Especially if the guard had ever served in the police or military. As was more than likely the case.

Might as well just cut to the chase, then, Danny thought.

He reached the turnstile and stopped.

'I'm really sorry,' he said, smiling awkwardly, as English as could be, making a show of going through his pockets, 'but I think I've left my wallet and card upstairs.'

He knelt down and opened his rucksack. But even as he began searching through it, he saw the bearded guard's shadow falling across the scuffed lino in front of him, meaning he'd already clocked that something wasn't right and had just peered over the turnstile to get a better look.

Danny became excruciatingly aware of the tips of the red tracksuit jacket's lapels rubbing at his throat. He felt as if the guard's eyes were burning like lasers into the back of his head.

'Jesus, mate. What the hell is that smell?'

'All things, for all people, everywhere,' Danny said, looking up.

'You what?'

'It's your store motto,' Danny said, again keeping his accent all English and smooth, smiling broadly now as he got to his feet. 'I read it on the way in.'

'So . . . ?'

'So . . .' another smile, 'so as an employee of this store, I think you're now going to have to give me exactly what I want.'

'What are you on about?' The security guard's wide brow furrowed as he tried to work out if Danny was playing some kind of a joke. 'Hey . . . do I know you?' he said.

Danny didn't answer. Out of the guard's line of sight, he slipped his hand into the rip in his rucksack.

'Here, Alan . . .' The bearded guard half turned to the bald guy over at the desk, who'd just taken a bite out of his sub and was idly watching Danny through heavy-lidded eyes. 'You ever seen this fella, before?'

Danny knew he couldn't just vault the turnstile and run past these two. Not because he wouldn't make it ahead of them through those swing doors. Because he would.

No, he couldn't run, because if he did, one or other of these guys would either activate an alarm or chase him out on to the street. In each case they'd end up alerting the police.

Which was why Danny had already reached the regrettable conclusion that his best option was just to get on and neutralize the pair of them now.

The intercom on the fat guy's desk suddenly burst into life.

'This is a store-wide security announcement. Code fourteen twelve. I repeat, code fourteen twe—'

Danny didn't need to know what the number actually signified to know that it added up to trouble. His internal clock told him that it was just over four minutes since he'd first entered the store.

Meaning he'd been too slow. Someone, somewhere had just ordered the whole place locked down.

He used the cop's baton again. Was used to its weight by now. Rearing up, he vaulted over the turnstile and slid across the table, simultaneously bringing the weighted end of the baton sailing round and cracking into the bearded man's face.

Blood cascaded from his shattered mouth. Danny landed beside him, balanced, and kicked out hard into his ribs. The guard fell, clutching at his face. Then Danny was running again, a sprinter out of the blocks, smashing the overhead CCTV camera clean off its fittings with a sweep of the baton as he charged directly at the fat guy behind the desk.

This was all about speed. About shock and awe. His plan was simple. To make a big enough mess of the first guard to knock any thoughts of resistance clean out of the second guy's mind. To move up on the second man fast, before he'd even thought about triggering any alarms.

It didn't quite work out like that.

While the bearded guy he'd hit stayed right where he was on the floor, the bald guard kicked himself back from his desk on his wheeled swivel chair with surprising speed.

He got up – even bigger and wider than Danny had expected – and wiped the mayonnaise off his mouth with the back of his hand. Then he did what Danny could never have foreseen.

He grinned.

CHAPTER TWENTY-EIGHT

It was a type of grin Danny had seen before. Late at night. Outside bars. On the faces of junkies and street thieves. But on plenty of soldiers too. It was a primeval grin that had nothing to do with friendliness and everything to do with turf.

All of which Danny realized too late. He was already rounding the desk and closing in on the guard way too fast to be able to slam on the brakes.

The bald guy was waiting for him, and shifted his bulk sideways at the exact moment that Danny brought the baton swinging down.

Danny missed. The baton powered on through the block of air that the bald guy had vacated. Danny's momentum hauled him down after it, sending him crashing to the floor.

He got lucky. Didn't hit his head. Managed to take the worst of the impact on his shoulder. But as he crash-rolled and got to his feet, his luck ran out again.

The bald guy had already turned to face him. And had already thrown a punch. And timed it well. Danny never even saw it coming. It was only the fact that he wasn't yet steady on his feet that saved him. As he staggered sideways, the blow glanced off the left side of his jaw with enough power for him to realize that, if it had connected with its full force, it would most likely have knocked him out.

Danny tasted blood. He lost his grip on the cop's baton and watched helplessly as it spun skittering across the floor.

A shadow to Danny's right. A vibration in the air. He side-stepped just in time to avoid getting caught out by a follow-up left uppercut from the bald guy, who, Danny now saw, was already closing in for the kill.

Trained, Danny thought, crabbing sideways and backwards, keeping the hell out of the big guy's impressive reach, while simultaneously trying not to get cornered or pinned against a wall.

'Yeah, that's right, mate,' the big guy said in a deep, gravelly voice, almost as if he were reading Danny's mind. 'I used to box. Harrow Road All Stars Boxing Gym. You not heard of it?' A gold tooth flashed as his upper lip curled back. 'You're going to remember it after today.'

Two paces, three. Keeping his guard well up, the bald guy shadowed Danny every step. Then he started circling round him, was clearly aiming on driving Danny back towards the bag inspection table, maybe hoping his fallen colleague might bushwhack him from behind.

He watched as Danny tore the shattered sunglasses from his face and let them fall to the floor, and then he grinned again.

'You know what?' the sucked in spit off his lower lip. 'This job's a piece of shit. Most boring thing I've ever done. I've been praying for some stupid yuppie fuck like you to flip out on me for over two years.'

Yuppie fuck? So much for the designer suit giving Danny a veneer of respectability. Seemed like his choice of attire had instead become a red rag to a bull.

This guy wasn't doing this because he knew who Danny really was. He was no hero, trying to do right by the store. He was doing this for *fun*.

He swayed gently as he came forwards. A tree in a breeze. *Well balanced for such a big fucker*, Danny thought. He was three stone heavier than Danny . . . four inches taller . . . a different boxing class . . . And yet . . .

This is no ballet. It's all about putting the other guy down.

That was what the Old Man had always told his new recruits at West Point. That was what he'd told Danny too, when he'd first started teaching him how to fight.

How to *fight*, not box. For *survival*, not fun.

Guard up now, in a classical stance, Danny feigned a left-right jab combination. Like he was willing to box this one out too.

And the bald guy bought it. Again he smiled.

That was when Danny kicked him hard in the balls.

The big guy stumbled. He gasped and wheezed and doubled right up.

Danny stepped in close then with his left foot, bringing his left arm tight across his torso, part counterbalance, part defence. He shot a hammer-fist straight towards the bald guy's nose. But missed and split his lip wide open instead.

The big guy staggered again, his right arm pinwheeling uselessly now as he fought to regain his balance.

Along with the contorted look of pain on his face, Danny saw a flash of betrayal in his eyes.

That's right, Danny thought. *Fuck your Queensberry Rules, and fuck you.*

He fired a left into the big guy's throat, then dropped into a crouch, simultaneously seizing his opponent's left heel and twisting hard counterclockwise. The bald guy spun clean round. He hit the floor flat on his front, a wheezing, twisted pile of flesh.

Danny snatched two power cables from the back of the printer and computer on the control desk, and used them to hog-tie the bald guy. Then he went after the other guard. He'd just spotted him crawling out from under the inspection table in an effort to haul himself away. The man froze when he heard the squeak of Danny's trainers coming up from behind. He shrank up into a ball. Danny used two phone cables to strap his throat and ankles to the table.

Danny tried to collect his thoughts. He was still fizzing with adrenalin. Eight minutes since he'd first entered Harrods. Had he been fast enough? Or was he already totally screwed?

Only one way to find out. He collected up his broken sunglasses and the cop baton and stuffed them into his rucksack. He took the

bald guard's reading glasses from where he'd spotted them on the
control desk, next to a timer sheet with the name 'Alan Offiniah' at
the top.

The world went blurry as he slipped the glasses on. He perched
them on the end of his nose. Then he grabbed a bottle of Coke off
the desk, along with what was left of the bald guy's sandwich.

He drained the Coke and ate as he hurried up the steps to the
swing doors at the top. He could have drunk another ten bottles.
Could have done a lot of things, in fact. Like volunteered to be
shipwrecked. Or joined a monastery. Or slept in a hammock for a
month.

Anything not to be here.

He looked back over his shoulder at the bald guy before he went
out through the door. He was glaring up with a look of absolute
defiance on his face. Like he'd been cheated. Like all he needed was
one more shot and this time the title would be his.

No doubt about it, Danny thought. On a different day, under
different circumstances, he'd definitely have given Alan Offiniah
a job.

CHAPTER TWENTY-NINE

13.13, KNIGHTSBRIDGE, LONDON SW1

Two steps out on to the pavement and Danny saw he was completely surrounded.

A roadblock facing Harrods had been set up across Hans Crescent less than five metres to his left. Two unmarked cop cars, blue lights flashing, parked at crazy angles alongside a line of abandoned civilian cars. A long-wheelbase Ford white riot van had been ploughed up on to the pavement.

Upwards of fifteen police were manning the makeshift barricade. Three of them were armed and had taken up sniper positions.

To Danny's right, another wave of police was coming in. More hardcore. CO19. A squad of them on foot. Bustling between abandoned civilian vehicles. Running awkwardly like a bunch of Fat Camp escapees. Fully geared up. Bulletproof vests. H&K single-shot carbines at the ready.

Danny got a flashback memory to a piece of flickering First World War archive footage he'd watched in a military history lecture, showing a platoon of doomed British youth charging the German trenches, only to be mown down by machine-gun fire.

But no one was going to stop these guys today. And they weren't gunning for Germans. They were all looking to waste whoever they thought had shot all those civilians outside the Ritz. They were all looking to waste *him*.

'You.'

Danny spun. The word had come at him as more of a scream than a shout. The burly cop running at him from the direction of the roadblock was wearing a riot helmet. Visored. One arm was outstretched, pointing at Danny. The other gripped a Glock 17 semi-automatic pistol.

Two other cops – one of them armed with an MP5 – had seen what their colleague was doing. Others were turning to face Danny, distracted by the first cop's shout.

Even if Danny managed to take the first cop out, he'd never get away. The man with the MP5 would take him down.

This is it.

He knew it then. Accepted it, strangely. He felt the last of his energy running off him like water as he stood there in his own personal no-man's-land. His whole body sagged.

He thought about Sally in that moment. He thought, as he so often had in the long hours and days and months that had followed her death, that she wasn't really dead at all. That she was waiting for him somewhere. Somewhere normal. On that stone bridge in Central Park, where they'd used to meet at lunchtimes when they'd first begun dating. Or in their one-bed apartment in Queens that summer they'd moved in together, where she'd put down her paintbrush on the windowsill and pressed his hand to her denim dungarees, so he could feel his daughter Alexandra kicking for the very first time.

'Move!' the cop running at him shouted.

Move?

The sun burned down. Sweat trickled from Danny's brow. The cop grabbed him by the collar of his suit jacket. He jerked him aside, out of the way of the oncoming police. He gripped the back of Danny's neck.

'That way.' The cop was pointing Danny in the opposite direction from the roadblock. 'Go. Get the hell out of here. Now.'

Then before Danny had hardly had a chance to accept what was happening to him – let alone thank his lucky stars – the cop was running back towards the roadblock.

They think I'm just another civilian.

The change of clothes . . . it had been enough to fool the cop. Witnesses, police, you name it, most people only cared about the big details of the way other people looked. It was a fact Danny thanked God for then.

He saw another cop frantically waving at him from beside a flashing squad car parked across the next road junction.

He remembered what the Kid had said. About the civilians leaving the Ritz being kettled in Berkeley Square. Quarantined until they could be interrogated. Was that what was happening here? Because Danny couldn't afford to get caught up in that. Not with the potential DNA match still waiting to be picked up by forensics at the Ritz.

No time to think about it now . . . No choice but to go with the flow . . . Not with all these cops watching.

Danny ran to the waiting cop. He noticed the street sign as he did. Pavilion Road. The name struck a chord. Another thing the Kid had said. Down south that way was where the Kid was waiting.

The cop didn't give Danny a second glance as he reached her. She was too busy looking past him at the roadblock and the sliver of Harrods façade beyond that. She grabbed him, pulled him past her, passing him on to another cop, who unceremoniously shoved him further west.

So they still think that I – that the guy in the red tracksuit – they still think I'm inside Harrods . . . Which means they're not trying to quarantine me anywhere now . . . They're just clearing the area of civilians . . . setting themselves up for a siege . . .

The cops spat Danny out through a wall of riot shields into a short street jammed with stationary vehicles and panicking civilians.

'That way. Keep moving,' the last cop who'd manhandled Danny yelled.

Keep moving – how?

Because something was wrong. Bodies were pressed up against gridlocked cars. Hundreds of people had been jammed into this short stretch of street, siphoned off from inside and around Harrods. But the crowd wasn't moving. None of them could get out.

They were starting to shove each other, to panic. News of the massacre outside the Ritz had clearly filtered through. These civilians' terrified faces all told the same story. Their recurring group nightmare, the one they'd collectively been having since 9/11 and 7/7 . . . they'd woken up bang in the middle of it now. There'd been a terrorist attack right here in central London. And not just on some diplomat. Civilians like themselves had been indiscriminately slaughtered. One of the masked gunmen was now on the loose.

And all these people were convinced that if they didn't get the hell away from here now, they'd be the next ones to die.

Danny wanted to call the Kid. To find out what the bigger picture was. How many central London streets had been kettled like this? What was going on back at the Ritz? But he couldn't use his phone. Not if the networks were meant to be down. Not if he couldn't even hear himself think.

It was over an hour since the attack outside the Ritz had taken place. But it was less than fifteen minutes since the cops had opened up on Danny in Harrods. He remembered the poor woman who'd got hit and wondered how many others had too.

Jean Charles de Menezes.

The name leapt up like a flame in Danny's fevered mind. He'd attended a conference on urban policing a year ago in Geneva. De Menezes had been given as a perfect example of what cops shouldn't do.

Menezes had been a young, unarmed twenty-seven-year-old Brazilian electrician whom the cops here had wrongly mistaken for a terrorist. He'd been shot in the head seven times at Stockwell tube station on the London Underground in 2005 by members of CO19, the same Metropolitan Police specialist firearms unit Danny suspected he was being hunted by now.

The London cops had tried to wriggle out of any blame. Meaning those bodies back in Harrods would probably be attributed to the masked gunman too.

Forcing his way forward through the crowd, Danny now saw why the civilians weren't all just running away as fast as they could. Another roadblock was hemming them in. Some miscommunication between the police. At the end of the street was a row of dark blue unmarked pursuit cars with blacked-out windows. A solitary marked squad car. Ten or twelve uniformed police had formed another riot line. One of them was shouting through a megaphone at the crowd to stay calm.

Danny scrummaged his way forward, cracked someone hard in the ribs with his elbow and hauled his way past. He worked his way up steadily along the side of the street.

All the shops he passed were rammed with people taking cover. A fight had broken out in one doorway, with two guys dressed in suits refusing to let an old woman in.

People were clutching desperately, furiously at their phones, like kids with broken toys, clearly cursing the fact that the networks had now either been deliberately taken down – as the Kid had predicted – or were jammed from too much traffic.

Danny was panicking too. This street was one bottleneck he couldn't afford to get stuck in. The moment the police spoke to those two trussed-up security guards, they'd run the time codes on whatever CCTV cameras were outside.

They'd see which way Danny had gone. The clothes he'd changed into, too. Any ideas he had of making that dream getaway, they'd be history after that.

A screech of rubber. A warning clatter of batons on shields rose above the angry noise of the crowd. The first of those unmarked pursuit cars leapt backwards, wheeled right and out of sight. The others followed. Leaving only the white squad car and the now hopelessly isolated and exposed line of police.

In Danny's mind's eye, it was like one of those plastic tile puzzles he used to get in his stocking from Santa Claus as a kid. All you had to do was clear the right part of the puzzle and you could suddenly move everything else.

He wasn't the only one who'd spotted the opportunity. The whole crowd surged forward as one.

It was like the removal of a dam from a pool of water. People rushed out of the street and Danny let himself get swept along. In under a minute he was past the abandoned white cop car. Out on to Sloane Street.

More sirens to the left. The crowd veered right and started to break up. The sense of panic and fear dropped too. These people weren't potential victims any more. You could see it on their faces. They were survivors. They were the ones who'd got away.

With each step forward, the crowd felt less like a scene from a disaster movie and more like a sports crowd leaving a stadium.

Another hundred metres and the collective rhythm of the people had become almost normal. They'd started to talk again, not shout. Danny even heard somebody laugh.

He nearly snatched out his phone and called the Kid. To tell him he was OK. To work out where the hell they should meet. But equally he knew that he couldn't exactly start chattering into a phone.

And besides, there was someone he wanted to talk to first. *Crane* . . .

The first opportunity Danny got, he cut off Sloane Street and into Cadogan Place.

He spotted the moped chained to a railing outside a boutique hotel. He could only see one CCTV camera nearby, and that was turned away from him, monitoring the entrance to a bank.

Danny popped the bike's panelling and got it started. The owner had been kind enough to secure a helmet in its equally easily opened pannier. And had left a full fuel tank.

Half a mile and thirteen turns later, heading due south along Passmore Street at a steady twenty-five miles an hour, Danny finally got what he'd been wishing for since he'd first gazed down on that burning black limousine outside the Ritz.

He was just another blurred face in the crowd.

CHAPTER THIRTY

'Hi there. Welcome to Pasta Pronto. Can I interest you in any of today's specials?'

'No. Get me two litres of still water. Two strong black coffees. Spaghetti. Fries. Bread.' Danny spoke in English, but his accent was now French.

The waitress – Argentinian, dyed red hair piled high and knotted on top of her head – glanced from Danny to the three empty chairs at the table he was sitting at, clearly wondering how many other people would be joining him. Flushed cheeks and a bright smile, she couldn't have been more than eighteen.

Danny had already taken a brand-new black leather wallet from his brand-new rucksack. It contained a full set of credit cards and a photo ID matching his face but in the name of Louis Barthes, a Parisian businessman, whose crumpled expense receipts clearly demonstrated that he regularly spent time in London for work.

Danny opened the wallet now for the waitress to see and smoothly removed a twenty-pound note, before sliding it beneath an upturned wine glass.

'That's for you,' he said, 'so long as you persuade the chef to get my order here in the next five minutes. I've got a meeting I need to be at and I can't be late.'

'Yes, sir.' The waitress was already punching Danny's order into an electronic pad.

Danny watched her scurrying away. Then he started a quick three-sixty visual sweep around the concourse again.

He'd chosen this Italian franchise in the middle of a busy shopping mall in Chelsea because it was out in the open, easy to see people approaching, and near to the escalators, the fire exits and the doors leading out on to the rooftop car park, should he need to make a hasty escape.

He was barely a few miles from the chaos of that penned-in crowd, but looking round now, he could have been on another planet. There were some apprehensive-looking people, sure. But others were laughing, drinking coffee, shopping, just getting on with their lives. London was a network of separate villages, his wife Sally had always told him. More like separate continents, he thought.

Danny had ditched the stolen moped in an underground car park half a mile away. He'd washed in a public convenience, scrubbing his face and hands with caustic liquid soap. He'd used the medical kit in his rucksack to tend to the multiple cuts he'd sustained after entering the sewers, and had patched up his blistered, torn feet as best he could with bandages and antiseptic cream. Then he'd carefully cut out the security tags from the suit he'd stolen from Harrods, in case they set off an alarm in some other store.

In a high-street menswear store, he had then bought himself a fresh set of clothes. Blue jeans, grey socks, a white T-shirt and a hooded khaki jacket. New running shoes. Black Nikes. Exactly what the mannequin in the store's display window had been wearing.

He'd also bought a black baseball cap, rucksack and new shades. The only time his face had been uncovered throughout the whole process had been when he'd switched outfits in the store's changing booth, after first having checked that there'd been no prying CCTV cameras there to record the event.

Exiting the menswear store, he'd ditched the stolen suit, along with his soiled tracksuit, rucksack, gloves, trainers, cap and the guard's spectacles – all of which he'd earlier transferred into one of the menswear store bags – in the first bin he'd passed on the high street.

He'd spotted this shopping mall from two hundred metres away and had entered it via a street-level cinema foyer, before walking straight through into the shopping concourse beyond.

He reckoned he'd done enough to buy himself some time.

He peered back into the restaurant. The waitress was now busy working the coffee machine, transient plumes of steam hissing up past her face. Noticing Danny watching, she flashed him a perfunctory smile. Meaning, he hoped, that she'd already incentivized the chef to get his ass into gear.

Danny grimaced, his stomach cramping. He was ravenous. As in sweating, starting to shake ravenous. Two guys at the table next to him were digging into a couple of steaks. The smell of Dijon mustard and meat was making Danny's stomach growl. It was all he could do not to snatch their plates right out from under them.

Both guys were in their mid twenties. Well groomed. Suited and booted. Bankers, Danny was guessing, or hedgies, or City-boy slickers – or whatever the hell else the media was calling them now.

Guys like that no longer had any impact on Danny's world. He didn't invest in anything he couldn't manage himself. The majority of his wealth was tied up in a bunch of properties, with the rest carefully distributed through a web of cash accounts, and safety deposit boxes, accessed via a correspondingly complicated web of fake IDs. The whole financial system could implode again tomorrow and it wouldn't make a scrap of difference to him.

Not that he'd gone into this business for money. He'd started out working for Uncle Sam for kicks and because of the Old Man. Then once he'd switched from the military to the Company, he'd done it out of addiction. Arrogance and competitiveness too, he now recognized – because he'd thought he could one day be the best.

But all that had changed after Sally and Jonathan's deaths. When he'd gone freelance after that, he'd done it to protect people like them, to stop those who would do them harm. He'd done it to correct the failures of his past.

But the money was unavoidable. Crane had taught Danny that. If you didn't charge the market rate, private clients wouldn't consider you worth paying for. Then they'd end up employing someone not as good. Someone who might let them down. Which Danny never would.

Crane . . .

Danny snatched up his phone again. After he'd finally given the police the slip, he'd discovered that Crane had left him four coded messages during the course of the morning.

The first was logged on his phone as having arrived a half-hour after the shooting – by which time, Danny assumed, the news of what had happened must have broken in the States, or wherever the hell else Crane might be. The other three messages had come through at roughly thirty-minute intervals since.

Danny had unscrambled all four the moment he'd sat down in the restaurant, using an encryption key on his phone. Each of them had read, simply, 'CONTACT ME.'

Which Danny had done the second he'd read them, replying: 'DRINK. NOW.'

As soon as he'd pressed 'SEND', the software on his phone would have automatically encrypted the message, before firing it off to Crane. Crane would then have used a twin encryption key on his own computer to unscramble the message his end.

Since Crane and Danny were the only two people in possession of the twin keys necessary to unscramble these coded messages, Crane would know that the reply to his own messages was genuine. Leaving them free to arrange a meeting where no one else could hear.

Plenty enough time had now passed for all this to take place. *So why the hell hasn't Crane even got back in touch?* He'd clearly already have worked out that Danny must have been in the hotel at the time of the attack, which was why he'd been repeatedly trying to get hold of him since. So what was he doing now that was more important than talking to Danny? Did he already suspect that the people Danny had gone to meet had been involved with the hit? Was he even now talking to his US government contact to find out what the hell was going on?

Never trust in anyone fully but yourself. Another of the Old Man's aphorisms sprang to mind. Because could Danny really trust anyone else now? He'd never met Crane, or Crane's US government contact. So how could he know for certain that they weren't somehow involved in this too?

The waitress returned, balancing a tray loaded with Danny's coffees and water. Danny's nostrils flared as she put the steaming coffee cups down. She unscrewed the lid of one of the water bottles and started pouring it into a glass of crackling ice. Too slowly.

'I'll do that,' Danny said, gripping the bottle.

'Sure.' The waitress let the bottle go. 'Your food won't be long,' she said.

As Danny lifted the bottle to his lips and started to drink, his stomach twisted with fresh discomfort, the icy-cold liquid burning like whisky as it poured down his throat.

He noticed the waitress staring. Probably at the bruise forming on his cheek below his left eye, he guessed. A reminder of his encounter with Alan Offiniah, which would stay with him now for a week, and which even his new tinted Aviator shades didn't fully conceal.

He glared hard at the waitress. She hurried away.

He did another three-sixty security sweep as he drained the bottle. The electronics store on the other side of the concourse had several TVs in its window, which were still showing footage of the 'Mayfair Massacre', as they'd now tagged it. Always from the same angle. From across the street where that TV crew had been. Only now the TV people had added computer graphics, showing the angles of fire. They'd made it look like a video game, Danny thought. As if no one had really been hurt at all.

The hawk-faced man. He'd been dressed in a tracksuit when Danny had met him, and Danny now knew for sure that he'd been one of those two shooters out there on the balcony.

Danny had watched the whole sequence up close outside that store only a few minutes ago. After they'd wasted the limo, one of the masked men had started shooting in a spray-and-pray pattern, missing some groups of civilians entirely, ripping others apart.

But the second man – the shorter, stockier of the two – had remained completely focused throughout, drilling controlled burst after burst first into the vehicle's occupants as they'd tried to escape, and then into the crowd of panicked civilians, taking them down in ones and twos, hardly wasting a single round.

He'd looked as casual, in fact, as if he'd been standing on a boat deck with nothing more incriminating than a fishing rod in his hands.

And there at his wrist – between the end of his sleeve and the beginning of the black glove on his right hand – Danny had seen something flash in the bright morning sun. A gold chain. The same one the hawk-faced man had been wearing.

Oh yeah, that sicko had been having the time of his life.

Danny checked his phone as he snatched up the nearest coffee and burned his lips at the very first sip. Still no word from Crane.

He felt his vision darken, like someone had just turned down a dimmer switch on the world. His temple throbbed. Dehydration, he hoped. Not the start of a migraine, because sometimes those could get him too.

He grabbed a packet of sugar from the dull metal bowl on the table, tore off its top and tipped its contents into the coffee. He splashed in water from the second bottle and drank greedily, wincing at the heat, shocked by the sudden influx of taste. For a second he thought he was about to spew it all back up.

He stared down at his hands. They were shaking. Clenching his fists, he tried to make them be still. But he could not. He checked the phone again. Still no answer. He felt exposed, completely alone.

This is the worst day of my life . . .

But even as this thought entered his head, anger rose up through him. Hatred at himself for having thought it. Hatred and shame.

This wasn't the worst day of his life. Nor would tomorrow be. Nor any other day yet unlived. The worst day of his life had already happened. A nightmare that was a memory. One that began with a walk in the woods and ended with blood on the snow.

CHAPTER THIRTY-ONE

SEVEN YEARS AGO, NORTH DAKOTA

Danny was sweating, trembling. From where he and Lexie were crouched down behind the thorn bush, through the falling snow, he could see there was snow right there on the doormat beneath the cabin's eaves, snow that must have dropped from the boots of whatever uninvited stranger had come to call.

No third set of boot prints led away from the cabin and there was no other door. Meaning that whoever had walked this way had to still be inside.

The cabin's curtains remained drawn. It was dark as a cave in there this time of year. Danny knew Sally wouldn't have let anyone in without afterwards opening them wide.

'Daddy, you're hurting me.'

Beside him, Lexie shifted her weight. The crunch of her boots in the snow rang out like a cymbal crash in Danny's mind.

He looked down at her hand gripped in his. He saw the blood-red puckering of his skin and forced his fingers to relax. She grimaced, jerking her hand back like she'd just been stung. She clenched and unclenched her little fist.

'What is it, Daddy?' She spoke in a whisper. She'd not yet seen the boot prints, but he could tell just from the way she now glanced across at the cabin that she too knew something was wrong.

'We're going to play a game, princess,' he whispered back.

'But I thought you wanted to get back . . .'

'I know. But it's just for a minute.'

Danny started stepping slowly backwards, taking Lexie's hand, gently this time, so that she had no choice but to do the same. He didn't take his eyes off the cabin. He watched the curtains. He didn't blink.

'What kind of game is it, Daddy?'

'A hiding game.'

'Who are we hiding from?' A note of excitement in her voice. But apprehension too.

'Just your mother and your brother.' He kept walking backwards, holding her firmly by the elbow, preventing her from turning. 'See if you can't step into your old boot prints,' he said.

'You mean so Mom and Jonathan will think we've just disappeared into thin air?'

'That's right.'

Danny did the same, keeping them moving backwards, both of them glancing back over their shoulders to make sure they hit the mark. Ten paces, twenty.

Better to look a fool than be one, his father would say.

The snow had started falling even harder now. Danny felt his chest tightening as they finally reached the hawthorn clump and the cabin dropped out of view.

'OK,' he said, stopping ten paces later, 'this is far enough.'

The Old Man had helped Danny build the tree house. Originally it had been meant as a hide from which he would be able to shoot wood pigeons. But Danny had ended up making it more than that, building it into somewhere he could hang on his own, and even sleep out in on hot summer nights.

He lifted Lexie up into it now, to save her climbing up the cut-off branches – to keep the snow on them so it looked like no one had.

A small, dark opening led into the interior of the tree house. Danny had done a good job of camouflaging it when he'd been a kid. And now ivy had grown over its windows and floor and walls.

So much so that now you had to know it was there to see it. Even here below it, it just looked like another gnarled oak.

Lexie scrambled through, then twisted round to face him. He smiled up at her. But she didn't smile back.

'I won't be long,' he said. 'You stay inside. And don't you come out now. Not until I say.'

'Something's wrong, Daddy. You look . . . afraid.' It was clear from her face that she'd never thought of the word in connection with him before.

But she was right. Danny was afraid. Of something, *someone* he wasn't even yet prepared to name in his mind, because so terrifying – and, *please God*, absurd and unlikely – was the prospect of them having come here. Of this person being in there with Sally and Jonathan. His wife and his boy.

The two paths – one facing forwards, one back – of his and Lexie's boot prints led off towards the pastures, as if the two of them had walked this way and back to the house together and neither of them had stopped.

It wouldn't fool anyone for long, Danny understood. But it was the best he could do in the time. And he certainly couldn't send his daughter out into what now looked set to be turning into a snowstorm. Not when the nearest inhabited farm was nearly four kilometres away. Particularly not when he still prayed that what he was fearing was wrong.

But he wasn't taking any chances either. He set off as quick as he could, tracing his own boot prints again. Forwards this time. On to the hawthorn patch.

When he got there, he stopped. He crouched and parted the tangle of icy branches.

Through the thickening blur of snow, he could see that the cabin door remained shut, the curtains closed. Black smoke trailed up from the chimney and vanished in the white sky.

If Danny's cell phone hadn't been in the cabin, if he'd even had one in his car, he'd have called the police then. He'd have been happy to be proved to be just paranoid.

But there was no one to turn to for help.

He slung the drawstring bag, then unclipped his bowie knife from its scabbard. Inside were two smaller knives of identical design, one with a four-inch blade, one with a two.

He slid the four inch down the inside of his boot, where it might be easily found. With the two-inch, he nicked his trouser lining at the back behind his belt, and slid the tiny knife inside, where it could not be seen or felt.

He threw away the scabbard. The three empty pockets there would betray the missing blades. Then he ran right, using the hawthorn as cover. He moved parallel to the line of the stranger's boot prints, which had stopped at his front door, shadowing them back in the direction from which they'd come.

Thirty metres on and he passed his own car. A Chevrolet Sedan. Nothing but a blurred white lump in the snow.

Fifty metres further on and his stomach lurched as he saw the second vehicle. It was parked up in a small clearing in the woods behind a thicket of spruce, where it could not be seen from the cabin or the dirt track leading up from the valley.

The tree branches shivered in the wind as the snow continued to fall. But apart from that, all was still.

Danny circled round, then moved in closer to the vehicle, his bowie knife already in his hand, his breath rushing out fast in little white clouds. A cold clamminess had settled on the back of his neck. He'd become acutely aware of the passing of time.

There were no tyre tracks ahead of the car, he now saw. None behind either. Not enough snow had yet fallen this morning to account for that. And last night it had stopped falling at just gone midnight. Which meant this vehicle must have been parked up here all night.

Like Danny's own car, the horizontal surfaces of this vehicle were covered in snow. But unlike his car, as he closed right in, the lurid red of the driver's door of the vehicle was clearly visible. Because that was where whoever had been in this car all night had exited this morning, dislodging the snow from the door as they did.

Danny was close enough now to see in through the window.

There was no one inside. But the footprints he'd tracked back from the cabin, they'd started from here.

Meaning that whoever's car this was, they were now inside the log cabin with Sally and Jonathan.

A silent wail of desperation rose up inside Danny's throat, as again his worst fear leapt to the front of his mind.

He arrowed through the swirling snow and the white woods towards the cabin, as silent and swift as a bird of prey.

He prayed – *God*, he prayed he was wrong.

CHAPTER THIRTY-TWO

'Excuse me, sir?'

Danny looked up to see the Argentinian waitress staring down at him, a plate and bowl in her hands. He realized he was holding his breath. Looking down, he saw his fists clenched on the table. He forced himself to exhale, and felt his chest shaking as he did.

Come on, Crane, he thought, glaring at his phone. *The second I've finished with him, I can talk to the Kid.* He had already messaged the Kid to say he was OK.

He moved back a little from the table, so the waitress could serve him his food. Steam rose rapidly off the bowl of spaghetti. Its dollop of sauce was the colour of raw liver. Stacked up on the plate was a mesh of stringy fries.

'Thanks,' Danny mumbled.

He grabbed a fistful of fries and stuffed them into his mouth, then began forking up spaghetti, efficiently, like a mechanical digger clearing rubble from a construction site.

He slopped sauce across his chin and the already stained white tablecloth. One of the City boys shot him a look of disgust, but Danny just carried on staring right back at him and chewing until the bigger man looked away.

He started on the second coffee, tossed down more water after that. The warm feeling of food in his stomach, the idle chatter and piped mall music, and the softness of the padded chair on which he sat, for a second it almost made Danny feel normal.

He began to collect his thoughts. But the image of the hawk-faced man kept flashing into his mind.

The chiming of a glass bell – the alert noise for incoming mail. Danny's screensaver – a downloaded photograph of a Provençal villa, with a Photoshopped picture of himself and a nameless woman and child, all chosen to match his current French ID – vanished as he picked up his phone from beside his drained coffee cup.

He tapped in the phone's security access code. A bundle of indecipherable code scrolled across the screen. Meaning the message was encrypted. Meaning also that it had to have come from Crane.

Danny's heart began to race as he used another password to activate the phone's encryption software, allowing him to translate the garbled message into English.

The unscrambled message read: DRINKING. NOW.

Whatever Crane had been doing, whatever the cause of his delay in getting back to Danny, he was waiting in Harry's Bar now.

Danny pulled out of his mail program, tapped the InWorld icon on his screen, then logged in. He was relieved to see that 'CRANE' was indeed listed in green lettering on his 'Buddies' list at the bottom of the screen.

Now that his Bluetooth headset was broken, Danny was forced to switch his phone over to non-audio mode. Or else, without an earpiece, he'd risk being overheard.

Non-audio mode in InWorld meant that Danny and Crane's conversation would now emerge in the form of cartoon speech bubbles from their onscreen avatars' mouths.

The specially designed InWorld-compatible security software they'd both be using would ensure that bit by bit their conversation would also be automatically encrypted and unscrambled as it shuttled back and forth between them via the latest version of global instant messaging. And what with text encryption being faster and more accurate than audio, they'd end up communicating just as quickly and safely as any other way.

Danny did a final three-sixty check around the mall. Then the restaurant, the bankers, and the steam rising off what little was left of his food . . . it was suddenly as if none of it was there.

His entire focus was on Noirlight now.

CHAPTER THIRTY-THREE

Danny bypassed Crane's security MOBs – the alleyway doorman with his snarling Rottweilers, and the grizzled old barman – as fast as the InWorld engine and Crane's security protocols would allow.

Then he steered his avatar, F8, who was dressed as normal in blue jeans and a plain white T, past the floor-to-ceiling antique bookcase beside the bar, and on into Crane's private office.

The wood fire was still flickering ruby red in the cast-iron hearth, but Danny could no longer hear it crackling. In fact, stripped of its audio ambience, the whole scene had a flatness to it that made it feel even more illusory than it already was, and consequently even less suited to solving Danny's real-world problems.

But Danny wasn't here for the atmosphere. He was here for Crane. And there Crane's avatar was – dark hair, side-parted, dressed in a sombre grey suit, white shirt, black tie, like he was fronting a funeral parlour – sitting as per usual behind his wide mahogany desk, lit from above by the sapphire glow of art deco lights.

The effect was to leave Crane's avatar's face deep in shadow. A deliberate affectation, Danny had always thought. A joke even, to make light of the clandestine circumstances under which they always met.

But he saw nothing funny about it today. He was sick of deception. He wanted the truth.

Danny left F8 standing in the doorway as he started to type on to the small touch keyboard at the bottom of his phone's screen. A cartoon speech bubble emerged from F8's head, and steadily inflated as words scrolled through it.

◥F8: You seen the news?

A hesitation. Possibly due to a momentary confusion on Crane's part over the fact that they weren't using audio. Then, as Danny's avatar's speech bubble slowly faded and dissolved, a new speech bubble emerged alongside Crane's avatar's face.

◥CRANE: Were you in the hotel when the shooting started?

◥F8: In the room. Drugged. Set up by the people you sent me to meet.

Another pause. So long this time that, for a few seconds after Danny's speech bubble had faded away, he was left wondering if the InWorld system had timed out or bugged out and jammed up his screen

◥CRANE: Where are you now?

◥F8: That's not important.

Never trust in anyone fully but yourself . . . Danny couldn't think of a single reason why Crane might betray him. But until he got some answers about what the hell had gone down today, and until Crane had satisfied him that he was playing this straight, he wasn't giving any information away that he didn't need to – especially concerning where it was he'd gone to ground.

◥F8: Who is your US government contact?

◥CRANE. Come on, Danny. You know how it works.

Yeah, you protect their anonymity, even though they nearly got me killed.

◥F8: What department do they work for?

◥CRANE: The same people you once did.

The Company then, Danny thought. Or its Special Activities Division or Special Operations Group, at any rate. Either one of which was capable of instigating black ops abroad. But here? In London? In the capital city of one of the US's chief allies? And publicly murdering a whole bunch of civilians like that? Danny wished he could believe it wasn't possible. But he'd been involved in this game too long for that. Agents did go rogue. And sometimes big time, just like today.

◀F8: Do you think your contact knew what the client they fixed me up with was planning on doing?

◀CRANE: Are you asking me if I think the US government is actively involved in an international act of terrorism and mass murder? No.

◀F8: So what is your contact's take on what happened?

On how badly they screwed this up . . . on how they ended up hanging me out to dry, whether deliberately or not.

◀CRANE: I'm still trying to speak to them.

Trying . . . Danny could hardly believe what he was reading. Anger flushed through him. Crane *still* hadn't managed to get this jerk of a contact of his on the phone? Danny's fist clenched so tightly around his phone, he nearly cracked its screen.

◀F8: You're gonna need to do better than that.

◀CRANE: I've got other news. British special forces have recovered the body of one of the terrorists from the hotel room . . .

Danny felt his whole body tense. He'd not yet mentioned the dead man to Crane. There'd been nothing on the news feeds he had seen either. Nothing even about any special forces insertion. Meaning Crane must have mined this intel from some other source. Meaning he had an in. Most likely through British intelligence.

◀CRANE: Word is the guy died of natural causes, a heart attack in the wake of the shooting.

Giving more credence to Danny's theory that the guy's body had been mutilated by his accomplices in an effort to conceal his identity, because they'd not had time to dispose of it properly.

Meaning the card and data stick really might have been overlooked and could provide some solid leads. A frantic exit by the dead terrorist's associates would also account for how they might have screwed up on the sedative dose they'd given Danny.

And yet . . .

And yet something about it all still seemed too good to be true. A nagging doubt remained at the back of Danny's mind . . . because could someone as calculating and calm as the hawk-faced man really have made such mistakes?

There was still only one way to find out. And that was to get the stick and the card to the Kid.

◖F8: You let me know if they manage to ID him.

◖CRANE: We find that out, and we'll be a whole lot closer to discovering who set you up.

Danny thought about the swipe card and stick in his bag. Only now he thought of them like playing cards lying face down in a game of seven-card stud. Until he'd decided how to play them, he didn't need to reveal them to anyone. Including Crane.

A final pause. Crane's speech bubble faded. Another expanded in its place.

◖CRANE: Good luck.

Danny watched Crane's avatar dissolve into nothing behind the virtual mahogany desk, leaving F8 standing alone. He glanced down at the 'Buddies' list at the bottom of his screen and watched Crane's name fade from sight.

The real world – the stained tablecloth, the people out shopping, and the bright mall lighting – all that swung nauseatingly back into focus then.

He took the unmarked swipe card and the data stick from where he'd earlier secured them in his rucksack and turned them slowly over in his hand. The black ink smeared across the card had now dried.

His conversation with Crane might not have given him the answers he'd wanted, but it had confirmed one thing in his mind: these two items were now his greatest hopes.

Crane was right. The dead body. That was the key. Finding out who might also tell Danny why.

CHAPTER THIRTY-FOUR

Danny paid for his food and drink. The Argentinian waitress told him to 'Have a nice day,' and gave him a cracked smile as he picked up his rucksack.

Walking away, Danny glanced back to see her holding the twenty-pound note up to the light just to check that it was real. Meaning he still looked kind of dodgy, he guessed. Exhausted. Stressed out. Even so, she seemed satisfied and slipped the cash into her jeans back pocket. He paid her no attention after that.

'The Kid,' he said into his phone, leaning up against a pillar near the TV store, out of sight of most of the passers-by, still conscious that he didn't want to make a big issue about publicly using his phone.

He could already see from his phone's call register that the Kid had tried calling him a whole bunch of times since he'd messaged him.

'Jesus, Danny,' the Kid said now, with clear relief in his voice, 'it's harder getting through to you than to my teenage niece.'

So the Kid had a niece. A brother or a sister too, that meant, Danny supposed. The thought of the Kid at a family function, outside of work, barely made sense. But if Danny made it through this, he really would take him up on that offer to go and hang out.

'I'm guessing from the fact that you're in a shopping centre that you pulled off the practically impossible and got away,' the Kid said. 'Unless of course the cops did snag you and they've taken you there for lunch.' He clearly had Danny's phone's GPS signature right back there blinking on one of his screens.

'I ate alone.'

'Yeah, well you're fucking lucky.' The Kid's voice was brittle. Danny knew he was still angry that he hadn't taken his advice about cutting down that alley back by the school. He obviously thought he'd have got him safe by now. 'So who the hell *have* you been talking to all this time? If you were calling your lawyer, I hope you remembered to put me in your will.'

Danny smiled at the morgue humour. All ex-soldiers were the same. The worse shit got, the lighter you made of it. Sometimes it was the only way to get by.

He filled the Kid in on his conversation with Crane. The pertinent bits anyway. Not about how it had taken place in Noirlight. Or about how he still didn't trust Crane's contact. But about how the terrorist in the room had died of natural causes.

The Kid got the point straight away.

'You need to get me that swipe card and stick,' he said.

'What's your location?'

'South of you. Sleaford industrial estate. The other side of the Thames. Behind Battersea power station. Less than two miles from where you are now.'

Assuming the police were still concentrating their efforts to the north and north-west of him, and hadn't yet widened their net or roadblocked the Thames bridges, Danny estimated that he could probably reach the Kid within twenty minutes.

'You got the equipment there to read the card?'

'To scan it, sure,' said the Kid. 'But to read it . . . well, that kind of depends on what's on there.'

Which could still be nothing, Danny thought. Or something totally unimportant, like credits for a library photocopying machine. With no name attached. No paper trail. Nothing.

He just had to pray it was more.

'Jesus, Danny,' said the Kid, 'I can't believe how big this has gone already. "The Running Man", that's what they're calling you. After that Stephen King book and Schwarzenegger film. You're everywhere. CNN, Fox, China Central, Russia Channel One, Al Jazeera, you name it. You've gone global, mate. This is the biggest fucking manhunt in history. People are even betting on the result.'

'The result?' At first Danny thought he'd misheard.

'You know, on whether the Running Man is going to get away.'

Danny peered round the pillar over at the TV store. The Kid wasn't exaggerating. Over half the screens now showed images of him. Filmed from the chopper. Or blurred on foot exiting Hyde Park, caught on camera by some passer-by. Or on Harrods' CCTV, assaulting security guards, racing through the store, knocking down displays. Even him taking out the CCTV camera itself in the staff exit, before he'd ended up going through that round of sheer hell with Alan Offiniah.

Other screens focused on the wider story. On the fact that terrorists were still believed to be at large in central London. On whether suicide bombs would be next. On the mass murder outside the Ritz. On growing rumours that a gunman had gone on the rampage in Harrods. News reporters stood in flak jackets in Knightsbridge and Green Park.

Other channels were concentrating on the actual hit on the limo. On international reactions to the way it had been targeted. The White House lawn. Ten Downing Street. Tbilisi in Georgia. Moscow in the rain.

Even as he watched, Danny saw a hastily constructed animated sequence of a man in a tracksuit with a backpack on, running into a store, only for the store to then explode in a cartoon fireball.

'IS TERRORIST STILL INSIDE? IS HE WIRED TO EXPLODE?' the accompanying headline read.

And people are placing bets?

'But the scumbags that did this, they're all still at large,' Danny said. The thought made him sick to his core.

'I know that, Danny. But most people don't care. To them you're just another chunk of reality TV. Something for them to chew their popcorn to. Thirty-three thousand police, mate. That's how many are looking for you in London right now. Plus God only knows how many government operatives. At least nine intelligence agencies I can think of. Both here and abroad.'

Agency spooks. Danny had been spared them so far at least. And the military. He'd been lucky in that, he knew. Because it wasn't like the British weren't prepared to deploy soldiers into civilian areas. He remembered how just a few years back they'd sent tanks to Heathrow airport, following fears that a terrorist organization was planning on using a rocket launcher to shoot down a jet.

They'd no doubt use the same level of force on him too, if they could only work out where he was.

'Danny?' said the Kid.

'What?'

'Do me a favour and don't switch off your phone again. It makes my life a whole lot bloody simpler if I can contact you and track where you are.'

'Sure.'

Danny noticed that his phone's low power indicator was still flashing. There was a telecoms store across the mall. As soon as he'd finished talking to the Kid, he'd get in there and buy a new battery.

'Oh, and Danny?' said the Kid. 'You know those bets I was talking about . . .'

'On whether I get away?'

'Yeah. Well the odds on you making it are sky high . . . So you know what?' Danny heard the telltale crinkling sound of the Kid starting to smile.

'Let me guess: you're thinking of placing a bet.'

'Exactly right. But you know why?'

'Nope.'

'Because I got inside information.'

'And what's that?'

'That the Running Man's even faster than he looks.'

Danny smiled. Because even though it was only a joke, he knew there was some truth in it too. The Kid still believed in him. He still believed they could make this come good. And so long as

Danny could stay focused, then maybe he could prove the Kid right. Forget the nine intelligence agencies and the thirty-three thousand police. Those were just numbers, just stats.

Remember, he told himself. *This is what you and the Kid are good at. Staying invisible. Outwitting predators. Keeping alive.*

But then his whole expression froze.

A new piece of breaking news footage had just joined the others being shown in the TV store. But rather than having been filmed from afar, this latest one showed Danny up close, snatching up a piece of card from the ground.

A high-resolution image of Danny Shanklin's face filled the screen.

Danny's mind raced along with his heart. The guy in the pinstripe suit outside Harrods . . . the man he had run into, who'd been making that phone call . . . He'd somehow snatched footage of Danny right at the moment his face had been exposed . . . right after his sunglasses had fallen off.

Danny felt his throat constricting. His chest began to cramp. Because surely it was now only a matter of time before he'd be ID'd.

But then even that stay of execution was snatched from him. Because the photo was only a precursor to what else the media had. Now – as one by one the close-up image of Danny's face filled the other screens in the store – words flashed up beneath those images too.

And the Running Man now had a name.

CHAPTER THIRTY-FIVE

'Danny? Danny . . . are you still there?'

The words 'DANIEL SHANKLIN' glared out at him from beneath every single image of his face in the TV store window.

'Danny?'

The Kid's voice finally pierced Danny's mind. He tore his eyes from the screens.

He said, 'Wait.'

Stand, don't fall. For God's sake, don't fall. He felt as if the pillar against which he was leaning was made of sponge. He felt like the whole mall was no longer real, as if everything he saw was no more substantial than a digital environment clipped straight out of Noirlight.

He fought the fear rising up inside him. He forced himself to focus on the here and now.

Lexie.

His precious princess. The fact that he'd now been publicly ID'd meant that a link from him to her would happen next, just as sure as night followed day.

He'd done the one thing he'd sworn he never would. He'd put her life in danger again.

The first thing the police, the military, and whatever other agencies were hunting Danny would do was to run his now known real ID through every official database available.

They'd start pulling up his entire documented history – from his birth and marriage certificates to the births of his children and the deaths of his wife and son.

Which meant they'd soon enough find out about Lexie. How old she was, and how she lived here in London, and where she went to school. Then they'd come for her. To reel him in. Of that Danny had no doubt.

He had to reach her first. And get her somewhere safe. He had to do it now.

He turned towards the fire exit leading out on to the rooftop car park, already focusing on what kind of vehicle he'd be best off stealing. But then he stopped. It was too risky. There'd be CCTV covering the lot. Plus if he hotwired a car with a transponder fitted, he'd end up getting tracked by the cops double quick.

He opted for the escalator instead. Headed down, checking out his fractured reflection in the mirrored mosaic on the wall. He adjusted his cap further down his brow, turned up his collar and set his shades square on his face.

A face the whole world now knew.

He scoured the ground floor below him as he continued his descent, counting the CCTV cameras, looking for a blind spot. He saw one. A flower bed of plastic foliage and fake tropical blooms stood unmonitored in the far right corner of the mall, near its southernmost exit.

Danny marched straight for it as soon as he hit the ground floor, the swipe card and data stick already palmed in his hand. He sat on the flower bed wall and half turned to face the fake flora behind.

It was bedded with sand, he saw. He leaned back, propping himself up with the arm holding the data stick and card, and pushed them firmly into the sand, then glanced back to check that neither item could be seen.

'You still got me there on your nav?' he said to the Kid.

'Of course, but—'

'The mall's south exit. There's a flower bed on the left as you come in.' He got up and, turning, used his phone to snap a photo of the plant he'd buried the stick and the card beside. He punched the Kid's number and hit send. 'The data stick and the card are buried there. Come get them as quick as you can.'

'You mean you're not coming to meet me?' Confusion was rising up in the Kid's voice.

'Check the news feeds,' Danny said.

He was already pushing through the mall's glass swing doors and out on to the hot, crowded pavement.

Blaring car horns. The stink of petrol fumes. The traffic was moving, but only just. Bright sunlight burned down, glinting off windscreens and store windows. Danny turned right, walked fast. Again he had to use all his self-control, just to stop himself from breaking into a run.

The Kid's voice came back. 'Oh shit. Oh Christ, I can't believe this is happening.' He sounded more rattled than Danny had ever known him.

'How the fuck could they have matched up my name to that footage so quick?' Danny said.

Because there'd not been nearly enough time for him to have been ID'd from any forensics that might have been found back there in the Ritz. Meaning the link to his name could only have been made through that phone footage. Meaning also that someone must have run those images through US public records databases. But how could they possibly have got a match so fast?

'I . . . I don't know.' The Kid was reeling, clearly just as thrown as Danny. 'Maybe . . . maybe that footage broke somewhere else first . . . maybe even on a news channel in the States . . . Or, I don't know, maybe someone recognized you and rang in . . . That's the only thing I can think of, Danny . . . that it must have happened like that.'

It was possible, of course, Danny knew. But there was another possibility too, one he didn't want to believe but also knew he'd be crazy right now to discard. Namely, that Crane could have given up his real ID. Either naively, or out of some misplaced sense of trust to his US government contact, who'd in turn naively – or deliberately – then passed it on to the hawk-faced man.

Leaving the possibility that the hawk-faced man had now decided to give the police a helping hand to capture their man.

Danny wanted to be wrong about Crane. But he didn't know. What he did know was that anyone could be got to. Crane's contact. Even Crane himself. With the right leverage – financial or emotional – everyone had their price.

All of which meant that Crane was now a risk Danny could no longer afford to take. He would not contact him again.

'We need to get you somewhere safe,' said the Kid. 'Somewhere off the street. And find these fuckers quick. Forget about me coming in to pick up that data, Danny. The quickest thing is for you to bring it to me.'

But Danny was already a hundred metres from the shopping mall, and not turning back. Sweat was pouring off his brow. His clothes felt like wet paint sprayed on to his skin. Pressure, the heat, it didn't matter which . . . He felt dizzy, nauseous, like he was about to throw up or pass out.

All day it had been like he'd had a snare tightening round his neck. And the harder he'd pulled, and the more he'd struggled to escape, the tighter it had become. Until now he wondered if he'd live through this at all.

The traffic on this side of the street was still crawling at a snail's pace both ways. He considered going back to the underground car park to get the moped, but there was already the possibility that the police had by now used CCTV footage to trace his escape route there.

Instead he saw a black London taxi moving slowly towards him in a demarcated bus and taxi lane. The orange glow of its roof light meant it was for hire.

'And Jesus, Danny,' the Kid was saying, 'for God's sake keep your face covered. The rules have changed. All those CCTV networks I was piggybacking . . . the ones the police were tracking you on before, when you were wearing that tracksuit . . . well from here on in they're going to be double trouble. Not only are the cops going to be scouring the feeds looking for you, they're going to programme in your face and get the computers looking too . . .'

Danny already knew what he meant. Intelligent CCTV. As far
as spying on its own population went, the Brits were world leaders.
Half of London now incorporated facial recognition systems into its
surveillance networks. The systems were far from flawless, but they
could still trip him up.

'Another damn good reason to get you off the street,' said the
Kid. 'You need to get your arse over here now.'

But Danny was hardly even listening. He flagged the taxi down.

'Danny?' Another note of confusion from the Kid. 'What are you
doing? Why aren't you going back to pick up the swipe card and
stick?'

The Kid must have just seen that Danny's GPS signature was
still nowhere near the mall.

'Fetch them and find out what's on them,' said Danny. 'I'll call
you back when I can.'

'But Danny . . . Danny . . .' The Kid was shouting now. 'I'm
fucking serious. I can still get you through this. But you've got to
come in now, Danny. You've gotta—'

Danny cut him off. As he got into the taxi, he checked for
messages from Crane. There were none. Then his phone's screen
slowly faded to black as its battery finally died.

'Where to, mate?' said the driver, peering at Danny through the
rear-view mirror.

'The corner of Whelan and Peters Street,' Danny said. 'Get me
there in under ten minutes and I'll pay you triple, OK?'

Danny stared out of the window. The cab jumped a kerb and
turned into an alley. As it picked up speed and the buildings blurred
past, he hunched forward in his seat, his fingers locked up in two
fists.

Lexie. He had to get to her. He had to reach her in time. He'd not
fail his daughter again.

CHAPTER THIRTY-SIX

Icy wind crackled like static through the brittle branches of the pine trees. The air tasted of ozone, almost crisp to the bite. The snow was falling heavily now, swirling like interference on a TV screen.

Danny was desperately trying to control his breath, to clear his mind, to calm his stuttering heart. But all his training seemed to have deserted him. This wasn't work. This was home.

He was pressed up flat against the log cabin wall, edging sideways, pushing through the glistening cobwebs hanging from the eaves, spreading his weight carefully to avoid the giveaway snapping of twigs and the crunch of frozen leaves.

Inside the cabin was a Beretta twelve-gauge shotgun and shells, locked in a dry steel box, safe from the kids. But if he was right and someone had come here to do them harm, he'd never have the chance to get to it. He'd have to act faster than that.

He had the bowie knife in his right hand. In a fighting grip. He stopped at the corner of the cabin and listened. Nothing but the wind. He waited. Then stole a look round the corner. The porch was clear. Another look. The curtains and door were still shut.

A final look confirmed that no third set of boot prints had been added to the others leading outside. Which meant the stranger was still in there. Danny pressed his ear up hard to the cabin wall and listened again. If whoever was inside had been talking to Sally or Jonathan, he would have been able to hear the muffled vibrations of conversation.

But there was only silence.

Danny dropped into a crouch. One of the games he'd played here as a kid had been sneaking up on the Old Man when he'd been snoozing on a rocking chair outside the front door, after drinking too many beers with Danny's mother on a hot sunny day.

Danny had never once succeeded in goosing him. The reason was simple. The pine boards the Old Man had got cheap from the local sawmill to build the porch with were sprung. It didn't matter how many nails he had driven into them. They still flexed a little when you trod on them. They creaked.

Which was why Danny chose speed now over stealth.

He burst round the corner and ran for the porch. The closed cabin door could be blocked or barred. He'd get no second chance to spring this surprise.

He hit the door shoulder-down with everything he'd got. It busted wide open with no resistance at all.

The cabin consisted of a large single room, with a couple of head-height plywood partitions to separate the two sleeping areas. Danny's plan had been to execute a tight crash roll, protecting himself from the blade of the bowie knife, coming up in the centre of the cabin, six feet from the door, thereby giving him a combat circle with a maximum eight-foot radius.

From there he'd have been able to assess then neutralize any threat.

Instead the world lurched sideways as his legs were torn out from under him. He sprawled forward, smashed face down on to the wooden floor. He twisted up in pain, a burning sensation in his side. Straight away he realized the bowie knife had cut into him. He tightened his hold on its grip, jerking it free. Groaning, he got to his feet.

Sally was staring at him wide-eyed. Her white nightshirt was torn and stained with blood. She was strapped to one of their four wooden dining chairs, next to the table in the small kitchenette in the right-hand corner of the room.

Her left cheek was swollen from where she'd been punched. Duct tape had been wrapped round her mouth to gag her. Her legs, waist, forearms and the backs of her hands had been taped to the chair so she now couldn't move.

'Drop it.'

Danny spun, his blade ready to parry or strike. But no one came at him.

At first all he saw was Jonathan. His mouth had been gagged with duct tape just like Sally's. His eyes looked big as plates, wet with tears, red and raw around the rims. He seemed to be floating. Right there in his red pyjamas in the gloom of the unlit room.

Then Danny's brain brought him the message that his boy was being held. And the man who'd spoken, the man who was holding Jonathan, now stepped forward out of the shadowy alcove beside the hearth where the firewood was stored.

'Let him go,' Danny said. 'Now.' *Then I'll fucking kill you*, he thought. *I'll cut out your fucking heart.*

Then he saw the pistol. A Browning M1911 semi-automatic. The man had it pressed up hard against Jonathan's head.

Danny calculated the distance between them. Two accelerated strides was all it would take.

But the man knew Danny wouldn't rush him. Danny could see it right there in his eyes. Grey eyes, he saw, dull eyes, flat eyes, like the eyes of a dead fish. Eyes that knew no fear. *I'll pull the trigger before you reach me* . . . That was what those dead eyes told Danny. The man knew he wouldn't rush him, because he would not risk his boy.

'Drop the knife,' the man told him again.

This time Danny did what he said, feeling as he did his power being sucked from him, like he'd just been put in a vacuum, deprived of air. He laid the knife on the floor. Because he had no choice.

'Kick it away,' said the stranger. His voice was reedy and thin. His accent Southern. Educated.

Again Danny obeyed. The cut in his side sent a sharp stab of pain piercing through his ribs as he kicked out. The knife spun across the scuffed wooden floorboards, out of reach.

The man took another step out of the shadows. Danny took in all he saw. The broad shoulders. The powerful build. The sharply defined cheekbones. He might even have been called good-looking, if it weren't for those lifeless slate-grey eyes. Their size looked all wrong. As if they were somehow too small for his face. Like a seagull's. As if this man were part predator, part scavenger. As if given half a chance, he'd strip the meat from your bones and leave them to bleach out in the sun.

He was wearing a black round-neck jumper and dark blue jeans. No labels. Neoprene gloves. His head had been recently shaved. Clean skin. Scrubbed. His scalp was bald and white as snow. He'd shaved his head for this, Danny instantly figured. In case anyone had seen him pass this way. This was his killing face, the one he wore only for this. His naked disguise.

Danny's subconscious absorbed all this in seconds. But all he could think of was that the stranger was touching his boy. All he could think of was Jonathan's heart beating. And that pistol pressed to his face.

A terrified whimper. Sally's. Muffled by the duct tape.

'Lie flat on your front,' said the stranger.

Danny slowly lowered himself down. His senses reached out. For anything, *anything* he could use. But all he got was a gust of cold wind whistling through the open door. A stink of plastic melting on the open hearth. Sally's breathing coming out in short, asthmatic gasps. A soft moan escaped from his boy.

A footstep. Another. The stranger was moving in closer now.

'Put your hands behind your back – *NO*' – a sudden half-shout, the first sign of nerves – '*DON'T* try and look at me.'

But it was too late. Danny had already seen what the stranger was planning on next. He'd seen all he'd needed for his worst fears to have been confirmed.

The man had kept the pistol jammed up against Jonathan's temple, his elbow hooked round his throat. But he'd now also picked up a long metal pole, with a pulley mechanism fitted to it and a rope noose hanging from its end.

It was the knot the noose was tied with that frightened Danny. He'd seen that knot before.

'Press your palms together as for prayer,' the man said.

The word *prayer*. He intoned it differently. Reverentially. As if he meant exactly that. As if Danny should be praying to *him*.

Another cold blast of wind rushed through the open door. Danny stared up into Sally's frightened eyes. He watched them flash now with warning, with terror. And she was right. Any sudden movement, any attempt to evade the noose or attack, and the stranger *would* shoot their boy.

Danny knew this even better than Sally did, because he'd already worked out who this stranger was. He was the Director. Or that was the dumb name the press had given him. He'd murdered eleven families in six different states over the course of the last sixteen months.

He'd become the FBI's Elite Serial Crime Unit's top priority, so much so that Danny had been seconded in from the Company to help capture him. To track him. To trap him. He'd nearly done it, too.

But he'd failed. And now the Director had come for him. To meet the only man who'd come close. To meet him and kill him, of course. Of that Danny had no doubt.

But knowledge was power. And Danny was already thanking God that he'd acted on his suspicions outside. He thanked God for the knife.

So now think, he told himself. *Fucking think and fucking plan*.

The Director's male adult victims had all been restrained and positioned facing their families, with their ankles bound together and their hands tied behind their backs. In a downwards prayer position. To this dark god who now stood before Danny. They'd been made to act as audience – or congregation, even – to the fantasy he'd enacted before them with the people they loved.

That was why Danny had hidden that two-inch blade. In case this, his darkest fear, was confirmed. Because he'd been warned that this man might come looking for him. He'd been warned, but he'd not believed it. Not till he'd seen those footsteps outside, and that car.

And it was because of the two-inch blade that he wasn't yet prepared to risk Jonathan's life in a desperate rush. Not while this man had a gun to his head. Not while Danny could still regain control. Not when he might still break free of the noose and the knot.

He prayed the tiny blade wasn't visible now, as he felt the noose brush over the backs of his hands and close around his wrists. He fought the urge to twist over and fight. He squeezed his eyes tight and he thought of his boy. He swore to himself that they'd survive.

The noose tightened. A snapping sound. The wooden pole's mechanism; it had just tied the noose's knot off. When Danny tried to move his wrists apart, he could not. His fingers, though . . . his fingers could stretch . . . they could reach . . .

A scuffling sound. A clicking. Another snap. A second noose tightened round Danny's ankles. Jonathan whimpered. Danny couldn't see his little boy, but he could tell from Sally's eyes that he'd not yet been hurt.

'I've called the police,' Danny said. 'You can still leave. You've got time. If you leave now, you could still get away.'

'Liar.'

'You fuck! I've fucking called them!'

These words Danny screamed. Not because he thought it would make the stranger believe him more. But because he wanted the stranger to think he was desperate, that he was already beat.

'Liar.'

A whisper this time. So close. Danny felt the man's warm breath on his ear. A stink of carbolic soap, of mouthwash, of antiseptic cream.

A click of the pistol to let Danny know it was there. The stranger frisked Danny down. Efficiently. Like a cop might, Danny thought. *Is that what you are . . . why we couldn't catch you? Is it because you're police?*

'And what have we here?'

The man had found the four-inch blade in Danny's boot. The one Danny had left for him there.

'I'll fucking kill you, motherfucker. I'll fucking—'

Again Danny shouted the words. Another show of furious desperation. He struggled, screaming, bucking on the floor, twisting, trying to turn, fighting against the sudden weight of the man kneeling on his spine. Not because he thought he could tear himself free. But so the stranger would think the four-inch blade had been his last hope.

The man raised Danny up then by the scruff of the neck, and slammed him back hard on the ground. Without warning, he twisted the four-inch blade's tip hard and fast up into the bleeding wound on Danny's side.

Danny screamed again. No need to fake anything this time. He gritted his teeth and crushed the tears that sprang to his eyes, as the man twisted the blade in again.

The man stood and kicked Danny hard in the ribs, then stepped back and watched him writhe. He waited until he'd stopped.

'It's not deep,' was all he then said, calmly, as if there'd been no altercation between them at all. 'Your wound, I mean. And that's good, because it means you're not going to die on me yet.'

He yanked Danny's head up then by his hair. A shriek of duct tape. He wound it tight round the lower half of Danny's face, covering his mouth, trapping his tongue against his upper lip, but leaving his eyes and nostrils clear.

Digging his foot beneath Danny, he kicked out, flipping him over on to his back. In the reflection on the full-length wall mirror, Danny saw the wire the stranger had stretched across the doorway, the one that had tripped Danny up.

The stranger used the metal pole as a lever this time, flipping Danny over on to his front again, up against the cabin wall. He wedged his legs there with the Old Man's beat-up brown leather armchair.

'Stay,' he told him, as if he were talking to a dog.

Danny tried slowing his breathing. *Wait. Wait. Wait for your chance.* He couldn't risk working the two-inch blade free yet, not with his back still open to the room.

Footsteps. The sound of paper being torn and scrunched up. A glass of water being poured, then drunk, before being smashed hissing into the embers of the fire.

Jonathan started to whimper. Danny prayed he would stop, would not draw attention to himself. A scrape of furniture. More duct tape being ripped. Then a sudden thunder of hammer blows, but only for a second. Then another short burst of the same.

Danny thought the worst then. He felt himself disappearing, fading into nothing. He thought he might already have lost them both.

But then he heard Jonathan whimper again and sagged with relief. He was still alive. He told himself the same must be true of Sally. More footsteps came next, heading for the open door.

Lexie. No . . . Danny prayed the snow was still falling. He prayed for it never to stop. *Please, Lexie*, he begged silently. *Please don't have come down from that tree* . . .

The sound of the door slamming. Then another creak. Something being dragged. Elation leapt inside Danny's heart. The stranger hadn't gone out.

He doesn't know about Lexie. Or he's given up on finding her in the storm.

Pain tore through Danny's arms as the stranger hauled him up by the knot binding his wrists – as easily as if he were a child, as if he didn't weigh a thing – and dragged him across the cabin.

He gripped Danny's hair with one hand and hooked him under the elbow behind his back with the other. He jerked him up, nearly dislocating Danny's shoulder as he did, then shoved him down on to a chair positioned opposite Sally and his boy.

Danny stared hard into his young son's eyes. All the love he'd ever felt for anyone, he felt it for Jonathan now.

But then his heart sank. On the other side of Sally was another empty chair. For Lexie. The stranger had not forgotten her at all.

A creak of gloves. The stranger gripped Danny's neck, and exerted a sudden violent downwards pressure. He wound duct tape round Danny's torso, strapping him tight to the chair. Then taped his legs tight too.

When he'd finished, he gazed down at Danny and smiled. All teeth.

'Your little girl . . . Alexandra . . .'

The way he said it – like he was trying out the word for flavour – made Danny want to tear out his tongue. The bruises on Sally's face . . . He'd not just done it to find out if Danny had a phone . . . This man had beaten their daughter's name from her too.

'Did you hide her somewhere out there? Or did you tell her to run for help?'

The stranger wasn't expecting an answer, of course. Not now he'd taped Danny's mouth. He watched Danny's eyes instead. He watched them like a fisherman watches the sea for signs, searching for cormorants diving for fish, so he'd know where to cast his net.

He watched Danny, and then he smiled.

'Not help,' he said. 'Not in this storm. She's hiding. Somewhere dry and out of the wind. Just like those rabbits you've been busy gutting and skinning out back.'

Danny knew then for certain: the stranger had either been watching them the last couple of days, or he'd scoped the place out some time after he'd arrived. Either way, he'd know already that they had no neighbours near.

Without warning, the man turned to face Sally. He ducked down low and kissed her duct-taped mouth. A rushing sound filled Danny's ears. He threw himself bodily forward. Instinctively. Without thinking.

But neither he nor the chair moved. That was when he realized it. That hammering sound. The stranger had nail-gunned the chair to the floor. So that whatever came next, whatever he chose to do to Danny's family, Danny would have no choice but to *watch*.

Danny fought the blind fury rising inside him. He forced himself to focus instead on what he now knew he must do. He thought of the two-inch blade. How much time did he have? He couldn't be sure. This man's previous victims had sometimes been killed quickly, sometimes over days.

Never give up. Never say that you can't.

He would not surrender hope. He still had surprise on his side. The stranger no longer regarded him as a threat. That much was obvious from the way he now turned his back on Danny and put more logs on the smouldering fire, before continuing to tear up more newspaper and scrunch it into tiny balls.

Danny already knew what he was doing that for.

He felt for the two-inch blade with his fingertips then. He started to work it free.

CHAPTER THIRTY-SEVEN

Through a warren of one-way streets and back alleys, the taxi driver reached Whelan Street nine minutes later.

Danny paid him and hurried out. In case the driver was later questioned, he walked in the opposite direction to the one he wanted, before doubling back on himself once the taxi had vanished from sight.

St Peter's Girls' School occupied a large site near Brook Green. During the taxi ride there, Danny had seen no police, either in cars or on foot.

Because they're all still looking for me somewhere else.

Nine minutes . . . meaning it was now fourteen minutes since he'd been officially identified on British TV. It was possible, then, that news had not yet reached the school. Or if it had, then it had not yet been acted upon.

Despite having always paid the fees, Danny had had little contact with the school since his daughter had become a pupil here five years ago, shortly after her eleventh birthday.

He walked quickly though the open gates and set off along the hundred-metre gravel drive.

The turreted façade of the main school building gave it the air of an English stately home. A fountain with three stone dolphins frozen in the act of leaping drew Danny's eyes towards the building's entrance. Landscaped lawns and riotously coloured flower beds stretched away left and right.

London's wealthiest clamoured over places for their kids here. Lexie had got in on an art scholarship. She'd been a day girl here for her first four years, but had started boarding after her grandmother, Jean, had got ill. The one school holiday there'd been since Jean had died – this Easter just past – she had elected to spend with a school friend here in England, instead of with Danny.

Two cars passed him as he marched on, each of them moving too slowly to trigger panic. As they reached the turning circle surrounding the fountain, they were directed by a grey-haired groundsman into an already brimming car park, where a bunch of civilians were milling around several rows of expensive vehicles, as if they were all out visiting some kind of exclusive rural car dealership.

Most of the men were dressed in linen suits and ribboned panamas, the women in fashionable floral summer dresses. Danny, in contrast, in his hoodie and jeans, looked more like someone they might assume was about to break into their cars.

Beyond the lawns to the left of the main school building, a wide area of flat land had been given over to grass tennis courts, hockey pitches and an asphalt athletics compound. A hundred or so schoolgirls in running whites were engaged in a variety of sports. Their shouts of encouragement and excitement drifted across to Danny on the breeze.

He picked up his pace. If the police got to Lexie first, then at least she'd be safe, he was thinking. She might get wheeled out on TV in an attempt to entice him in, but she'd not be physically harmed.

But if the Kid was right and British intelligence agents were now involved, and *they* reached Lexie first, then the rules would be different, and a whole lot worse. Danny was the enemy. A mass-murdering terrorist in their eyes.

They'd treat Lexie any way they needed in order to bring him in, or find out where he was.

Ignoring the grey-haired groundsman, who called something half-heartedly after him, Danny marched up the worn stone steps into the cool entrance hall of the main building.

A marble staircase spiralled up. Bright sunlight shone down through lead-latticed windows. A couple of schoolgirls ran chattering past. Polished trophy cabinets and school photographs studded the walls.

In the three months since Jean had died, Danny had found himself officially directly back in charge of his sixteen-year-old daughter's life. But she'd wanted no more contact with him than before. Two lunches. That was all. Each of them awkward, passed in near silence. Just as bad as any of the others he'd irregularly been granted while Jean had still been alive.

Danny felt his parental failure bearing down on him like a rock. What did he really know about Lexie? Nothing. He felt sick with nerves over the thought of seeing her. He didn't know how he could even begin to explain what was going on. He just prayed she'd not seen the news since his name had been revealed. He prayed she would hear it from him.

His new trainers squeaked on the ancient red-and-white chequered floor tiles, as he hurried over to the reception, a panel-fronted mahogany counter behind which an immaculately groomed women in her mid forties sat leafing through a neat stack of paperwork. There were no TVs in sight.

As Danny reached her, she looked up. She had sharp brown eyes and wore her jet-black hair scraped straight back from her brow. Her professional smile faltered only slightly as she took in his hooded top and jeans.

'May I help you?' she said.

'My daughter.' Danny's accent shifted smoothly into Home Counties English. 'She's a student here.'

'There's a PTA picnic in the car park,' she said, 'followed by drinks in the pavilion at half past.'

Danny stared at her blankly.

'The pavilion . . . between the athletics track and the swimming centre,' she said. 'You are here for sports day, I presume?'

'Er, yeah.' Danny remembered again the letter he'd received about Lexie running in the fifteen hundred metres this afternoon. He remembered too how he'd planned to come here today after his meeting at the Ritz to watch her unseen. He couldn't believe how much had changed in just a few short hours.

He glanced over at the doorway and up the driveway. It was clear. Glancing back at the receptionist, he saw she was looking him over warily now. He smiled at her to keep her on his side.

'I've had a hell of a day,' he said, raising his shades an inch as he did, revealing his bruised face. 'Had an accident playing polo. Fell off my damned horse.'

She winced sympathetically.

'But I really do need to see my daughter now. Before the races begin.'

'I see.' The woman grimaced, glancing at her watch. 'The trouble is that most of the girls will already be getting changed.'

Danny pictured the school driveway in his mind's eye. He sensed trouble coming sooner rather than later. Those same cop pursuit cars that had nearly snagged him by Hyde Park, he envisaged them screeching up beside the dolphin fountain now.

He gazed into the receptionist's eyes and told himself to stay polite.

'Anything you can do to help, I'd be most grateful.' Another smile. 'And by the way, I've got to tell you, that shirt really suits the colour of your eyes.'

The receptionist's cheeks reddened. But the corners of her mouth were already pinching up into a smile by the time she reached for the intercom.

'Right,' she said, 'well let's see if we can track her down. Could you tell me what your name – what *her* name is?' she corrected herself.

'Alexandra. Alexandra Shanklin.'

'Lexie?' a female voice interrupted from behind, leaving the receptionist's hand hovering over the intercom system before she'd actually switched it on.

Danny turned to see a tall blonde teenage girl, skinny as a stork, with an iPad hooked nonchalantly under one arm.

'That's right,' Danny said.

The girl smiled at him brightly. 'I just saw her. In the quad. If you hurry, she'll probably still be there.'

'Er, thanks.' Danny turned back to face the receptionist, smiling abashedly this time. 'The quad,' he said. 'Would you mind telling me exactly where – and what – that is?'

CHAPTER THIRTY-EIGHT

The school's quadrangle was less than a two-minute walk through the oak-panelled corridors of the main school building.

Danny was taken there by the girl with the laptop, whose name was Sarah and who told him before she said goodbye that Lexie was one of her closest friends. As she pointed him out into the quad, she wished him the best of luck. From the look that accompanied these words, Danny guessed he was going to need it too.

Fifty metres long and open to the burning blue sky, the pillored, alcoved quad was boxed in on either side by tall Gothic buildings. Two decorative stone arches, both wide enough to drive a car through, stood at either end. Visible through them were the athletics track to the north and the dolphin statue to the south.

At first Danny didn't recognize Lexie amongst the group of ten or more teenage girls, all dressed in athletics kit, huddled chatting and laughing beside a black-painted door.

Three guys were with them, all basking in the attention they were receiving in this otherwise female environment. All same age, sixteen or seventeen. Out of school uniform. In jeans, T-shirts and boots. Most likely boyfriends or relatives from another school, Danny supposed.

It was only once he'd got up close enough to the group for several of the girls to have fallen watchfully silent that he knew for certain that the laughing girl slouched up against the wall beside the door was his daughter.

She was slim like her mother had been. But in contrast to Sally's elegance, Lexie was still bony-kneed, gangling, not yet fully grown. In profile, she was elfin-featured. So much like Sally, it wrenched his heart.

She'd still not seen him. She kicked off the dry, dusty wall, turning to face a dark-haired boy who'd just flipped a skateboard up vertically with a practised flick of his boot.

Seeing her at her full height, Danny reckoned she might even have grown an inch since he'd last seen her. It hit him that his little girl might one day be taller than him.

She'd dyed her hair and was wearing it tied up. Stripes of black ran like strips of liquorice through a tangle of strawberry blonde.

As the other girls – en masse a cloud of oversweet perfume – stepped back to let Danny through, Lexie finally noticed him too. He saw straight away that she'd got it all wrong. That she thought he'd just turned up here for sports day. Her estranged dad fumbling to make amends.

He could not have manufactured worse circumstances for a reconciliation if he'd tried.

He took off his shades and immediately regretted it. As she stared at the bruise Alan Offiniah had given him, her eyes grew harder still.

'What do *you* want?' she said.

A hiss of car tyres slewing through gravel.

Danny looked sharply across to the front of the school. What he'd dreaded was already happening. An unmarked black Mercedes – no, make that two – had just pulled up in a mistral of summer dust alongside the fountain.

Several men were already spilling out of the vehicles. Some of them in suits. A couple in jeans, T-shirts and shades. One sported a black leather jacket. Two of them ran for the school entrance. The others fanned out.

'You've got to come with me now,' Danny said.

'You can't just walk in here and tell me what to do—'

He grabbed her by the shoulder and jerked her aside so he could open the back door.

'Get your fucking hands off me.' She tried to break free.

He didn't let go. He had to get her out of here. Now.

'What the hell do you think you're doing?'

Someone shoved Danny hard in the back. When he turned, he saw one of the teenage boys, the one who'd been holding the skateboard – thin, but athletic-looking, with dark curly hair – squaring up to him.

'Don't even think about it,' Danny said.

The boy had his bony hands bunched up into fists.

Lexie stepped in between then.

'It's OK,' she said. 'He's my father.'

A cloud of confusion crossed the boy's face, but he stayed right there by her side, his fists not relaxing one bit.

More vehicles slewed to a halt at the front of the school. No sirens. Not cops. Car doors opened and slammed. This time Lexie heard. She looked that way, then back at her father. Her eyes grew wide with alarm.

'Dad, what is it? What's going on?'

Dad. She hadn't called him that in years. Not since the two of them had moved to California after Sally and Jonathan had died. Not since he'd sat there with her and TV and not speaking, and her living on pizzas and Dr Pepper, and him on prescription pills, drinking himself slowly to death.

He stared into her eyes. His little girl. She'd stroked his hair as he'd lain there slumped in his bed. She'd cleared away the bottles and put them chinking out into the trash.

An order shouted. One of the suited men – bald, squat and powerful-looking – set off jogging purposefully towards the quad archway.

The other kids began dispersing, sensing now that something was wrong. Apart from the curly-haired boy who'd fronted up to Danny. He'd not taken his eyes off the older man. He hadn't moved an inch.

'Lex,' he said. 'What do you want me to do?'

Danny saw the way his daughter's eyes softened when she looked into the boy's. The two of them, Danny could see it, were clearly much more than just friends.

'Wait here,' she said.

Lexie pulled open the black door. Danny followed her inside.

'I'm not going anywhere with you until you tell me why.'

Danny couldn't see her face. She was marching ahead of him down a gloomy corridor. A sign reading 'LIBRARY' pointed to the left, but Lexie led Danny right, as somewhere nearby a machine burst humming into life.

'Wait,' Danny said.

The rising noise of the machine drowned out his words. Lexie stormed past an empty classroom. Lines of desks and tucked-in chairs. A whiteboard with a series of mathematical equations half rubbed out.

Two metres on and the noise became deafening, as they passed another doorway, through which Danny glimpsed a bent-backed janitor in a blue boiler suit, polishing a scuffed wooden floor.

The corridor branched left, but Lexie carried straight on. Into a music practice room, Danny saw, as he hurried in after her. A piano stood up against the wall to the right. Danny ran to the head-height windows and peered out into the quad.

Lexie's friends had all vanished. Except for the boy, who, true to his word, had not taken his eyes off the door through which Lexie and Danny had gone.

The man in the suit who'd been jogging towards the quad hadn't yet entered it. He was poised beneath the quad's archway, a phone clamped to his ear, looking all around.

They're configuring . . . laying down a net . . .

Lexie slammed the door shut, cutting off the sound of the machine. When Danny looked across at her, there was nothing but hatred and rage in her eyes.

'Who do you think you are, coming here and—'

'You're in danger,' he said. 'You've got to trust me. We have to go.'

Just like that time in the woods, something in his eyes – a warning there – it stopped her dead in her tracks. Her own sharp eyes flicked towards the window.

'Those people at the front of the school. They're looking for you?'

'Yes.'

'Why?'

'They think I did something bad.'

'What?'

'They think I shot some people. A whole lot of people. They think I shot them dead.'

'My God . . .'

He watched her face crumple. Her defiance vanished. She looked like a kid, nothing more.

'All those people on the news . . .' she said. 'The Running Man. You're *him*? Oh Jesus. Oh God.' She looked like she was about to throw up. 'But everyone's been talking about it.' She shook her head, as if a part of her still refused to believe. 'There's meant to be . . . there's meant to be nearly thirty people killed . . .'

Through the window, Danny watched the squat bald guy moving slowly into the quad. His right hand was inside his jacket, as if he was reaching for something. Danny already knew what.

'Why can't you just give yourself up?' Lexie said. 'Tell them it wasn't you.'

A part of him burned for her then. She'd not asked if he was guilty. She'd not asked.

'Those men out there . . . they're not police,' he said. 'And even if they were, even if I did surrender to them – if they didn't shoot me first – I might never get out again. I've got to somehow first prove it wasn't me.'

Another man in a grey suit – blond, heavy, fast – now ran to join the squat guy. They entered the quad warily and marched to the kid by the door.

'Please, Lexie,' Danny said. 'Or they'll use you against me. They'll hurt you to get what they want.'

This was his last opportunity, he knew. She realized it too. And something in her changed then. He'd never know why. Maybe because of the way his voice had just caught. Or perhaps because the same defeat he felt now ballooning inside him, she somehow saw in his eyes.

'This way,' she said.

She jerked the music room door open and hurried out into the noisy corridor.

Father and daughter, they started to run.

CHAPTER THIRTY-NINE

Lexie turned right out of the music room and raced ahead of Danny down the red-tiled corridor, the noise of the polishing machine drowning out her steps. Danny caught up with her as she burst through a set of swing doors and ran on into an echoing, high-beamed auditorium.

Straight ahead he could see a set of closed fire exit doors that would lead them outside. Bringing them out at the back of the main school building, he reckoned, hopefully out of sight of where the unmarked Mercs had pulled up.

To the left, at the end of the aisle that bisected the rows of empty plastic seats, was the main entrance to the auditorium, a huge set of intricately carved wooden doors with smaller doors set within them, one of which was already ajar and through which a thin vertical line of daylight could be seen.

But Lexie ran right.

'Where are you going?' Danny hissed. He wanted out, not in. He wanted to get away from this place as fast as he could.

'The rafters.'

'What?'

'It's where we smoke. We'll be able to hide up there.'

She *smokes*?

'We can't hide,' Danny said. 'They'll find us. The second they discover I'm here, they're going to tear this place apart.'

As soon as he said it, Danny wondered, *Maybe they didn't come here to snatch Lexie. Maybe I wasn't as smart as I thought I was. Maybe they followed me.* But it made no difference now.

'I know,' Lexie called back, but she didn't stop. Instead she raced up the wooden steps leading on to the stage. 'But once we're up there, I can lead you right across the school. Through the roofs. Through the two buildings alongside this. We can get out through the chapel, by the teachers' car park at the back.'

The promise of transport . . . that clinched it for Danny. Plus, he was now also thinking that running straight back out of this building might mean running straight back into trouble. Those two guys back there in the quad had been equipped with comms. They could already have ordered the building surrounded.

He ran after Lexie across the empty stage, their footsteps booming out like cannon fire in their wake. Backstage, they switched right, moved into the wing, behind the runners for the heavy red velvet curtain.

A metal ladder stretched up towards the ceiling. They started to climb quickly, their footsteps ringing out on each rung like bells. Danny followed Lexie's lead, up past the lighting rigs.

He heard the sudden silence when they were three-quarters of the way up.

The janitor had just switched off his machine.

Danny gripped Lexie's ankle. He felt her leg flex and for a moment he thought she was about to instinctively kick him away. But then she peered back down the ladder towards him and the look he shot her through the gloom froze her as well.

The creak of a wooden floorboard. They both heard it then.

Danny slowly turned his head back towards the auditorium. Through a thin gap between the heavy stage curtain and where it pressed up against the wall, he could see the men now, twenty feet below, thirty feet away.

Three of them. They'd come in silent and fast. All of them armed with handguns. Sig Sauer P230s, they looked like from here.

Cold fury rippled through Danny. They knew he was with his sixteen-year-old daughter and yet they'd come in here ready to shoot.

The first guy in – heavily muscled, late thirties, with cropped black hair and ice-grey eyes – crouched down motionless to the right of the doorway through which Danny and Lexie had entered.

His two colleagues crept in after, listening, watching, with their Sig Sauers ready to fire. Steady hands, Danny noticed. No nerves there.

Danny counted off the seconds . . . three, four, five . . . then the heavily muscled guy waved his two colleagues forward with a series of swift hand gestures.

They moved quickly, silently, like sharks, the three of them spreading out now across the auditorium, checking the rows of plastic chairs, clearing them one by one.

Soon they'd widen their search to the stage, Danny knew. And the moment they stepped into the wings and looked up, they'd have him and Lexie right in their sights.

He squeezed her ankle again. As she glanced down, he could tell from her pale, drained face that she'd seen the three armed men as well.

Sweat dripped into his eyes as he nodded her on. He blinked the stinging sensation away. The sound of a jet flying somewhere nearby echoed through the room. When he next looked up, Lexie was already moving. She'd realized that this was their last chance.

They moved up rung by rung. Silently. Danny glanced back only once towards the auditorium. And that told him all he needed to know. The three agents were moving now towards the stage, exactly as he'd feared.

Lexie stopped.

Danny's heart sank as he stared up. Directly above he, he saw, was a closed trapdoor. A terrible pained expression spread across her face, as if she was about to cry. She bit down hard on her lip.

'Do it,' Danny mouthed.

She nodded once, determinedly, then turned away from him. Danny watched as, with excruciating slowness, she pressed her palm up flat against the trapdoor and gently began to push.

A tiny hiss. It sounded like an avalanche to Danny. A dust shower fell. He took the brunt of it on his head. But the rest drifted down. He waited for a face to appear below him backstage. But none did. He could no longer see the men through the gap between the curtain and the wall.

Then the floor polishing machine droned once more into life. When Danny looked up, he saw the trapdoor quickly opening into a widening sliver of hope. Then Lexie was moving upwards, squeezing on through as she continued to open it wide.

Danny hurried after. His heart was hammering now. He couldn't bring himself to look down for fear of seeing one of those agents looking right back up at him.

He watched Lexie's legs slithering out of sight. *At least she's made it*, he thought. And then he was hauling himself up through the gap.

A moment of terror. With his legs dangling below him. As if he were perched on an overhang, or sitting on the edge of a skyscraper. As if with just one slip, he'd know death.

Then silently, desperately, he raised himself fully up into the gloom of the roof space above.

CHAPTER FORTY

Danny lowered the trapdoor behind him, cutting off the noise of the polishing machine to nothing but a faint hum. Then silence. Someone had switched it off.

Smeared skylights illuminated a swirling galaxy of dust motes. The roof space was bigger than Danny would have guessed. High enough to stand.

Lexie had stepped aside to let him through. He pressed his finger to his lips, to ensure she didn't make the mistake of thinking that just because those men could no longer see her, they couldn't hear her as well.

But he needn't have bothered. She'd already worked it out. She squeezed past him without speaking and set off along a wooden walkway. Danny couldn't help noticing her balance. She crawled like a cat. A natural. Just the same as she'd been when he'd first started teaching her judo as a kid.

After ten metres, she stopped and turned to face him. 'We're above the library now.' A barely audible whisper. There were tears in her eyes. 'Those men . . . they looked like they wanted to shoot you. They looked like they wanted you dead.'

She was right. Whoever those people were, Danny was their problem. They'd come here to switch him off.

'The library roof,' she said, 'connects with the chapel. We can get down through there and then out. There's a back road that leads out of the school. Those people hunting for you, they might not even know it's there.'

It was a good idea – probably his only option. And she was right again to have used the word *hunting*. She'd recognized the scenario for what it was. Those men were the hunters, and Danny and Lexie were their prey.

'Let's move it,' he said, his voice a whisper too.

Lexie set off quickly again along the walkway. Silently. He glanced around as he followed. Rotting roof felt, assorted junk and the desiccated carcasses of trapped pigeons lay scattered across the rafters and blocks of decaying insulation. Grit cut through his trousers into his knees. A stink of rot. The gurgle of a water tank somewhere nearby. Dotted across the wooden beams, Danny saw the telltale black smears of scuffed-out cigarettes.

'This place is a fire trap,' he said without thinking. 'I don't want you smoking up here again.'

I don't want you smoking at all . . .

She glanced back over her shoulder – and sneered at him in open disbelief.

'Yeah, well maybe if you promise not to bring any more psychopaths into my school, then we can come to some kind of a deal.'

She had a point.

Another thirty feet and the roof space they were in terminated in a triangle of crumbling brick wall. The walkway branched left here, traversing the building. They followed it for five metres more.

'Here,' Lexie said then, crouching down beside a small closed wooden doorway.

She pulled the bolt across it and, without hesitating, crawled through into the darkness beyond.

Like the smoking, this was obviously something she'd done a hundred times before. So that was what he had on his hands, he now saw. An adventurer. A rebel. A real chip off the old block. It was crazy how they'd had to end up running together for their lives for him to have got even an inkling of that.

He wondered what else he'd get to find out about her, if they ever had the time.

The space they now entered wasn't nearly as dark as it had first appeared. In fact, the further along the dusty walkway they went, the more crepuscular light filtered down through the cracks in the tiled roof above.

Silence. It was all around them. As big and as wide as the sea.

'We're above the chapel now, aren't we?' he said.

'Yes. Look.'

She stopped momentarily two metres ahead of him ahead of him to point across at a thin shaft of light rising up through a gap in the roof insulation below.

When Danny reached it, he peered down past what he guessed must be a light fitting, and on into the depths of the chapel. Bright sunlight shone through stained-glass windows, scattering rainbows of coloured dots across the rows of wooden pews and the black-and-white chequered floor.

There was no one in sight, Danny was relieved to see. Which meant they still had the jump on those guys.

Lexie reached the end of the roof space and stopped at the top of another ladder. She didn't bother waiting for Danny or checking with him if it was OK to go down. She knew time was not on their side. And she'd already made her own choice, just the same as him, from looking down through that light fitting. She'd decided that the chapel was safe.

The ladder was only ten rungs deep. It terminated not at ground level, but in a raised gallery, a choir stall up beside the chapel's brass-piped organ. As Danny hurried down after his daughter, he peered over the gallery balcony and saw they were still the only people here.

Again Lexie didn't bother to wait. She raced ahead down a spiral of stone steps, and into the vestibule of the chapel below.

'Come on.' A loud hiss this time. She was clearly buzzing, adrenalizing. 'This way. Through the crypt. It's somewhere else where we—'

She stopped herself just in time before she actually said the word *smoke*. She glanced back at him, warningly, clearly expecting some authoritative remark. But Danny had learned his lesson. He didn't try parenting her again.

Ten steps later and they were down at crypt level, racing through a dark dank passage beneath the chapel. Then the passage ran out and Lexie lifted the latch on another wooden door.

They stepped into darkness. Danny couldn't see a thing.

His daughter shut the door behind them and switched on the light.

He'd been expecting stone coffins. Inscriptions on walls. Cases of communion wine. Maybe altar silver too. But what he got instead was synthesizers, electric guitars, basses and a full set of drums.

'This is where we do our band practice,' she said, breathless now. 'It's soundproof, you see, so—'

'You're in a band?'

'I'm the drummer.'

'Cool.'

He couldn't believe he'd just said that. Like that. Like he approved. And clearly neither could she. There it was again, that sneer. Him giving her his view on her life. He'd clearly not yet earned the right to do that.

He struggled for something to say, something that wouldn't put her nose out of whack. He saw the drum kit over in the corner and looked for a clue on the bass drum's skin, but there was nothing painted there.

'So have you guys got a name?' he said.

'The Mole Rodels.'

He nodded. *Cool*. He managed to just think it, not say it, this time.

Lexie started threading her way through the instruments. She said, 'The car park's out this way.'

And there it was. *Boom*. In an instant, whatever moment of father/daughter intimacy – of *normality* – they'd almost just shared, it vanished like a puff of smoke in a gale.

The men in the auditorium, the hawk-faced man at the Ritz, the hell Danny had been through in between, and that he still hadn't got away from yet . . . all of that now came back in a rush.

'From here on in, make sure you keep behind me,' he said, joining her now by the door. 'And no matter how much it might piss you off, when I tell you to do something, you just do it, no questions, OK?'

She swallowed hard. His tone of voice had killed stone cold any sense of this being an adventure. It had brought back fear instead. *But that's OK. That's good*, Danny thought. Because so long as you used it, fear could keep you sharp. It could keep you alive.

He took out the cop baton from his rucksack, then strapped his rucksack tight to his back. Lifting the latch on the heavy crypt door, he pulled it ajar, then stepped out blinking into the bright light outside.

CHAPTER FORTY-ONE

To the young blond man in the grey suit who came racing round the corner of the school chapel, it must have looked as though Danny were miraculously rising up out of a grave.

Danny had already been three quarters of the way up the stone crypt steps by the time he'd spotted him. But at least he'd got the advantage of seeing him first.

A split second's advantage. That was all he'd needed. He'd already got the cop baton gripped in his right fist. His brain did the maths, calculating that the blond man's current trajectory would mean he'd cross Danny's path less than three feet away.

He brought the baton round hard, whip-cracking its extension mechanism as he did. The blond man had no time to check his speed. Or dodge. Or pull whatever weapon he even now began reaching for from beneath his jacket.

He was way too late to avoid the baton, which Danny brought round fully now, pivoting his hips as he did to maximize its impact.

The baton's weighted end slammed into the blond man's right kneecap with a sickening crack. The man stumbled – almost cart-wheeled, he'd been moving so fast when his kneecap had popped.

Danny didn't wait to see him hit the ground. He was up the steps and on him in less than two seconds.

He thought the man was faking at first, just lying there like that, flat out on his front. Danny dropped down on to him, twisting his arm round and heaving back his head back.

That was when he noticed the blood trickling down the man's face into his closed eyes. A deep gash had split his forehead. Looking across, Danny saw a flower of blood on the stone chapel buttress beside him, where the man's skull had sledgehammered into it.

He rolled the man on to his side and knelt beside him. He recognized his face. One of the three sharks from the auditorium. His suit jacket was open. Beneath was his Sig Sauer, still in its sidearm holster. Danny couldn't hear him breathing. Was he dead or just knocked out?

He got no chance to find out. A footstep.

'Don't move, or I'll shoot.'

Idiot. Danny cursed himself. Why hadn't he looked?

A male English accent. Crisp and confident. Whoever this was, they'd done it before. And they were close. Two metres behind him, Danny estimated, not turning round. Close and confident. Not a good combination to be up against. If this guy pulled the trigger of whatever weapon he was holding, Danny did not believe he would miss.

'You'll do exactly what I say. Now crawl away from the body.'

The *body*. This guy thought his colleague was dead – that Danny had killed him.

Danny did what he was told, a sudden fatigue washing heavily over him. He remembered what the Kid had told him back in the mall. Thirty-three thousand cops. One innocent man. He knew he'd done well to survive as long as he had. But had it all come to this? Jumped from behind? Without even a chance to fight back? His mind whirred. Could it really just be over like that?

'Face down and spread them.'

Danny assumed the position. He lowered himself on to his belly. Then stretched out his legs. His arms, too. He pressed his left cheek to the concrete, trying to catch a glimpse of his captor, but the guy kept out of sight. Danny heard the scuff of a shoe in the dirt. Closer than the man's voice had sounded before.

But why wasn't he calling for backup? That was what Danny wanted to know. What was he dealing with here? Some kind of glory boy who wanted all the credit for the collar himself? It made no sense.

Then something else Danny would never have expected. Another scuff. Even nearer than the first. This man was actually closing in on him, unnecessarily exposing himself to the possibility of a counterattack.

Which Danny would be only too pleased to deliver.

But he'd have to be fast. If he didn't get it exactly right first time, he'd be dead.

He hesitated. *Lexie . . .* If he screwed this up, the guy would shoot and Danny would never see her again.

Another second passed. And still he didn't move.

Then even his breath froze. He felt the cold, hard barrel of the man's pistol press up hard against the back of his head, pinning his face to the ground.

Danny still couldn't see the man in his peripheral vision. But he must have been aiming at Danny all along. Waiting . . . *tempting* him to make a move.

If Danny hadn't thought of Lexie, he would have. And then he'd already be dead.

The man jerked Danny's left arm up behind his back, using his own left arm to lock it there.

Danny got his first blurred glimpse of his captor's face then, as he leaned in closer to Danny's ear. Cropped black hair. Heavily muscled. The leader from the auditorium. In total control again now.

Danny stared into his burning dark eyes. No fear. Only blood lust. Any doubts Danny had had, they vanished then. This man had wanted him to struggle. He'd wanted to blow him away.

'Not so fucking tough, are you?' he hissed in Danny's ear. 'Or so fucking clever.' A smile, then. A promise. 'Oh, I can't wait to have a little chat with you . . .'

Danny had seen that exact same look in another man's eyes before. A look of absolute power. The look of someone who believed themselves invulnerable. A man who thought he was a god. And all Danny wanted now was what he'd wanted then. He wanted his family to live. He wanted to keep Lexie safe.

'Now you're going to tell me where that little bitch of yours has gone.'

Bitch . . .

For now he just hoped Lexie had had the common sense to run. Because this man still wanted her. To help him make Danny talk. To help him make Danny confess to something he had not done. By hurting her, he could open Danny wide.

Lexie had other ideas.

Sunlight flashed off the electric guitar as she brought it swinging down hard in a glinting arc towards the back of Danny's captor's head.

CHAPTER FORTY-TWO

The man had seen the guitar coming too. He threw himself out of the way. But not far or fast enough. The guitar missed his skull, but it slammed into his neck instead.

He keeled over with a groan. Then managed to roll sideways, out of reach, just preventing Danny from snagging his neck.

'Get back,' Danny barked.

Already rising, he glared over at Lexie. She was standing with the guitar still gripped in her hands, raised above her head as if she were about to take another swing. Defiance flashed in her dark brown eyes. But Danny wanted her out of reach.

'I said move,' he told her, turning now to face the other man, who was already staggering to his feet, clutching at his head.

The man looked even tougher up close. Dense. Muscular. His eyes hardened as he stared at Danny. He'd adrenalized, had switched into fight mode. He was a killing machine who'd just acquired a target.

He wasn't the only one.

He and Danny were now five feet apart. Both unarmed. The impact with the fallen blond man had been so great that it had torn the cop baton from Danny's hand and sent it skittering away into a nearby flower bed. But this other man had lost his grip on his

P230 too when Lexie had struck him. It now lay in the guttering several feet away, equidistant from them both.

Whoever broke first would reach it. But to do that they'd need to first turn their back on the other. And it was a risk neither of them was prepared to take.

Danny was still conscious of Lexie being somewhere close behind him. *But where?* He couldn't see her. He couldn't risk her getting hurt.

The other man must have seen these flashes of concern in Danny's eyes. He tried to take verbal control.

'We don't have to do this,' he said, rocking gently on his heels, shifting between a defensive and aggressive stance, deliberately keeping Danny guessing as to his real intent.

The man's palms were upturned in a gesture of conciliation. But his eyes betrayed him. They moved fractionally to the left, in the direction of the pistol, to map its position. He began edging that way.

That was when Danny knew he had no choice. His opponent would go for the weapon.

He shrugged off his rucksack and let it fall to the ground, knowing he'd impede his balance and movement by keeping it on.

The man understood Danny was coming for him then. He had one eye on Lexie. He knew he'd have to fight. He closed in fast, without warning, savagely grabbing the back of Danny's neck. With his right hand he seized Danny's left sleeve, intending to throw him off balance.

But Danny had anticipated the move and grabbed the other man's head as he closed, jerking it down, aiming to smash his own forehead up into his opponent's face.

The man tilted his head just in time. He took the worst of the blow on the top of his skull. A sound like a piano being hit with a hammer rang out through Danny's mind. The two of them staggered apart.

Danny was the first to recover. He caught the man's fist in his hand and used his foot to sweep the man's legs sideways from under him. He followed him down, adding his own weight to that of the heavily muscled man as they fell, ramming his elbow deep into the other man's diaphragm just as they crashed to the ground.

The man twisted sideways, gasping, just managing to avoid Danny's attempt at a cross-body armlock.

Swiftly regaining his breath and his balance, once more revealing his training, the man then reached out for a foot lock. He wrapped his arm round Danny's ankle as they grappled on the ground.

Danny slammed his free left foot hard into the man's exposed neck and succeeded in driving him away.

They scuffled then, with the dark-haired man trying and failing to pin his leg down across Danny's body. Until finally he overreached himself, and overbalanced, exposing his back to Danny for a fraction of a second.

That was all it took.

Danny tore the other man's left arm up behind him into a chicken-wing position, then hooked his free arm round his head. Keeping the chicken wing in place, he then locked his own hands behind the other man's shoulder blade.

He arched backwards, pulling sharply back on the man's forehead as he did, bending the stunned man's neck swiftly back to a point where another couple of millimetres and it would snap.

The man's breathing stuttered and slowed. He knew Danny had him in a neck crank and could kill him whenever he chose.

Danny's own heart was beating as fast as a bird's. He could taste blood in his mouth. Pain resounded through his skull.

'Tell me who you work for,' he said.

He marginally slackened the pressure on his neck to allow the heavily muscled man to respond.

He made a gargling sound. Two letters. A number.

'M . . . I . . . 5 . . .'

'What do you know about the people who carried out the massacre?'

'It . . .' the man said, 'it was you . . .'

'Wrong.' Danny gave him a fraction more squeeze. 'I've been set up. Who else are you hunting apart from me?'

'No one . . .'

Considering the amount of pain this guy must now be in, considering the fact that he knew that all Danny would need to do to snap his neck like it was made of balsa was to arch swiftly back and squeeze with both hands – taking into consideration all that, Danny decided he was probably telling the truth.

So there it was. Danny and the dead guy back in that hotel room – if they ever managed to ID his disfigured corpse at all – they were the only ones now who were going to take the blame.

Which meant that, dead or alive, Danny was going to have to bring the hawk-faced man in. He was going to have to prove who he was and what he had done.

'Tell your bosses there were at least five people in that hotel room who were involved in that hit,' Danny said. 'Tell them they're probably hiding amongst all those people who got out. And tell them that I told you that I'm innocent, and I will bring you proof.'

The heavily muscled man grunted something. It could have been a *yes*, or a *no*, or *fuck you*. It didn't matter which. This conversation was now at an end.

Danny switched his grip to a stranglehold. He squeezed down tight, bringing sharp and sudden pressure to bear on the MI5 operative's carotids, rendering him unconscious within seconds.

Death would have followed if he had held the grip, but as it was, he just pushed the man's limp body away.

CHAPTER FORTY-THREE

A tortured twang of broken, twisted strings. As Danny got up, he turned to see Lexie standing there shaking. She'd just dropped the guitar.

'Is . . . is he . . .'

She couldn't get the words out. Her eyes were locked on the motionless body of the heavily muscled man.

'He'll be fine.'

Danny took her hands in his and stared deep into her eyes. Her breath was coming in short, sharp bursts. She was shaking. She couldn't stop.

'It's OK,' he said. 'It's all going to be OK.'

Tears started streaking down her face. She didn't seem to be aware of them at first. Her eyes just glazed over. But then she jerked her hands free and wiped the tears away.

'We should go,' he said. 'The others . . . they'll be coming.'

He grabbed the baton from the flower bed, snapped it shut inside his rucksack. He decided against taking the pistol. Again he didn't know who he might end up instinctively using it against. Maybe an innocent cop. Something he just couldn't chance.

'What about him?'

Lexie was staring at the fallen blond guy. But then the man

answered her himself. He groaned and rolled over on to his side, facing away from them. Not dead. Coming round. The second his mind cleared, he'd reach for his radio and weapon.

Danny grabbed Lexie's hand. 'Quick. The teachers' car park,' he said.

She led him fast past the flower beds, and on through a clapboard-sided alleyway that ran between two single-storey maintenance buildings. A stink of fresh creosote. A bird shrilled startled up into the sky.

As they branched right at the end of the alley and broke through a line of tall poplar trees, Danny saw forty or so cars were spread out across a gravel car park. A badly surfaced private road ran due north away from the school buildings, into the suburban streets beyond. No cop cars anywhere, as far as he could see. No reason why his daughter's plan might not work.

'That one,' he said.

He'd already selected their ride. A powder-blue Saab. Fast, but old enough not to have been factory-equipped with a transponder linked up to a stolen-car tracking service.

'But you can't. That's Miss Heap's,' Lexie said.

'Who?'

'The headmistress.'

'Tough.'

He smashed the driver's window with the baton, snapping off the remaining jagged shards of glass before reaching in and manually popping the lock. The car might not have been modern enough to come fitted with a transponder, but he had just made the unfortunate discovery that it was definitely fitted with an alarm.

A high-pitched whooping rose up from somewhere deep within its bonnet as Danny climbed into the driver's seat. A whiff of fresh mountain pine from the little deodorizer tree hanging from the rear-view mirror. A packet of biscuits beside the gearstick. He reached across and opened the passenger door.

'Buckle up,' he told Lexie, as she clambered in.

He shoved his rucksack into her arms as she pulled the door shut after her.

'Inside's a small grey box,' he said.

'A what?'

'Just find it.'

She looked up sharply at his tone of voice, her expression flaring, reminding him of the rebellious teenager he'd met in the school quad. But then she glanced away, must have remembered their pact. She set about rifling through his rucksack.

Danny got busy himself, ripping out the panel under the steering wheel, tracing back the wires. Less than ten seconds later, the engine rumbled into life.

Sitting up, he checked the rear-view mirror, the side mirrors too, searching for any signs of pursuit. Nothing. Looking across at Lexie, he saw she'd done what he'd asked. She had the grey box in the palm of her outstretched hand.

'Switch it on and stick it on the dash,' he said.

As she did, he reversed the car out of its parking space. He checked the mirrors again. But the staff car park was empty. A circle of red LEDs began spinning round the display on the top of the grey box, then switched to amber, then turned to green. And the car alarm switched off.

Lexie stared at the little grey box like she'd just discovered fire. 'Did that just—'

'Yeah, now put it back in the bag.'

'What is all this other stuff?'

'Stuff you don't need to know anything about.'

Danny steadily built up speed as they drew out of the car park. He stopped accelerating when he reached thirty m.p.h. and kept it steady there. No point in drawing attention to themselves by squealing off in a cloud of dust. He looked out across the playing fields and saw why the car alarm hadn't brought anyone running.

A brass band was marching across the athletics track. St Peter's Girls' School sports day had finally begun.

'What now?' Lexie said.

'We get you out of here. Somewhere safe.'

Danny already had somewhere in mind. He initiated the sat nav and punched in an address, at the same time switching the machine's audio off, so the route just showed on its map.

The machine did the maths and flashed up the distance south-west to their destination. Get away from the school fast, without picking up a tail, and they might just be in with a chance.

'Where?' Lexie said.

'A friend's place. Just until I've fixed all this.' He tried to sound reassuring. Normal. But his mind was whirring. What the hell was he meant to say to her to help her deal with what she'd just seen? She'd just watched him nearly kill two men. For Christ's sake, she was only sixteen.

They reached the end of the private road. Another mirror check. No one in pursuit. Danny turned right into a tree-lined residential street, again checking his mirrors, and the sky for choppers too.

He checked the sat nav route and memorized the next ten turns he'd need to take, and then they set off on their run.

'That man I hit with the guitar . . .' Lexie said, her voice small, like she was suddenly much further away than she really was.

'What about him?'

'He said he worked for MI5 . . . and they're the government, right?'

'Yeah.' And he was an asshole, Danny thought.

'Does that mean I'm going to be in trouble for hitting him?'

'He didn't identify himself. You did what you had to do.' However all this turned out, Danny was determined she shouldn't feel guilty or bad about what she'd done. 'You know, you really should think about taking up baseball,' he said, again aiming for normal, trying to leave behind what had just happened. 'Because you've really got one hell of a swing.'

He glanced across at her, and though he couldn't be certain, he thought – he hoped – he detected the trace of a flummoxed smile breaking through that serious expression of hers. Morgue humour. There it was again. In times of strife, sometimes your only friend.

'Over here they call it rounders.'

This time it was Danny who smiled. 'Yeah, well you still gave him one hell of a shock.'

Lexie fell silent then. She stared out of the window, her face turned away from his. Danny wished he could magic them both away. To somewhere safe. A beach in Thailand. Somewhere nobody knew their names. The only trouble was, he doubted there was anywhere left in the world where that was possible now.

A car turned into the street up ahead of them and drove towards them. Fast. Danny's grip tightened on the steering wheel. But the car shot past without incident, loud music blaring, a couple of young guys laughing up front, just out for a ride.

He checked the sat nav again. He was seven turns into his initial sequence already. A third of the way. He memorized the next ten turns.

'I can't believe what you just did,' Lexie said. 'To them . . .'

The two men, she meant. The ones they'd left sprawled out like wind-tossed laundry on the ground.

'They'll be OK.'

'I mean, I know that what you do for a living is dangerous . . . and that's why Mum wanted you to stop . . .'

Danny couldn't remember the last time he'd heard anyone speaking out loud about Sally. Jean hadn't thought it was good for him to talk about Sally and Jonathan in front of Lexie, in case it upset her. And the old lady had flatly refused to talk to him about them at all. Not because she'd hated Danny. Or had even blamed him, he reckoned. But maybe because by not talking about it, she hadn't had to deal with it herself.

'What you saw today,' Danny said. 'It's not what I normally do. I don't hurt people for a living, Lexie. I do the opposite. I try to make people safe.'

In truth, he felt sick, having had her witness that fight. Even if he'd had no choice. But there was no point in bullshitting her now.

'Sometimes when people come for you, you've got to defend yourself,' he said. 'And sometimes that means you've got to fight.'

She didn't answer. When he looked across, he saw she was staring outside. He could see her reflection there in the car window, as the blur of the houses washed by. She wasn't crying. But there was an emptiness, a hollowness to her young face that he'd give anything to wipe away.

He didn't need to ask to know what she was thinking. She was thinking about back then in the cabin. She was thinking of blood on the snow.

The second his eyes switched front again, he saw the silver BMW swerve into the street a hundred metres ahead of them. It shot towards them like an arrow that had just been unleashed from a bow.

He knew it was coming for them.

CHAPTER FORTY-FOUR

'Hold tight,' Danny said through gritted teeth.

The BMW was still hurtling towards them down the long, straight residential street. Accelerating. Sixty metres and closing. It shifted on to Danny's side of the road. Didn't look much like it was planning on stopping, either.

With their combined velocities, a collision would leave the occupants of both vehicles dead. But Danny doubted that whoever these people were, they were intent on an actual kamikaze mission. More likely whoever was driving that car was assuming Danny was going to chicken out of the collision first.

He reckoned they'd already worked out his weakness – his daughter was with him, and he wouldn't risk her life. They thought he'd just slam on his brakes. Or would maybe even panic and lose control and plough into the line of parked cars that he was whipping past now.

They'd have been better off watching their sat nav screen. Because then what Danny did next wouldn't have come as quite such a shock to them.

He slammed the gearstick up into third and floored the accelerator. The car bucked a little, then surged forward. Right at the BMW. Thirty metres. Twenty. Danny watched until he could see their faces.

'Dad.' Lexie started to shout. 'Dad. Stop.'

He hung a hard right. The car slewed screeching across the street, right across the path of the oncoming BMW.

For a split second, Danny thought he'd misjudged it. But then the side street the sat nav map had predicted opened up right there in front of him. Silver flashed in the rear-view mirror as the BMW sailed past.

Miss Heap's Saab shot forward, jumping the kerb momentarily before Danny hauled it back round and down on to the road.

'Are you OK?'

Nothing.

'Lexie. Answer me.' He needed her to respond. He couldn't have her going into shock.

'Yes,' she finally said.

Looking across, he saw both hands gripping the top of her seat belt where it disappeared into the car's roof.

The cobbled mews they'd entered was deserted apart from one or two parked cars. Danny floored the accelerator and they raced past a row of craft shops and art studios. Hot summer air rushed in at him through the broken car window.

Nothing in the rear-view mirror. The BMW might have crashed, he hoped, but without much faith. More likely it would either be screaming in reverse back up that street they'd left it in. Or it would already be cutting through another series of turns to intercept him somewhere else.

As they reached the end of the cobbled road and shot out into the street beyond, Danny heaved the car hard round to the left.

A flash of red this time in the rear-view. A bus. A double-decker. He had missed ploughing into it by less than ten feet. Its driver angrily flashed its lights, blasting its horn.

Another movement. The silver BMW was back.

It dipped out to the right just to the rear of the bus, then straight back in, narrowly avoiding a head-on collision with a truck at the head of a column of traffic coming the other way.

Danny gunned the Saab up behind a small green Nissan driving in front of him. He searched the oncoming traffic for a gap so he could pass. He spotted one coming. In three cars' time. A space of maybe forty metres.

The second the gap reached him, he slung the car out wide, tyres squealing, across on to the other side of the street.

He floored the accelerator in third. The engine shrieked. The forty-metre gap shrank almost to nothing in less than two seconds. An oncoming Land Rover rushed towards him. Its driver stared out at Danny in horror as she slammed on her brakes.

But whatever impact she'd been expecting never came. The exact instant the rear of Miss Heap's car drew level with the front of the little green Nissan, Danny twisted the steering wheel hard left, bringing him sweeping back across on to his own side of the road.

Looking back, he saw the BMW, with its vastly superior acceleration, had already successfully managed a similar manoeuvre, and had already cut past the bus.

Only the Nissan was now keeping them and Danny apart.

'Get down,' he said.

Lexie didn't react. She was too freaked out. He grabbed the back of her neck and pushed her head down roughly between her knees.

'And stay down.'

Any second now, he was expecting the BMW to be right on his tail. And then what? An explosion of glass behind his head? A bullet slamming into the dash? Or something infinitely worse?

He tried not to think of the dangers. He focused on working out how the hell he was going to lose the BMW instead.

He was stuck behind another car already. A Citroën. Doing less than thirty miles an hour.

But worse was what was happening up ahead. Fifty metres on, the traffic in front of Danny was already slowing, brake lights glowing as they backed up in a column at a set of red lights.

The last of the oncoming traffic on the other side of the street would be passing Danny any second. Then the BMW would pull into the gap. It was less than ten metres behind them now. Within seconds it would be past them. It would box them in. And then they'd be toast.

Danny moved first, crossing on to the other side of the street the first chance he got. He floored the accelerator. The car hit forty m.p.h. Then fifty. He was doing sixty by the time he sailed through the set of red lights on the wrong side of the road, and out into the major intersection beyond.

Headlights flashed, horns blared, vehicles swerved and shunted into one another to get out of his way. The wind rushed past his face through the open car window. He twisted the steering wheel sideways and missed flattening a motorcycle by inches, before sliding, skidding, towards a jackknifing truck.

He missed that too. Or it swerved to miss him. The speed he was going at now, it was impossible to tell.

A gap opened up ahead, and suddenly he was clear of the tangle of colliding traffic, and barrelling along an empty stretch of road.

But he wasn't the only one. Whatever miraculous guiding hand had steered Danny through that intersection, it had steered his pursuers through too.

The BMW was rushing up behind. Twenty metres. Now ten. It pulled out alongside him. Then powered forward. Drew level. He could hear its engine scream.

Lexie was staring terrified out through Danny's busted window. She let out a whimper of fear.

Danny looked across. The gap between the two cars was less than three feet. The guy in the BMW's passenger seat, a ginger-haired man in a violent red shirt, was pointing a Browning high-power 9mm handgun at his face.

'I said down,' Danny shouted at Lexie.

The best way to lose a tail if it was faster than you, Danny had learned a long time ago, was not to try and outrun it, but to run it off the road.

He gave no warning. He looked straight ahead, and focused everything he'd got now on how he'd pull out of this spin. Then he slammed on the brakes and simultaneously twisted the steering wheel right.

He couldn't have timed it better. He clipped the back of the BMW hard. A screech of burning tyres. An explosion of rending metal. The BMW was easily the heavier of the two vehicles. But that didn't save it now.

The collision sent it spinning anticlockwise across the front of Miss Heap's car, so that the Saab's left wing clipped it hard again, this time on the passenger door.

Another agonized shriek of buckling metal. The Saab's front crumpled and tore. The BMW catapulted off to the left.

Danny and Lexie span anticlockwise too. The world lurched sickeningly round. But Danny had had one big advantage over the BMW's driver. He'd known what was coming. He'd turned into the spin, and now he set about controlling the skid.

He fought the steering wheel as they hurtled towards a crash barrier. At the last second, he managed to right the Saab once more and arrowed it back along the street.

'Jesus Christ, Dad.'

Danny glanced across, surprised. It seemed like Lexie had rediscovered her voice.

'Are you OK?'

'Oh Jesus, Dad. Please don't do that again.'

A pneumatic hissing noise. Something wrong with the engine. Danny slowly applied the brakes as they pulled up towards another queue of traffic at another set of lights.

His heart was racing. His fingers were aching from gripping the wheel. A slick of sweat trickled down his brow.

In the rear-view mirror he spotted a glint of silver metal in the sun a hundred metres behind. The BMW was on its side, its wheels spinning, smoke pouring from its engine.

A door burst open and a man crawled out.

CHAPTER FORTY-FIVE

The lights turned green. Danny cut quickly through the line of traffic crossing the next intersection and headed north-west.

'Are we safe yet?' Lexie said.

'No.'

They'd already been a mile from her school by the time the BMW had intercepted them. It had been driving in the opposite direction. Which meant it couldn't have tailed them. It must have been sent there instead.

And whatever electronic eyes had guided it, they were probably still watching Danny and Lexie now.

With intelligence agencies leading the chase, it was possible they'd deployed a surveillance satellite. Danny knew for a fact that there were several in geosynchronous orbits over western Europe, all of them capable of conducting square-metre-by-metre search patterns, and able not only to photograph a postcard from space, but also to track it blowing across someone's backyard.

They'd certainly have no trouble following a car like this through the streets of London, once they'd locked on.

Even if the people hunting him were only using CCTV, they now knew what he was driving, so it would just be matter of time till they located him again.

Meaning he still needed to make like Houdini. And vanish. And quick.

'I don't believe it,' Lexie said. 'Miss Heap smokes . . .'

Glancing across, Danny saw that sometime during the chase, the passenger glove compartment had burst open and disgorged a bunch of the headmistress's belongings on to Lexie's lap. She was holding up a silver packet of cigarettes.

'Wait,' Danny said. 'What's that?'

He snatched a metal canister from her hand. Lighter fuel. It was full.

'What about matches?' he said.

She held up a small brass object. 'Just a Zippo.'

He took that too. Another glance at the sat nav. They could make it to the safe house on foot from here.

Up ahead he saw a sign for an industrial estate. He took the turn. It was exactly what he'd wanted. A confused road layout, heavy on warehouses and light on traffic. Plenty of buildings and alleyways. The perfect place to ditch the car.

As he drove beneath a bridge running under a raised train track, he spotted a spiral of railings leading down into an underpass. Again he checked the rear-view mirror. Again the road was clear.

'Get out,' he said, screeching the car to a halt.

'But Dad . . .'

'Now.' She was shaking; he reached out and squeezed her hand. 'We've got to lose the car,' he said. 'To buy ourselves some time. Go down into the underpass and wait.'

She nodded, steeling herself, then got out and ran. He watched her as far as the underpass railings, then jerked the door shut. The car screeched away from the kerb.

He caned it out from under the bridge in second gear, then shifted into third. To the left up ahead was a row of five faded roadside advertising hoardings. A wasteland of rubble and half-demolished warehouses stretched out behind.

Bracing himself against the wheel, Danny jumped the kerb and took his foot off the accelerator. He ploughed the Saab's left wing hard but laterally into the hoarding, tearing a gash through the half-rotten boards, further crumpling the front of the car.

As the Saab shuddered hissing to a halt, he snatched up Miss Heap's can of lighter fluid and her Zippo. Grabbing his rucksack, he got out and set about squirting lighter fluid all over the the dash, carpets and seats.

He flicked the Zippo into life, tossed it on to the passenger seat and – WHOOMPH – the lighter fluid caught, sending flames licking hungrily out across the upholstery.

Danny ducked through the gap the car had ripped in the advertising hoarding, so that he could no longer be seen from the road. He heard a pursuit car coming then, gunning along the street from the east. He pressed himself flat against the hoarding as the vehicle – a black Mercedes – overshot him.

He kept the row of hoardings between himself and the Merc and edged his way along, arriving back at the entrance to the underpass less than thirty seconds later.

Checking up the road to where the burning car was, he saw two suited men standing with their backs to him, edging closer to the car and trying – daring each other it looked like – to get near enough to peer through the billowing black smoke to see if anyone was inside.

He slipped into the dark mouth of the underpass. It was time to collect Lexie and finally get them somewhere safe.

CHAPTER FORTY-SIX

They'd headed south from the road where Danny had torched the car.

'You're pretty fast,' he said, catching his breath.

'You're not so bad yourself.'

They were resting up in the scented shade of a magnolia tree in full blossom, in the large walled front garden of a multi-million-pound house that backed on to the Thames.

Sunlight filtered down through the thick web of branches, sending shade patterns shimmering across Lexie's flushed face. Both she and Danny were panting, sweating, exhausted. Danny reckoned they'd just run just over three miles.

He'd done his best to make their journey here complex to track – sticking to densely populated areas. He'd taken Lexie into two shopping malls. Safe beneath the cover of metres of concrete.

In each mall they'd bought new clothes – with Danny accounting for his filthy condition following his fight by telling the first perplexed-looking sales assistant he'd encountered that he'd slipped during a visit to a nearby construction site. They'd switched their route and had doubled back on themselves more times than he could count.

But now they were here, and he hoped no one else knew.

Danny was wearing running clothes, a black baseball cap and shades. Lexie had kitted herself out in an outfit she'd got from a store called Topshop, the style of which was alien to Danny.

Out of her school running kit, he thought she looked more like twenty than sixteen. It made him feel even older, like he'd missed out on more of her life than he actually had.

His phone was still dead. He cursed himself for not having remembered to pick up a battery. The Kid would be frantic by now. But with any luck, he'd already have picked up the data stick and card by the time Danny did get to speak to him. And then, depending what he'd mined off them, they could plan their next move.

'I was meant to be running the fifteen hundred metres today,' Lexie said.

'I reckon you would have won.'

The first mile they'd run, they'd done almost flat out. He'd assumed he'd have to help her, or adjust his pace, just to stop her from falling behind. Especially considering she smoked. But she hadn't complained once. All through the industrial estate. Along the canal towpath. Into the first shopping mall.

She'd not freaked out either. Not at the dull *thwack-thwack* of the unmarked grey chopper that had lurched into the skies above Miss Heap's burning car as they'd run on beneath tree cover in a park less than half a mile away. And not just now when he'd walked her into a stranger's garden and told her to hide behind the front wall.

'You did good, you know,' he said.

'Thanks.'

She smiled then. From relief, he supposed. And for a fleeting moment she looked just like her mother, like Sally had on that subway carriage as she'd been filling out that crossword clue the first time they'd met.

But just as quick, the smile vanished. Zipped. Withdrawn. Taken from him again.

He wanted to tell her that no matter how horrific today had been, in some crazy way, sitting here with her now in this beautiful place somehow made it all worthwhile. He wanted to tell her how much he'd missed her. How he wished he'd never let her go. But he feared what she'd say if he did.

'You know, this has got to be the longest time we've spent together, just the two of us, for quite a while,' he said.

'It's certainly the most memorable.'

He couldn't believe it. She was making a joke.

But as she blew her black-streaked fringe from her face, he again felt the fading of her smile, like the sun going in behind a cloud.

'That lunch after grandma's funeral was longer,' she said, a deep frown now creasing her brow.

When you hardly spoke a word to me . . . when you barely acknowledged I was there . . .

He'd wondered then if that was the end for them, if she'd ever want to see him again.

'You must still miss her. Your grandmother,' he said. He pulled a bottle of water from his rucksack and handed it over.

'Yes.'

He watched her as she drank. 'She was a good woman,' he said.

Lexie handed back the bottle and pulled her knees up to her chest. Wrapping her arms tightly round herself, she stared down at her new trainers.

'Grandma once told me that she thought you were self-destructive,' she said. 'She told me when she first took me away to live with her that you were a danger to yourself . . .'

She turned to him then. Danny couldn't hold her stare. He looked away. All that shame he'd felt after she'd left, after he'd got himself off the pills and had quit drinking, when he'd finally realized he'd lost her, he now felt that terrible weight bearing down on him again.

'She was right,' he said. 'But I've changed.'

'But that's just it.' Lexie's voice flared. 'Have you? Because what happened then . . . in the woods . . . when that man . . .'

Even after all this time, neither of them had a name for him, any more than they would ever be able to name between them the terrible things he had done.

'. . . when that man came looking for you then . . .' Lexie said, her voice cracking, 'he came looking for you because of what you do . . . because he wanted you dead . . . and these government people today . . . .don't they want just the same thing?'

'This isn't my fault.'

'Neither was what happened to Mum and Jonathan, Dad. I know that. But it still happened, didn't it? It happened all the same.'

Danny saw it then in her eyes. The tears shining that she wouldn't let fall, that she hated him seeing, that she even now started wiping roughly away. He saw there reflected in them just how much she still hurt. How she would always hurt.

And maybe she was right to blame Sally and Jonathan's deaths on his work. Because that job he'd been seconded to do for the FBI, it had brought the stranger right to their cabin door. And maybe she was right about now, too. Maybe nothing had changed. Because here his work was again, ripping her world apart.

He understood then. As she tore her eyes bitterly from his. Everything he'd tried to do, every way he'd tried to protect her, he'd failed. His work might have saved him, might have given him purpose again. But it had kept him and Lexie apart.

For a moment, as she sat there hunched up, staring across the small neat lawn, he thought she was about to just get up and go. But then she bit down on her lip and shook her head. As if reminding herself that that was no longer a choice.

'So whose place is this?' she said, staring up at the tall, whitewashed Georgian house.

'Someone you can trust,' Danny said. He stood and reached out to take her hand. 'Come on. Let's go see if she's in.'

There was a moment's hesitation, as Lexie stared into his eyes. Then she pushed herself up, not accepting his help, hooking her thumbs into her pockets instead.

They set off together up the short pathway that led to the front door. Lexie didn't take his hand, but she did walk by his side.

CHAPTER FORTY-SEVEN

If Alice De Luca hadn't been at home, Danny would have had to break in and try to contact her. But as it turned out, she opened the door barely seconds after he had pressed the enamel bell.

Even in bare feet, she was a tall woman. Taller than Danny. Striking with it. Red hair, green eyes and something fierce about her high-cheekboned face that had always reminded him of an engraving he'd once seen of Boadicea, ancient Queen of the Britons.

Her hands were muddy – from gardening, Danny guessed. She was wearing blue dungarees and a dirty apron with the words 'Domestic Goddess' written on it in pink lipstick writing, along with a white cotton shirt with its sleeves rolled up, showing off her muscular arms.

She stared at Danny and Lexie like they'd just dropped out of the sky.

'Oh Jesus, Danny,' she finally said. 'Please don't say you've brought her here.'

'I take it you've seen the TV.'

'The TV. The radio. The internet. Come on, sweetie,' Alice said, addressing Lexie now, 'you'd better get yourself inside.'

Danny and Lexie hurried past Alice into the airy red-tiled hall. It was exactly as Danny remembered. The same huge oil painting of Alice and her much older Italian husband Francisco was the first thing to confront you as you stepped inside.

'Is Frank home?' Danny said.

'No. Away in Milan on business.' Frank was an art dealer. He had galleries in England, Italy and France. Alice's accent was Texan. Moneyed. She hadn't lost a trace of it, even though she'd been living here for years.

Other paintings – mostly oils, a couple of watercolours, all of them originals, several worth each as much as a normal family home – drew the eye deeper into the richly furnished house.

But Alice led Danny and Lexie through the first door they came to, into a spacious sitting room furnished with a harpsichord and sofas, and lined with wall-to-ceiling bookshelves crammed with leather-bound volumes.

Peace, normality, the smell of clean carpets. The moment Alice shut the door behind them, it was like she'd locked the craziness out.

'You must be Lexie,' she said, reaching out to shake Danny's daughter's hand.

Lexie glanced at Danny, confused, clearly wondering who the hell this woman was. But she took Alice's hand nonetheless and shook it, firmly but mutely, before glaring back at Danny.

'I used to work with Alice,' he said.

Which was true. Alice now worked for a London-based VIP close protection firm. She'd brought Danny in four years ago as a consultant following the attempted kidnapping of one of her more famous clients.

She'd grown her hair down past her shoulders since then and had it in a ponytail now. She was also wearing her wedding ring, something she'd always used to take off whenever she and Danny had spent time alone.

She smiled at Lexie. 'Are you hungry?'

Lexie nodded.

'Thirsty?'

Another nod.

Alice noticed Lexie eyeing the packet of Marlboro Lights on the card table in the corner of the room.

'Do you smoke?'

Lexie's brow creased in irritation as her eyes flicked from Alice to Danny and back. It was a tell Alice didn't miss.

'I'll take that as a yes, sweetie. You help yourself.'

'Thanks,' Lexie said. 'I will.'

'Come on.' Alice took Danny by the elbow and steered him towards the door. 'You can come help me fix us something to eat.'

Danny decided he'd probably be best off dealing with the smoking issue another time. He followed Alice through to the kitchen. Even after all he'd eaten at the mall, he was already hungry again.

Shopping bags stood unpacked on the table. A computer screen glowed on the polished granite of the kitchen worktop. News footage played. Of the shooters on the balcony again. Of Danny's face.

A heavy scent of flower blossom filled the room. An open door led out into a conservatory. Beyond that, a well-kept back lawn sloped gently down towards a low red-brick wall, over which an enormous weeping willow stood sentry. Through its gently swaying foliage, Danny glimpsed patches of blue sky and the wide grey sweep of the Thames.

'Lexie's beautiful,' Alice said.

'I know.'

'Must have got it from her mother.'

'Thanks.' She'd meant it as a joke, Danny knew. But even so, it was true.

'She's feisty too,' Alice said. 'Probably got that from you.'

She poured Danny a drink of water. He drained it. Accepted another. Outside, a mournful boat horn sounded on the river. Alice stared out that way.

'You're a fugitive, Danny. I should call you in.'

'You should . . .'

'But of course I won't.'

No matter how much time she spent these days working with London police, Danny knew in his heart that she remained his friend.

'All those people who got shot. I had nothing to do with it.'

'I figured as much.'

The way she gazed steadily into his eyes said the rest. She knew him well enough to be sure he wasn't capable of doing what the news had said. He glanced warily back towards the front door.

'You think someone could have followed you?' Alice said.

'No.'

But that didn't mean he could hang round here for long, he knew. Every moment wasted, the hawk-faced man and his team would be getting further away. Tougher to track.

'What are you going to do next?' Alice said.

Danny pictured the data stick and the card back there in that flowerbed. Would the Kid have retrieved them by now? 'I've got a lead,' he said.

'And what if it doesn't come off?'

'Then I'll find another way.' He said it stoically. 'The people who've done this . . . I won't let them win.'

Alice's gaze remained steady. 'So what do you want me to do?'

'Take care of Lexie. Just for a while. Until I sort this out. I can't take her with me, Alice. I can't have her getting dragged any deeper into this than she already is.'

'Why me?' Alice said. 'Why here?'

He told her the truth. 'Because I didn't know where else. Because you were nearby. And because I needed to get her somewhere safe.'

In fact, he had considered taking Lexie to Anna-Maria, but had decided against it. Who knew how long the people who'd set him up had been tracking him? They could have been tipped off by Crane's contact as to when he was entering the UK. They could have followed him from the airport. Maybe where he'd gone out for dinner. Who he'd gone out with.

Again Danny remembered the grey Range Rover that had cruised past him and Anna-Maria as he'd walked with her towards Regent's Canal last night.

Alice, though, was a safe bet. The job he'd done for her hadn't come through Crane, and had been completely off the books – a favour for a mutual friend. There was no paper trail to lead anyone to her. Their brief affair had been secret, and since they'd broken it off, they'd only spoken rarely on the phone.

His heart skipped a beat. His eyes flicked back to the computer screen. He'd just heard his name. And now he saw it printed there too, under an old photo of him in Army Rangers uniform. A summary of his military record flashed up after that.

Alice picked up a remote control and zapped it at the screen. The newsreader's voice got louder. A grey-haired guy with a Welsh accent addressed a studio camera.

'. . . and further confirmation is now coming in concerning the prime suspect's abduction of his sixteen-year-old daughter from an exclusive west London girls' school . . .'

An outside TV broadcast filled the screen, showing police cars parked outside the main school gates.

He turned to Alice.

'I need to get going,' he said. 'Frank's boat . . . Does he still keep it here?'

Alice's husband had used to keep a rib in a sling hanging off the back garden wall. Travelling by water was probably Danny's safest bet now, he reckoned. A possibility the police might overlook. Plus, Battersea power station, behind which the Kid was waiting for him, was only a few miles downriver from here. He could probably be there in a less than an hour.

'Sure,' Alice said, 'and the outboard's got fuel in it too. But you're not going anywhere yet.' She crossed her powerful arms adamantly across her chest. 'Not until you're fed and watered. And showered too. You look like shit, Danny,' she told him, taking his hands in hers and studying the cuts and bruises on them. 'You're only going to draw attention to yourself. You don't smell too good either, I'm afraid.'

She was right. The stink of the sewers was still on him, in spite of his earlier efforts to wash it off in that public convenience. The chase through the school and in the car had taken its toll on his physical appearance as well. He stank of smoke, and his face and hair were filthy from where he'd crawled through those attics. A clean-up now might save him plenty of further scrutiny down the line.

'OK,' he said. 'But it's going to have to be quick.'

He already knew where the shower was. In the six months or so their affair had lasted, he and Alice had often spent time here together while Francisco had been away.

Alice had never told her husband about them. But she'd told Danny all about Francisco's own affairs, enough for him not to have felt guilty about what they'd been doing.

He had known it wouldn't last anyway. Not because of him, because of her. Because he'd been an adventure to her, an enigma, and the more she'd got to know him, the less like lovers they'd become, and the more like friends.

As he stripped off now in her bedroom's en suite and stepped into the shower cubicle, he left his open rucksack in easy reach on a chair with the cop baton handle sticking out.

He did it more out of habitual caution, than fear. Because he really didn't think anyone could have followed him here.

He should have relaxed, then, as he switched on the shower and a jet of cool, clean water rushed down on him. But instead his mind started racing, thinking first of Lexie downstairs, then of Lexie as a child, and then of how much time he'd lost in between.

And then as the cool water continued to pummel his aching, sweating skin, he thought of another cold place, so long ago. He thought of woods, and of blood on the snow.

CHAPTER FORTY-EIGHT

'You're wondering how I found you.'

The stranger wasn't expecting an answer. Danny's tongue was bleeding, still trapped by the duct tape. Sally and Jonathan were both also gagged, strapped to the two chairs facing him. Less than four feet away.

A bitter odour of urine and sweat. A clock ticked dully on the shelf above the stove, between a half-finished bottle of red wine from last night and a photo of Lexie holding Jonathan, newborn, in her arms.

Jonathan was in shock. His eyes were flickering, half closed, in REM. His chest was rising and falling in a stuttering motion. His nostrils were clogged with mucus. His breathing crackled. He needed his inhaler. Danny could see it on the table.

On his red pyjama top was a torn Super Mario sticker, which he must have got off a yoghurt he'd eaten after Danny had gone out. It was flecked now with his mother's blood.

Sally eyes were stretched so wide it seemed like she no longer possessed eyelids at all. Sweat seeped down her brow and tear-scorched cheeks. She kept trying to hold Danny's stare, but she couldn't stop her eyes from flicking constantly sideways towards the man who had beaten her. Her face had been warped by the duct tape stretched across it, so that it looked like she'd suffered a stroke.

Don't look at him. Don't let him scare you. I'll get us out of this, I swear.

That was what Danny was trying to tell this woman he loved. And he was trying to make this wish come true, trying not to acknowledge his own fear. He was focusing on the problem instead, on working that two-inch blade free from the waistband of his trousers.

He could almost touch the knife's grip with his fingertips now. The kicking the stranger had given him had pushed the knife further from the slot through which Danny had initially inserted it. So that he now had to flex his back and arms almost to breaking point each time he attempted to edge its grip back towards the opening.

He had to be careful. So careful. Because each time he moved, he risked alerting the stranger. The duct tape tugged at the hairs on his arms. Fresh pain cut through him as the cut in his side opened and wept like a clam.

The stranger was a dark, hunched shape in Danny's peripheral vision. Over to his left. He was still squatting beside the hearth, scrunching up more pieces of paper. He'd been doing this for nearly five minutes now.

Each piece of paper would be the size of a pea. Danny didn't need to view them to know this. He'd seen others this man had made before. He already knew how his mind worked. He knew exactly what he planned to use the paper for.

'It must seem impossible to you . . . for me suddenly to be here,' the man said.

It didn't. Danny had already worked out how. Special Agent Karl Bain. He'd brought Danny across from the Company to work alongside the FBI's Elite Serial Crime Unit, in order to help capture this man. Two months ago, after Danny and Bain had failed in their attempt to snare the killer, Bain had been found dead. An apparent suicide in a motel room, alongside the brutalized body of a male prostitute.

But Bain's death had been faked. Danny understood that now. And this stranger had been the one who'd faked it. And before he'd jammed that pistol barrel up into the roof of Karl Bain's mouth and pulled the trigger, he'd got Bain to tell him how he could track Danny down.

Sally's eyes locked on Danny's again. He'd not told her about the FBI investigation he'd been seconded to. But now she would know this was personal. That this man had come here because of Danny's work.

I should have quit before, Danny thought. He told his wife this with his eyes. *I shouldn't have waited for you to beg . . .*

If he'd already done as she'd wanted, this lunatic wouldn't be here doing this to them now. Instead he and his family would be eating breakfast. Danny would be sitting with his arm around Sally at the kitchen table, basking in the aroma of coffee and bacon, chairing the inevitable debate between the kids over whether to have a snowball fight or go tobogganing first.

More blood seeped from Danny's wound as he contorted his body again. The grip of the tiny knife, he snagged it then in the opening of the waistband. He pinned it between his fingertips. He started to ease it through.

'The answer is, I'm smarter than you,' said the stranger.

A statement of fact. Danny refused to listen. He would not let this man's abhorrent self-belief defeat him or undermine his own.

He concentrated on controlling his breathing instead. He continued to work the blade free.

Jonathan twitched in his chair and groaned. His head lolled forwards, before snapping upright again. There was a dreadful innocence to the action that churned Danny's guts, as if Jonathan were in no more peril than an exhausted commuter who'd fallen asleep on a train. But then the boy's eyes rolled back once more in delirium. His breathing crackled on.

A creak. The stranger got to his feet. As his footsteps came towards them, Sally's fingers flexed like spiders against the wooden arms of the chair to which she'd been taped. One of her fingernails snapped.

A barking noise. Wood on wood. The stranger dragged the kitchen table over alongside Danny, his wife and his son.

The stranger was now wearing a blue gauze surgical mask. He snapped on fresh surgical gloves. He knew all about DNA. All about what forensics would try and sniff out. Just as he'd left no evidence of his presence at the motel where he'd murdered Karl Bain, so he was planning on leaving this cabin clean too.

Again Danny thought, *You must be police. Police or Bureau or Company. You've got to be one of the three.*

The stranger swept the packet of Cheerios, Jonathan's Spiderman bowl, his inhaler and a milk carton off the table and on to the floor, where the milk glugged noisily out.

In a neat row at the centre of the table, he then set about placing one by one a pair of shears, a Tupperware box full of tiny paper balls, a copy of Maxim, and finally a rough-edged fist-sized rock – still glistening wet from where he must have picked it up from the snow.

Paper, stone, scissors . . .

That was when Danny first understood what his FBI and CIA colleagues had not. Why each of the stranger's previous victims had been killed in the ways they had. Some stabbed in a frenzy. Some with their throats slit or entirely cut out. Others bludgeoned. Many choked.

It wasn't because their murderer had been attempting to differentiate his crimes' signatures in an effort to throw the police and FBI off his trail. It was because it had been part of a game.

The stranger walked round behind Jonathan and Sally so that he was facing Danny. His fish eyes glinted in the dim cabin light, as dangerous and tarnished as sharp metal shards in a stream.

He slid the glove free from his left hand, then reached out and touched Sally's left ear. She flinched and jerked her head away. He gripped her blonde hair tight with his gloved right hand.

She froze then and let him do what he wanted. He slowly stroked the tip of his bare left forefinger around the curve of her ear, before gently massaging her ear lobe between his forefinger and thumb.

Danny stared through him. As if he were nothing. As if he were a ghost. As if this stranger were already dead. He still had the two-inch knife's grip between his forefingers. He'd now got the weapon almost entirely through the gap in his waistband.

Once he'd slit the tape binding his wrists, he'd have to wait for his chance. He'd only get one. The second the stranger turned his back, Danny would whip his arms round to the front, allowing him to slash through the tape binding his legs and his chest. He'd have to be quick. The quickest he'd ever been.

But then he'd be free. And armed. The stranger had left his pistol lying over by the fire.

And Danny would kill him long before he reached that.

The stranger pulled his glove back on, and stepped in between Danny and Sally. He turned his back on Danny for a second. But then – a sickening jolt of his heart – the tiny knife got snagged behind Danny's back as he tried to pull it fully free.

Danny froze. The stranger was facing him again.

Eyes locked on Danny, he placed his hand gently over Sally's right wrist. Then tore off the duct tape pinning it there.

She grimaced in pain. Her fingers flexed. A look of puzzlement crossed her face. Then hope. She thought he was going to release her.

She was wrong.

'Paper, stone, scissors,' the stranger said, at last turning away from Danny. He held up his clenched fist before Sally. 'Let's begin.'

Danny twisted the knife grip over in his fingers, and once more tried to slide it free.

As the stranger gestured up and down three times with his fist, Sally's face crumpled in confusion. She could not believe what he wanted from her. She didn't move her fist at all.

'Stone,' the stranger said. His fist had not unfurled.

He punched Sally hard in the mouth. Her cry of shock was swallowed up inside her taped-up mouth.

Danny twisted. He bucked. He tried to turn the knife.

'Again,' said the stranger.

Sally stared at Danny in desperate appeal. He was hyper-ventilating, edging towards panic. *Too fast.* This was all happening too fast. He could feel the sweat trickling down his wrists on to his fingers. On to the grip of the knife.

He *had* to get free. He had to stop this animal now. He turned from Sally, twisted his torso, desperate to work any space that he could.

'Stone,' said the stranger a second time.

A hesitation.

Then Danny heard the judgement: 'A draw.'

So Sally had realized what she must do. She'd started to play along.

Danny gasped as he felt the knife finally pull fully free from his waistband. For a terrible instant he felt its grip swinging slowly back and forth between his fingertips like a pendulum, as though it might drop.

Drop it now and it would fall to the floor. Drop it now and Sally would die.

'Again,' said the stranger.

Danny wasn't looking at them, was still twisted round. But he could hear the dominance in the stranger's voice. Control. That was what this was all about. Total control. Sally was not his equal. She was his plaything now. She was no more important than a plastic character on a game board.

The swing of the knife was slowing. Danny desperately willed it not to fall.

'Scissors,' said the stranger.

Another hesitation.

And then the result: 'You win.'

Sally whimpered.

But Danny knew there could only be one true winner in this game. And that it would never be her.

The swing of the knife finally stopped. Danny still had it. He edged another two fingertips on to it. *Steady. For God's sake, don't drop it.* He started to walk it up between his fingertips. The second he felt the end of its grip where the sharp blade began, he began to pivot it round.

'Again,' the stranger said.

Sally's breath was hissing hard and fast. Danny no longer cared about the crackling of the duct tape behind his back. Every muscle in his contorted body was working to the same end now. He was burning up with sweat, choking on his own phlegm. Using all his fingers and thumbs in unison now, he turned the downwards-pointing blade fully out and away from him, and started to edge it up. Towards the duct tape binding his wrists.

'Paper,' said the stranger.

Again that hesitation. Danny still couldn't see.

He heard a sudden frantic gasping of Sally's breath.

Then came the verdict: 'You lose. She loses . . .' the stranger said.

Danny realized that now the stranger was talking to him

'Turn round and watch,' said the stranger, 'or I'll kill the boy first.'

First . . .

Danny slowly turned to look. The stranger was staring at him. So close, Danny's fingers froze on the knife's grip again.

Danny looked past him. He stared desperately into Sally's eyes instead.

I love you, was all he thought, as he prayed for the stranger to look away so that he could work the knife again . . . so he could cut through that tape and—

Then he saw that the stranger already had the magazine from the table rolled up into a thin cylinder in his left hand. He didn't take his eyes off Danny. He stepped behind Sally and gripped her head. Then he tore the duct tape from her face and forced her jaw apart, ramming the rolled-up magazine deep down inside her screaming throat in a series of violent stabbing motions.

A wave of horror rolled through Danny. Sally was choking. *That fucker . . . that fucker . . . he wouldn't pull it out . . .* He threw himself forward as she started convulsing, panic tearing through him.

And in that instant, the knife slipped from his grip and fell.

The stranger already had the plastic box in his hand. He held Sally tighter, and poured its contents down the makeshift paper tunnel into her lungs. Light danced in his dead-fish eyes as he watched Danny.

A hideous gargling noise erupted from Sally's throat.

Danny twisted, enraged, and silently screamed, *I'll kill you I'll kill you I'll kill you*, as his fingers groped blindly for the fallen knife. The knife he could not find.

Please! Danny was screaming through his gag. *PLEASE. NNNNUUGH . . .*

Then it was over. Her body went rigid. With one terrible last shudder, she slumped.

A roar of blood in Danny's ears. Tears coursed down his face. He was swallowing down vomit, biting through his cheek. His heart clenched as violently as his fist. As if it would never open again. As if he could not breathe.

A look of absolute power, of ecstasy, settled then upon the stranger's face. He turned to Jonathan and tore the tape from his right hand.

And then he said, 'Next.'

NURGHHHH . . . NURGHHHHH . . .

A bolt of adrenalin. Danny's fingers raced again to find the knife. He twisted his body sideways. He twisted himself until he thought he would snap. Until . . . *there* . . . *THERE* . . . He felt something. The edge of the two-inch blade.

The stranger was shaking Jonathan hard by the shoulders now, trying to wake him, determined to snap him out of his trance. Jonathan's eyes flashed open. Rolled back. Then flashed open again. He stared unblinkingly ahead. Catatonic. Past the stranger. Past Danny too. Into thin air.

'Play,' said the stranger.

Jonathan didn't respond. He didn't even blink.

Danny's fingertips dragged the knife from the edge of the seat towards him, then turned it and began to drag it up his back.

The stranger moved his hands up and down three times. His fist stayed locked. Jonathan still hadn't moved.

'Stone,' said the stranger. 'You lose.'

He did it as Danny's sweat-drenched fingers scrabbled to grip the knife blade tight enough to cut, only for it to slip once more and fall. He walked round behind Jonathan and reached over his head, and held the open shears to his throat.

The boy stared then into Danny's eyes. And that was when Danny betrayed him. He knew what would happen next, and he knew he could not stop it, and he knew he could not watch.

A coward, he looked away. He looked away, and his little boy died alone.

CHAPTER FORTY-NINE

'Are you OK?' Alice asked Danny as he walked back into the kitchen.

'Why?'

'You look pale.' She walked to the stove and stirred the pan there. 'You need to eat,' she said.

'I'm not hungry.'

She pushed a bowl and fork across the table towards him, then left him, walking through to the conservatory to be with Lexie, who was already out there, smoking another cigarette.

Danny sat down, feeling the weariness coursing through his legs the moment he took his weight off them. He stared into the bowl: penne, fresh tomatoes, black olives, basil.

He pushed a forkful into his mouth. She was right: he needed food. As he chewed, he stared at the computer on the kitchen work surface. But the news feed's loop was the same as before.

He stacked his empty bowl on top of the two others already in the kitchen sink. Three glasses and a carton of orange juice stood on the table. Danny finished off what was left of the juice, then reached into his rucksack and took out a heavy black leather belt with a metal buckle.

He'd had it made specially five years ago in Tokyo. He now threaded it through the trousers of one of Francisco's pale linen suits, which Alice had laid out for him while he'd been in the shower, along with a clean white shirt and a panama.

He picked up his rucksack, walked though to the conservatory and checked his reflection in the mirror hanging there. He adjusted his shades and the hat. He looked like a well-to-do businessman. An architect, perhaps. Or an attorney.

Through the aspidistras and cacti of the conservatory, he saw that Lexie and Alice were now waiting for him at the end of the garden, perched on the wall beneath the weeping willow.

On his way out to join them, he glanced down at that morning's *Times* newspaper, which lay neatly folded on a rattan chair. It showed a photo of the UK prime minister, but Danny knew that by tomorrow his own photo would have taken its place.

Alice had left her phone on the glass-topped table beside the chair. It was the same make and model as his. He picked it up on his way out into the bright sunshine.

The Kid . . . Danny needed to speak to him. To decide on their next move.

Whatever Lexie and Alice had been discussing, they stopped talking as soon as Danny approached. But just seeing them there, already at ease in each other's company, he couldn't help wondering what it would have been like if Sally was still alive, and whether she and Lexie, as well as being mother and daughter, would by now have become good friends.

'Thanks for the lunch,' he said to Alice. 'And for the record, it was at least a fifteen.'

An old joke between them. Whenever they'd cooked for one another in the past, they always used to say how much they'd be prepared to pay for the same food in an uptown restaurant.

Alice smiled. 'Perhaps next time we should try it under less stressful circumstances,' she said.

Danny held the twin phones up. 'My battery's dead,' he said. 'Needs charging. Is it OK if I switch it for yours?'

'Sure.'

He flipped the backs off the phones and swapped their batteries. The second his phone went live again, it began to ring. He checked his call register. It was the Kid. He'd left a whole bunch of messages.

Danny messaged him quickly to say he was OK and would call him in a few minutes' time. His mind was racing with unanswered questions. Had the Kid retrieved the data stick and the card? What had he found on them?

But first Danny would say his goodbyes.

'You're in luck,' Alice said. 'The tide's high, just starting to go out. We've already lowered the boat.'

Danny leant across the mossy garden wall and peered down. The two metre hard-hulled rib was tied to a metal ladder that led down from the top of the wall into the dark oily waters. Waves from a passing tourist boat slapped against the crumbling brickwork. The outboard engine had already been fitted on to the boat's transom. It was ready to go.

'Thanks, Alice.' Danny turned back to face her. 'For everything,' he said.

When he gave her back her phone, she kept hold of his hand and gently squeezed it. She leant into him and kissed him on the cheek, then went one better and hugged him tight.

'Be careful, Danny,' she whispered in his ear. 'I'll leave you guys to say goodbye,' she then said aloud, pulling back. 'You come find me when you're done, Lexie. I'll be inside. I'll put some coffee on.'

Danny watched Alice walk away and disappear through the conservatory door. When he turned to Lexie, he saw she was staring up at him.

'You and her . . .' she said. 'Are you . . . ?'

'No.'

'But you used to be, right?'

Danny didn't even know how to start talking about something like this with his daughter. The last time they'd had a heart-to-heart, she'd been into Pokémon and he'd been happily married to her mom. He didn't know the rules any more. He had no idea how

Lexie might react. He decided to prevaricate instead, to answer her question with one of his own.

'Why do you ask? Did Alice say something?'

'No. It's just obvious, that's all.'

Female intuition. Her mother had been the same. Danny had never been able to lie to her either.

He stared into Lexie's intelligent eyes, trying to work out what she was thinking. Whether she'd hate him for having been with someone else after her mother. He thought about Anna-Maria too, and his crazy idea last night about what it might be like one day to have a normal relationship with her. Could that ever include Lexie? The way he'd just seen her getting on with Alice suddenly made it seem possible after all.

He decided to tell Lexie the truth. And not just because he reckoned she'd guess if he was lying, but because he wanted to be honest with her. To talk to her as an adult. He wanted this moment with her now to be one she could always look back on and understand that he'd tried opening up to her. No matter what might happen next.

'We did see each other for a while,' he said. 'But not lately.' Not since he'd started seeing Anna-Maria whenever he was here in London. Not since Alice had started seeing someone else too.

He didn't know what he expected Lexie to say next. But certainly not what she did.

'I'm glad,' she said. 'She's cool. It's good you got to spend time with someone so nice.'

Danny smiled. Here she was. His little girl. Suddenly all grown up. His heart went out to her then. He remembered watching her back there at the school with her friends. Her kicking off that dry, dusty wall. A part of a whole world that she lived in that he knew nothing about.

'And what about him?' Danny said.

'Who?'

'The boy – I mean, the *guy*,' he corrected himself. 'The guy in the quad at school. The one who would've tried to punch my lights out if you hadn't intervened.'

'He's no one.'

A no one who makes you blush, he thought.

Just the same as she had with him, Danny could tell when Lexie was hiding something. Not because it was something he'd been trained to do. But because she was his daughter. And he could see that she was in love.

'Well I liked him too,' he said. 'And I'm glad you've got someone like him around.' He meant it as well. The curly-haired boy had looked like the kind of kid who'd still be waiting there by that door for Lexie, because that was what he'd promised he'd do.

'Don't . . . don't let anything happen to you.' Lexie blurted the words out, her face simultaneously crumpling, as if she wished she could take them right back.

'I won't,' he said. It was a promise. 'That phone call was from a friend. He's going to help me. I'm not alone.'

She started trembling then, as if they were back in those icy woods. Danny heard her crying before he saw the tears. A tiny whimper, deep down inside her. A sound she tried to swallow before it came out.

'Why?' she said finally.

'Why what?'

She wiped away her tears and looked up angrily. 'Why do you have to be so bloody nice?' She sniffed. She gasped for air. 'I've tried to hate you,' she said. 'I've tried so hard.'

'I'm sorry.' Danny searched for better words. He wished he knew how to express himself, how to make all this right, how to take her sadness away. 'I'm sorry for what I did. For who I was. For not taking proper care of you.'

He'd written to her about this, years ago now. But who knew if she'd ever even read those letters? They'd probably ended up in a bin.

'I don't care about that,' she said. 'You were just sad.' She wasn't even trying to hide her tears any more. They were streaming down her face. A flash of confusion – of more anger too – deep inside her eyes. 'What I mean is, why did you let Grandma take me? Why did you let me go?'

'But . . .' Confusion rippled through him. 'But I thought you loved her . . .'

'I did. But I loved you too. You were my dad. You'll always be my dad. You should never have sent me away.'

The realization hit him then like a hammer blow. For a second she looked like she wanted to punch him too. But then her shoulders slumped. She stared at the ground.

He wanted to tell her that he'd thought sending her to England had been for the best, but the words seemed too lame to say to her face. And also because they weren't true. He'd never made that decision. Grandma Jean had. She'd taken Lexie from him and he'd just let her go. Only now did it occur to him that she might have wanted to stay.

'It'll never happen again,' he said. 'You'll never lose me again.'

He felt his breath tightening. Everything he was saying, it was coming out wrong. It was all too late. But as he gazed down sorrowfully at his daughter, she looked up at him and reached into her pocket.

'There's something I need to give back,' she said. 'I took it when I got that grey box out of your bag.'

She held out a square of card towards him. It was the old photo, of Danny pushing her high on that playground swing, with her long blonde hair blowing in the breeze.

'I remember where we were that day,' she said, staring wistfully down at it, her thumb rubbing at its corner as if she were trying to magic those days back. 'It was in New York, wasn't it? In that little park near where I went to grade school . . .'

She tried handing it back to him. He shook his head.

'You look after it for me,' he said. 'You can give it to me the next time you see me. I promise it won't be long.'

Another promise. She didn't question this one either. She just turned with him to face the river, and they watched for a moment in silence as the water flowed slowly by.

'When this is over,' she said, 'when you've proved to everyone that you've done nothing wrong. When the summer holidays start . . .'

'Yes?'

'Can I come and see you? You know, where you live?'

'Of course.' He didn't tell her how much he'd hoped for this, how he'd already got everything waiting for her there on Saint Croix. How he'd fixed her up her own set of rooms. He still prayed he could make it all come true.

She reached out to him then. She pulled him in tight. And as her chest heaved against his, he knew that everything between them could be good again one day. He'd do everything in his power to make it so.

'You'd better get going,' she said, smiling up at him now, wiping the tears from her eyes. 'You don't want to miss the tide.'

'I love you, princess,' he told her.

'I know. And Dad . . . I love you too.'

CHAPTER FIFTY

Danny watched Lexie shrinking into the distance as he motored the boat downstream, riding the outgoing tide towards Battersea on the south side of the Thames.

There were many emotions he knew he should have been feeling. Guilt about having dragged his daughter into all this. Rage at the people who'd given him no choice. Relief over the fact she was now somewhere safe. Fear that he'd never see her again.

But as he raised his hand to wave goodbye, what he actually felt was pride.

He twisted round in his seat and faced front, maintaining a steady pace, not wanting to draw any attention.

Not that anyone seemed to be looking for him here. The only other river vessels in sight consisted of a coxless four rowing boat arrowing hard against the tide, and a line of houseboats with stained hulls moored alongside a trio of riverside pubs.

In the city, though, the hunt still raged. Sirens rose and fell on the breeze. Choppers scoured the skies above Brook Green and Hammersmith. But the most immediate threat to Danny now was Hammersmith Bridge, a hundred metres ahead. Where police lights flashed either end.

Soon Danny could see the police themselves. Their fluorescent jackets. Up there lined along the riverbank railings. And the roadblocks they were manning. But none of them looked down at the river. And Danny drove thankfully on.

He dropped the throttle almost completely off as the rib slipped through the sanctuary of the dark shadows thrown down by the bridge. He didn't look up as he emerged into the glittering waters beyond.

Heart beating audibly in his ears, he waited for some cop to shout down for him to come back, knowing that if they did, he'd need to dispose of his rucksack – somehow sink it unseen – and become the visiting Parisian businessman his ID now claimed him to be.

Because there was no way he could outrun anyone from here.

But no one did call out. And gradually he picked up speed again. He steered a course close to the silt-rimed riverbank, and followed its lazy curve round. Another two hundred metres and the bridge had disappeared entirely from sight.

Taking his phone from his suit jacket pocket, he saw that he once again had a range of networks to choose from. Normal service across the capital must have been restored. Suggesting that SO15, the Metropolitan Police counterterrorism command, must have decided that Danny was not part of any larger guerrilla force that was attempting to redeploy itself. Meaning that from now on they'd be focusing all their resources solely on him.

Just like the MI5 guy he'd fought had said.

Danny checked his phone's call register function. Two more missed calls from the Kid since Danny had checked his phone in Alice's garden. But nothing from Crane. It was like he'd dropped off the face of the earth.

Danny pictured his other phone. The one he kept for personal calls. He'd left it on the shelf by his cabin porthole on the barge. He wondered who'd have tried calling him on it, now his name had been released. Anna-Maria for certain. Candy Day from Saint Croix.

He couldn't return to the barge. Not until he'd cleared his name. Even though *Pogonsi* wasn't registered to him, with that footage and those photos of him now out there, and with more sure to follow, any one of the other Regent's Canal residents could have recognized him and tipped off the police.

The same went for Saint Croix, of course. The press would end up descending on his home there too. He thought about Lexie and the old tractor shed he'd fixed up as a studio for her to paint in. He hoped that what was happening now would one day calm down enough for her to be able to visit. He hoped that even after he'd cleared his name, he wouldn't be forced to sell up and move on.

Other locations he frequented and resources he kept – both here in the UK and at home and abroad – would have been compromised too. Certain banks. Certain assets. But not all. Keep clear of the police and he would still have the ability to regroup and strike back.

The phone trembled in his hand. Another incoming call. The Kid, he saw. He switched the phone off mute.

'Kid, I'm sorry . . .'

'Jesus, Danny . . . Are you still all right?'

'I'm fine. Listen, there was someone—' Danny caught himself in time. 'There was *something* I had to do.'

'Right . . . kidnap your daughter . . .'

Danny shook his head. *Idiot*, he thought. Of course the Kid would now know. He imagined the whole news media would now be focusing its attention as much on her and her past as on him.

'I needed to get her somewhere safe,' he said.

'Bloody hell, Danny, you've known me nearly six years. And you never thought to mention that you had a *child* . . .'

'I'm not turning out to be much of a friend today, am I?'

'It's all right,' said the Kid.

But he didn't sound all right about it. He sounded hurt.

'I'll make it up to you once this is all over,' Danny said. 'I promise.'

'It's all right, bruv. You don't need to promise me shit.'

Bruv. There it was again. The Kid's cast-iron guarantee that as far as work was concerned, they remained rock solid.

'So this daughter of yours . . . she with you now?'

'No.'

'But she's OK?'

'Yeah. And like I said, somewhere safe.'

Just as when Crane had asked Danny the same question about himself in Noirlight, Danny gave no details about Lexie's whereabouts now, and the Kid didn't ask.

'You totally dropped off my sat map back there, Danny. What the hell happened to your phone?

'Battery died. I got a new one.'

'OK, so how about you tell me what the hell you're doing in the middle of the bloody Thames . . .'

It must have looked weird all right, Danny thought. His GPS signature floating merrily down the river on the Kid's map.

'Coming to see you, of course. I thought I'd take the scenic route.'

'And avoid all those nasty checkpoints. Nice thinking. I like your style. Only problem is, bruv, if you're heading for Battersea power station, I've had to relocate.'

'Why?'

'Too many boys in blue hanging round. I decided to get off the street. They'll have started running the licence plates of all the vehicles caught on film near the hotel at the time of the shootings. Even fake ones like mine. Meaning the van's now too much of a risk.'

'Where are you now?'

'Driving south. But not for much longer. I got keys to a mate's place. A slice of warehouse. He's been out of town for a while, if you know what I mean . . .'

Prison, Danny guessed. For people like the Kid, who liked snooping round other people's virtual fortresses, it was one of the traps of the trade.

'What's the address?'

'I want to check it out first,' said the Kid. 'I'm not the only one with keys, so I want to make sure there's no one else around. Aim for Clapham High Street. There's a small cinema there by Clapham Common tube station. The Clapham Picture House, it's called. I'll phone you and tell you where to meet me once you're there. Just get there quick, all right? The sooner we've brought you in, the safer both of us will be.'

Danny felt a wave of guilt then. It hadn't even crossed his mind that him getting caught would mean the Kid ending up forever compromised too.

'Thanks,' he said.

'What for?'

'For sticking with me.'

'What else are bloody friends for?' The Kid sniffed the compliment away. 'Now . . . do you want to hear about that USB stick and card, or what?'

Danny felt a pulse of adrenalin. 'You mean you picked them up?'

'Yep.'

'And?'

'And there's data on them both. And even better for you, mate, the names of the files on that stick . . . they look like they're in Russian.'

'That's fantastic.' Danny had to fight the urge to punch his fist in the air.

'Yeah, but the bad news is they're encrypted,' the Kid said.

'Something you can fix?'

'Planning on.'

Again Danny canned the urge to celebrate just yet. But even so, he couldn't fight the waves of optimism rising up inside him. Because if anyone could pull this off, it was the Kid.

'I've got a program stripping both the stick and the card down right now,' said the Kid. 'It's going to take a little time, Danny, but with a bit of luck I should have something to show you by the time we hook up. And if not, this mate of mine's place . . . he's got a hundred times the computing power I've got here in the van. So we can always have a crack at it there.'

The click of a lighter. The hiss of cigarette smoke being inhaled.

Shit, Danny couldn't help thinking, *with the kind of day I've had, I might just break my promise to Anna-Maria and buy myself a pack if*

I make it through to tonight. A smoke and a drink. He'd kill for them both right now, vows and promises or not.

But then something caught his eye up ahead. A police riverboat. It was heading upstream straight for him.

'I've got to go,' he told the Kid, as he quickly cut him off.

CHAPTER FIFTY-ONE

The police riverboat powered straight past Danny, on towards Hammersmith Bridge and into the fray. The cop standing on its prow even gave Danny a friendly nod as it ploughed by, kicking up a V of foaming waves in its wake.

Half an hour later, he moored Francisco's rib at a pier on the south side of the Thames, right alongside Battersea Park. Even though the Kid had already moved out further south, this was still the nearest Danny had been able to get to where he'd be.

From a tourist stall on the towpath next to a giant statue of Buddha, he bought a blue baseball cap adorned with the legend 'I LOVE LONDON'. He ditched the panama in a bin, telling himself that if one day all this came good, he'd need to find a replacement for Alice to give back to Francisco.

From the river, Danny had seen the police setting up roadblocks across Albert Bridge to the west and Chelsea Bridge to the east, no doubt to enable them to begin searching vehicles and checking pedestrians for ID.

Looking nothing like him, the Kid might have been able to cross over and back to collect the data stick and card from the shopping mall on the north side, but for Danny, being anywhere near the police was way too risky. Every single one of them would by now have an image of his face on their phone.

He entered the park itself, avoiding both the main roads either side running across the bridges, in case any further ID checkpoints had been set up along them.

Once out of the park, he set off on the three-kilometre journey to Clapham on foot. The roads this side of the river were slow-moving anyway, and the risk of facial recognition systems snagging him on public transport was too high – even if the tubes or trains were running at any useful capacity, which he doubted.

He stuck to the back streets wherever possible, further limiting his exposure to CCTV. The deeper south of the river Thames he went, the less scrutinized he felt, and the more normal his surroundings became. Less police. Less gridlock.

By the time he'd cut through Killyon Road on to Clapham Manor Street, where he passed by a pub called the Bread and Roses, he felt he was leaving hell further behind him with every step he took. Through the open pub window he saw people crowded round the TV, watching what had been happening across the river. But it was clearly a case of something happening there, not here.

Outside the pub, people were drinking, chatting, unconcerned about what was happening elsewhere. For Danny, it was as if he'd stepped into another city entirely. One where he was no longer running for his life. One where he'd finally almost escaped.

Which I have, he told himself ten minutes later, outside the small side-street cinema the Kid had directed him to, as he finished off a Styrofoam cup of pungent black coffee and waited for the Kid to call. *So long as nobody recognizes me. Hopefully I've bought myself some time.*

Another twenty minutes went by – enough for Danny to start to feel once again on edge – before the Kid's name flashed up on his phone's screen.

Fifteen minutes after that, and Danny was walking past a parade of run-down 24/7 food stores and low-rent cafés and bars in Streatham. Burger wrappers and gnawed chicken wings littered the gutters. A police siren whooped in the distance. From somewhere closer came a muffled shout and the tinkle of breaking glass.

Danny turned down a short alley. A reek of blocked drains filled the air. Gang tags and graffiti patterned the crumbling brickwork like tattoos on an ageing boxer's musculature. Distorted snatches of TV shows and drunken disputes in a dozen different languages drifted down from the tenements above.

He was tiring again by the time he reached the shabby three-storey redbrick the Kid had described. He pressed the buzzer. The Kid must have been watching out for him through the private CCTV camera peering down from the guttering above. Because less than five seconds later he opened the reinforced, security-alarmed door.

'Nice to have you back, bruv,' he said with a wide grin, slapping his hands down on Danny's shoulders before pulling him in and hugging him hard.

The Kid looked relieved and exhausted and about as fried as Danny felt. He was dressed in an oversized, scuffed black leather flying jacket and had a lit cigarette clamped between his teeth.

'It's good to be back,' Danny said. 'And thanks again, Kid. For everything. If it wasn't for you, I'd be locked up or dead by now.'

'All part of the service.' Another grin from the Kid.

The stink of cigarette smoke funnelling from his nostrils was like sweet perfume to Danny right now. He could hardly believe it, that here they were, finally face to face again. The van this morning seemed a lifetime ago.

'Come on, man. Quick,' the Kid said, stepping back into a gloomy whitewashed corridor lit by a single bare bulb. 'I've got something to show you.'

Danny followed him inside and pulled the door closed behind them. A wave of relief and fatigue swept over him, as if he'd just got home after a twenty-hour flight. He wanted to collapse. To lie down. To sleep for a week. But the Kid was right. They needed to move on the stick and swipe card now.

He followed the Kid's lumbering gait down the corridor and on through a set of white swing doors.

A huge bare-brick open-plan work space. Harsh halogen lights shone fiercely down from a high metal-girdered ceiling. Looked like they been rigged in a hurry. Bare wiring ran down from them into a wall socket. Pieces of plaster were missing in the ceiling where they'd been fitted.

The only natural daylight came from three small rectangular windows set up out of reach at the back of the room. All of them were barred. Another set of swing doors stood opposite the ones the Kid had led Danny through.

Not much in the way of creature comforts, Danny noticed. A bunch of mattresses stacked up in one corner. Several utilitarian grey plastic-backed chairs and a chipped beige Formica refectory table. No heating, he realized, breathing in the cool air.

Whoever the owner was, they clearly weren't much interested in interior design. Only work. Four desks stood piled high with screens and tech. The floor was a jungle of cables leading between them. A series of lifeless plasma monitors hung on the wall to the right like a weird modern art installation.

Two long wooden desks had been pushed together to form an L, behind which the Kid now squeezed. He sat with his back to the wall.

'Pull up a chair, bruv,' he said.

Danny did. He sat opposite the Kid.

'This place looks like it's got more tech than NASA,' he said.

'Better tech too,' said the Kid with a smile.

The room reminded Danny of intelligence command posts he'd worked from in Kuwait and Iraq.

The Kid was already typing. Glancing up, he checked his watch, then his phone. In spite of the cool temperature in here, Danny watched a trickle of sweat run down his brow.

'Shouldn't be too long now,' the Kid said, almost to himself, without looking up.

Danny noticed a microwave oven over on a sideboard. A bin beside it was stacked high with empty food packaging. Instant meals. But there was no garbage stink, meaning that none of it could have been there long.

'Looks like someone's been living here,' Danny said.

The Kid stared blankly round.

'Several someones, in fact,' Danny said, nodding over at a bunch of sleeping bags rolled up beside the mattresses.

The Kid shrugged, as if he hadn't given the matter any thought. His phone beeped on his desk. When he looked down, he smiled.

'Good,' he said, 'we can finally begin.'

CHAPTER FIFTY-TWO

'So . . . the data stick?' Danny said. 'What have you got?'

The Kid sat back a little in his chair. The glow from his computer screen cast dark shadows across his face that for some reason made Danny think of Crane in his equally eccentrically lit office in Noirlight.

'Nothing,' said the Kid. 'It's blank. Here, you can have it.'

Without warning, he tossed the data stick to Danny and pulled a black leather attaché case across the desk towards him.

A wave of confusion washed over Danny as he turned the stick he'd just snatched out of the air over in his hand.

'But you told me on the phone that you'd found files,' he said. 'Encoded Russian files.'

'I know.' The Kid smiled awkwardly. 'And that *was* the plan. For me to shoot you a bunch of horseshit. About how I'd cleverly worked out that the data signatures on the swipe card and data stick both belonged to one Colonel Nikolai Zykov, the military attaché to the Russian embassy here in London. AKA the dead guy in the hotel room.'

Horseshit?

Danny replayed in his head what the Kid had just told him. It made no sense. What was he doing? What was he saying?

The Kid flipped his laptop round so that its screen faced Danny.

'Look. I'd even gone to the trouble of getting hold of a photo of the colonel for you.'

A magnified newspaper article filled the screen. Something about a state visit three months ago by some high-powered female Russian official to London. A photograph accompanied the article, showing two women and a uniformed man.

Danny stared into the man's face. He was sixties, gaunt-looking. The two women in the photograph were smiling. But not him. Was this really the man whose shredded face Danny had stared down at in that hotel room?

The Kid spun the laptop back round to face himself. Then he opened the attaché case, its lid concealing its contents from Danny.

'I was also then going to tell you that Zykov had a reputation as a communist hardliner,' said the Kid, reaching into the attaché case, 'which is true. And that he'd subsequently become involved with a number of clandestine Russian nationalist military groups prior to the dissolution of the Soviet Union in December 1991 – also true. All of which would then have made it entirely possible for you to believe that he might have been involved in today's assassination plot to kill Madina Tskhovrebova outside the Ritz, thereby allowing him to stir up another expansionist war between Georgia and Russia . . .'

Danny felt as if the room were somehow shifting away from him, as if he wasn't really here at all. This *couldn't* be real – could it? – what the Kid was saying. Because if it was true, then the Kid had been planning on lying to him, manipulating him, controlling him – but *for what*?

The Kid pushed the lid of the attaché case away from him, letting it fall down flat now on the desk, whilst simultaneously removing a Glock 18 machine pistol and a fully loaded magazine from its moulded-foam bed. He rammed the Glock's extended magazine home.

A rushing sound filled Danny's ears.

'I was then going to tell you that there was an encrypted file on the data stick named Tskhovrebova,' the Kid said. 'You know, the same as the assassinated writer.' He spoke of her like she was nothing but a piece of deleted data herself. 'And then I was going to tell you that the file had been created by Colonel Zykov only hours before the assassination took place this morning . . . giving you further proof that he had to have been involved in the hit.'

The Kid flicked the selector switch on the machine pistol's slide from semi-automatic to full, giving it a cyclic rate of 1,300 rounds per minute. With the thirty-three rounds in its extended magazine, that gave it more than enough punch to rip a man in half. Twice.

He stood and aimed the weapon right at Danny's heart.

'Don't worry, Danny. I'm not going to shoot you just yet. Not unless you give me no choice.'

A flood of adrenalin had swept through Danny's body. Every muscle tensed. His brain felt like it was on fire. *This is really happening*, he told himself. *The Kid's betrayed you . . . He's threatening to execute you too.*

'Then,' the Kid said, 'just when I'd got you all royally pissed off at poor old Colonel Zykov, I was going to drop the bombshell on you that I couldn't actually open the file, because the encryption software that had been used to create it was of a type only ever used on the secure internal operating systems of Russian governmental offices. Thereby allowing me to help you reach the conclusion that the only way for us to decrypt the file would be for you to break into the Russian embassy and plug me in direct.'

'But . . . but why?' Danny's voice was cracked. He tried to swallow. Couldn't. His mouth had turned dry as cement dust. 'Why would you want to do that?'

The Kid half grimaced, half smiled, like a teacher growing frustrated and bored with a child who was failing to grasp some obvious concept.

'Well naturally,' he said, 'because there really is something on Colonel Zykov's computer in the Russian embassy that I want you to help us steal.'

Us . . .

Danny looked round. This room. The layout. The fact that it had reminded him of an intelligence command post. The bead of sweat he'd seen trickling down the Kid's brow. The way he'd glanced with relief at his phone. No way was he working alone.

A swish.

The swing doors to the right of the Kid opened and the blonde woman from the Ritz walked in. Her fawn linen suit was badly crumpled, the dark bags beneath her eyes were even more pronounced than before. She had a twenty-one-millimetre armour-piercing Russian pistol in her hand, which she now pointed at Danny's face.

Another click.

This time behind Danny. He turned to see the bearded man who'd searched him in the hotel suite. He was still wearing his black suit and black shirt. He was armed with an H&K MP7 submachine gun. It was aimed at Danny's back.

When Danny looked back at the Kid, he saw that the man he'd thought of until barely a minute ago as someone he could trust with his life was no longer smiling.

Never trust in anyone fully but yourself.

Danny should have listened harder to the Old Man. Because the only other person Danny had trusted this whole long day had been playing him right from the start.

'And now of course you're wondering why the fuck I'm telling you that I was planning to trick you,' said the Kid. 'Because there's no way you're going to break into the Russian embassy and plug me into their government intranet now, right?'

'Right.'

A snort of laughter. The Kid shook his head. There was something close to deep personal satisfaction in his eyes. 'Wrong. You see, my devious little plan to trick you into going in there no longer matters. Because we've found a much better way to make you do exactly what we want.'

'What?'

The Kid's eyes narrowed now as he watched Danny's face for a reaction. 'You really shouldn't have put that new battery in your phone till you were way past that address you left her at,' he said.

Danny's skin turned cold.

'Because the second you switched your phone back on, your exact location popped up on my screen, Danny. And that's when we worked out where it was you must have dropped her off.'

Her . . .

The Kid watched Danny as the implication sank in.

'So really it's all thanks to you that we've got your little girl now . . .'

The Kid turned his laptop screen round to face Danny again. This time the view was of the back of his van. And now Danny saw why the hawk-faced man wasn't here.

He was sitting beside Lexie. She'd been blindfolded, and her hands were tied. The hawk-faced man cocked his head and gazed up at the camera filming him. He stared into deep into Danny's eyes. Oh yes, he knew Danny Shanklin was watching him now.

And Danny knew he'd been right about the man all along. He did not make mistakes.

On the other side of Lexie was the tall, thin, bespectacled man, now dressed in an oversized blue raincoat, with his black attaché case on his lap.

Danny turned to the Kid. He fought every atom in his body that wanted to throw itself at him. Three weapons were covering him. He wouldn't even get close.

'You son-of-a-bitch. I'll kill you for this.'

The Kid adjusted his grip on the machine pistol and slowly shook his head.

'No, Danny. You're going to do exactly what we say. Or first we'll kill her. And then we'll kill you too.'

CHAPTER FIFTY-THREE

The front of the Russian embassy on Kensington Palace Gardens was besieged by TV crews, as well as the furious relatives of dead British civilians, and placard-bearing pro-Georgian protesters, accusing the Russians of state-sanctioned mass murder.

But the back of the building was quieter. No press. Just police. They'd set up two temporary manually operated road barriers either side of the back of the row of diplomatic buildings, to control access and curtail media intrusion.

The light was fading. In an hour or so it would be dark.

As the deceased colonel's black Mercedes carried Danny relentlessly forward towards the westernmost barrier, he felt like he was in a submarine drifting down helplessly into the depths.

The Kid . . . Lexie . . . They've got Lexie . . . Fail, and Lexie will die . . .

Thirty metres to the barrier. Twenty. One car in front of him – a silver SUV – waiting to be let through. A cop was talking to the driver through the window of the vehicle. Danny slowed to a halt behind.

Right from the start. There in the back of the VT Media van. The Kid had already known what Danny had been walking into. Throughout the chase. All that time Danny had thought he had been his only hope.

The son-of-a-bitch. Danny had worked with him on more than ten previous assignments. But none of that meant anything now. If he got through this in one piece, he wouldn't quit until he brought that bastard down.

If . . .

There was still so much to do. And so much Danny still didn't understand. Who were these people? How did the hawk-faced man know the Kid? What could he have possibly offered the Kid to betray Danny? What was the data they now wanted Danny to steal from the dead colonel's computer? And what, if any, had Crane's part been in all this?

Danny had a few answers only – as the Kid had explained what he'd wanted Danny to do, he'd been unable to stop himself gloating about just how well he'd played Danny already today.

What it came down to was this. The hawk-faced man had wanted as much publicity as possible for the assassination. He'd wanted to stir up as much hell between the Russians and the Georgians as he could.

And he'd wanted the Russians to get the blame. So he'd chosen to set up a member of the Russian embassy staff at the scene of the crime. He'd picked Colonel Zykov. But to get the media attention he wanted, he'd needed to make London panic. Meaning he'd also needed to murder those civilians. And he'd needed a fall guy to run.

The Kid had volunteered Danny. Because he knew he'd be able to manipulate him. And because he knew Danny was good enough to lead the police on one hell of a chase. But also because he knew Danny had worked for the Russian government before – on a hushed-up retrieval of the daughter of a minor Russian diplomat who'd gone missing in Chechnya – something the Kid was now planning to publicize, to make Danny's involvement in the hit all the more plausible.

And so today they'd woken him up with a shot of Adrenalin, and then the Kid had gone zealously about his job, running Danny away from the police and out across the city. Like a fox before a pack of baying hounds. Like he'd turned Danny into a one-man blood sport. Witnessed by as many TV news camera crews as the Kid had been able to tip off anonymously in time.

The hawk-faced man had wanted the hunt to become a global media event. With Danny Shanklin as its star.

And so the Kid had obliged. He'd become Danny's puppeteer, jerking him this way and that.

First out through that sewer. Danny now couldn't believe he'd been so dumb as to accept the fact that the Kid had simply got lucky and discovered that route out. Weeks of careful planning had gone into this. And those boot prints he had seen down there ahead of him . . . they hadn't belonged to sewer workers. That was the way the hawk-faced man and his crew had got out of that hotel too.

It had been Danny's own fault he'd come up through that Hyde Park fountain's maintenance drain. If he'd listened to the Kid's instructions, he'd have emerged in a quiet alley, from which they could then have run him again. With the aim of always keeping him one step ahead of the police. To make the chase last longer. And drive the media coverage up to the max.

In fact the Kid had been keen to point out – on a note of professional pride, it seemed – that the only times Danny had nearly got caught had been when he'd ignored the Kid's directions and gone it alone.

Such as when he'd run into Harrods. Or when he'd cut the Kid off and gone to fetch Lexie. The fact that Danny had been ID'd had been his own fault too. Something else that had nearly got him snagged.

The hawk-faced man's original plan had been to let Danny get caught once the desired media storm had been generated – preferably in some violent confrontation with the police, thereby garnering yet more publicity.

But then the plan had changed. Last night, under torture, Colonel Zykov had revealed the whereabouts of valuable data – the Kid had refused to tell Danny what. And that was when the hawk-faced man had decided not only to use Danny as his runner, but if he survived the chase, to then also deploy him as his thief.

The SUV at the barrier slowly performed a three-point turn, having clearly been turned away. Danny drove forward into the space it had vacated and pulled the colonel's Mercedes up at the barrier. Taking off his gloves, he buzzed the tinted driver side window down a third of the way, as a uniformed male cop – early thirties, clean-shaven, exhausted – leaned down to talk to him.

'I need to get through,' Danny said. In Russian. Then, in heavily accented English: 'I work at the embassy. Here is my identification.'

The young cop looked him over. Danny didn't remove his tinted Aviator shades or black cap. He kept his face in profile to the cop, his bruised cheek hidden. He handed the cop the dead colonel's laminated plastic ID card, the photo of which the Kid had already switched for a photo of Danny that he'd Photoshopped to no longer look like the Danny the police had pictures of, but to have enough feature collisions in common with the dead colonel to get past someone like this cop.

The cop studied the card slowly, then peered in at Danny.

'One moment, please, sir,' he said.

Danny felt his heartbeat rising as the cop walked over to his superior officer at the barrier and handed the ID card across.

Danny felt powerless. Numb with it. The Kid had already explained how he and the hawk-faced man had come up with a plan to get him safely into the colonel's office. But how that plan would come to nothing if the colonel's body had already been ID'd.

Because then Danny would get caught. And the hawk-faced man would have no further use for him. They'd leave him to take the blame with the dead colonel for the assassination.

The hawk-faced man would no longer have any use for Lexie either. She'd be a liability. Nothing but a loose end that needed to be tied up.

The sense of sickness, of falling, it intensified now, as Danny watched the cop's superior slowly turn the fake ID over in his hand.

After what seemed like an age, he finally returned it. And in the very instant the young cop began to march back over to the barrier alone – Danny knew it . . . he'd passed the test. The colonel's body had not yet been ID'd. They were going to let him through.

For now, at least, he and Lexie were safe.

He watched as the weighted barrier rose up.

'Thank you, sir,' said the young cop as he reached the Mercedes. 'Have a good evening.' He passed Danny back his ID.

Danny buzzed the window up and put his gloves back on. Wiping down the window button, he drove on.

'Five more metres, then turn right,' said the Kid. 'And keep cool, Danny. Remember, your daughter's life depends on it.'

Danny was wearing a transmitter in the breast pocket of the colonel's grey linen suit. A Bluetooth audio bead was tucked inside his left ear.

He forced himself not to react to the sound of the Kid's voice. But even so, he couldn't help himself picturing Lexie in the back of that van. Just like he couldn't prevent himself picturing his foot stamping down on the Kid's exposed neck.

Focus . . .

Work, he reminded himself. *This is work*.

That was what he'd repeatedly tried telling himself from the moment he'd been taken away from that warehouse in Streatham in the back of the transit van. And as the blonde woman and the bearded man had driven him out of central London and looped round to the north. And as they'd dropped back into central London again and Danny had been transferred to the colonel's stolen car. And as they'd given him one final glance of the laptop screen showing Lexie sitting alongside the torturer, to remind him of what they'd do if he in any way deviated from their plan.

He wouldn't screw this up. He was going to see it through. He'd get through this, and then somehow get Lexie back.

He turned right. Down a concrete ramp leading beneath the back of the embassy.

The Mercedes' radio-frequency ID tag automatically triggered the security barrier at the bottom of the ramp.

During Colonel Zykov's torture, and under the influence of an SP-17 truth drug, convinced that his own daughter had been about to be butchered, the colonel had been kind enough to furnish the hawk-faced man with a foolproof guide to getting in and out of the Russian embassy undetected.

Danny set about putting that plan into action now.

Thanks to the police guarding the back of the embassy and the protesters besieging the front, with any luck no one inside would be monitoring the underground car park CCTV too closely.

But even if they were watching Danny as he parked the Mercedes in the colonel's space now and exited the vehicle . . . the shades, cap and the suit he was wearing had all been taken from Zykov's apartment. And Danny now also made sure to run further visual interference, keeping the new phone the Kid had given him pressed up to his face as if making a call, thereby concealing his features.

There were two elevators at the far side of the car park. Precisely where the colonel had said. One was accessed via a standard numeric code pad and would get Danny as far as the staffed security point up on the embassy's ground floor.

The other was reserved solely for the use of diplomatic VIPs and accessed all floors, including the top floor where only the ambassador, the colonel and the deputy ambassador worked.

The elevator was operated via a fingerprint recognition pad, which only these three men were able to use.

Danny popped the lid of the Petri dish in his pocket and removed the colonel's severed right forefinger. He ignored its odd weight, telling himself it was just a cold piece of meat. He pressed it up against the fingerprint recognition pad on the wall beside the elevator's brushed-steel doors.

A beep.

The doors silently parted. The elevator was empty. Danny stepped inside.

He hit the button for the seventh floor. The doors shut and the elevator rose. Danny stepped out of sight to the side of the doors as it slowed to a halt. He pressed the door open button. The doors slid apart. He pressed the hold button to keep them that way. He listened. He heard nothing. He used a mirror to check outside. He saw no one in the empty corridor. He stepped out.

Plush red carpet. Paintings on the wall. He already had the floor plan memorized. Ten paces later and he was at Zykov's office door. The ink-stained swipe card really had been the colonel's. He slid it now through the door's locking mechanism.

He opened the door and slipped in.

CHAPTER FIFTY-FOUR

Danny silently closed the door behind him.

The colonel's office was three metres square. A lingering odour of coffee and cigars. Embossed invitations on a cork pinboard: diplomat parties the colonel would never now get to attend. The rattle and hum of an air ventilator. An antique mahogany armchair and a green velvet-covered sofa. Nice artwork too on the plain white walls, Danny saw. One of the Matisse cut-outs looked real.

Two windows. A view out of the back of the building. Danny stepped up and peered out into the thin evening light. He could see the police below. No other vehicles approaching. Everything looked fine.

He pulled the curtains closed and went over to the desk. Another antique. Expensive. Polished crystal glasses in a holder. An ashtray. An empty silver ice bucket and an unopened bottle – of Diaka vodka, Danny noted, the most expensive damned vodka in the world, distilled through diamonds, no less. A computer. A nice one too. Twenty-four-inch LED screen. State-of-the-art. The colonel had obviously appreciated the finer things in life.

'OK, we're inside,' Danny said.

'How many terminals?'

'Just the one. Like the colonel told you.'

The colonel that you and your friends murdered in cold blood, Danny thought. *The colonel whose daughter you threatened just like you're now threatening mine.*

The Kid said, 'Switch it on.'

Danny did as he was told. The computer chimed and hummed into life. Its log-in screen appeared along with a request for a password.

The Kid read out a nonsensical series of ten letters and numbers. Danny typed them into the keyboard and hit return. The log-in screen vanished.

A few seconds later, the computer's desktop blossomed across the screen. Its background was a photograph of the colonel. He was standing with a stern-faced grey-haired woman, who Danny assumed was his wife. Between them was a plain-looking teenage girl. Their daughter, Danny guessed.

Icons for various applications and a number of yellow and blue Stickies popped up across the screen.

'Now put my phone down facing the screen like I showed you,' said the Kid.

Again Danny obeyed. He sat down on the ergonomic wheeled desk chair. He propped the Kid's phone up against the colonel's crystal tumblers, so its camera could now film the screen live and transmit everything it saw back to the Kid. The sound of the Kid's keyboard rattling.

'OK, I'm in,' he said a few minutes later.

A white rectangular icon appeared on the screen, indicating that a remote device had been plugged in. The icon was labelled 'APHEX'. Danny remembered the Kid's T-shirt. As in Aphex Twin. His favourite musician. Meaning the Kid had just jacked into the colonel's computer via his phone's Bluetooth.

Without Danny touching the keyboard, the computer's system preferences began booting up from the dock at the bottom of the screen. Danny guessed this meant the Kid had taken full remote control of Zykov's computer now.

The screen turned white, as its operating system flashed open. Through his audio bead Danny heard the Kid's keyboard begin

to rattle again. Lines of code raced first across then down the
screen. Alien poetry. Danny wouldn't even know how to begin to
decipher it.

The speed of the Kid's typing grew steadily faster. Was he still
back there at the warehouse? Danny wondered. He had no way of
knowing. And what about Lexie? The last time Danny had seen
her was in the Kid's van. But going where? To meet the Kid back
at the warehouse? Or was the hawk-faced man taking her somewhere else?

My princess . . . with those scum . . .

And what about Alice? What had happened to her? Christ,
Danny hoped she was OK.

The Kid had told Danny when he'd said goodbye that the hawk-
faced man would release both Danny and Lexie so long as Danny
got them what they wanted. He argued that they'd have no need to
keep them afterwards, since Lexie knew nothing at all, and what
little Danny did know he could not prove. Plus if Danny went
anywhere near the police, the Kid had reminded him, he'd get
arrested. If he wanted to stay free, he'd have to go to ground for the
rest of his life.

A nice enough argument. But Danny didn't believe a word of it.
Once he no longer needed them, the hawk-faced man would kill
them both.

Which was why Danny had to find a way to *stay* needed. Until
he could get to Lexie. In order to be able to save her, he first needed
to discover where she was. And so he watched. He listened. He
waited for his chance.

'Got it,' said the Kid.

The code stopped moving. A small rectangular graphic icon
flashed up in the centre of the screen.

It was labelled 'C332'.

Above it was a tiny flashing red padlock symbol: 🔒.

Danny heard another muffled voice coming at him through the
audio bead. It didn't sound much like the Kid. Meaning the Kid
was no longer alone.

Then the Kid's voice came back: 'OK, so now let's see if the colonel was telling us the truth about how to decrypt the file so we can read what's inside . . .'

As the lines of code continued to sputter across the screen, the sound of the Kid's rapid typing seemed to blur into one continuous whirring sound in Danny's mind.

Beside the onscreen padlock appeared a timer symbol: ⏳. It began to slowly rotate.

'This might take a couple of minutes,' said the Kid.

Danny assumed the Kid wasn't speaking to him. But the fact that he was talking out loud at all gave Danny an idea.

'I've been thinking,' he said.

He needed to get the Kid talking. Just like old times. So that maybe he'd drop his guard. Give Danny more information about what was going on than he should. Give him something he could use.

'Don't go breaking the habit of a lifetime,' said the Kid.

'Very funny.'

The Kid laughed.

'I'm serious. There's something that's been bothering me.'

'What?'

'How did you set up the meeting in the first place?' *What was Crane's involvement?* in other words.

Another snort of laughter at the other end of the line. The now unmistakable sound of the Kid's ego swelling up.

'Oh come on, Danny. I'd have thought even you would have worked that out for yourself by now.'

Danny's eyes stayed glued to the screen. The timer continued to turn.

'Nope,' he said.

'Well I suppose there's no harm in telling you now,' the Kid said. 'You see, the funny thing about virtual meetings, Danny . . . is you never really know who you're talking to.'

Danny once more pictured the Kid in the warehouse, sitting in the shadows behind his desk. He pictured Crane's avatar in Noirlight, the same.

No . . .

'But that's not possible,' he said. 'I was working for Crane before I met you. You can't be the same person.'

'No, Danny. You're right. Not the same. Not for all that time. Not for that long at all, as it turns out. Just the last five days, in fact. Just for long enough to get you over here to the UK for that meet.'

Five days ago. That was when Crane had first contacted Danny about coming here. Only it hadn't been Crane at all.

'But what about Crane's security protocols?' Danny said. He still couldn't believe this was how he'd been duped. 'My link to him has always been encrypted. Completely secure.'

'Yeah, and it would have remained that way too, if you hadn't been stupid enough to let me borrow your damn phone. Everything I needed, I hacked it from there.'

Danny cast his mind back two months, to the last time he and the Kid had met up. It had been at Hong Kong Kai Tak International. They'd both been heading home from a job. The Kid had borrowed Danny's phone for a couple of hours after he'd claimed his own had run out of juice.

Like that would ever happen, Danny now saw. As if.

'It was pretty easy from there,' said the Kid, 'to get into that virtual office of Crane's and clone it as well as his avatar, and then re-route your pathway through Noirlight so that every time in the last five days when you went there looking for Crane, you actually found me.'

No wonder 'Crane' had been unable to track down his US government contact, Danny thought. There'd never been one.

'And when you spoke to Crane today in that shopping centre,' the Kid said, 'of course you were really speaking to me. You see, as well as jacking Crane's avatar to set up the meet, we then decided last night to use it to stoke you up about the importance of the data stick and the card . . . you know, to stop you being so suspicious about them having just been left there on purpose . . . to help steer you here into the embassy.'

And that was exactly what would have happened too, Danny now saw. If they hadn't decided to use Lexie to lever him instead, he'd probably have ended up here anyway, just like the Kid had planned.

But even in this darkness, Danny glimpsed a spark of hope. The real Crane had never betrayed him at all. Meaning that if Danny ever got out of here, he would still be there to help.

Danny felt air on the back of his neck. He froze. Behind him, the door to Colonel Zykov's office had just swung open.

'Wow, Danny, that's some silence,' said the Kid through Danny's audio bead, clearly not having heard the door opening. 'I mean, I've heard of the penny dropping, but that sounds more like Fort Knox.'

Danny ignored him, his whole being tensing now as he heard the creak of a footstep behind him.

He'd assumed the door to Zykov's office would have locked itself automatically as it had shut. He should have checked.

'Nikolai?' a man said in Russian. 'I thought I saw your car downstairs. But aren't you meant to be sick?'

Thank God Danny had his back to the man. And thank God he was still wearing the colonel's cap and sombre suit.

But if the intruder took another step forward, the illusion would be destroyed.

Danny pushed up fast from the chair. He stepped sideways, turning as he did. Fast enough to take the man standing in the doorway completely by surprise. One stride and Danny was on him. He struck him hard in the throat, silencing his vocal cords. He spear-handed his solar plexus next, depriving him of breath.

The man was older than Danny had anticipated. Mid to late sixties. Untrained. A diplomat, not a soldier, thank God. Danny grabbed him round the throat as his knees sagged. He turned him and hauled him inside the office, then turned them both round so he could push the door shut behind them with a flick of his heel.

The man didn't struggle. Partly because he was still gasping for breath, but also because he'd already worked out that he was completely outmatched.

So what to do with him now? Cut off his oxygen until he fell unconscious. But with a guy this age, that might just finish him off. Danny saw the gold ring on the man's wedding finger. He could have kids, grandkids.

Stepping back to lock the door, Danny tore a scarf off the hat

stand beside it and used that to gag the man. He pinned him to the
floor and hog-tied him with his own shoelaces, then dragged him
over behind the colonel's desk and used it to pin him up tight
against the wall.

'Any noise and you're dead,' he told him in Russian, before
taping over his gagged mouth and ears.

Danny sat back down on the chair. The timer, he saw, was still
slowly turning over.

'Danny? What the hell *was* that?' hissed the Kid. He must have
heard the struggle and had now glimpsed Danny's reflection in his
view of the screen.

'Someone came in. It's dealt with,' Danny said.

'Jesus, Danny. You'd better not fuck this up now.' The Kid
sounded panicked. Terrified even. Making Danny wonder once
again how the hawk-faced man had turned him. 'OK,' he then said.
'The decryption's complete.'

Onscreen Danny saw that the ⌛ symbol had vanished and the
red 🔒 icon had become a green 🔓.

The white operating system screen disappeared and was instantly
replaced by the desktop showing the photograph of Colonel Zykov
and his wife and child. Immediately, dead centre, up popped file
C332.

'OK,' said the Kid, 'we're nearly out of here. First up I'm going
to sling in a worm that'll wipe the colonel's hard drive the second
we pull out, so there's no way anyone can ever discover what we
just took.'

There . . . The Kid was still doing it, still talking, still thinking out
loud. Just as Danny had hoped.

'And now we've got that out of the way,' said the Kid, 'all we
need to do is copy our nice decrypted data over on to my phone and
we're done.'

And bullseye . . . There it was. The information Danny had been
praying for: information he could use.

He felt his whole body tense as he unblinkingly watched the
screen. The decrypted file marked 'C332' was dragged remotely over
to the icon marked 'APHEX' that represented the Kid's phone.

A green light on the top of the phone's casing flickered.

An onscreen message on Zykov's computer warned: 'File Copying In Progress . . . Do Not Disconnect'.

The green light on the top of the phone faded.

The onscreen message on Zykov's computer switched to: 'File Copying Complete'.

The second it did, Danny snatched up the phone and told the Kid, 'I'll bring it in person.'

And with that, he tore off the phone's backing and ripped its battery out. Before the Kid would have had a chance to transmit the data he'd stolen back to himself via the phone.

Leaving me still useful, Danny thought, snatching the blank data stick the Kid had given him from his pocket and getting to work, moving fast now. And just fast enough, before the bright colours of the colonel's desktop melted and died into impenetrable black, as the worm set about its dark work.

But much more importantly, he was thinking, as he slipped the phone into his pocket and headed for the door, *keeping myself useful keeps Lexie indispensable too. Meaning now I've just got to find a way of getting her back.*

CHAPTER FIFTY-FIVE

Danny exited the Russian embassy the same way he'd got in. Down through the VIP elevator and then back out on to the street in the dead colonel's Merc.

The same cop who'd raised the barrier to let him through the first time did the same again now, waving him on. Danny headed straight for the address in Kensal Rise, north of Notting Hill, where the blonde woman had told him she'd be waiting.

He passed by plenty of uniformed police on his way, but no more roadblocks, and none of the police flagged him down. The manhunt, it seemed, for the time being, had halted. At least while their quarry had gone to ground.

Danny kept the car radio switched on to a BBC rolling news service. Views on where he and Lexie had vanished to were currently split between theories of him still being at large in London, or having already somehow escaped the city, or even having fled abroad. Various so-called experts were speculating on who else he might have been working with. And, of course, there were stories – many terrible, moving stories – of the civilian dead and their grieving relatives.

Meanwhile the Russians were continuing to deny any involvement in the assassination of the Nobel Prize-winning writer.

The UN General Secretary had described the assassination and massacre as 'A tragedy of the highest order. An affront to democracy'. The British prime minister had announced that no expense or effort would be spared in hunting Danny Shanklin down.

It was estimated that over seven hundred million people worldwide had watched Danny run. A statistic that made him feel physically sick.

The BBC's latest breaking news was that the SAS had now fully occupied the Ritz and cleared it of any further terrorist threat. And that a body had been recovered from the room from which the shooting had taken place.

Breaking news . . . As in information that had only just been made public right now.

In other words, when the Kid had earlier used Crane's avatar in Noirlight to tell Danny that the colonel's body had already been recovered and its cause of death by natural causes established, that had just been more bullshit. To convince Danny of the plausibility of the data stick and card having been left behind accidentally.

After a thirty-minute drive, Danny reached the address the blonde woman had given him. Mostyn Gardens. A terraced street in a quiet residential area. The sky was grey and darkening. The Transit was waiting for him, parked on the street corner. Its lights flashed once as Danny drove the Merc towards it. He slowed and parked up in front of it. The bearded man and the blonde woman got out.

'Give me the phone,' the blonde said, as Danny walked towards her.

The bearded man had positioned himself six feet away from her. He'd made sure to leave the long dark coat he was wearing open enough to ensure that Danny could see the machine pistol, fitted with a sound suppressor, gripped in his hand. He clearly wanted there to be no doubt in Danny's mind that he could shoot him dead right here, right now, and none of the civilians sitting at home in these houses watching their TV shows and eating their suppers would ever even know.

'First I see my daughter,' Danny said.

It was a gamble. That they wouldn't kill him, not until they knew he actually had the phone on him. And not until they'd checked he hadn't somehow corrupted the stolen data.

'Suit yourself,' said the blonde. No emotion. Nothing. Danny may as well have been debating the price of some piece of junk up for sale on eBay. 'He wants to check it's all on there anyway,' she said, 'before he lets you go.'

Lets you go . . . Danny still didn't believe either the Kid or the hawk-faced man had any intention of that.

He got into the back of the van and sat down cross-legged on the cold metal floor. He had no choice. There was no point trying to overpower these two. He'd never find his daughter then. The best he could hope for now was that they actually would take him to Lexie, and not to some other location, where they'd take the phone from him and check its data was intact before executing him.

So long as he got to Lexie, he might still just figure out a way to get them both out alive.

Not might . . . *Would*, he corrected himself. Because he couldn't just hope. He had to *believe*.

They slammed the Transit doors shut, locking him inside. The Transit engine rumbled into life and drove away. There in the darkness, Danny tried not to think of all the things that could now go wrong. He concentrated instead on clearing his mind. On readying himself for what was to come.

He knew that when an opportunity did arise to save his daughter, he would only get one shot.

One shot.

He tried to think of the future, but he felt himself dragged into the past.

CHAPTER FIFTY-SIX

SEVEN YEARS AGO, NORTH DAKOTA

A ripping of duct tape. A hissing of air. A buzzing noise inside Danny's skull. Nonsensical words flowed from his bleeding tongue. He couldn't look at Jonathan and Sally. He would not look.

His skull jarred. It snapped back, struck. It jarred again. Purple and red flashes blossomed and died before his eyes. More pain. The stranger was staring into his eyes.

'Where is . . .' the stranger began to say.

'Ker-murgh . . .'

Danny's tongue wouldn't frame the words. The stranger relaxed his hold on his jaw.

'KIIIILLLLLMEEEEE.' Danny screamed it. He wanted death. He wanted to be dead like Karl Bain. He wanted the top of his skull blown off.

The stranger tightened his grip.

'First tell me where she is . . .'

'Gurghterhellll . . .'

The second the stranger released him, Danny bit at his gloved hand, then spat at him. A gobbet of blood and drool slipped from his torn lower lip.

'Fukyaou . . .'

The stranger punched Danny's head back and watched it loll

forwards again. He walked to the table and picked up the blood-drenched shears. He snapped the blades shut so that they turned from an X to a Y. He plunged them down two-fisted into Danny's right thigh.

Danny roared, choking on his blood as he writhed. The stranger twisted the shears slowly, then pulled them out. Danny bit down so hard he cracked his back teeth. The stranger stood and watched, and waited for Danny's hyperventilating to subside.

'Don't die,' he said. 'I need you.'

To watch.

He didn't need to say it. He knew Danny already understood.

The stranger pulled on a thick winter coat. Knee-length. Navy blue. He slowly buttoned it. Then he took off his face mask and folded it neatly away in his coat pocket. He checked his appearance in the mirror on the wall. He slowly wiped the blood from his brow back across his shaved head, as if slicking back invisible hair with some new cosmetic product. He smiled.

A keening noise started deep inside Danny's throat, a wailing he could not stop.

The stranger knelt beside the fire and picked up the Browning semi-automatic. Danny's eyes stayed on him, his neck twisted and cramped. He watched the stranger instead of what was closer . . . instead of what was over there . . . *Them* . . . the two red shapes on the chairs, both silent as a scream . . .

The stranger vanished from his line of sight. Footsteps crossed the floorboards. A click. The cabin door creaked open. A blast of chill wind raked across the sweat on the back of Danny's neck. His head lolled again. A pale shaft of winter daylight stamped itself on to the wooden floor. Blood. There was so much blood.

Danny prayed he was actually dying. That he'd been in a crash. That he'd imagined all this. That he was in a coma. That he would soon be dead. But that Sally and Jonathan were both somehow still alive.

He begged God to let him take their place.

The door slammed shut and he was alone.

Only not alone. Because they – *they* – were still here with him.

Sally's dead eyes stared back at him. The stranger had cut off and removed her left ear. Danny could not look at his son.

A coldness filled him then. As if he were no longer made of flesh and blood. As though he were made of stone.

But looking away, he saw the photograph of Lexie holding Jonathan as a newborn, and he remembered his son alive . . . He remembered the first time he'd walked and stumbled into Danny's outstretched arms . . . he remembered the love that still burned for him and Sally . . . And *Lexie* . . . he remembered her.

He would not let the stranger take Lexie from him too.

The knife . . . He reached for it . . . *nothing*. He twisted and turned. Then something . . . wedged up tight against the wooden strut of the chair back . . . *a blade* . . .

He gripped it, turned it, slitting his finger to catch it, then dragged it nearer, snagged it between his fingers . . . and finally raised it upwards, then round, pinning its grip tightly between the cups of his bleeding palms.

The tip of the blade snicked the duct tape that was binding his wrists. He started to saw.

Sally's dead eyes watched him, begging him even in death to succeed. Blood ran freely from his wrists as he finally cut through the tape binding them and tore them free.

He still had the knife gripped in his right hand. He slashed through the duct tape securing his torso to the back of the chair. He severed the noose binding his ankles. When he tried to stand, he nearly fell. He sliced through the tape binding his knees to the chair.

Then he stumbled forwards, free.

He checked Sally and Jonathan. Robotically. Without hope. He was too late. He did not look at them again.

He focused on the living. On Lexie. The stranger was hunting her down in the snow.

He used strips from one of the shirts Sally had hung up by the fire to dry the night before to bandage his waist and tourniquet his right thigh. The killer had aimed carefully with the shears. He'd not severed any arteries. He'd not wanted Danny to quit his game yet.

Danny dragged himself to the front of the cabin. He slumped

against the wall between the closed door and the window to its right. He moved the curtain fractionally aside and wiped the condensation from the glass with his fingertip, before wiping at it again with the front of his jacket to clear the streak of blood away.

He checked outside. Heavy snow was falling. Almost a white-out. Only one set of fresh boot prints was now visible leading away from the cabin. The stranger's. Danny prayed that Lexie's and his own would also have been obliterated out in the woods.

His cell phone was no longer where he'd left it on the bedside table. Sally's was gone too. He snatched up his bowie knife from the floor and hurried out into the cold.

Twenty metres from the cabin and Danny felt his strength failing. Blood trickled down his thigh, leaving tiny red splashes in the snow. With each step forward, he felt his leg getting heavier.

It wasn't hard to find the stranger. He saw him thirty metres away through the trees. He was shouting. To himself, it looked like, when Danny first spotted his blue coat in amongst all that white. But then Danny realized where the stranger was standing. Beneath the tree house. He wasn't shouting. He was calling out.

He was telling Lexie to come down.

Danny edged forward, keeping low, using bushes and rotting tree trunks as cover. The trees . . . they must have sheltered the ground here more than outside the cabin. Danny's boot prints must still have been visible, enough for the stranger to have puzzled over. Before working it out.

So long as the stranger didn't turn round, he might not see Danny until it was too late. But Danny's movement was sluggish. He stumbled and fell twice. He was only saved by the wind from being overheard.

Twenty metres to go.

Between the gusts of wind and the shocking hisses of his clothing on the brambles he was edging past, Danny caught snatches of what the stranger was telling Lexie.

'They asked me to come out and get you. They're all waiting for you inside by the fire.'

Lexie shouted something back. Danny didn't catch what it was. Fifteen metres.

Danny saw the blood on the stranger's gloved hands then. He was gripping the Browning pistol behind his back. The blood slicked back on his scalp as well. Perhaps Lexie had seen it too. Perhaps that was why she was refusing to come down. Because she realized what this man was.

Or perhaps she'd heard the screams.

Ten metres. Danny steeled himself against the pain that would rip through his leg the second he started to run. He'd get up as close as he could. If he could, he'd slit that bastard's throat from behind. If not, he'd knock him down.

'Please don't make me come up there and get you, Alexandra...'

Five metres.

The crack of a twig.

Too late, Danny remembered the Beretta twelve-gauge shotgun and shells locked in the dry steel box inside the cabin.

Too late.

The stranger started to turn. Danny broke into his run.

His leg buckled beneath him on the third stride. It was like he'd stepped into a hole. Even so he somehow kept going, lurched forward two more steps, another after that.

But now the stranger was facing him. He was bringing the Browning up. Danny knew he wasn't going to reach him in time. If the man pulled that trigger, the hammer blow of the bullet would be the last thing he ever felt.

And Lexie would die.

He threw the bowie knife as hard as he could.

He watched it tumble over and over as he fell. His face smashed into the snow. Then he heard the stranger scream.

Dragging himself up, Danny saw that the knife blade had lanced deep into the stranger's shoulder, just to the right of his neck, where his coat collar had slipped to one side. The pistol he'd been holding was nowhere to be seen.

Danny roared. Pain ripped across his leg, but that no longer mattered. He ran at him hard again.

The stranger got a grip on the knife handle. He began pulling it out. He didn't see Danny coming at him. Not until Danny's forehead smashed him straight between the eyes.

The collision sent both men crashing to the ground. He screamed out again. Danny forced himself up. The stranger did too. He still had the knife in his fist.

Where's the pistol?

Danny stared desperately round. Then saw it. A glint of metal in the snow. He dived for it with the last of his strength.

The stranger was already running by the time Danny reared up and turned. A rush of motion between the trees. Danny fired once. Twice. The gunshots echoed through the wood. But the stranger didn't stop. He ran on.

A crackle of branches.

Danny saw Lexie falling. An angel from the sky. He saw his daughter fall from the tree and land on her feet in the snow.

He lurched sideways. He fell against a tree. She rushed to him and clung tightly to him. He locked his body up against the trunk, and raised the Browning, once more tracking the racing, crashing figure of the stranger through the nest of woodland branches and the swirl of driving snow.

Die.

Danny locked on to his target. He squeezed the trigger slowly. Fired. The stranger stumbled. But still he didn't stop.

Gritting his teeth to breathe through the pain, Danny brought the pistol round again, getting the stranger back in his sights, waiting for an opening between the trees.

One came. He fired again. This time the stranger shuddered sideways. Danny waited for him to fall.

Die.

Die.

But the stranger just grew thinner. Became blurred. Vanished into the snow storm like a chalk figure that had just been rubbed out.

CHAPTER FIFTY-SEVEN

It was nearly two hours before the Transit doors opened up again. Danny blinked in the moonlight. His muscles ached. His eyes stung. He'd kill for something to drink.

He'd *kill* . . .

'Get out,' a tall, burly skinhead said. A pale, deep-lined face. Jeans, a white shirt.

The bearded man stood beside him, watching, his machine pistol steadily trained on Danny as he crawled forwards across the clanking van floor.

The skinhead was carrying a Glock 30, also known as a 'pocket freight train' on account of its awesome stopping power. It was fitted with a state-of-the-art sound suppressor.

Not that he'll need that out here, Danny thought. Because they were now in the countryside. He could sense that even before he climbed fully out. The smell of the hot city streets – the drains, the rotting food – had been replaced by the scent of hedgerows and cut grass. The city noises were absent too. No more engines, car horns and bass. Instead Danny heard only the trickle of a nearby stream.

Grit crunched beneath his shoes as he got out. Looking up, he saw that the sky was starry, with a full moon on the rise above a cobweb of trees.

The Transit was parked in front of an old stone farmhouse. In a large, flat twilit field alongside it, Danny saw the unmistakable silhouette of a Cessna light aircraft, standing at the end of a makeshift runway lined with battery-powered flares.

A block of light appeared in the centre of the farmhouse. The front door had just opened. A figure walked towards them through the gloom. Danny felt a jolt of hatred burn through him as he picked out the features of the hawk-faced man.

He was dressed in a dark, well-tailored suit. A primrose-yellow shirt. He looked totally legit, like someone who'd just stepped out of a business brochure, a captain of industry.

He walked up to Danny and struck him hard and without warning across the side of the head with the aluminium grip of his PSM pistol.

A burst of red pain behind Danny's eyes. A ringing noise in his ears. He staggered sideways and fell to his hands and knees in the dirt. A boot stamped him down flat.

'Search him. Find the phone,' the hawk-faced man said in Russian.

The click of a machine pistol's selector switch. Danny braced himself. He thought for a moment they were just going to waste him there and then.

But instead he felt himself being pinioned to the dirt, then frisked. They found the Kid's phone in his suit jacket pocket. They took it.

They didn't bother to check his shoes.

'Take him inside to the girl,' the hawk-faced man said.

Lexie . . .

Danny's dread dissolved into relief. So she *was* here.

Meaning this wasn't over yet.

He swallowed down the hope that flared inside him as he was jerked upright. He sagged, feigning semi-consciousness. The less strength they thought he had now, the better chance he'd have.

The huge skinhead hauled Danny up towards the farmhouse. The hawk-faced man and his bearded foot soldier followed, their weapons locked on Danny.

A flagstoned hallway. Cold. A smell of burnt food. A lamp on a plain wooden table beside a plain wooden chair. Two bodies on the floor. A man and a woman. Early fifties. Civilians. Probably the owners of the farm, Danny guessed, sickened by the way they'd been dumped there like so much trash to be put out. They'd both been executed, he saw. Shot through the back of the head.

Danny was dragged stumbling down a corridor into a much bigger room. Where someone smacked him again round the side of the head. His vision strobed. A deep voice laughed.

Low-wattage bulbs glowed in opaque ceiling lights. No Lexie. A bunch of cardboard boxes stood stacked in the corner. A dining table and several chairs had been pushed up against a whitewashed stone wall. Two dining chairs had been positioned side by side, facing a sideboard above which ran a long rectangular mirror. Smashed china littered the floor.

'Sit him down,' the hawk-faced man said, in Serbian this time. 'Shoot him if he moves.'

The skinhead shoved Danny down on to one of the two isolated chairs. Danny watched in the mirror's reflection as the skinhead and the bearded man positioned themselves behind him. A wink of metal on the skinhead's left wrist. He was wearing Danny's watch.

The bearded man returned the Glock to the skinhead, along with a Taser X3. Then he aimed his machine pistol at the centre of Danny's spine.

The door burst open.

'Dad . . .'

Danny's heart leapt as Lexie stumbled through. He scanned her face and body. No bruises on her face. No blood. No torn clothing. Relief surged through him. So they'd not harmed her yet.

The blonde woman marched in behind her, armed with the Russian pistol. Lexie tried to rush to Danny. The blonde woman wrenched her back by her hair. Danny's fists closed. He nearly went for her then. But if he did that, he knew they'd both be dead. He forced his body to become still as a rock.

The blonde woman pushed Lexie down on the chair to his right. 'Don't look at each other. Don't speak,' she said.

Lexie's chair creaked. Danny felt her there, shaking with fear. The hawk-faced man was blocking his view of the mirror. But he guessed she must have already seen the two men standing behind them, as well as the weapons they held.

The Kid sauntered in. He nodded at Danny, nonchalantly and smiled. Like they were just two old buddies who'd bumped into each other in a bar.

Danny wanted him dead. Wanted it bad.

'Check it's all there,' said the hawk-faced man in English, handing the Kid the phone.

While the Kid set to work on it, the blonde woman started packing up various pieces of hardware – machine pistols, cell phones, laptops and the Kid's Glock 18 – into a brown leather holdall.

She reached out to take the Russian pistol from the hawk-faced man. He let her, but when she tried the same with his PSM, he waved her rudely away.

The hawk-faced man watched the Kid working the phone. Danny checked the mirror's reflection. The two men behind him were still watching. Their weapons were still locked on.

Time . . . Danny felt it slipping through his fingers then, fast running out . . .

· *Patience*, he told himself. *Watch and wait.*

Another pulse of adrenalin – of hatred – rushed through him, as the tall bespectacled man in the ill-fitting suit walked in. He stopped and stared at Lexie and Danny in turn through his watery brown eyes.

He put his black leather attaché case down on the dresser and opened it. Danny glimpsed its contents reflected in the mirror. Scalpels. Syringes. Needles. His tools of the trade.

But what does he need those for? Neither Danny nor Lexie had any information that could possibly be of any use to these people.

Sweat broke across Danny's brow. He prayed Lexie wasn't looking at the case.

'It's all here,' the Kid finally said.

The hawk-faced man took the phone from him. He slipped it inside his suit jacket pocket.

'I'll see you at the plane,' he said to the Kid in English. 'Come,' he said in Russian to the blonde woman.

She followed him out without another word. Neither of them even glanced back at Danny.

Right then, Danny didn't know what he hated them for more. For having set him up. Or for having written him off, dismissed him as an irrelevance, as already dead.

They'd left the leather holdall containing most of their weapons behind, he now saw. So that wherever they were heading, when they got there they'd be able to pass legitimately through customs and security.

Judging by the length of Danny's journey in the Transit and the fact that there'd been no nearby city glow in the sky when he'd arrived, he reckoned this farm must be somewhere on the south coast.

The Cessna had the range to get them from here to France, Belgium or the Netherlands in a single hop. From where they could then simply disappear.

Danny guessed that the hawk-faced man would probably toss the PSM pistol out into the English Channel once they were safely on their way. But until that moment arrived – like Danny would have done if their situations had been reversed – he was keeping it just in case.

Danny saw the Kid staring at him, smiling, slowly shaking his head, like he couldn't quite believe Danny was actually here.

'So how does it feel to be famous?' he finally said. 'To be the most wanted man in the world?' He wasn't looking for an answer. Knew he wouldn't get one. Instead he carried on. 'You were right, of course,' he said.

'About what?'

'Cutting me off back there in the embassy. A clever move. Because if you hadn't, I would have mailed that file right out from under your nose. And then we'd have put in a call to the cops to let them know where you were.'

Danny watched as the Kid swapped his leather jacket for a designer linen number from the brown holdall. He slipped it on and adjusted its baggy fit over his broad-shoulders and T-shirted belly. He looked like a wedding guest, as if he was planning on doing nothing more sinister than drunkenly hitting on bridesmaids all night.

'You said you'd let me go. That I couldn't prove any of this anyway. That I'd have to go to ground . . .'

The Kid grimaced. 'Oh, come on, Danny. I know I *said* that. But you never really believed me, did you? I mean, I know you'd never quit. You'd come looking for me and – you know what? – I think you might even find me too. That's your problem, you see, bruv. You're just too dangerous to leave hanging around.'

Bruv . . . How can we have gone from that to this? Danny thought. How long had the Kid been planning on betraying him? How much had Danny ever really known about who he really was?

'Who are they?' Danny said. 'These people you're working for?' It had to be worth a shot. He and the Kid must still have some kind of connection. Maybe there was still a chance he could talk him round.

'Who says I'm working for anyone?' the Kid said, leaning back against the dresser, folding his arms and staring down at Danny. 'Who says they're not working for me?'

Danny remembered the terror in the Kid's voice when that man had stumbled in on him in Colonel Zykov's office and the op had nearly been blown. Oh, the Kid was working for the hawk-faced man all right, and not the other way around.

'Why are you doing this?' Danny said. 'For money?'

The Kid smiled. That old smile. The same one that used to make Danny want to smile too.

'I'm not even going to try justifying myself to you, Danny,' he said. 'Because you'd never understand. And besides, none of that's important any more. All that really matters now is that you've lost.'

GOD IS A PROGRAMMER.

It had been written right there on the Kid's arm all along. Power. A bunch of code to manipulate. A game played with real flesh and blood. Was that all this really was to him? Just the same as killing had been for the stranger who'd come that day for Sally and

Jonathan? Was there really so little difference between these two men?

Danny still couldn't bring himself to believe that in his heart.

'What was the data I stole?'

'Forget it, Danny. I'm not going to tell you.' The Kid checked his watch. 'In fact, I'm not going to talk to you any more at all. Because you're only asking me this shit to buy time. In the hope that you'll figure a way out of here. Which you won't.'

He buttoned up his jacket and smiled down at the fit, pleased.

'Anyway, I gotta go now,' he said. 'Got a plane to catch. But my friend here' – he nodded towards the torturer, who was staring studiously into his briefcase – 'and his companions, they're getting out of the UK by another means.'

'It's not too late to change your mind,' Danny said.

The Kid laughed. 'Oh, trust me, Danny, it really is. But Mr . . . Smith . . .' he said, clearly using the first arbitrary name that came into his head as he glanced across again at the bespectacled man, 'he'll take care of you. Tidying up is kind of one of his perks . . . you know, a bonus, if you like.'

Danny stared into the Kid's dark, glittering eyes. He wished them lifeless and cold.

But not yet. Wait, he told himself. *Wait till the Kid's gone. Then it'll just be you up against the three of them. With possibly only two of them armed.*

As the Kid turned his back on him and walked out of the room, Danny swung round and stared deep into the torturer's eyes. Dead eyes. Loveless eyes. Eyes that sparkled now with excitement at the thought of causing pain.

Danny had stared into eyes like those before.

CHAPTER FIFTY-EIGHT

The torturer blinked first. He looked down into his attaché case at the metal inside and started to hum.

Danny started shaking. The chair he was sitting on creaked.

The torturer looked up sharply. A thin smile played across his lips. He thought he could see fear and surrender flashing in Danny's eyes.

The second the torturer looked back to his case, Danny's eyes switched back to the reflection. To the bearded man. He was still standing two feet behind Danny's right shoulder. With the machine pistol gripped in both hands.

But the skinhead had moved. Further left. So he could *watch* . . . so he could see what the torturer was doing.

He was no longer covering either Danny or Lexie with the Glock. Only the Taser was raised and ready to use. Danny guessed what he was planning. To first Taser Danny. Then Lexie. Then tie them both up so the torturer could begin.

'Shut your eyes,' Danny said.

'Wh . . .' A noise, not a word, hissed out through Lexie's lips.

'Just do it,' Danny said, his hands closing in on his belt.

Even though they'd made him change into the dead colonel's suit before setting out for the embassy, they'd not stopped him from threading his own belt through its trouser loops.

'And keep them shut,' he said. 'No matter what you hear.'

The torturer looked up again, cocking his balding pale head like a dog that had just had its interest snagged by some low-frequency sound.

He stared at Danny, trying to read him. Danny locked eyes with him, holding his gaze, so the torturer wouldn't look down and see his hands move.

But it wasn't only the torturer's watery brown eyes Danny was seeing now. It was the eyes of the hawk-faced man. And the eyes of the man he had fought and defeated outside the school chapel. It was the eyes of the man who'd come hunting for him and his family in the woods.

Danny was staring now into the eyes of everyone who'd ever come to hurt him and his.

He saw the comprehension dawning on the torturer's face then. When he'd watched Danny shaking earlier, he'd been mistaken, he was now realizing. It wasn't fear and surrender he'd seen in Danny's eyes.

It was retribution.

It was death.

Danny rose, spinning clockwise out of his chair. As he pirouetted on his right foot, he tore the six-inch stiletto knife free from his belt.

The buckle-hilted knife was double-edged, designed for stabbing as well as cutting. It was made of tamahagane steel, a combination of high and low carbon, flexible enough to bend inside a belt, but vicious hard when straight.

The bearded man never saw it coming. Danny completed his turn – a move he'd practised a thousand times before – in less than half a second. He slashed the blade backhanded across the bearded man's throat.

It cut clean through his windpipe and carotid. A red jet of arterial spray burst out, hitting Danny in the face.

Danny's turn had brought him round in between the bearded man and Lexie, his intention being to shield her with his body in case the man fired. But this now put him in a position to seize the bearded man's right wrist and drive it into a lock, to ensure the machine pistol was also now pointing down.

The skinhead had meanwhile had a chance to react. He was raising both the Glock and the Taser up to fire. But he was overadrenalizing. His finer motor movements were fractionally out of whack. Enough to leave him momentarily off balance and totally exposed.

Danny stabbed him fast in the face. Through the mouth. To the back of the throat. The blade skittered and glanced off his teeth. Danny brought it back in a piston movement and stabbed him again. This time through his right eye socket, into his brain. He felt the blade tip catch and scrape on bone.

The skinhead slumped sideways to the ground as Danny withdrew his blade. He was still locking the bearded man's right fist, keeping the machine pistol pointed down. He hacked deep into his spurting throat again, then threw him, dead, aside.

A flash of movement to Danny's right. The torturer was breaking for the door. To warn the others.

'Keep them shut,' Danny shouted at Lexie, heart thundering now as he snatched up the fallen Glock. He grabbed her and carried her over his shoulder across to the open doorway through the which the torturer had run.

By the time Danny spotted him, the torturer was already halfway down the corridor that led straight on into the front hall.

Danny twisted Lexie to face the wall and pushed her down. Then he turned, slipping the blade into his jacket pocket.

He brought the Glock up in a double-fisted grip, locking his entire body as he aimed. He caught his breath, making sure to compensate for the added weight of the sound suppressor, as the torturer reached the front door.

Exhale . . .

He double-tapped the trigger. A *tock-tock* noise. Heavy recoil.

He'd been aiming for the torturer's thigh – he wanted him alive – but the first round missed him entirely, slamming into the door frame just past his right knee.

The second round thumped straight into his lower back. The torturer was slammed forward into the farmhouse door – like he'd been hit by . . . a freight train, just like the Glock ads said.

Danny ran to him, keeping the Glock trained on him. No need. The torturer's spectacles were smashed, lying in a widening pool of blood already seeping out across the flagstones. He was still alive, but only just. He was crying out in Russian and German. Danny checked the entry wound on his back. It had smashed right through his spine.

Danny searched him for weapons. Found nothing. Then he heard the low growl of the Cessna starting up outside. His instinct told him to run back and get the machine pistol off the dead bearded man. He'd have a better chance with that of shooting out the plane's engines before it got into the air.

He ran to Lexie instead. He couldn't leave her here among the dead. He lifted her up in his arms. Her hair was spattered with blood. But even now she kept on doing what he'd asked. Her eyes were still clamped tight shut.

'It's OK, princess. I'm getting you out.'

He raised her on to his shoulder and carried her away, out through a kitchen and on through an unlocked back door. He staggered with her into the warm night air.

The plane's engine was rising in pitch, preparing for take-off. The runway was on the opposite side of the building from where Danny now crouched beside Lexie in the inky blackness of a bramble patch.

'Don't move,' he said. 'I'll be back.'

He could hear the aircraft engine reaching its climax. It had to be starting its run.

He cornered the building at a sprint, just in time to see the Cessna building up speed across the uneven ground. He targeted a point two-thirds of the way along the runway and ran towards it.

He slowed as the plane drew level, and raised the Glock with both hands. He took aim, the front sight wavering. Sweat – or blood – trickled down his brow.

It was too far away, he knew it, but he still squeezed off a shot. Then another. And another after that.

With zero wind, totally relaxed, out on a range . . . it was possible he might have made it.

But he missed.

As he watched the plane rising into the air, he saw the hawk-faced man look out from the cockpit window. Maybe he'd glimpsed Danny there. Or had even caught a trace of some residual muzzle flash that the sound suppressor had failed to conceal.

Danny would never know for sure. But for an instant he thought their eyes met.

And in that instant he made the hawk-faced man a promise. He'd come find him. He'd not rest until he had.

Then the plane was gone, into the night.

Danny turned and ran, not towards Lexie, but to the front door of the farmhouse, behind which the torturer lay dying. He squeezed the Glock tight in his right hand. In his left he gripped the belt buckle knife.

It was time to find out exactly who 'Mr Smith' was, and what it was that he knew.

WEDNESDAY

CHAPTER FIFTY-NINE

Five days had gone by since Danny had loosed off those shots at the Cessna and missed. He and Lexie were now three hundred miles away, on the west coast of Wales.

Danny looked up from the contents of the torturer's wallet he'd been sifting through at the kitchen table, and gazed out at Lexie through the holiday cottage window.

She was sitting cross-legged in khaki slacks and a red hooded top in the overgrown front garden, using a sharp stone to draw on a broken roof slate. Beyond the garden wall, a deserted dirt track meandered up through a rocky valley towards the rugged hills and grey sky.

After Danny had finished with the torturer at the Sussex farmhouse, he'd fetched Lexie from where he'd hidden her behind the bramble patch and taken her to the Transit. He had then returned to the house and removed the bodies of the murdered owners and put them outside, so that their relatives would be able to give them a decent burial.

He'd then searched the dead Russian and Serbian mercenaries, as he now knew them to be. He'd got his watch back off the skinhead. Luckily it hadn't been broken in the fight.

He'd collected up their bags and possessions, stowing these items in the back of the Transit. He'd left their bodies inside.

After cleaning himself up and changing his clothes, he'd burned the farmhouse down, knowing that otherwise his DNA would be found and he'd be blamed for what had happened there too.

In addition to the weapons, documentation, computers and phones he'd found inside the mercenaries' brown leather holdall, Danny had recovered his own stolen wallet and jacket from the Ritz, along with its set of fake ID and credit cards in the name of Samuel Wilson Jones.

He and Lexie had driven through the night. They'd ditched the Transit in Bristol city centre the following morning and had bought an SUV from a used car dealership with an Amex. They'd then sold that vehicle at another dealership for cash. In a third dealership Danny had paid cash for an old VW camper van, which was now parked at the side of the cottage out of sight.

Lexie had handed over a month's rent up front for the use of this property, along with a large cash deposit. She'd given one of Danny's new disposable cell phone numbers as an employer reference to the small-town agent she'd rented the property through, but they'd not even bothered calling Danny to check.

Lexie looked different now from the girl whose face had been plastered across the media for the last five days. Her hair was cut short. She'd done it herself, at Danny's request, along with home-dyeing it black in a motorway service station bathroom the morning after they'd fled from the farm.

The media had, of course, by now matched the Danny and Alexandra Shanklin on the run here in England to the Danny and Alexandra Shanklin who'd been attacked by the Paper Stone Scissors killer in the States. None of Lexie's school friends had known a thing about that before. Yet another part of her life he'd screwed up. And yet another reason he was determined to see this through so she could once more hold her head up high.

He'd altered his own appearance too in the last few days. Fair hair. New clothes from a store in Bristol. Glasses. His jaw was thick with stubble. His plan was to let it run to a full beard, and grow his hair longer too.

It was a start, but he already knew he'd have to do a whole lot better. Every airport and cross-border facial recognition system across the world would have been programmed with his features.

The London manhunt might have ended, but the global search for Danny Shanklin had only just begun.

Colonel Nikolai Zykov's mutilated body had eventually been ID'd through dental records two days after the assassination and massacre had taken place. Danny's work in Chechnya for the Russian government had now been leaked to the press by the Kid.

It was still assumed that Danny had been hired by the colonel. Meaning that – again, just like the UK spook Danny had fought outside the school chapel had claimed – he was the only person still being hunted in connection with the Mayfair atrocities.

The Russian government continued to deny all involvement. They had issued a statement that Colonel Zykov had recently been seeing a psychiatrist for chronic depression, and that an internal investigation had also now revealed connections between him and certain illegal clandestine nationalist organizations, and certain already imprisoned Russian billionaires.

Zykov, in other words, had been officially disowned.

They'd denied any knowledge of Danny too.

Meanwhile the diplomatic storm triggered by the assassination was whipping up into a hurricane. Russian and Georgian troop reinforcements were mobilizing around South Ossetia and Abkhazia. European stocks and currencies were sliding on the fear of regional destabilization, as well as the renewal of terrorist attacks in the West. The hawk-faced man could not have scripted it better if he'd tried.

Except for one thing. Danny Shanklin was still alive.

He looked back at Lexie. She'd finished the slate she'd been drawing on and now placed it on the grass at the end of a row of other slates. Each had different designs on them. Some were patterns made up from combinations of Celtic symbols, taken from a book of Welsh history the cottage's landlord had left along with a stack of well-thumbed paperbacks in its living room. Others were views of the isolated hillsides surrounding the cottage. Or of wildlife, of buzzards circling high up on thermals, of rabbits and foxes and deer.

It was good to see her doing something normal, something that she liked. And her grandmother, Jean, had been right, Danny thought. Lexie really was talented. He felt humbled watching her work, both startled and amazed by his own flesh and blood.

Lexie said she was planning on taking the slates back to school to use as part of her coursework. He'd like that. If something good were to come out of all this.

It still astonished him how quickly she'd adapted. She hadn't complained. About the fact that she couldn't yet return to school, or contact her friends. About how the only way for him to protect her was to keep her hidden until he'd cleared his name.

Danny wasn't only worried about intelligence agencies wanting to get their hands on her to use against him. She was still a loose end that the hawk-faced man had failed to tie up.

Danny wasn't kidding himself either, though, about how well she'd coped. He worried about the psychological impact the events of the last week would have on her. He feared she could still end up suffering from some kind of post-traumatic anxiety. He needed to get her somewhere secure as soon as he could. And get her help, someone neutral she could talk to. A professional. Someone who could do a much better job than him.

Once all this was all over, he needed to take proper care of her. To make up for all that lost time. To become a real father again.

He still couldn't forgive himself for having fired up his phone while he'd still been at Alice's home. If he'd not committed that one careless, unthinking act through which he'd been traced, then Lexie would still be safe, and Alice De Luca would still be alive.

According to Lexie, the hawk-faced man had shot Alice in the face as soon as she'd opened her front door. According to the newspaper article Danny had read, she'd died instantly. The machine pistol she'd been killed with had been fitted with a sound suppressor. No one outside Alice's house had heard a thing. No one had come to help. The hawk-faced man had left her face down in the hallway and had caught up with Lexie on the stairs.

Last night Danny had dreamt of Alice, as though she'd still been alive and they'd still been together. They'd been walking through Green Park hand in hand towards a setting sun. They'd been busy making plans.

The police hadn't yet identified Danny's fingerprints at Alice's home. But they would. He'd be blamed for that too. Of course Lexie would be able to act as a witness to what really happened. But would the police believe her? Not if they still believed Danny was responsible for the hit and the Mayfair massacre. They'd assume she was covering for him, or had somehow been involved as well.

Danny had dreamt last night of Sally also, but in his dream she'd still been dead, strapped to that chair in the cabin with her mouth gaping wide and her eyes as deep and dark as burrows.

Watching now as Lexie lay down on the grass and stared up at the swirling grey sky, Danny scratched at the scar where the Paper Stone Scissors killer had driven the shears deep into his thigh.

The Paper Stone Scissors Killer. That was what the media had taken to calling the Director after the details of Danny's family's ordeal had been leaked. Danny and Lexie had been the first to survive one of his attacks.

After he'd faded like a ghost into that snowstorm, Danny had collapsed. It was Lexie who'd saved him. His nine-year-old daughter. If he'd been on his own, he would have died.

She'd gone back into the cabin. She gone back in *there*, where Sally and Jonathan had been. She'd gone back in on her own and she'd found Sally's cell phone and had dialled 911.

The police had combed the valley for the stranger's body, in case Danny really had clipped him with that Browning as he'd thought. But they'd found nothing. Forensics had gone over the cabin and the stranger's abandoned car. But they'd turned up nothing.

Danny and Lexie had been offered protection after that. A new beginning. But Danny had taken his daughter away to California instead. To a rented apartment in Santa Monica. He hadn't wanted anybody's protection. He hadn't wanted anyone near them. He'd gone there to look after his little girl. But what he'd done instead was collapse into drinking and pills.

Time had passed. One day Sally's mother, Jean, had come to stay. Then one day soon after that she was gone, and Lexie with her. Danny had been too doped up on drink and pills to remember the how and the why.

One night months later, he'd thought about killing himself, but had instead made a phone call asking for help. It had been the first step on the long road to getting himself well again, a road he knew he'd one way or another continue to walk most likely for the rest of his life.

Two years after Sally and Jonathan had been murdered, the FBI began to theorize that their killer must already be dead. The Director had never surfaced again. Or at least not in the way he'd done before. No more paper, stone, scissors. No more tortured mothers and children. No more executed fathers who'd first been made to watch.

Danny did not believe the FBI were right. Not in his heart. Not for a second.

He'd hired one of Karl Bain's best men – an FBI investigative profiler who'd recently retired. He put him on a retainer. To keep trying to fit the pieces together. To cross-reference any and all convictions that had occurred since the time of the attack on the cabin. In case the stranger was not attacking because he was already doing time. To search for similar murders abroad and at home. To never stop looking.

So far there'd been nothing. But one day Danny believed that would change.

A movement caught his eye. There in the distance on the dirt track road. A vehicle was coming their way.

Danny quickly got up. He took the Glock 30 from the locked drawer of the desk in the corner of the room. He'd disassembled the other weapons he'd brought from the farmhouse and had buried them up in the hills, so that they could never be used to link him to the murders at the farm or at Alice's. He'd destroy this weapon too before he left here. But not until he knew he was safe.

He checked the window again. The vehicle – a black Land Rover, it looked like – was coming closer. It would have passed the 'No Through Road – Private Property' sign by now.

It was not slowing down.

CHAPTER SIXTY

WEST WALES . . .

As Danny hurried for the side door of the cottage, he watched Lexie waking from her daydream with a start. She must have heard the Land Rover pulling up on the rough dirt turning circle just beyond the garden wall.

By the time the vehicle's door slammed shut, Lexie was already on her feet, staring at the giant of a man coming towards her.

He had shoulders not quite as wide as a truck, thick dark hair scraped back in a ponytail, and a long shovel of a face, which tapered down into an unkempt and prematurely silvered beard, making him look a little like a werewolf, and a lot like someone you'd cross any road to avoid.

He was dressed in a bespoke black suit, black leather shoes, pale blue shirt, no tie. All of it Armani. The curling tip of a green flame tattoo showed just above the collar line of his tree trunk of a neck. A large platinum and diamond-encrusted ring glistened on his left index finger, big enough to make a street thief's eyes bulge with desire – not that even a crackhead would be dumb enough to think they could steal it from this particular man and live to tell the tale.

His dark eyes sparkled like wet pebbles in the sun, locking on Lexie as he marched up to her and stopped.

'You must be Alexandra,' he said.

His accent was Russian. Lexie's eyes widened with fear. Her knees began to sag.

'It's OK.' Danny stepped up beside her and put his arm around her. He'd left the Glock inside when he'd seen who'd got out of the car. 'He's a friend. He's here to help.'

'My name is Spartak Sidarvov,' the man said, not taking his hooded eyes off Lexie. He leant towards her, deliberately lowering his height. 'I met you once before. When you were much younger. When your mother was still alive. You look like her.' He gave Lexie a lopsided smile and gently placed his hand on her shoulder. 'Apart from your hair, I think,' he said, 'which I imagine was your father's idea.'

Lexie exhaled, smiling as she did – largely, Danny guessed, from relief.

Spartak turned to Danny. 'And so, by the devil's poisonous shit. This is what a man with a million-dollar price tag on his head looks like . . .'

'It's good to see you too,' Danny said.

Spartak's face split into a grin. 'Come here.' He bear-hugged Danny so hard the air hissed from his lungs.

Danny forced a smile as the big man released him, but at the same time he couldn't stop himself from thinking about the Kid. About how he'd betrayed him. About how he'd never even seen it coming. He thought about the Old Man too. About his advice: *Never trust in anyone fully but yourself.*

And yet here he was already doing the opposite. Because he had no choice. Because he'd known Spartak longer than anyone. And because he needed backup for what he was planning to do next.

And not just Spartak either. He'd need to find a new techie to replace the Kid. And, of course, he somehow needed to re-establish safe contact with Crane.

'I guess you two need to talk,' Lexie said.

Danny nodded.

'I'm going to finish my slates,' she said. 'Call me when you've got lunch ready,' she added, with a sly smile that made Spartak grin.

'Just like her mother,' he said, as he set off with Danny towards the cottage.

They went inside. Spartak weighed nearly eighteen stone. As the two men sat down opposite each other at the kitchen table, his wooden chair creaked like it was about to splinter.

Danny cut straight to the chase. He told Spartak everything that had happened to him from the moment he'd met the Kid five days ago outside the Ritz. Right up to when he'd fired those shots at the Cessna.

He then told Spartak abut his little conversation with the dying torturer. About everything he'd revealed.

He'd given Danny his real name. But he'd not known the identities of any of the others, in spite of having worked with them before. The hawk-faced man – Glinka was the only name the torturer had ever known him by – was a Russian mercenary, who the torturer claimed had been approached three months before by certain elements within the Georgian secret service.

They'd hatched a plan to assassinate their own supporter, the writer due to address the UN – Madina Tskhovrebova – and blame it on the Russians. To reinvigorate international political pressure demanding Georgia's reunification with her former territories. To help them get back what they thought of as theirs by right.

Glinka had decided to pin the assassination on a member of the Russian embassy staff. Its military attaché had been the obvious choice. But as his team had set about researching Zykov prior to his abduction and the hit, Glinka had realized he might have met the colonel before.

When he had come face to face with Zykov on the night before the assassination, his suspicions had been confirmed. In 1990, Zykov had illegally raided the Biopreparat chemical weapons facility at which Glinka had been stationed.

Fearing the imminent collapse of the Soviet Union and the subsequent neutering of Russia's security and power, Zykov and his fellow nationalist hardliners had taken it upon themselves to preserve certain secret chemical weapons for the potential future exclusive use of the Russian state. It was these which they'd gone to the Biopreparat facility to steal.

Five nights ago, Glinka had tortured Colonel Zykov in his apartment to discover where those stolen chemical weapons were being kept now.

The colonel didn't know, since the weapons had been regularly moved since their original theft. What he did know, however, was the name of the hidden and encrypted file on his government intranet computer that was regularly updated by his co-conspirators with the weapons' current locations.

The discovery of the existence and proximity of this file was what had led Glinka to change his plan. As well as carrying out the assassination he'd been paid to do, he would now steal the stolen weapons data too. For his own personal gain.

'And so they mutilated the colonel's body,' Spartak said, quickly guessing ahead. 'To buy themselves more time. Because the second Zykov was discovered missing, the embassy would be locked down and the opportunity to steal that data would disappear.'

'And the colonel's co-conspirators, as part of the protocols of their own web of trust, would have remotely destroyed his copy of the file.'

'All of which leaves us with one big problem,' Spartak said. 'They have the data and we do not. We don't even know what these chemical weapons are they are planning to steal.'

'Smallpox,' Danny said.

Spartak looked up sharply.

'Six different formulations,' Danny continued. 'Against which current vaccine stockpiles are completely ineffective.'

Spartak's expression darkened as he did the maths.

Danny must have looked the same when he'd first researched the ramifications himself, about the kind of cataclysmic damage a chemical weapon like this could wreak.

In the event of a hybrid smallpox outbreak, current ring vaccination and quarantine containment measures would only slow, not stop, the development of a pandemic. The death toll could reach not just into the hundreds of thousands, but into the millions. Economically it would cost governments billions. Only one in three people exposed to the disease would survive.

'My God,' Spartak said, 'but this is terrible . . .'

God had nothing to do with it. The Biopreparat Zykov and his co-conspirators had tricked their way into back in 1990 had been an unofficial repository for dozens of smallpox formulations developed as part of the Soviet biological warfare programme. The effectiveness of these weapons had increased exponentially over time, due to the fact that the otherwise globally eradicated smallpox virus was no longer vaccinated against.

'And I don't suppose there's any way to prove any of this?' Spartak said.

Danny had thought about that himself, about tipping off the current Russian government, the Americans, Chinese, Indians and British too. But why would any of them believe him?

'Not even if anyone was listening to us,' he said. 'Which they're not.'

'And there's no way to tip off Zykov's friends either that Glinka is coming for them . . . and what's theirs.'

'We don't even know who they are.'

Spartak threw up his hands, exasperated. 'Then we're completely and utterly fucked, my friend.'

'*Were* . . .' Danny dug into his jeans pocket and pulled out a black data stick, the same one that had been left there for him five days ago, hanging round the dead colonel's neck.

Spartak's hooded eyes narrowed to slits. 'What's that?'

Danny handed the stick across. It looked as insubstantial as a twig in Spartak's huge hand as he slowly turned it over.

'It's the stick the Kid gave me,' Danny said. 'The one he was going to use to lure me into raiding the embassy before they kidnapped Lexie. The one he said didn't have anything useful on it.' He paused. 'Well, now it does.'

Spartak smiled slowly. 'You stole the data . . .'

'Copied it,' Danny said. 'I knew they'd check on the phone to see if it was all there. But while I was still in the colonel's office, just before that worm took effect, I copied the file directly from the colonel's computer and onto the stick. Then hid the data stick in my shoe.'

Spartak kissed the stick. He clenched it tightly in his fist. 'So we now know what they know . . .'

'What they're going to try and steal . . .'

'And where they're going to try and steal it from . . .'

'And let me guess,' Spartak said, unfurling his fist again before returning the data stick to Danny, 'some of these seriously deadly and priceless biological weapons are in Russia . . . which is why you've called me in.'

'And because I was missing you.'

'But of course . . . because you are only human,' Spartak said with a shrug.

Danny smiled. But he felt no true happiness then. Only nerves. Spartak had a family of his own. He had every right to walk away from this now. Danny watched and waited as the Russian stared out of the window, processing and assessing all that he'd heard.

'I never did like the Kid,' he said finally. 'He was a slob. He had no sense of style. It will be a privilege and a pleasure to track him down.'

Danny looked up sharply. 'Then you're in?'

'Oh yes. We will go together and we will find them. Trust me, Danny boy,' he said, 'we will make these bad-boy fucking bastards pay.' He clapped his hands together then, as if sealing his decision in his mind. 'And meanwhile,' he said, 'we must also stop you falling into the hands of MI5, the CIA, the FSB and every other goddamn dickhead security agency who will be trying to nail your head to the wall.' Again that wide, wolfish smile. 'It should be a piece of piss for men like us, don't you think? To clear your name once and for all.'

'Thank you.' Danny felt his throat tightening. Spartak being here, agreeing to help him . . . He knew the fightback could now begin. 'You must be thirsty after your journey,' he said. 'I put a bottle of vodka in the freezer for you.'

Spartak raised his thick dark eyebrows at Danny inquisitively.

'Sorry, not Diaka,' Danny said. The world-famous vodka he'd last seen on Colonel Zykov's office desk. 'Funnily enough, they didn't have that in stock at the local village store.' He ignored Spartak's exaggerated look of disappointment. 'But I did manage to procure you a bottle of Stolichnaya, so don't feel too hard done by, eh?'

Spartak grinned, 'An excellent choice.'

Danny heard music. He turned and looked out through the open window at Lexie. She was whistling as she drew. An ache filled his chest. A pang of regret. He'd recognized the old tune. It was called 'Lullaby of Birdland'. Sally's favourite. She'd taught it to Lexie and Jonathan. The four of them had used to sing it together on long journeys in the old Chevy Sedan.

'I'll be back in a minute,' Danny said.

Outside the weather was turning. A cold wind had started to blow. Dark clouds scudded across the sky. A storm was gathering in the east.

Danny listened to Lexie whistling. He watched her as she drew. He thought of what was gone and what was yet to come.

I'll be there. Nothing can stop me.

'Dad,' she said, noticing him there. 'I've finished. Come and see.'

Danny Shanklin's story continues in 2012 in the heart-pounding sequel

WANTED

ACKNOWLEDGEMENTS

A big thanks to James Gurbutt, my terrific editor, for the best email I received last year. Thanks also to Rob Nichols for so many smart ideas. And to Jonny Geller at Curtis Brown, as always, for keeping knocking on those doors.

Thundering applause go to Kevin Whelan for his expertise in all things military and technological. Every conversation is an education.